Straight On 'Til Morning

"A dramatic and funny coming-of-age story. . . . A horrific and ultimately sorrowful thriller. A bizarre combination of *The Wonder Years* TV series and *The Lost Boys* film, this fantastic tale entertains."
—*Publishers Weekly*

"The *Stand By Me*-cum-*The Outsiders* feel of the first half of the novel is real, and honest, and a great read in and of itself; add the twisted fantasy element . . . and this book becomes perfectly unique. A grown up, odd, compelling journey through adolescence, and heartache—and of course Neverland . . . a fascinating and completely engrossing book. One that makes you read and read . . . straight on 'til morning."
—*The 11th Hour*

Strangewood

"Christopher Golden gradually brings into being a world of haunted and perilous fantasy which, while moving into greater solidity, never loses touch with its painful, sweet embattled human context. [*Strangewood*] is a notable achievement—Christopher Golden has written a beautiful and wildly inventive hymn to the most salvific human capacity, Imagination." —Peter Straub

"I read *Strangewood* in one sitting . . . a daring and thoroughly engrossing blend of wonder and adventure, terror and tenderness. *Strangewood* is what Oz might have been if L. Frank Baum had grown up on a steady diet of Stephen King." —F. Paul Wilson

continued . . .

More praise for *Strangewood*

"If Clive Barker had gone *Through the Looking Glass*, he might have come up with something as imaginative and compelling as *Strangewood*. It's been a long time since I've read such an original novel."
—Kevin J. Anderson, *New York Times* bestselling coauthor of *Dune: House Harkonnen*

". . . a tour de force that examines the themes of love and faith, revenge and retribution. Truly frightening, and inspiring."
—Nancy Holder, Bram Stoker Award-winning author of *Dead in the Water*

"Enthralling . . . The imagination that it took to create this world—well, I am in awe of Christopher Golden."
—*Midwest Book Review*

". . . will lead readers to wonder if Christopher Golden is actually a pseudonym for a collaboration between Dean Koontz and Peter Straub. . . . Do not read just before going to bed unless you want to journey to *Strangewood* while you sleep."
—BookBrowser

"Original, suspenseful, and often genuinely creepy."
—*Science Fiction Chronicle*

"Excellent dark fantasy."
—*Locus*

More praise for *The Shadow Saga*

"An intriguing adult mystery, not for the faint of heart." —*Murder Under Cover, Inc.*

"Passionate . . . Excellent . . . Golden has written one of the best . . . a deep probe into the inner workings of the church and a surprise explanation for vampires. [A] brilliant vampire novel in a blizzard of bloody tooth bites this year."
—LitNews (published on Compuserve) and *Dark Channel*

"Golden stands many time-honored concepts about vampirism on their heads."
—*The Overlook Connection*

"Golden has created a new myth. A real treat for those who are tired of ideas that are as old as yesterday's blood . . . worthy of the praise it has already received, and more." —*Eclipse Magazine*

"A fast-paced action thriller that will hold the reader's attention from the first page to the last."
—*The Talisman*

"Golden combines quiet, dark, subtle mood with Super-Giant monster action. Sort of M. R. James meets Godzilla!" —Mike Mignola, creator of *Hellboy*

THE
FERRYMAN

Christopher Golden

A SIGNET BOOK

SIGNET
Published by New American Library, a division of
Penguin Putnam Inc., 375 Hudson Street,
New York, New York 10014, U.S.A.
Penguin Books Ltd, 80 Strand,
London WC2R 0RL, England
Penguin Books Australia Ltd, Ringwood,
Victoria, Australia
Penguin Books Canada Ltd, 10 Alcorn Avenue,
Toronto, Ontario, Canada M4V 3B2
Penguin Books (N.Z.) Ltd, 182–190 Wairau Road,
Auckland 10, New Zealand

Penguin Books Ltd, Registered Offices:
Harmondsworth, Middlesex, England

First published by Signet, an imprint of New American Library,
a division of Penguin Putnam Inc.

First Printing, May 2002
10 9 8 7 6 5 4 3 2 1

Ⓢ REGISTERED TRADEMARK—MARCA REGISTRADA

Printed in the United States of America

PUBLISHER'S NOTE
This is a work of fiction. Names, characters, places, and incidents either are
the product of the author's imagination or are used fictitiously, and any resemblance to actual persons, living or dead, business establishments, events, or
locales is entirely coincidental.

For my children.
Swim.

Acknowledgments

I am grateful to so many for so much. First, of course, to my wife, Connie, and my children. The story echoes, but echoes fade.

To my editor, Laura Anne Gilman, and my agent, Lori Perkins.

To Joelle Corcoran, for talking about what it was like to almost die.

To Hank Wagner and Bill Sheehan (and Connie again), all of whom read this novel in various stages and offered both enthusiasm and very helpful suggestions.

To my family, those still with me and those long departed.

And, at the last and always, to my friends, those who swim with me against the current and lend me their strength when I grow weary. I hope I do the same. I am grateful to all of you, and most especially to: Tom Sniegoski, Bob Tomko, Stefan Nathanson, Jose Nieto, Rick Hautala, and Megan Bibeau.

PROLOGUE

❧

It's not a dream.

On the banks of a broad, roiling river, Janine Hartschorn turned in a wild circle, searching for a familiar landmark, anything that might jog her memory, help her figure out where she was and how she had gotten here. Failing that, she'd have been happy to simply find a path that led away from the rushing water, a path to somewhere—anywhere—else.

But Janine couldn't see a damn thing.

A thick, damp mist enshrouded her and spread its tendrils through the trees and across the river. If she looked straight up, she could see a few breaks in the fog, but she tried not to pay attention to them. If she did, she would have to think about the stars. The night sky seemed somehow closer here, wherever *here* was, and the stars that punctured the darkness were red like scarlet tears against the face of the night.

Or wounds.

They might have been wounds.

Something brushed past her in the mist. Janine gasped and turned quickly to peer deeper into the damp shroud around her, but she could see nothing. A branch, perhaps. It might have been only a branch, yearning toward her under the press of the wind. But there was no wind.

Her breathing quickened, yet each breath was more shallow. Her eyes shifted in sudden spasms of paranoia as she gazed around her at each swirl of fog. Out there, within the cloud that lingered upon the marshy ground that squelched beneath her feet, someone watched her. Suddenly Janine was seven years old again and her older brother and his friends had led her into the wood behind their house and left her, like Hansel and Gretel's parents. They crouched snickering behind trees as she called out into the sunless forest.

She called out now. "Hello? Who's there?"

Of course there was no answer. They would not confess their presence. The mist had texture, shadows within shadows, and she imagined she saw figures there, that she was being watched not by one but by many, and that they were all people who knew her. People who knew that every step forward put her in peril and yet urged her on regardless.

She did not trust them, those shades and specters.

"I'm sorry," she said, though she could not have said why. "I can't stay here. Can't be with you. I have to—have to go."

Janine's skin was moist with the condensation in the air, but her skin prickled as though she were draped in rough, heavy wool. Her feet had sunk so deeply into the mire that she found it difficult to move them. She struggled against the muck that entrapped her and her heart began to beat faster. Once again she felt like a child, held against her will but capable only of whining and lashing out for her freedom.

"Please," she whispered.

Tears like melting ice dripped down her cheeks, stinging her flesh. The taunting specters who lingered just beyond her vision only made her feel more lonely. More alone. Again she struggled to free her feet. With a sound like helium leaking from a balloon, she tore her right foot from the sucking mud, leaving one brown sandal behind. The other foot came loose more easily now, so that she wore only one shoe.

Get your bearings, Janine, she told herself. *And get out.*

Paranoia dissipated, but fear remained. It felt as though the fog around her had infiltrated her mind but was now clearing. Janine forced her breathing to slow, took long hitching breaths, and managed to calm her body down. Her heartbeat still resounded through her body, but slower now, not hammering against the cavern of her chest.

The water. She had to get away from the water.

Whatever was coming for her, haunting her in this dreadful, claustrophobic territory, it was coming across the water. Retreat was her only option. Overwhelmed by the desire to distance herself immediately from the muddy shores of the fog-enshrouded river, Janine turned and blindly walked into the mist. The ground beneath her feet still squelched with dampness, and the bank did not seem to rise up before her as she had expected.

The sounds of the river receded slightly behind her, and the wind rustled the leaves of the trees as she moved into denser wood. Branches swayed and seemed to dip across her path as if they were sentries warning her to turn back. But Janine did not turn back.

The prickling of her skin began to subside, the dread to recede from her heart. Even the mist seemed thinner around her and the air blowing through the trees smelled fresh, without what she now realized was the fetid scent blowing off the river.

At last the ground seemed firm beneath her feet, one bare and one still shod in brown leather. With a ponderous sigh of relief, Janine looked down to see that, even with the mist, she had begun to follow a path through the wood. Stones and roots jutted from the path and yet it seemed familiar to her.

Somewhere in the back of her mind, a child she had once been recognized that this was the path home.

I was lost, she thought. *Lost. Now I want to go home.*

With a smile and a shake of her head, Janine picked up her pace, unmindful of the hazards that might lie along the path for her one bare foot. A stubbed toe or a twisted ankle were a fair price for a bit of extra speed, for a single minute less time spent in this dark and dreary wood.

Her smile evaporated. Something was not right.

Janine stopped and peered through the mist all around, more angry now than afraid. There were still eyes upon her, figures lingering just beyond her vision in the mist, watching her plight. She ignored them, for she was almost home. Their presence had become almost familiar now, like the mist itself, the trees around her, and the sound of the river.

The river.

It's not behind me anymore.

Somehow the sound of the river had migrated. It was off to her left now, rushing past rocks and burbling along the marshy shore. Once again, her breath came too fast and her heart began to skim along far too quickly. Janine shook her head and took a step backward. She cast a glance back the way she had come but knew it would be foolhardy to reverse direction. Only the river lay back that way . . . and whatever it was that was coming for her.

Pulling at her.

Yes, she thought. That was the feeling she had been struggling to identify. The foreboding that filled her was not merely the presence of the thing but a kind of magnetic draw that seemed to drag at her limbs as she moved. She felt it pulling to her from the water, pulling her in.

Grimly determined, Janine pressed on. She had barely walked a dozen feet farther into the mist when her bare foot touched soft, damp earth that squished between her toes. With a whimper she looked down and saw that the firm ground of the path had given way to mire again. Hesitant, she nevertheless continued, her single sandal and bare foot making almost obscene noises in the mire.

It turned, that's all. It will turn again. I'm on a path. It must lead away from the river eventually.

But a moment later she stepped forward and her

right leg plunged to the knee in blood-warm water and she stumbled and nearly fell face-first into the river.

The path turned, that's all.

Holding her breath, Janine took a step back . . . and found herself impossibly deeper than she had been a moment earlier. She spun around, searching through the mist for the shore, but the river rushed all around her now and she could feel it pulling at her. The water had reached her waist and she felt its undercurrents caressing her skin, tracing the lines of her legs. It felt as though something tugged on her under there, and she batted at the water around her.

Coins jangled in the loose pockets of her skirt, where the fabric had begun to float up around her. Janine frowned.

Out in the river, something moved through the water. A light appeared, tiny but growing larger, cutting toward her across the suddenly calm surface of the river.

"No," Janine whispered.

Her limbs felt heavy and cold despite the warmth of the water. A single step back and she only plunged deeper, nearly fell into the river and found herself turned around, facing the light again. Metal clanked against wood and the light seemed to swing from side to side and it grew nearer.

It was a boat. Narrower than a rowboat and roughly the length of a canoe, it came on toward her with a flickering lantern hung from its prow. No sail, no oars, nor even any rudder that she could see. The darkened figure that stood at the fore of the tiny boat made no effort to propel the vessel nor navigate its course.

Janine bit her lower lip hard enough to draw blood, and she tasted its copper tang in her mouth. Her insides had stopped churning with fear and become instead a hard-packed core of ice and stone. A step in any direction would only plunge her deeper, bring her farther into the river. She could not escape him.

Come for her was the Ferryman.

How she knew this was a mystery to her, but she did not question it. Inescapable fact loomed before her on the rippling surface of the river. Through the clearing mist she could see him now, draped in a scarlet hood and robe, a golden sash about his narrow waist. Beneath the hood his countenance was hidden, yet she imagined some horror beneath, some grotesque visage with burning eyes in skeletal orbits.

The lantern clanked against the wooden boat. The light cast by the flame within skittered insectlike across the swirl of the river. Janine stood frozen, watching the Ferryman come. He had stood as if hewn from granite upon the prow of the vessel but now reached up with narrow hands, thinly tapered fingers, and pulled back the cowl that had hidden his face.

Janine gasped, suddenly remembering to breathe.

The Ferryman's flesh was pale and marbled and offset by his eyes, orbs of blackest indigo set into his thin face as if each of his pupils were its own full and devastating eclipse. His dark hair hung to his shoulders and his beard was lush, though pulled to a point some seven inches below his chin and bound with a metal ring.

Not the grotesque she had feared. But chilling just the same.

The ferry drifted to a stop perhaps a foot from where she stood, an island to herself in the river, and floated no farther but instead remained there as if hovering just above the water.

The eclipsed stars that were the eyes of the ashen creature turned upon her, and Janine felt for the first time that perhaps its desire for her to accompany it, to accompany him, might not be an end to things but a beginning. Yet even as the thought dawned upon her, she also felt a new magnetism tugging at her from behind. Some other force had touched her, and it was powerful indeed.

She gazed across the river, squinted to see the land from which the Ferryman had come, but she could see nothing.

The slim, dreadful figure upon the ferry held out its right hand, palm up. It gazed down upon her and it made its single demand in a voice that seemed to ripple with the flow of the river.

"The coins."

Janine shook her head. Any hesitation was gone. "No," she said, barely a whisper at first but then more powerfully. "No."

The Ferryman narrowed its gaze, the burning rims of fire around the black centers of its eyes disappearing now to leave only wells of darkness there.

"The coins." More insistent.

Nausea roiled in Janine's gut and bile rose in her throat. She choked it down and took a step backward . . . and did not slip deeper into the river. Another step, and she knew she was moving closer to the shore, though she dared not turn her back on the Ferryman.

"The coins?" A question now, accompanied by an expression that might have been amusement.

Janine snaked a hand into the sodden pocket of her skirt and withdrew three silver coins. With a powerful snap of her arm, she tossed them out across the river as though she were skimming stones. But they did not skim. They sliced the water's surface and then sank quickly below.

The Ferryman's expression changed instantly. Fury rippled across his white stone features and his eyes went wide, revealing the twin suns behind the eclipsed irises. They flared and seemed about to burn her.

She ran. With great effort she surged up out of the water onto the muddy banks of the river.

A tug from behind and Janine turned one final time.

The Ferryman had not moved. He only stood in the prow of the ship glaring at her. In one arm he held a squalling bundle wrapped in white cloth close against his slender form.

Janine tripped. She went down face-first into the sucking mire and it covered her face, pushed up her nostrils and into her mouth, and she found she could not breathe. Nor could she see. The mist and the filth that covered her eyes had made her effectively blind. She tore wildly at her face, at her mouth, struggling to take a breath. Even just a single breath.

Her chest burned with the need for air; her lungs felt as if they were about to explode.

I'm going to die, she thought.

Then, simply, *No.*

Janine gasped. *Air. Sweet Jesus, air.*

Her eyes fluttered open.

Doctors, nurses, machines, sterile whiteness and you're going to be all right, Miss Hartschorn. Just relax now, you're going to be all right.

The baby? What about the baby? That was her voice, her rasping, raw-throated voice.

The sad faces of the nurses.

The doctor glances away.

We did everything we could.

CHAPTER 1

✿

David Bairstow was at war.

A warm breeze blew in through the open windows, but the smell of chalk lingered defiantly in the air. The clock ticked off the seconds with an almost petulant persistence, but David did his best to keep from even glancing at it. It was a bad precedent to set, but worse, it might be seen as a form of surrender.

He stood at the head of the classroom, his back to the blackboard, and faced his students. His hands were thrust casually into his pockets and he stood with his head cocked at a devil-may-care angle, eyebrows raised.

"Anyone?" he prodded.

The response was less than overwhelming. David sighed and straightened the tie he wore only because he felt it would not be fair to go without one when the boys of St. Matthew's did not have the option. He scanned the forty-two faces before him, hoping to stumble across one—only one—that seemed alert and interested.

Nothing.

David Bairstow was at war.

But his students were not the enemy. Rather, he faced a disembodied creature known by various names: Senior Slump, Spring Fever, Senior Slide. It was late April. They had already applied to colleges and been accepted or wait-listed. Whatever they did in these last two months of school would not change the fate each of these seniors had waiting for them in the fall. The result, whatever cute name one wanted to put on it, was nothing short of apathy.

David smiled thinly. "You guys are unbelievable," he told them, abandoning the pretense that nothing had changed in their demeanor.

After all, this was an Advanced Placement English class. The kids in here were the brightest St. Matthew's had to offer. But they all had a swagger now, the smart ones even more so, that said they cared not a whit about anything but gliding toward graduation on whatever little updraft would carry them the rest of the way.

The thing was, that was not good enough for David. His job was not to get them into college; it was to teach them. Though some of his colleagues would have joined in the slide, David simply was not built that way. He loved to teach. One of the reasons he had worked so hard at getting the AP classes was that he wanted students who actually had a desire to learn. But every spring . . . he had to take drastic measures.

"All right, listen up, folks," David said, his voice growing louder.

A number of students snapped out of the malaise that had set in. Christi McCann even had the decency to look embarrassed at the way her eyelids had been drooping, though David noticed that Brad Flecca's did not so much as flinch. The kid was slumped in his seat, eyes closed, a bit of drool at the corner of his mouth.

David wanted to toss him out the window. On the other hand, he could remember his own senior year at St. Matthew's, could recall with startling clarity how it felt to walk the corridors in those last few weeks, feeling on top of the world, and bored by anything that might kill that buzz.

So . . . no killing the students. At least not this time.

"One last time," he announced. "Can anyone . . . and I do mean anyone . . . tell me about the dichotomy between language and structure in the presentation of the roles of protagonist and antagonist in *Moby Dick*?"

They were paying attention now. All except for

Brad Flecca, of course. But still no answer was forth-coming.

"Did anyone actually read *Moby Dick*?"

So quickly he was literally startled, all but half a dozen or so hands shot up. David shook his head and laughed, which seemed to take several of his students aback.

"What's funny, Mr. Bairstow?" Christi asked.

"Ah, they speak!" David replied.

He studied the girl, trying not to be aware of how sweet she looked in her St. Matt's uniform. It was a constant struggle, teaching seniors, particularly the brighter ones. But he was thirty-three, and knew full well the difference between admiration and perversion.

"Give me that show of hands again," he asked.

The hands shot up. Again he shook his head.

"I just want to thank you all," David told them. "I mean, here you are cruising toward graduation. I'm heartened to see you have enough respect for me to give me the courtesy of lying."

Dry chuckles all around, though very few students would meet his gaze. For her part, Christi looked miffed at the mere suggestion, as did Gordon Libertini, who was likely to be valedictorian of the class when all was said and done.

"Cards-on-the-table time," David went on. "Melville was a semigreat writer. *Moby Dick,* though, is dense and excruciatingly boring. Do you think my brain is wired so differently from all of yours that I don't know that? So, listen, who really read the book?"

Christi. Gordon. Half a dozen others.

"Bravo to you," he told those faithful few. Then he glanced around the class at the others. "For the rest of you . . . nothing I can say will make you read the book. So what I'm going to do instead is answer my own question. I'm going to tell you what fascinates me the most about *Moby Dick* from the point of view of story and structure."

He glanced at Gordon. "Who is the protagonist of the novel?"

Christi's hand shot up, but it was clear the question was for Gordon, who replied in a tone that suggested it was an insultingly simple question.

"Ahab."

David nodded slowly. "And who is the hero?"

In the back of the class, Ashley Garbarino shot up her hand and spoke without being called on. "Aren't they the same thing?"

"Are they?" the teacher replied.

"I get it!" Christi said quickly.

With a soft, proud smile, David nodded toward her. "Christi? Go ahead."

"The way the story is structured, Ahab is the protagonist and the whale is the antagonist. But what you said before? About language? Melville always describes Ahab as this, like, dark devil, storming around the deck, terrifying his men. And the whale is this pure, white, innocent creature. Almost, like, angelic or something. So even though they function like that—"

"In those traditional roles," David prompted.

"Exactly," the girl said quickly. "Even though they function in those traditional roles, the language is telling you it isn't true, that Ahab is the villain, and Moby Dick is the hero."

David smiled broadly. "Bravo," he said, and offered her a little golf clap.

Though he was pleased both with himself and with Christi's intuitiveness, he could see that the class was slipping away from him again. And who could blame them? They were supposed to be discussing a literary classic whose density and archaic language were a chore for all but the most devoted literary scholars.

He clapped his hands together loudly. "All right. Everyone clear on what Christi was just saying about *Moby Dick*? It's going to be on the final."

Groans all around.

David walked around behind his desk and grabbed

the cart upon which sat the TV and VCR he had retrieved from the audio-visual department.

"However, there's more to it than that. You are all, at the very least, going to skim *Moby Dick* for its essence, and for its structure. But it gets better. I am also going to introduce you to a modern example of the very point Christi just so eloquently expressed. We'll spend our next few class meetings viewing a film in which the traditional protagonist/antagonist structure and relationships exist, but in which you will also find that the director and cinematographer have purposely used the language of film—music, camera angles, lighting, et cetera—to undermine those traditional roles and give us a very different idea about who is the hero and who is the villain."

David turned to face the class. Even Brad Flecca was awake now, and staring at him with an expression of surprise that was almost absurd in its childlike honesty.

During that single school year, David had blazed through Greek and Roman mythology, Poe, Shakespeare, Robert Frost, James Baldwin, Raymond Chandler, and John Irving, all to teach them about the nature of stories. But this was the first time he had brought in another storytelling medium.

Olivia Costa raised her hand.

"Yes, Olivia?"

"What's the movie?"

David smiled, savoring the question. "It's called *Blade Runner*."

In the teachers' lounge, Lydia Beal scraped the last spoonful out of her plastic yogurt container and shook her head in amazement. "I swear to God, David, I do not know how you get away with it every year."

They sat together at a small round table, one of several in the room where the teachers congregated during free periods and in shifts at lunchtime. Much like the old granite school itself, the room was a featureless, rectangular box. There were three windows on one side and Catholic school–themed posters on the one opposite, a television and VCR, a microwave oven, a coffeemaker, and a refrigerator.

The microwave oven timer dinged loudly and he rose to retrieve the popcorn he had made. The smell of it filled the room, rich with butter and salt. Half the pleasure of the stuff was the scent, as far as he was concerned.

"Get away with what?" he asked as he returned to the table.

"That movie," Lydia replied, narrowing her eyes. "Every year."

"Hey. *Blade Runner* is a classic." David popped a few pieces of microwave popcorn into his mouth to cover his grin.

Lydia rolled her eyes.

The only other person in the room was Ralph Weiss, an enormous, fiftyish man with thinning hair, thick glasses, and a mountainous gut. Weiss was an officious man of intimidating size who lectured his students and thought that was the same thing as teaching.

Weiss had been perusing a magazine on American military history—probably for things to read aloud in class—but perked up at Lydia's remarks. It would have been impossible for him not to have overheard the conversation, and it was just as impossible for him to keep his opinion to himself. He settled his reading glasses on top of his head, where his graying rust-colored hair had receded like the lowest of low tides, and he scratched thoughtfully at his beard.

"Miss Beal is correct, Mr. Bairstow," Weiss intoned. "You have a responsibility to teach those children until such time as they have graduated."

"I *am* teaching them, *Ralph*," David replied curtly.

Weiss flinched. He was an old-fashioned sort of man, but only when it suited him. One of his eccentricities was that he insisted upon addressing nearly every-one—and certainly everyone younger than he—in formal fashion. He always seemed to put particular emphasis on this quirk with David, who imagined it had to do with the fact that Weiss had taught *him* world history so many years before.

Though the last thing David wanted to do was ruffle feathers, he could not bear the older man's condescension. Yet he was forced to fight back in small ways. Calling him Ralph, for instance. Drove the big man absolutely crazy.

"What you are doing, Mr. Bairstow, is wasting valuable class time by letting these children sit and watch a science-fiction movie that has nothing to do with teaching English. In addition, the film contains violence and nudity, not to mention profanity. I have no idea why Sister Mary allows it, but I suspect if the archdiocese were aware of it, they would be scandalized."

At David's side, Lydia Beal inhaled sharply, her teeth whistling a tiny bit. "Mr. Weiss, maybe you should take that up with—"

"No, Lydia. It's fine," David interrupted.

He glanced at her, saw the worry in her eyes, and knew she feared that he would overreact. A tiny smile lifted the edges of his mouth. Those who knew him well would have realized there was no humor in it, nor even a trace of amusement. David Bairstow prided himself on being a good guy, but part of that included not backing down from a fight. Not ever.

"Y'know, Ralph," he began, "maybe you're right. Maybe I should go in there every morning and do them the favor of *reading Moby Dick* to them like they're still in grade school."

Angry lines appeared on Weiss's forehead along with a few drops of sweat as he bristled at David's words. In almost surreal fashion, David noticed that one of the drops of sweat was magnified by the thick reading glasses propped on the enormous man's head.

"Mr. Bairstow," he began, with the same reproachful tone he had used when David was in the tenth grade.

"*Mis-ter* Weiss," David replied pleasantly. His smile

twitched ever so slightly. "I don't tell you how to teach history—though God knows someone should—so I would appreciate it if you wouldn't try to tell me how to teach English."

Practically spitting in rage, Weiss stood up. His chair scraped the floor and nearly tipped over; only by some miracle did it remain upright. He grabbed his books and the magazine he had been reading from his table, folded his glasses and slid them into his pocket, then crossed the space between them in two strides.

The door to the teachers' lounge opened and Annette Muscari came in with several other teachers. The group were chatting happily amongst themselves and did not at first notice the tension in the room. David glanced at them only once, but he knew the very moment they realized something was going on, for their voices trailed off almost instantly.

"You, sir," Weiss began, towering over him and glowering dangerously. "You, Mr. Bairstow, are a blemish on the face of Catholic education. An embarrassment to this school and to the archdiocese."

David nodded slowly. "That may be so, Ralph. But if so, we've got a lot more in common than I ever realized."

Weiss opened his mouth, perhaps about to attempt a sharp retort, but all that came out was his dragon breath, which stank as though he had been eating putrefying meat. He pursed his lips, his face growing redder, a few more beads of sweat popping out on his forehead.

Then he simply groaned, turned on his heel, and left the room. He banged the door shut behind him like a petulant teenager.

"Holy shit," Lydia muttered under her breath.

David snickered. "You're in a Catholic school, Lyd."

She laughed and buried her head in her arms on the table. Annette came over immediately, eyes wide with fascination. The other teachers, including Clark Weaver, a meek, bespectacled man who had been at

St. Matthew's even longer than Weiss, kept to themselves. They spoke in cautious tones; David imagined they were speculating about what had happened, but none of them were friendly enough with him just to ask.

Except Annette, of course. The two of them had started the same year and become fast friends. She was a lesbian, cute and waifish and just a little butch, but she and the school administration had established their own Don't Ask, Don't Tell policy, so despite the archdiocese's position on homosexuality, it had never been a problem. Sister Mary did not necessarily see eye-to-eye with the cardinal.

Thank God, David thought.

"What was that all about?" Annette asked cattily as she pulled up a chair. "I don't think I've ever seen Ralphie that pissed off."

"You didn't have him as a teacher," David reminded her.

"True," she admitted. Her green eyes sparkled beautifully, her blond bob giving her an almost elfish countenance.

David stuck a hand into the bag of microwave popcorn, which had cooled enough now that the so-called butter on it was a thin layer of grease. Not that that would stop him from eating it.

Annette grabbed his wrist. "Talk to me, Dave," she commanded. Her eyes ticked toward Lydia. "What happened?"

"*Blade Runner,*" Lydia replied calmly, her tone grave, as if those two words were enough to explain it all.

Oddly enough, they were.

Annette started laughing. At the table nearest the windows, the other teachers now turned to pay attention to the proceedings. David caught them looking and offered a tiny shrug. Mr. Weaver seemed to chuckle a bit as he pulled a banana out of a brown paper bag. It was an endearing response, and David liked him a great deal more in that moment than he ever had before.

"I can't believe Sister Mary lets you get away with that every year," Annette told him.

"I just said the same thing," Lydia noted.

David raised an eyebrow at Annette, wondering if she was aware of the irony of her questioning the things Sister Mary indulged from *him*.

"Look, it's a legitimate teaching tool. All right, so it's got some questionable content. But they're seniors. Seventeen- and eighteen-year-old American kids. I'm pretty sure they've seen worse. The first year, Sister Mary dragged me down to the dungeon afterward and read me the riot act. Then I explained what I was getting at, what the lesson was that I was trying to teach about storytelling. She thought about it, and she agreed with me."

Lydia put a hand to her mouth, her eyes wide in a scandalized expression that would have been tiresome on most people but was almost precious from the wholesome forty-five-year-old divorcée.

"You mean Sister Mary has seen the movie?" she asked.

Clark Weaver cleared his throat noisily, drawing the attention of all those in the room. "Actually, she's quite the movie buff," he revealed. "Got a bigger DVD collection than most of the students, I'd wager."

"You learn something new every day," Annette said, a bit awed.

David sighed. "Unless you're in Ralph Weiss's class."

"Good comeback, by the way," Annette noted as she stood and went to get her lunch from a cabinet.

"Well, you should have heard them at it before you came in," Lydia replied. Then she also stood. "Almost time for our shift on lunch duty, David."

He glanced at his watch. They had a few minutes, but he suspected Lydia was going to visit what the teachers still called "the lavatory" first. There was a bathroom right off the teachers' lounge, but Lydia never used it.

David smiled fondly at her. "I'll meet you down there."

After Lydia left, Annette slid into the chair she had vacated. Even when she ate, she did so almost demurely. That, combined with her thin lips and somewhat pointed ears, only added to the otherworldliness of her appearance. All those things had led him to give her a nickname only he and one other person ever called her.

"So what else is up with you, Elf?" he asked.

Annette smiled sweetly at his use of the pet name.

"Not much. We still on for tonight?" she asked.

They had planned a trip into the North End for dinner, an early celebration of her birthday, which was still a week or so away.

"Wouldn't miss it," he told her.

With a mouthful of peanut butter-and-banana-sandwich and a cup of coffee in her hand, Annette turned to him abruptly, sloshing a few drops of coffee onto the table.

"David," she mumbled, her mouth full. "I wasn't sure if I should tell you this or not, if you'd want to know, I mean."

He understood her, though just barely. Annette chewed quickly and then swallowed.

"I heard from Janine last night," she said, her expression now serious.

Janine. The only other person in the world who called Annette Elf. David knew the news was not good. The sparkle had disappeared from Annette's eyes.

In his life, David had had many good friends. Somehow, though, they all seemed to slip away. Even those he still cared deeply for were not really a part of his life anymore. Most of his high school and college friends were married and had children, and thus had lives too complicated for such frivolities as a movie or a few beers with an old buddy. Only Vince Piselli still sought him out regularly, but Vince was divorced, and seemed to be trying to recapture the drunken debauchery of their college days.

So, almost by attrition, Annette had become his best

friend. None of which lessened the degree to which he cared for her. Perhaps it was because she was gay and he knew that there could never be anything sexual between them, but David adored her more than almost any other woman he had ever met. One exception was his sister, who lived in California and with whom he spoke at least twice a week. The other was Janine Hartschorn, the woman he had almost married.

Janine had been teaching mathematics at St. Matthew's for only a year before David and Annette came along. The three of them had quickly become almost inseparable. Not long after, David and Janine fell in love. For fourteen months it seemed perfect. They talked about the future. Then the past came back to haunt them in the form of Janine's ex, who had broken her heart not long after college.

He could still remember the words she had used to tell him the best thing in his life was gone. *I love you,* she had said, her voice quavering. *But if I don't give this a shot, see what I can make of it, I'll regret it for the rest of my life, and I'd end up resenting you for that. We'd both be miserable.*

With regret, he also remembered his response, the bitter words he still wished he could take back. *Yeah. At least this way only one of us is miserable.*

"What happened?" he asked hesitantly.

"She lost the baby."

A twinge of pain shot through his heart and he closed his eyes for a moment. The asshole had gotten Janine pregnant and had left her. Annette had told him that much, had even suggested that he call, but David thought that if Janine wanted to hear from him, she would let him know.

But this . . .

"How?"

Annette bit her lip slightly. She dipped her head toward him, then shot a quick glance at the other teachers. When she spoke again, her voice was almost a whisper, intimate and pained. "You sure you want to hear all this?"

David nodded.

"Okay, maybe one in ten first pregnancies, women have what's called preeclampsia. Blood pressure goes way, way up, and circulation to the fetus drops precipitously. It's dangerous stuff. But for Janine, it was worse. She developed another condition, or syndrome, or whatever. I don't even remember the name. Anyway, with the blood pressure up, the liver goes into overdrive and starts almost attacking the red blood cells and the platelets, destroying them.

"The short version of that is that with a really low platelet count, your blood won't clot. That means they can't perform a C-section and take the baby without having the mother bleed to death. I'd guess even vaginal birth is dangerous at that point, but the baby's coming out one way or another. But when the mother's system goes into distress—and we're talking critical—so does the baby's.

"Janine almost died, but she pulled through. The baby didn't make it. Now they've got her on all this antidepression medication and stuff. She sounded pretty bad."

"God," David whispered, dropping his gaze. He shook his head, unable to understand how things for Janine had come to this. He could not even begin to imagine how devastated she must have been.

Deeply saddened, he raised his eyes again. "Annette? Do you . . . do you think it would be too awkward for her if I went to see her?"

Annette reached across the table and twined her fingers within his. "I think that's a wonderful idea."

He thought on it for a minute, reluctant but at the same time driven by love and compassion for Janine. What they had might be in the past, but that did not mean he had to stop caring for her, particularly now, when she would need support the most.

"I'll go tomorrow afternoon," he decided. Quickly, he glanced at his watch. "I'm late, though. I'll catch up with you after school."

Annette gave him a nod. "Great."

As David pushed back his chair and rose, the door to the teachers' lounge swung open abruptly and Lydia Beal walked in, a stricken expression on her face.

"Ralph Weiss just had a heart attack in the cafeteria," she said, her voice strained.

"He's dead."

It was not sleep. At least, not in any meaningful way; not in any way that would have provided the sort of replenishment of body and soul, the sweet solace of dreams, the retreat to blissful oblivion, that people gave themselves over to each night.

Ever since she had first regained consciousness in the hospital and seen the despair on the faces of her caretakers, Janine had not had a single moment of the precious sleep that she had once taken for granted. She slept, certainly, but it was a shallow thing, haunted by the voices and rattles and tiny disturbances of the world around her. Yet she retreated to that unsatisfying limbo state again and again, if only to avoid the tears.

For when she was awake, she wept.

Depression, the nurses called it. A doctor had prescribed a drug called Zoloft for her. It was meant to regulate her mood. Janine took the pills they gave her and the drug did seem to dull her mind, to numb her ever so slightly. But it could not relieve her of the burden she bore. Perhaps if it really were depression, the drug might have had another effect. But it was not that at all.

It was grief. Bone-deep, heart-wrenching, soul-searing grief.

How could they not know that? she had thought at one point.

But slowly she came to understand the truth. They did know, of course, but they talked their way around her grief because there wasn't a pill for that.

Even the therapist or psychiatrist or whatever she was that the hospital sent in to speak with her seemed to know the truth of it. She talked about grief, clinical observations about spiritual agony, statistics and analogies and recovery forecasts worthy of a spreadsheet, or at the very least a display of augury more appropriate to such predictions, such as a throwing of the bones or a glance at a crystal ball.

Talk. All talk.

Grief had no cure.

Her body recovered more quickly. Though she had been through a massive physical trauma, the nurses seemed pleased to find no sign of long-lasting effects. No stroke, no brain damage, no need for a replacement liver or kidney.

Janine did not see the doctors much.

Rest, they told her. All she needed now was rest.

She laughed at that one, but nobody seemed to get the joke. They seemed not to understand that the periods of time she spent with her eyes closed were more like a trance than actual sleep. Rest played no part in it at all.

At least she stopped crying, however. By the end of the third day after her own body had killed her baby, she had run out of tears. She had even begun to make phone calls to a few close friends—all of whom she had badly neglected during her catastrophic reunion with Spencer. They were good friends, though. Not one of them reminded her that they had warned her; not one brought up what a stupid bitch she had been to fall for him again.

Not that she needed reminding.

There was a merciless, unforgiving voice in her head that seemed to be with her all the time, crucifying her for allowing herself to be swept back into Spencer Hahn's vortex.

And, of course, there was her mother.

Mother.

On Friday morning, four days after Janine Hartschorn had nearly died, she lay in that limbo state, not deep enough for dreams but not awake, and her subconscious mind became aware of an intrusion. The soft hiss of panty hose scraping together, the rattle of the blinds being opened, the slight redistribution of weight as someone sat on the end of the bed.

Her eyelids lazily parted once, twice, a third time. Then she frowned. At the end of the bed sat her mother, Ruth Vale, in a dark jacket and skirt that might have been an advertising executive's power suit or mourning clothes.

"Mom?" she rasped, stretching weakly. "I didn't expect you so early."

Ruth had once had hair as raven black as Janine's own, but when it had begun to gray she dyed it auburn and almost always wore it up in a severe braid. Power suit. Power hair to match.

"It isn't early, Nina," her mother corrected, hazel eyes surrounded with lines of disapproval. "It's nearly ten. You did say that lesbian girl was going to pick you up this afternoon, didn't you?"

Right, Janine thought. *Today's the day they send me home.* The thought left her with an even hollower feeling, and she was grateful that Annette was going to be there with her.

"Her name's Annette, Mom," Janine replied, growing even more tired, as though her mother were sucking the life out of her. "Yes, she's picking me up."

"Good," her mother said with a tiny nod, as though marking something off on some mental checklist.

She stood and brushed imaginary lint off her skirt, then straightened it. "I have a meeting later today, so I'm afraid I'm going to have to catch the shuttle right away."

Janine frowned, her mouth open just slightly, the air traveling in and out drying her lips. Her mother had been just as inept at comforting her these past days as the doctors and nurses, even more so, in fact. But simply having her there had at least given Janine something to hold on to.

"I'll be back for the service, of course," Ruth Vale added hurriedly, as though she knew she had to apologize for something but was not quite sure what. "Larry and I will both be here."

Larry. Janine's father, a pharmacist, had died young. Two years later, when Janine was only ten, her mother had married Larry Vale, another exec at the ad agency in Manhattan.

"I told you, I don't know if I'm going to do a . . . a memorial."

Ruth sighed. "Whatever you think is best."

When her mother bent over the bed to kiss her forehead, the way she had always done when Janine was sick as a girl, it was all she could do not to scream at the woman for being such a coward, too afraid of her daughter's pain to share the burden.

Then she was gone.

Like a phantom limb, Janine felt the weight against her body where she would have been holding the baby if he had lived. Her breasts ached with milk she would never provide. As she sat there in the sterile hospital bed, gray light filtering through the industrial windows, she held her arms up as if cradling the child. David Hartschorn, that would have been his name.

She had wanted to name him David.

On Friday afternoon, two days after Ralph Weiss's untimely death, David sat behind his desk and stared out the window. The bell had rung only a handful of minutes before, but the exodus of his students had been swift and he had been left completely alone.

At the moment, alone was good.

The pleasure he usually took as he watched his seniors march toward their final days at St. Matt's had been drained from him as though he had worked up a decent beer buzz and was coming down. His eyes burned a little and his head ached. Yet this was no hangover.

Several swallows adorned the branches of the tall oak just outside the window of his classroom, and

David watched them hop nervously about, whistling to one another as though each were on sentry, eternally vigilant. They seemed inelegant, those birds. Almost ridiculously anxious. They reminded him of people. All his life David had felt that way, always worried about where the next turn in the road would lead, always running on nerves, not instinct.

That knowledge pained him, but he could not escape it. A breeze blew into the classroom, strong enough to ruffle the papers on his desk, and he moved a pencil holder over to weight them down. His name was spelled out in gilt letters on the pencil holder: DAVID J. BAIRSTOW. As a kid, he had sometimes been Dave or even Davey, but mostly David. Except to his grandfather, who had always just called him *boy*. His mother had told him that the old man was disappointed David had not been named after him, but David didn't believe that, even back then.

As a child, David had been coddled almost to suffocation by his parents. His father, James, had been an accountant, and his mother, Rita, had stayed at home. A good life, no question. Even without closing his eyes, it was easy for him to bring to mind richly detailed snapshots of his childhood. The trees in the front yard he and his little sister Amy had loved to climb, one of which he had fallen from at the age of seven, biting nearly all the way through his lower lip. The tiny hill in the backyard where they had gone sledding in the winter; the way they had shoved their frozen feet under the baseboard heaters to warm up. The weekends—or entire weeks—they had spent with their parents on Cape Cod or up on the coast of Maine, when his father had said, "Damn the cost, it's time for the family, not the clients."

But too many of those trips to the coast of Maine had been to stay at Grandpa Edgar's in Kennebunk. The old man had been a firefighter in the town for forty-seven years before he had retired to a life of whiskey and cigars and reading the obituaries to find out who wouldn't be showing up to the weekly poker game.

Edgar Bairstow had showered his family with all the love he knew how to give. His gruff manner and rough play had always terrified Amy, yet Grandpa Edgar had loved her to distraction.

He had hated David.

It had taken him forever to stop making excuses for his grandfather. The old man had been dead three years and David had already graduated college when he finally accepted the truth of it. His grandfather had taken an instant dislike to him as a child, and had made no secret of his disdain for his grandson for the rest of his life.

The knowledge made David sad, but it also made him angry. What right, he had thought time and again, did an old man have to stain a young boy's world and self-image with such confusion and doubt? He could look back upon his life and recall all the times when he had found reason to celebrate, and too many of them were eclipsed by the dark cloud of his grandfather's derision.

It may have been that Edgar Bairstow thought his grandson's interest in books and his decided lack of involvement in sports of any kind was a sort of betrayal. David could distinctly remember his mother telling him, with a roll of her eyes, that his grandfather was happy he had a date for the eighth grade dance because the old man had thought David was gay.

Grandpa Edgar had died in his sleep the summer between David's freshman and sophomore years in college, and David had been secretly happy to see him go. That emotion both surprised and disturbed him, which was why he had held it so close. But once his grandfather was dead, David had hated him even more.

Hated him because he still loved him. Despite everything, he had craved the man's affection his entire life, and that had built up a kind of love in him.

Edgar Bairstow had been his grandfather, and even after his death he still wanted the man's blessings.

David hated him even more for that. It was an endless cycle of guilt and sorrow, a trap too simple to become mired in, and so he rarely let his mind wander there.

Today, in the aftermath of Ralph Weiss's sudden death, he could not help it.

Down the hall a door slammed and he glanced up to see one of the janitors, Melvin Halliwell, squeaking by with an ancient metal bucket and broom. Broken from his reverie, David reached into the top drawer of his desk and withdrew the book he had scoured the school library for earlier that day.

It was his high school yearbook.

The previous night he had searched his entire house for it but come up with nothing. That morning he had not been able to let the quest slip from his mind, and so had gone to the library. They had an archive of yearbooks from every graduating class since St. Matthew's inception.

David had not had time to look at it before his classes resumed, only shoved it into the desk. Now he studied the cover, the blue cloth and the image of the mustang inscribed there. The school mascot, the mustang.

Surprised to find his fingers hesitating, he forced himself to open the book. He flipped past the early pages at first, went right to the roster of students, the rows of photographs from the eighties that looked so silly now. Though there were a few faces he barely recalled, he was pleased with how many of his classmates' names popped immediately to mind before he had even read the words beneath their images. Lisa Farrelly. Colin McCann. Chris Franzini. Nicole Rice.

A tiny spike of sadness shot through him as he saw a picture of Maggie Russell.

Death, it seemed, was all he could think about today. Too many reminders. Whole months went by without his ever thinking of Maggie Russell, but whenever he did, he still missed her. More than fifteen years gone, and still, when he thought of her, Maggie's smile was fresh in his memory.

David Bairstow did not want to die.

He recognized it as a foolish thought. Certainly it was no breakthrough in human consciousness. Nobody wanted to die. But as he lingered over memories of those close to him who were no longer upon the earth, he could not help but wonder where they were now.

Where he would one day go.

He did not want to go. Not anywhere.

Reluctantly, as to a roadblock, he came to the conclusion that he could no longer avoid the thing for which he had retrieved the yearbook in the first place. Still, he put it off one moment longer, to glance out the window. The sparrows were gone.

David flipped back to the faculty section of the yearbook and quickly found the photograph of Ralph Weiss. He'd been thirty pounds lighter then, and though in David's memory of high school Mr. Weiss never seemed anything less than profoundly aggrieved about some matter or other, in the picture he wore a warm, genuine smile.

Now that Ralph Weiss was dead, it pained David to realize how much simpler it would have been, how much less energy it would have cost him, to just accept the teacher as he was. Ralph Weiss had been officious and barely competent as a teacher, but he had also been a benevolent and lonely soul.

"You had to go and die on us, didn't you, Mr. Weiss?" he said to the fifteen-year-old picture.

With a half smile and a shake of his head, he began to page through the yearbook again. Some minutes later, he was not sure how long, there was a rap on the open door.

David glanced up to see Annette standing just inside the classroom.

"Hey, Elf."

"Penny for your thoughts?" she ventured, her brow furrowed in an expression of grave concern.

"Pretty morbid, I'm afraid," he revealed.

"Just wanted to say good-bye. I'll see you at the funeral tomorrow, yeah?"

"Yeah," he agreed. "Maybe we can get something to eat after?"

Annette pushed a stray lock of hair behind her pointed ears. "Maybe. Janine's sort of on her own starting this afternoon, and I'm going to be spending a lot of time with her in the next week or so."

David raised his eyebrows. "She's home already?"

"I'm actually heading over to the hospital to pick her up now, bring her home."

A lengthy silence ticked past. A lone sparrow alighted upon a branch just outside the window and peered in, as if David's earlier scrutiny had driven them off and this solo bird had been sent to see if he'd left yet.

"Do me a favor?" he asked.

"Anything."

"Ask her if she'd like some more company tomorrow. Maybe I'll ride over with you. If she wants me to."

Annette smiled a bit sadly. "I'll ask, but I'm sure she'll be more than happy."

David nodded, pleased with his decision, and with Annette's reaction. She walked over to him and slid onto his lap to stare into his eyes.

"You're a sweet guy, Bairstow. Don't let anyone tell you different."

"Thanks, Elf." He gave her a short, sweet kiss, and amused himself by wondering what Melvin the janitor would think if he spotted Mr. Bairstow with the cute, blond science teacher on his lap.

The good feeling spurred within him by this musing dissipated quickly, however, as his thoughts turned back to Janine Hartschorn, and the baby she had lost. Both of them had been touched by death, though Janine's recent loss was far more tragic and intimate than the death of a colleague. Death was suddenly omnipresent.

David knew there was no way to escape it, but he hoped he would soon be able to return to the bubble of denial most people lived their lives in. The only way to combat the looming inevitability of death was to live.

Just live.

CHAPTER 2

❧

By the time Annette turned the car into Janine's driveway it was after four o'clock. The day had already grown long, but the sun's rays still streamed through the trees whose branches hung out over Winthrop Street. Janine had her window cracked a few inches, and the scents that were carried to her on the breeze were delicious. The landscape of the world seemed to have changed in the week she had spent in the hospital. Spring had truly arrived.

As best she could, she tried to grasp and hold on to the hope the season always provided.

Annette pulled into the small lot beside the rambling old white house and parked. "Home again," she said, and offered her friend a sweet smile before turning off the engine.

"Yeah," Janine agreed. "Home."

To her great surprise, the word resonated in her. This was not really her home. Her father had been born in Medford, but Janine had been raised in Elmsford, New York. That was home. Not her stepfather's house in Scarsdale, and not really her current apartment. Still, ever since college, the Boston area had seemed to wrap its arms around her, to cradle and comfort her in a way that New York could never seem to after her father had died.

Janine stepped out of Annette's weathered SAAB holding the cup of Starbucks cappuccino her friend had so thoughtfully provided, and stared up at the

house. It had been used as offices once. A dentist and
a doctor, brothers. The idea that they had shared the
space seemed wonderful to her, so very New England.
The family still owned the property, but it had been
converted to apartments, one on each of the three
floors. There was an enormous barn in back—left over
from the home's earliest days—and Dr. Feehan, the
landlord, had a million stories about playing in the
barn when he was a child.

A warmth spread through Janine as she stared up
at the house, and she felt a smile beginning to light
up her face. Her heart was heavy with the pain of her
loss, and she knew it would not leave her soon, if ever.
But for the first time she believed that there was room
in her heart for other feelings, other emotions. Home,
at least, was something she could hold on to. In so
many other ways, she felt cast adrift. Over the course
of her pregnancy she had come to mentally identify
herself as a mother. Now, without the baby, she wasn't
sure *what* she was. What her life was supposed to
be now.

"You coming, Janine?"

Annette had paused at the front steps of the apartment house and turned to watch her. With a nod,
Janine followed her into the foyer and they walked
upstairs together.

Her apartment was on the second floor, a two-
bedroom with a small but serviceable kitchen and a
lovely living room with high windows that caught the
sun from three different angles all day long. When she
turned the key in the lock and pushed the door open,
Janine felt a rush of relief. The sunlight gleamed off
the hardwood floor and the windows were open a
crack, letting in the spring breeze.

Inside, she dropped the small bag she had brought
home from the hospital and just wandered around the
place for a moment. All her plants had been watered,
and somehow that seemed important to her. In the
corner of the living room, where she could look down
upon the trees and the barn in the back, her music

stand waited for her. On an antique bench beside it, her violin case lay open, the instrument resting inside.

Home, she thought again.

As if sensing she wanted a few moments to herself, Annette had gone into the kitchen. She could be heard banging about in there, and after a short time Janine became both curious and a little concerned.

"Hey. What's going on in there?" she called.

"Dinner. Or it will be."

Janine's eyebrows shot up in alarm. With an ironic grin, she hurried into the kitchen to find Annette on her knees rifling through a cabinet full of pots and pans.

"Stop right there," Janine ordered. "Not that I don't appreciate your help, but let's face it; in the kitchen, you're a danger to yourself and others."

Annette turned and sat on her butt on the linoleum floor. She shot a baleful glance at Janine. "You know, that whole thing about lesbians not knowing how to cook? It's a myth."

"You make it true," Janine said bluntly.

With a sigh, Annette relented. "My mother made lasagna, okay? I just need a pot to heat up the extra sauce."

"Whew," Janine replied. "You had me scared there for a second."

They shared a bittersweet moment together then, both of them aware that it was likely the first time Janine had smiled in days, the first glimpse of sunlight breaking through the black cloud of her grief. Janine grimly accepted the knowledge that it was only a momentary reprieve, that the numbness she had felt would likely be her regular state for quite some time.

But it wasn't the *only* thing she could feel. Annette had reminded her of that, and she was more grateful than she could ever have put into words.

Though Annette tried to scoot her out of the kitchen, Janine stayed and together they quickly cobbled together a salad to go with the lasagna. Both of them wanted music—Janine especially—but it had to be something uplifting rather than the melancholy songbirds they both often listened to. Janine slipped in Barenaked Ladies' live album, *Rock Spectacle,* and, at odd times during dinner, they both sang along.

A bottle of Corvo Bianco had lain dormant in the fridge for months, and they polished it off between songs and servings of lasagna. Annette never brought up the baby.

After dinner they moved into the living room and Janine put a classical compilation into the CD player. Her violin called to her from the corner as if inspired by the music, but she resisted the temptation to play. There would be time for that. She would rebuild her life one moment at a time.

Janine studied Annette, there beside her on the sofa, and felt a deep and abiding love for her. She had never had a sister, nor in truth any girlfriend in whom she had ever felt she could confide completely. But the day Annette had first come to teach at St. Matthew's, Janine had felt a connection. She had known they would be friends. She cherished the other woman's place in her life, sometimes so deeply as to wish she herself were gay. They had joked about it often enough. And yet somehow, at times to her dismay, she simply could not conjure even the slightest interest in having sex with another woman, even one she loved so deeply.

"Hey," Annette protested, squirming under the intensity of Janine's examination of her. "Do I have sauce on my chin?"

Overwhelmed by emotion, Janine slid closer to her on the couch and laid her head on Annette's chest, holding her tight. She bit her lip to keep tears at bay and sighed heavily.

"Thanks, Elf," she whispered. Janine turned her face up toward Annette's, eyes wide, letting all her pain and affection show through. "I don't think I'd be able to survive this without you."

A kind of uncertainty transformed Annette's face. Her eyelids fluttered a moment, as though she were reluctant to hold Janine's gaze. Then she smiled weakly, and bent to kiss Janine softly on the forehead.

"I love you," she whispered. "You'll get through."

Janine basked selfishly in her friend's dedication for a moment; then she sat up. Her fingers twined with Annette's, and they shared a look of deep regret. Though she knew it was arrogant to think it, Janine had the idea that Annette might care for her as more than a friend, and she tried her best never to imply anything she did not feel.

"I love you, too," she told Annette, her mouth twisted into an expression of the irony she felt.

Annette chuckled softly and shook her head as if erasing something from her mind. "So, what's next?"

"Ben and Jerry's New York Super Fudge Chunk?" Janine suggested.

"Good answer. But I meant for you. Tom Carlson said you could take the balance of the year off, start up teaching again in the fall, right?"

"Yeah," Janine replied slowly. Carlson was the principal at Medford High, where she had taught since leaving St. Matthew's. "I'm torn, though. I don't know what I'd do with myself, you know? I think it might be worse, having that much time to think. I'm leaning toward going back, maybe in a couple of weeks."

"I'm sure your students will be happy," Annette said.

"You kidding? They think I'm Attila the Hun. I wish I could have even a fraction of the rapport with my students as David always has with his."

At the mention of David's name, Annette's eyes lit up.

"What?" Janine asked.

A mischievous smile appeared at the edges of Annette's mouth. "I told you Ralph Weiss died?"

Janine was horrified. "That's something to smile about?"

"No!" Annette quickly protested. "It's just that, well, I talked to David earlier, and he wondered if it would be all right if he came over with me after the funeral tomorrow."

For a moment, Janine could only stare at her. A million thoughts whisked through her mind, leaving her mouth open in a tiny *O* of confusion. *David,* she thought. Her gaze and her memories seemed to ricochet around the living room, resting for only a heartbeat on spots where David had left traces of himself upon her life, a dozen artifacts of their time together.

"Janine?" Annette prodded. "I didn't want to upset you."

"You didn't," Janine promised, glancing shyly away.

"Do you want me to tell him no? I can. He'd understand, you know."

Janine shook her head, a flutter in her chest. "No. No, please tell him I'd love to see him."

The intensive-care unit was quiet, save for the steady beep of monitors and pumps. Not that there was generally a lot of noise in ICU beyond the conversations between doctors and nurses, but often enough, there would be the sounds of despair. Stefanie Harlow was always relieved when she could finish a shift without losing a patient or hearing someone sob. Though she had chosen the ICU, and she believed that she brought some comfort to all her patients, both those who survived and those who did not, it was a constant drain on her emotions.

Two days earlier she had heard a teenage boy singing softly to his unconscious mother. An hour later the woman had died. Stefanie still could not get the song out of her head.

But this evening it was quiet. That was always good.

Then, almost as if summoned by her thoughts, an alarm went off on one of the monitors.

"Damn it," she hissed.

Mr. Haupt was a cancer patient. He had been undergoing radical chemotherapy and had had a heart attack that put him into a coma. Less than two days had passed, and hope for his recovery had dwindled to almost zero. His wife and children had gone home for dinner and a shower, and were due at eight, less than half an hour away.

Stefanie wondered if perhaps he hadn't just grown impatient. Despite all they had done for him, she knew that he must be in a lot of pain.

Chaos erupted in the curtained-off unit around Mr. Haupt as nurses and doctors rushed in. With one look at the patient—and without any need to look at the monitors—Stefanie knew that the man had had another cardiac episode. She also knew that it would be his last.

It's not fair, she thought.

Dr. Pulaski glanced at the monitors, studied Mr. Haupt for a moment, and then held up one hand.

"Don't," he said. "He has a DNR order."

As if a switch had been thrown, the chaos dissipated. Though the monitors still showed the man's fast decline, the alarms were shut off. Stefanie knew that with a do-not-resuscitate order there was nothing more they could do for the man. It just seemed so wrong that his family—who had spent two days in vigil at his bedside—had gone home for a few hours only to return and find him dead.

The others milled around, beginning in advance the work that would need to be done once Mr. Haupt was dead. Stefanie thought it in exceptionally bad taste. She sat on the edge of the bed and held tight to Mr. Haupt's limp hand as the old man's life slipped away.

"Don't go," she whispered to him. "Wait for them, just a little longer."

"Did you say something, Stefanie?" one of the other nurses asked.

"Just a shame they won't get to say good-bye," she admitted.

"It always is," the other woman replied.

On the monitor, Mr. Haupt's pulse flat-lined. Stefanie did not need to see it to know the man was dead. His cold hand had twitched once, squeezing her fingers as though trying to send her a signal. Then it had been still.

Almost instantly, at least it seemed to her, his skin had taken on the waxy sheen of dead flesh. No longer was the thing before her a human being, but a dried husk, a hollowed-out shell.

Tenderly, Stefanie reached her fingers up to touch the man's cheek. When she did, she hissed and pulled her hand away. The dead man's skin was not simply cold; it felt icy, frozen.

"Karen?" she said, softly at first. Then louder. "Karen, could you come over here?"

The other nurse approached. Even as she did, Stefanie watched in horror as Mr. Haupt's skin began to change. He had been drawn and pale at the end, of course, but now his flesh began to look mottled.

"What is it?" she asked.

"I don't know," Karen said quickly, alarm in her tone. "Could be some sort of virus or something."

For the dead man's skin had lost its mottling, but now had become even paler, with the webbing of blue veins beneath the surface clearly visible.

Like marble, Stefanie thought.

Mr. Haupt's right hand darted up, snakelike, and locked in a vise around her wrist. His eyes opened wide and stared up at her. The irises were huge and almost completely black, ringed with burning halos. It was as though the dead man's eyes were a window, and something was peering through from the other side.

Stefanie screamed.

Mr. Haupt sat up and tore the tube from his throat with a gagging noise and the sound of tearing as the tape came away from his face.

"Janine," the dead man rasped in a heavily accented voice. It sounded as though he were speaking on a bad telephone line, tinny and far away. *"Where is Janine?"*

Out of reflex, she reached out a hand to try to stop him from standing. Those black eyes like dying planets bore down upon her, and Stefanie fell backward and sat heavily upon the floor. A chill raced through her that seemed to come both from without and within.

Her breath fogged the air in front of her face.

In her peripheral vision, she saw the cardiac monitor. It still showed nothing but a flatline.

With a single thrust of his outstretched hand, he propelled her face into the monitor, shattering both glass and bone.

"Come on, come on."

Shane Dowling bounced a little on the balls of his feet as the elevator creaked slowly upward. At six-foot-seven and two hundred and sixty pounds, he made the ancient contraption sway unsteadily with just that motion.

"Shoulda taken the goddamn stairs," Shane grumbled. He ran an enormous hand over the black, gleaming skin of his shaven scalp. "Told you, Noah."

Beside him, Noah Levine was the picture of calm. He was more than half a foot shorter than Shane, and thin, but he was strong and quick. The only similarity between the two men was the dark blue security uniform each of them wore.

"Fourth floor, Shane. Stairs wouldn't be much faster, and we'd be winded, then. Got to conserve energy in a crisis."

"*You'd* be winded," Shane retorted, a wry grin on his face. "Crisis, my ass. We don't even know what we're dealing with yet."

"My point," Noah replied.

Their conversation ended abruptly when the elevator dinged and the doors slid open on the fourth floor. Without a word, the two guards hustled out into the corridor and sprinted toward the ICU. Shane held a hand on the billy club attached to his belt as he ran.

The scene in the corridor ahead of them was not one of chaos, but of aftermath. Nurses and orderlies darted into the ICU, though some milled about in the hall, attempting to get a look at what was going on inside. No one seemed frightened, however, which meant that whatever had happened, it was probably already over.

Shane was disappointed.

Noah took the lead slightly, and Shane let him. Though he loved his job, loved being associated with the hospital, he relished the few times when they were actually called in to do more than intimidate some poor sap who wanted to visit a patient outside visiting hours.

His huge rubber soles squeaked on the linoleum as he slowed down. An aging, withered nurse stood in the hall outside the ICU, her eyes wide with voracious fascination as she tried to get a better view. The arrival of the security guards seemed to excite her even more.

Noah pushed past those lingering around the door and into the ICU. Staff members pressed themselves against the walls like spectators at a marathon. Shane followed without enthusiasm, his gaze drifting toward the old nurse; she reminded him of a vulture, circling for prey.

"In there!" she told him.

No shit, lady. I'm not blind, he wanted to say. Instead he offered a thin smile and followed his partner.

The ICU was a shambles. Most of the units had curtains drawn around them, though Shane could clearly see figures moving within, likely doctors and nurses checking on all the patients. One of the units had been thoroughly trashed, monitors shattered, a crash cart overturned, tubes and things scattered on the floor. Even as Shane glanced at it, the light in that unit was turned out.

The cleanup would have to wait until after the police had a look at it, he knew.

In the main traffic area, things were even uglier. A doctor with thinning hair and round glasses with one lens cracked was having stitches sewn into his lip while another doctor checked his left arm and wrist for bone damage.

The worst was the nurse, though. A cute little thing

Shane had noticed plenty of times around the hospital, she lay unconscious on a gurney while Nelson Ramos, a doctor Shane knew, plucked small shards of glass from her face.

"What the hell . . ." he began.

But Noah had already questioned the doc with the stitches in his mouth. The man had been a real sourpuss, but Shane could not blame him. Those stitches had to hurt like a son of a bitch. The nurse tied off the stitches, and the doc turned to them, his brow furrowing with anger.

"What the hell you standing here for?" he asked, his voice muffled by the swelling of his lower lip and his effort not to move it too much.

"Dr. Pulaski," Noah replied, "if you could just—"

"Geoffrey Haupt, seventy-six. He's a cancer patient. He just took off a couple of minutes ago, but he can't get far. He's dying. Hell, we thought he was already dead."

With his right hand, Shane reached up to cover his mouth to hide the grin that spread across his face. All this trouble over some poor old guy about to die from cancer; it was pretty absurd. On the other hand, it was not the first story he'd heard about people at death's door going on a short walkabout before finally heaving their last. The doc was right about one thing, though: Haupt wouldn't get far.

"I'll go after him, Noah," he offered. "If he's not on this floor, he must have taken the stairs. Probably collapsed on the stairwell somewhere."

With a sigh, Shane strode out into the corridor again. Nurses and orderlies cleared out of his way. He glanced around at them, searching for eyes that held answers instead of questions. Every single one of the onlookers had an identical, mystified expression on their faces; all save one.

The vulture, the older nurse who had seemed almost too interested when they arrived, stood against the wall across the corridor. The corners of Shane's mouth twitched up in a rough approximation of a smile.

"Which way?" he asked.

As though she had never imagined such a piece of information might be important, the woman blinked several times, then slowly pointed along the hall toward the exit door at the far end.

"He went for the stairs?" Shane asked.

She nodded. "But . . . he was dead," the woman rasped. He studied her eyes and began to wonder if whatever she had witnessed here had put her into a state of shock.

On the other hand, that wasn't his job. They were in a building filled with people who were supposed to worry about such things, but he was not one of them.

"Thanks," he replied, smiling politely.

"He was," she chided, a bit defensively. "I saw him go. His heart stopped."

"Then it shouldn't be too hard to catch up with him, huh?" Shane asked.

He jogged down the corridor, grateful that the disturbed woman had seen the man make his exit. The last thing he wanted to have to do was check all the rooms up here.

When he banged through the door to the stairs, the lights flickered on the landing. Shane had expected to see the old man right off, and frowned when he realized the place was empty. Out of reflex, he took a quick look up, but gave little credence to the idea that the patient might have gone that way. The guy was on his last legs. Taking off like that likely meant he either wanted to escape, or just wanted to be outside again, one last time. Both options would have led him down. Outside.

'Course, no way's he gonna make it all the way down, Shane thought.

But at the third-floor landing, there was still no sign of the guy. As he started down toward the second floor, he hesitated slightly. It was possible he had chosen the wrong direction; that Mr. Haupt had gone up after all.

His left foot shifted and dropped down to the fourth step.

An alarm screamed up from below.

The emergency exit, Shane thought immediately.

"You've got to be fucking kidding me." He groaned. Then he started to hustle, taking the steps two at a time and leaping the last four or five at each turn of the stairs.

No more than twenty seconds later he jumped down to the first-floor landing—the red bell above the door screamed furiously—and slammed through the emergency exit. The metal door clanged against the brick exterior of the hospital and Shane stalked out into the parking lot.

Phillips Memorial Hospital stood on a small hill in the Lions Gate section of Medford, which had been considered swank in the 1940s and still carried a certain air about it despite the faded quality of the Colonials and Victorians that lined the streets. The hospital, though equally faded, also enjoyed a certain reputation, mostly a holdover from earlier days, though with a somewhat well deserved thanks to its staff.

One benefit it had over Boston-area hospitals was that it had been built in an age and in a neighborhood where few people were willing to encroach upon the sanctity of a place of healing.

Which meant that though Phillips Memorial was filled to brimming with patients and staff, the narrow spillover lot at the rear of the hospital was almost always hauntingly empty save for enormous blue Dumpsters and hazardous waste-disposal units, and the vehicles that routinely arrived to empty them.

A cold wind blew across the empty lot. An empty McDonald's takeout bag whirled and eddied in a dust devil that swirled beneath a distant lamppost as though performing in the spotlight. The door swung shut behind Shane, muffling the alarm bell within. The light above the door had burned out, but the lamps scattered across the lot gave him enough illumination to see.

To see nothing.

But how could there be nothing?

The thumping bass of a car radio cranked all the way up to "deafen" reached him as he stood in the darkness just outside the door and glanced around the lot, utterly bewildered. The alarm bell still wailed inside—he could hear it as if at a distance, or as if it were his morning wake-up and he had buried his head beneath the pillow. Still, it was tangible testimony to the fact that someone had come out this door. It was certainly possible that it had been someone other than the fugitive from the ICU, but the odds against that were astronomical.

On the other hand, how far could a guy dying of cancer get minutes after the ICU staff had been convinced he was done for?

With a sigh, Shane unclipped the two-way radio from his belt. He stepped away from the door and glanced both ways along the length of the back of the hospital. Sanitation containers. That was all he could see. Grimly, and feeling more than a bit absurd, he realized that the old guy might be hiding behind one of them.

He flicked a button on his radio with his thumb. "Noah, you there?"

A moment later, the radio's static was interrupted by his partner's voice. "Here. What've you got? Alarm went off down there. Did the old guy really get that far?"

"Even farther, I think," Shane replied. "I'm at the back door now and I don't see a goddamn thing."

"You don't have visual?" Noah asked.

Shane rolled his eyes, then glared almost angrily at his radio. "You watch too much fucking cable," he snapped. "No, I 'don't have visual,' you moron. I just told you, I don't see anything. If he came out this way, I think he's gone. I'm going to look around a bit, and—"

"Walk the perimeter," Noah instructed. "Report back if you find anything."

With a snicker, Shane thumbed the button on the radio again. "Yeah. I'll do that."

He clipped it to his belt, then glanced around the lot, shaking his head. "Walk the fucking perimeter," he whispered to himself. "Look, Ma, I'm in *Platoon*."

By random choice, he turned left. Thirty feet along was an enormous blue Dumpster with BFD stenciled on the side in letters two feet high. Shane's hand rested comfortably on the haft of his nightstick again, though only by instinct. He was curious about the missing patient, but also amused. It was going to make a hell of a story to tell.

As he passed the Dumpster, he glanced behind it.

The corpse lay sprawled in the sickly yellow lamplight, arms and legs jutting at impossible angles, almost covering one another. Blood had splashed the side of the Dumpster and the pavement all around, and the hospital johnny the patient had worn was drenched crimson and ripped to tatters, pieces of it hanging from the body.

"Holy shit," Shane muttered breathlessly.

The guy had been a patient, and he knew it was probably safe to assume this was their runaway, but he needed to take a closer look. He narrowed his eyes and peered into the semidarkness at the face.

The two faces.

Or more accurately, the two halves of the man's head. Shane blinked, holding his breath as he realized with mounting horror that the corpse before him was not sprawled out, or radically twisted. The dead man had been ripped in half from head to toe: torn right down the middle. His internal organs had spilled out, intestines landing in a wet coil, piled with the halves of the corpse.

Something moved in the dark mass of flesh and viscera, twitched beneath the raw, bloody flesh.

It poked its nose out and its eyes glowed yellow in the low light. A rat. And from the way the dead man's guts began almost to undulate, Shane knew there were many more rats where that came from.

He turned quickly away, fell to his knees, and violently puked his dinner onto the pavement.

CHAPTER 3

❧

The weather the day of Ralph Weiss's funeral was blasphemous. Funerals, David had always believed, were meant to be accompanied by gray skies on the verge of weeping. But that Saturday morning was perhaps the most gloriously beautiful day the spring had proffered thus far. The sky was crystal blue and utterly cloudless. The sun shone down brightly, but softly, without the vigor and even brutality it would adopt when summer blazed in. The lawn at Oak Grove Cemetery was freshly mowed, and the flowers and trees, newly budding, laced the light breeze with sweet, warm scents that made David think of childhood.

As he did so often, that morning he felt like a man comprised of two beings, two David Bairstows. One was the child he had been: the young man lingering into adulthood with the certainty that growing up, becoming adult, was nothing but a myth told to children, no more real than the bogeyman. The other was the David of now: older, forcibly grown wiser by the specter of death and the knowledge of his own imperfections. His attitude toward Ralph Weiss, for one. His inability to make things work with Janine, for another.

The unfortunate truth was that people did, eventually, grow up. Though he knew the process had enriched him, had made him more fully human and more fully aware of the world outside that which his selfish childhood mind had created, he was never quite certain if he was relieved to be quit of that foolish child, or if what he felt was an endless, aching grief.

A snatch of song came into his head. An old one, from his own school days, it was a Bob Seger song. "Against the Wind." "Wish I didn't know now what I didn't know then . . ."

It never ceased to amaze him, all the things he thought he understood as a child that took on entirely new meaning to him as an adult. That song was one of them.

Ralph Weiss's funeral was heartbreakingly small. In addition to the man's wife and grown children, as well as their little ones, there were a handful of friends from the man's private life. Most of the teachers at St. Matthew's had appeared for the mass and the burial, as had half a dozen nuns from the convent by St. Matthew's and a small clutch of only the kindest-hearted and most dedicated students.

It was a sad counterpoint to the last funeral David had attended. The year before, a student named Steve Themeli had been knifed in an argument over drugs. Themeli had been a rough kid, a troublesome student, and raged at every teacher who gave him the low grades he deserved—he had been particularly upset about nearly failing Mr. Bairstow's English class—but seemingly half the student body had turned out to pay their respects when he died. Themeli had been despised by the faculty, but the students had loved him.

It seemed wrong to David that so many would appear for the funeral of a drugged-out tough guy with an attitude the size of Texas, and so few for the old history teacher who had been a bit pompous, but had meant well. Wrong, and sad.

The priest had come from Weiss's own parish, but his words at the church had cemented David's suspicion that he had not known the dead man very well. Any one of Weiss's colleagues could have delivered a more thoughtful eulogy, but of course it would have been most appropriate had Father Charles been asked to do it.

Hugh Charles was the chaplain at St. Matthew's, an eccentric, wise man with sparkling eyes and a storm cloud of a brow when his wrath descended upon unruly students. Many people at St. Matthew's felt that Father Charles was the school's greatest treasure. But there were those among the staff—mostly elderly nuns whose sole function was to monitor study periods— who thought that Father Charles was far too relaxed with his students, and did not engender the proper respect for the clergy in them.

David thought that was pretty much bullshit. It was the very warmth the nuns disdained, combined with a firm, even stern, insistence upon scholarship, that inspired the students to show him more respect than David had ever seen young people give a clergyman. During his own days at St. Matt's, the chaplain had been Father O'Connor, a grim little troll of a man who inspired only dismay and trepidation amongst his charges.

So it was that as the final blessings were said over the casket that held the mortal remains of Ralph Weiss, David kept his eye on Father Charles. A small procession formed of people who desired to pass by the casket to cross themselves and perhaps whisper a parting prayer. Though David had no such desire he would have felt out of place hanging back.

Annette had stood beside him throughout the graveside service, their bodies at times brushing against one another in silent, subconscious communication. *We're here together. Isn't it awful? Let's get out of here as soon as possible. Feel that I love you, and know that it will keep you alive, that love.*

Of course it wouldn't. But the two of them lent each other the comfort of that reassurance.

When the procession began, Annette stepped forward first, breaking that link that had sustained them. With a frown, she turned to glance at him, eyes bright with the expectation that he should follow her. After just a moment, he offered a flicker of a smile and stepped into the procession behind her.

One by one they passed the casket, there beside the hole in the ground where Ralph Weiss's mortal remains would lie until they crumbled to dust. The hole was covered, of course, treated as though it were something obscene, the way some Muslims insisted upon women covering every inch of their flesh.

Garish.

The word came unbidden to David's mind, but he could not banish it. The flowers that bedecked the casket seemed too bright, the sky too blue, the sun too warm with hope and the promise of life.

As David passed the casket, he surprised himself by bending down to pull a single rose from an arrangement near his feet and tossing it onto the casket. Others ahead of him had done it, but he had not known he would follow suit until he felt himself moving.

A whisper of prayer passed his lips and he glanced to his left and saw Weiss's widow, supported by her children, dabbing at her eyes. As though she could feel his eyes upon her, Mrs. Weiss glanced up and stared at him a moment. A flicker of recognition seemed to wash over her face and her brow furrowed slightly. David wondered how many times her husband had complained to her at home about the former student who had come back to St. Matt's to teach and thought he could do it better.

Suddenly flushing with guilt, he broke the gaze and put a hand on Annette's shoulder, rushing her a bit so that they could escape into the small knot of mourners now gathered on the grass near their cars. Annette turned to look at him and blinked in surprise.

"What?" he asked immediately.

She glanced away. "Nothing. I'm sorry. I'm just . . . I guess I didn't expect to find you crying for him."

Baffled, David wiped a hand across his eyes and was astonished when it came away damp with salty tears. He had not even been aware that he was crying.

Annette's gaze was upon him again, and David shrugged.

"Maybe they're not for him, y'know? Maybe they're

for his family. Or maybe they're for me. I sort of feel like I've lost something. Kind of twisted, I know, when I didn't even like him"—he whispered that last—"but still. It's like part of my past has been taken away."

With a sweet smile, Annette reached out to take his hand. She stood on her tiptoes to kiss him, and he still had to bend slightly for her to peck at his cheek.

"You're a good man, David Bairstow. Trust me. I'm pretty objective."

David wiped at his eyes again but found no new tears. He nodded. "Thanks, Elf."

Even as he said it, he saw Father Charles striding across the lawn toward them. Annette followed his gaze and her expression changed a little. She was probably the only person at St. Matt's who didn't get along with the priest. Father Charles had never been anything but nice to her, but he had also admitted to her once that he supported the church's teachings about homosexuality. Annette had been cold to him ever since, though David thought it was more to protect herself emotionally than that she was angry.

Still, they both turned to greet the priest as he hailed them.

"Well, now, two of my favorite teachers," Father Charles announced as he reached them. "You're both well, I trust?"

They assured him that they were. The priest eyed them one at a time, then glanced sidelong toward the casket and the grieving family.

"A teacher is an extraordinary thing," he told them in a tone that would brook no argument. "To draw into the world the mind of another person, young or old, to educate, to provide form and a method of understanding experience. Glorious."

Now he studied them again, a small, beatific smile on his face, though his eyes were stern. "Don't ever forget that, either of you. We are, all of us, teachers. As we are all students. We never stop learning, or teaching. But those who dedicate their lives to the pursuit and the cultivation of knowledge and understanding are God's own instruments. Even one who is less than eloquent, for he still teaches by example, by dedication, the value of learning. There's a special place in heaven for teachers, I believe.

"I really do."

As though trying to determine if they had understood, he eyed them one last time. Then he nodded once and turned to go. With the second step, he paused and faced them again. He went to Annette, touched her gently on the shoulder. Then he took David's hand and leaned in to whisper to him.

"He knew," Father Charles told him, his words hushed and intimate. "Despite your sparring, Ralph knew you still respected him, David, and he respected you as well."

Then he walked off, leaving David to stare after him mutely. He felt the warm sting of another tear slipping down his cheek.

This time, however, he did not pretend to be surprised.

"You're not going to rub it in, are you?" Annette asked. "That she made a mistake leaving you?"

With an embarrassing snort of laughter, David turned to stare at her in shock and amazement.

"Jesus, Annette, no!" he said, snickering a bit. "You're unbelievable."

"Well, she did dump you, after all."

He adopted a hurt expression that was only half-feigned. "It was a mutual decision."

"Yeah, mutual 'cause she wanted to give Spencer another shot at the brass ring," Annette replied.

David had no response for that. He stared at Annette for a moment. She sat behind the wheel of her aging SAAB and sipped at her coffee as she waited for the red light to change. Medford Square traffic was arrayed all around them, creating an illusion that they were jammed up. But David knew from experience that as soon as the light turned green, it would flow.

Annette pushed a lock of her bobbed blond hair over her left ear and turned to gaze back at him.

"That wasn't meant to hurt you," she said, studying him. "I'm just saying there's nothing wrong with being a little angry at her. You guys had a good thing going and she fucked it up."

David nodded. He remembered the night Janine had revealed to him that Spencer wanted to be back in her life, and that she intended to let him. Her perfume had a cinnamon scent that insinuated itself into his nostrils and his brain, sparking instincts both romantic and lustful. Even now he could never inhale the aroma of cinnamon without forming illicit pictures of their lovemaking in his mind.

A tiny smile flickered across his lips as he thought of that scent now. But it was a fleeting thing, that smile. For his mind was on their words that night, her telling him it did not mean that she did not care for him, and him declaring that he believed, wholeheartedly, that a day would come when she would regret it, regret abandoning what they'd shared.

That day had most assuredly come. Yet David found only sadness for Janine now that it had. He certainly had never imagined something like this when he had spoken those words.

"I'd never do anything to hurt her, Elf," he said.

"You still love her?"

David glanced at Annette. She cradled her coffee between her thighs and rested both hands on the wheel.

"You know I do," he said. "But I've moved on. You don't just freeze in place when a relationship ends. Or, okay, you do, but not for long. Life happens when you're trying your best to wallow in your misery."

Annette chuckled at that. "Now, there's a bumper sticker slogan." She shook her head. "It's going to be fine. Really. No pressure. You care about her. She's had a rough time. Anything else is just subtext."

The light turned green and Annette accelerated, nosing her way through other cars until she was headed up Winthrop Street toward Janine's apartment. David watched the familiar storefronts and houses ticking by, the sweet spring breeze in his face. Though he was a teacher in a Catholic school, he was not in the habit of praying. Yet in that moment he silently thanked God for the weather. Between the sadness of Ralph Weiss's funeral and the anxiety he felt over seeing Janine again, a rainy day might have just about done him in.

He had removed his jacket and tie after they had left the cemetery. Now he unbuttoned and rolled up his sleeves. The air was full of the smell of growing things; David liked that. An old seventies song came on the radio. Just the opening chords of "Brandy" were enough to make him chuckle and turn up the volume. Softly, David began to sing along.

Annette laughed and joined in.

The brakes on the SAAB whined in protest as Annette slowed to turn into the driveway of the old house where Janine had an apartment. Oak and maple trees dotted the property, and in the back, beside the barn, wild lilac bushes were already beginning to bloom. There were only a couple of cars in the small parking area, but he spotted Janine's familiar Toyota in the farthest spot. A wicked flash went through his mind. *Oh, the things we did in that car.* They'd been like teenagers.

A twinge of guilt made him close his eyes a moment. There was a lot more to his feelings for Janine than such memories, though he cherished them. She needed him here as a friend, not her ex-boyfriend. David opened his eyes, cast a sidelong glance at Annette as she pulled the car into the nearest spot, and wondered if men really were the sex-obsessed pigs modern culture cast them as, or if women were just better at hiding it.

"The eagle has landed," Annette said, mostly to herself.

As they climbed out of the car, David looked

around again at the house and the yard. There was a kind of electricity in the air. His surroundings were both familiar and yet surreal, the way he felt every time he drove past the places he had played as a boy, as though a wrinkle had formed in time.

As that thought crossed his mind, a rare cloud passed across the sun and its light dimmed, casting the world around them in a pall of gray. David shuddered as though chilled. Something in motion caught his attention off to the right, and his gaze flicked toward the barn again. One of the enormous old doors was open and in its recesses he saw the MG convertible stored there by the retired doctor who owned the place.

Beyond the car, though, that was where something had moved.

A figure—a person—watched him from the shadows beyond the car. In that moment in which the sunlight was occluded, he caught the hint of a beard and thick, knitted eyebrows. But then the cloud passed and the rays of the sun made everything glow brilliantly once more. In the barn, the shadows deepened, and he could no longer see the man.

Still, the chill he had felt in that moment without the sun remained.

"What is it?" Annette asked.

David started a bit, then turned. She stood on the top step, the door to the foyer open, and waited for an answer. He had been so distracted that he had not even heard her press the buzzer for Janine to let them in, though she must have.

"Nothing," he replied as he shook off that chill. "Just saw someone in the barn. Probably Dr. Feehan, right? It's mostly his stuff in there, I think."

"Probably. Though I don't know that I've ever seen him," Annette said as they stepped into the foyer and closed the door behind them. "Damn shame to leave that sweet little car gathering dust in there, though. Janine should get in his good graces; maybe he'll will it to her."

"Maybe he'll will it to *you*?" David suggested.

"If God weren't so grumpy, He'd be doing stuff like that for people all the time," Annette replied, a wistful grin on her face.

"God's grumpy?"

"You taken a look at the world lately?"

"Wow, good afternoon, Miss Pessimist," David teased.

Annette shot him the middle finger over her shoulder as she went up the stairs to the second floor. At the landing, she barely paused before she knocked on Janine's door. David took a deep breath.

He heard her footsteps as she crossed the apartment. The click of the lock quickened his heart, and he was startled by the realization of exactly how much trepidation he felt about this meeting.

The door swung open. Janine wore a tight, white, ribbed cotton top and burgundy Levi's. Her feet were bare, finger- and toenails painted a dark, bruised red. Her black hair framed her full, pale features in a way that had always reminded him of old-style Hollywood glamour. Even in jeans.

But it was her eyes that caught him. Though they seemed brown most of the time, they had a way of shifting color with the light, or even with her mood. Gold and amber and copper, Janine's eyes were all those colors, if you simply caught her at the right moment.

When she opened the door, her gaze went to Annette first. Janine smiled tentatively. Then she looked at David, and her smile turned sad, wistful. To him, frozen in that moment, she seemed diminished somehow, fragile and tentative, as though she had learned a terrible secret.

He supposed that she had.

"Hey," she said.

"Hey."

"I'm really glad you came."

Then the melancholy seemed to burn right out of her, her smile sparkled, and he thought of the cloud that had passed over the sun just before they had come inside.

Janine stepped out into the hall and embraced him forcefully. Her body felt full and *right* against him. Where Annette was petite and girlish, Janine was tall and full-bodied; not exactly voluptuous, but doubtless in that neighborhood.

They fit together like the pieces of a puzzle. He recalled the way they had lain together at night before drifting to sleep, when she had nuzzled against him, his arm around her, her leg thrown over his. A puzzle, yes, and how well the pieces fit had seemed to hold some divine truth of the universe then, as if there really were such a thing as destiny.

And maybe there is, he thought.

He kissed her cheek. She smelled like cinnamon.

I want to live with a Cinnamon Girl. I could be happy the rest of my life with my Cinnamon Girl.

He smiled a bit sadly when he thought of that old song. David held Janine at arm's length and felt something pass between them. All of his nervousness dissipated in that moment.

"You look great," he said. "As usual."

"I'm a wreck," she replied with nonchalance. "It must be the Zoloft the doctor's got me on, but thanks for saying."

With that, she led them inside.

The apartment brought back even more memories. He spotted the elegant glass sculpture he had given her after they had been together a few months. It was of a dancer in a beautiful gown. It still held a place atop the entertainment center in the living room.

The spring breeze made the leaves of Janine's jungle of plants quiver and sway. Something soft and jazzy played on the sound system in the room. Deliciously spicy odors filled the apartment.

"What's that smell?" Annette asked. "I thought we were just going to have sandwiches."

"I felt like cooking," Janine said with a small shrug. "Kung Pao shrimp with cashews."

"You didn't have to do that," David said quickly.

"No big deal. I haven't cooked in a while. The mood struck me. I'm unstoppable when the mood strikes me."

"Yes, we know," Annette put in.

Janine shot her a withering glance, then strode toward the kitchen. Annette glanced at David and rolled her eyes. She wore a tiny smirk.

"It's just about ready," Janine called from the kitchen.

"Hey," David said softly.

Annette frowned at his tone of voice.

"Maybe she doesn't need that right now," he suggested.

"It's exactly what she needs," Annette replied. "To be with her friends, and to think about something else."

A moment later, Janine called them in to fill their plates and they sat around the living room quite informally, eating Kung Pao shrimp and studiously avoiding any talk about Spencer Hahn, past relationships, or the baby Janine had carried inside her.

Its ghost lingered in the room with the Oriental spices and the soothing jazz music. And yet David thought that was probably all right. That loss was part of Janine's life now, part of who she was. Though they never discussed the pain she so obviously felt, it did not seem awkward to him that they avoided it. It was *her* pain, after all. She would share it if and when she wanted or needed to.

What are you doing here?

The words echoed through Janine's mind time and again during David and Annette's visit, but she dared not speak them. As they ate, and later as they simply sat in the sun-drenched living room, the temperature just cool enough for steam to rise from the cappuccino she had made, she sneaked glances at him from time to time and just marveled that he had come at all.

I hurt you, she wanted to say. *Why are you here?*

The answer that kept coming back to her was a simple one: He was there because she was hurting, and he cared. Somehow she was managing to survive despite the huge, agonizing wound torn in her heart by the loss of her baby son, and yet David's presence—and the forgiveness implied by it—was enough to bring her nearly to tears.

In so many ways, she felt like an imposter there in that apartment. Smiling, participating in small talk, showing interest, and all of it a mask to cover the numb, frozen core of her where nothing mattered anymore. And yet, whether she could truly feel it or not, this did matter. These friends mattered, or she would not even have made the attempt at normalcy. The pull of anxiety and depression dragged at her, but with Annette and David there—and, she had to admit, with the drug her doctor had prescribed—she knew there was more to the world than mourning. It felt as though she were trapped in some impenetrable bubble with her grief, but now, at least, she could see what lay beyond it.

For the most part, they talked about St. Matthew's, and a little about Medford High. They talked about their students and about teaching, and though the subject of Ralph Weiss's death came up, they spent only a few minutes on that subject, as though death were too nearby at the moment and might overhear them and be drawn down to listen more closely. And nobody wanted that.

David seemed blissfully unaware of her complicated feelings about him, and Janine was glad. She had a lot to work through before she could focus on something so trivial as romance.

Still, it was a comfort being around him. David seemed so relaxed within himself, and Janine envied that easy confidence. He sprawled in his chair in the living room in gray pants and a white shirt, the remnants of the suit he had worn to the funeral, and he focused on her. After the time she'd spent with Spencer Hahn, whose attention had always seemed to be turned inward, just a few hours with David was refreshing.

Annette noticed, of course. Janine caught her smiling a few times as the conversation turned in lazy circles. It made her love Annette all the more. She did not think she had ever had a better friend.

The afternoon rolled on and the sun shifted in the sky so that the windows threw bright silhouettes onto the floor that seemed to stretch out and warp like reflections in a funhouse mirror. Janine grew tired. She did her best to hide it, but Annette noticed. A little after four o'clock, she glanced over at David.

"We should probably get going," Annette said.

Janine expected more, some comment about how tired she looked or how much she needed her rest. But Annette added nothing to her declaration. David did not need the situation clarified to him. He glanced once at Annette, once at Janine, then nodded in understanding and stood up.

"We really should. I need my beauty rest."

The women both laughed and David gave them an injured look that Janine remembered well.

Annette stood as well, and Janine walked them both to the door. She could feel the empty apartment behind her back, the silence that awaited her when they were gone, and a bit of melancholy settled in. Yet somehow she did not mind. If she could only take the time to become accustomed to her pain, on her own, Janine thought she would be all right.

"Thanks so much for coming. Both of you." She pulled Annette into a tight hug and whispered in her ear, "You're the best."

"Someone's gotta be." Annette kissed her cheek before stepping out onto the second-floor landing.

Janine took both of David's hands in her own. They were warm and strong, and she squeezed tightly.

"It means a lot, you coming to visit. There are so many things I—"

"Hey," David interrupted, his voice soft. "You don't have to."

She raised her eyebrows, dropped his hands, and poked him in the chest. "No interrupting. It's a guy thing, I know. But no interrupting."

With a thin smile, he raised his hands in surrender and nodded once for her to continue.

"I did a lot of things wrong. Not just wrong, but stupid," Janine said. She hugged herself a moment, then let her arms hang limp, her hands fluttering awkwardly, unsure what to do with them.

She allowed herself a tiny shrug. "I guess what I'm saying is, I'm glad you don't hate me. I'm glad you came."

David gazed at her expectantly, as though making sure she was through speaking. He did not want to risk interrupting her, apparently. Then he nodded again.

"Me too." His wistful smile disappeared then, and a flicker of pain passed over his features.

Janine stepped in to slip her arms around him. David held her close and she could feel the heat of his breath on her neck, the power of his hands on her back.

"I'm sorry, Janine," he said, his voice low. "For all of what happened to you, but especially for the baby. If you want to talk at all, or you want to just get a coffee or whatever, call me. Nothing complicated. I just want you to know I'm your friend."

They ended the embrace, but she held on to his hands again. "I know that, David. I really do."

Annette promised to call the next day, and a moment later Janine closed the door behind them.

She took a long breath and leaned against the door. Tears began to slip down her cheeks. Janine wiped them away quickly. It had grown chilly as the afternoon waned, but her windows were still wide open. Goose bumps rose on her arms and she hugged herself tight.

Nothing complicated, David had said.
"Too late," Janine told her empty apartment.

That night, she dreamed of a river.

*The place is familiar. Janine has been here before.
The air is heavy and damp and the ground beneath her
feet is a wet, gritty mire.*

It is dark; so very dark.

*Her eyes adjust slowly, and she finds that there are
stars in the sky. But they do not look like real stars. It
is almost as though they are painted there, pinpricks in
a sky ceiling that feels much lower than it appears. She
can almost feel the weight of it pressing down on her,
just as the oppressive feeling of the place itself seems
to close in on her, suffocating her.*

*Only the sound of the river can be heard as it whis-
pers along its ever-changing route. How can something
be both eternal and ephemeral? And yet it is. It
stretches out before her as far as she can see, as far as
she can imagine seeing. Wide as an ocean, yet it flows
past her, rolling toward some unfathomable destination,
or perhaps simply in a circle, ringing whatever lies
across its breadth in a never-ending current.*

*Janine does not want to be here. She wants to go
home. She wants to wake up.*

Wake up, for she knows this is a dream.

*But the damp, and the mire between her toes, and
the sound of the river are all so real. Behind her is a
dark wood where the trees grow too close together, as
though standing fast against intruders. Or anyone who
might retreat from the river.*

Retreat. That's what she had done.

*Janine had not crossed the river. She had run, and
thrown the coins, and . . .*

*Somewhere, close by, a baby cried. The sound
pierced her and she held her breath for long minutes
until she felt as though she no longer even needed to
breathe. Down here, on the bank of this river, perhaps
that was true.*

The clanking of metal made her jump.

She stumbled back, away from the riverbank, and the ground was more solid under her feet. Warm and dry. Janine stared out at the river at the lantern light that shone from the darkness like the single eye of some beast from the riverbed.

But she knew. She knew because she had been here before, heard that clanking of metal before.

Panicked, she reached into her pockets, but found no coins. Nothing to pay for her passage. She did not want to cross, and now she could not even if she did.

The wailing of the infant seemed closer than before. The baby crying for its mother. Warm, salty tears cut paths down her cheeks and Janine could taste them.

But this was a dream. She should not be able to taste her tears.

The clanking of metal moved closer, and she saw the prow of the small boat now, illuminated by the sickly light from the lantern that thunked against its post.

Slowly, the vessel glided up against the bank of the river and grounded with a hush against the grainy earth there.

Janine backed up a few more steps, but she stared at the small boat, a dark pain rippling across her chest.

The lantern stopped swaying.

Abruptly, the baby stopped crying.

The boat was empty.

A sudden, unreasoning fear swept over her. Janine stumbled backward, lost her footing, and then scrambled to her feet to flee toward the trees.

Where is he? *she thought.*

This isn't right.

She glanced back at the boat, rocking ever so gently on the river's edge. The lantern gleamed, the empty vessel haunted by the absence of its master.

Janine ran, breathing again, but in ragged gasps. She was frantic with the terrible dread that seeped into her bones just as the damp of this place had done.

She ran into him, nearly fell down as she struck his chest. He gripped her arms to hold her up, and she gazed into those black eclipse-eyes and knew she had to run from him.

Yet she could not.

Her body would not obey her, as though she had been frozen to the spot by the touch of those long, tapered fingers. His pale features seemed carved from marble, expressionless, inhuman. But then his mouth twitched and his lips parted, and it seemed he wanted to speak to her but hesitated.

The Ferryman kissed her then. Lips rough and dry on her own, so cold that it hurt. His breath was like frost.

Janine swayed, helpless a moment. Then the kiss ended and the Ferryman gazed down upon her.

"Do not fear me, Janine," he said, voice like the clanking of his lantern against wood. "I am here for you.

"I am here."

A tiny sound escaped Janine's lips as her eyes opened abruptly. There was no passage between sleeping and waking. Rather, she was instantly aware of the room around her, the streetlamps outside just enough to deepen the shadows and cast a sort of gloomy illumination upon the floor and the edge of the bed.

Something rustled in the shadows by her door.

Janine sat and stared, wide-eyed, around her room, unnerved by the dream, which did not dissipate the way most dreams do after waking. Her heart thumped loudly in her chest as she peered into the dark around her, gazing at every corner, convinced that she was not alone.

It would be more than an hour before she would be able to sleep again.

Her lips were so cold.

CHAPTER 4

❧

On Sunday morning, little more than a week after she had come home from the hospital, the phone woke Janine from out of a dream in which she cradled her baby boy against her chest and sang a lullaby. A discordant ringing disrupted her song. At the third ring her eyes fluttered open and she glanced down at her empty arms with a sense of loss unrivaled by any she had felt thus far.

The dream began to slip away but she could still feel the weight of her infant in her arms.

A quick glance at her alarm clock revealed that it was after ten a.m. The sun had warmed her bedroom and the sweet smells of spring and growing things were carried in on the breezes that billowed the curtains. The day was moving along without her.

Had she thought about it only a moment, she would have let the answering machine pick up. But Janine was angry—at herself for sleeping so late, and at the caller for taking her dream child away. After the fourth ring, even as the machine clicked on, she picked it up.

"Hello?" she said, her voice raspier than she had expected.

"Oh, Janine, did I wake you?"

Her mother. Janine closed her eyes and pressed her head deeper into her pillow.

"You did, actually, but I should be up anyway."

"Is everything all right? Why are you sleeping so

late? It can't be good for you to become some sort of recluse now. You should be out. Doing something. You know—"

"Getting on with my life?" Janine suggested tiredly.

"Exactly," Ruth Vale replied.

"Thank you for the advice, Mother. It never occurred to me."

Her mother was silent a moment on the other end of the line, and Janine could practically see the perfectly coiffed woman with her lips pursed in stern disapproval.

"I don't think sarcasm solves anything," Ruth told her.

Yet you fall back on it again and again, Janine thought.

Idly scratching the back of her head, she sat up and stretched. A moment later she rose and went to the window, pushing aside the curtains with two fingers to gaze out at the sparklingly bright day.

"You're right," Janine said, as she leaned against the wall and watched a pair of bluejays flitting from one tree to another. "I'm just not sleeping that well, Mother."

"Maybe it's the medication," her mother suggested quickly, their momentary conflict already forgotten. "You know you have to be careful what they prescribe for you."

"I'll look into it."

Portable phone in hand, Janine opened the curtained French doors and went out into the living room. It was so bright she had to blink a few times and she felt energized by all that sun. Just as her plants seemed to lean toward the windows to soak up the rays, so was Janine drawn that way a moment.

"So what's going on, Mother?"

Janine spun on one heel and strode into the kitchen, where she began to put water on for tea as her mother hesitated on the phone.

"Well, I've talked to Larry about it, and we both think it's time you had a fresh start. I wonder if you've considered that. It might be just what you need, Nina. You could move back here, even work at the agency."

Stunned, Janine tightened her grip on the phone. She held a box of tea bags in the other hand and stared at it stupidly, as though she had forgotten why she had taken it out.

"And do what?" she asked.

"There's no need for that tone," her mother said with a sniff. "I'm only offering to help. Not everyone has the chance to start fresh, you know. I'd think you'd be grateful."

Janine swallowed hard, took a deep breath to compose herself, then set the box of tea bags down and opened the cabinet to reach for a cup.

"I am grateful, Mother. It's very kind of you to suggest it. But I like it here. I don't know what I'd do at the agency. I'm a teacher, you know? It's what I do."

"Now, Janine, it isn't as though teaching has made you happy. It may be what you do, but it isn't who you are."

The kettle began to whistle on the stove. Janine only glared at it for a moment. Her right hand fluttered a bit in the air and she shook her head before plucking the kettle off the burner.

It isn't who you are. So who am I? Janine bit her lip. *Mommy, that's who I was supposed to be.* Her mother was right, in a way. She had never defined herself by her status as a teacher the way David and Annette both did. It was much more important to them than it was to her. So what was she?

Shallow as it seemed to her, she had felt that the baby she carried would have given her a certain identity, at least in her own mind. But that was not to be.

"You know what, Mother? I can't do this right now. I'm not ready to have this conversation."

Ruth paused a moment. The empty, hollow sound on the phone seemed to Janine to speak volumes about the real distance between them.

"If you change your mind, we're always here for you, Janine," her mother said.

"I appreciate that."

"So you'll be returning to work soon?"

"One more week out, then I'm back," Janine replied, though it was a decision she had made only as the words came out of her mouth. It felt right to her, though.

"Have you given any more thought to a memorial service for the baby?"

Janine poured water for her tea. Her hand wavered only a little. "Not really."

"We all need—"

"Closure, Mother, yes I know," Janine snapped. She hauled open the refrigerator door and snatched a yogurt from a shelf. With her hip, she bumped the door closed.

Then she stood, frozen, in the middle of the kitchen phone in one hand and yogurt in the other, with her eyes squeezed shut. When she spoke again, her voice was almost a whisper.

"Has it occurred to you that maybe I don't want closure on this?"

Ruth began to respond.

"Good-bye, Mother," Janine said.

She hung up and left the phone on the counter while she stirred granola into her yogurt. At her kitchen table, she ate her meager breakfast and pretended to herself that the conversation had never happened at all. When she was through, Janine walked into the living room.

The violin case stood against the wall, lonely and accusatory. She had not played since before . . . since *before*. With a wan smile, she drifted as though hypnotized across the sun-drenched room and lifted her instrument from its case.

It nestled, so smoothly textured, so familiar, under her chin. In her right hand, she held the bow out like a wand. Then she began to pluck at the strings, and then to tune, and finally to play.

For just a little while, the music took her somewhere else, far away.

* * *

Winchester, Massachusetts, was an old-money town with tree-shaded streets lined with brick Colonials, driveways populated by BMWs and Benzes, and the best public schools in New England. It might rub shoulders with Medford, but Winchester was never going to take its neighboring town home to the parents.

On Sunday, just after noon, David drove his modest Volkswagen out past the Winchester Country Club for the birthday party of six-year-old Lucas Kenton. The boy's parents, Geoff and Lily, had been high school sweethearts all the way back in St. Matthew's, and had rediscovered each other after college graduation brought them home again.

As a single guy in his early thirties, David found it awkward whenever he ended up at something like this. Lucas was a good kid, but most of the grown-ups there were married with children of their own. When he had a girlfriend, it had made him feel less out of place.

Today he planned to grin and bear it. Geoff and Lily were just about the only people from his high school class with whom he had regular contact, and he liked them both a great deal. They had the money to live in Winchester, but had managed to avoid adopting the attitude many of the town's residents seemed afflicted with.

The Kentons' house was a traditional brick New England home with a detached garage and a modest yard. Even the house itself was not as enormous as one might expect given the expense of living there. But it was in an old-money neighborhood and it backed up to the lake, with cement steps that went down from the backyard right to the water.

No playing football back there. Not unless you wanted to swim for the ball.

Perhaps a dozen cars lined the street on either side of the road. David found a spot three houses down. Most of the cars he passed on the way up to the house had child safety seats in them. With a small sigh, he tucked his present for Lucas—a LEGO submarine—under his arm and rang the bell.

When the door opened a wave of chattering voices swept over him. Warm, seductive aromas wafted from the house, and David's stomach rumbled. Though most of her friends probably would have had something even as small as a kindergarten birthday party catered, Lily Kenton liked to cook, and she did it very well.

"Dave!" Lily cried as she opened the door.

As usual, she looked wonderful. Lily was always perfectly coiffed, even if she had been cooking since the day before. Her dyed-auburn hair was cut in the latest style and her clothes never seemed less than brand-new. But David had known her most of her life; Lily's nearness to perfection was not some affected persona, but a notch away from obsession that she had been dancing around since childhood.

"You look great," he said as he stepped inside to give her a quick squeeze. "Smell great, too. Or is that lunch?"

Lily's eyes sparkled with mischief. "Nope, it's me."

"Rrrowrrr," David growled.

She whacked him on the arm, then led him down the front hall and into the massive kitchen. Women sat at the table and leaned against the counter, most with coffee mugs or wineglasses in hand. Children shouted happily and zoomed by. Lily and David had to step over toys as they moved amongst the gathered friends and neighbors.

"Most of the guys are out back," Lily told him. "Lunch will be ready in just a few minutes. There's beer back there, or can I pour you some wine?"

"I'm good, thanks." David held up the present and raised his eyebrows.

"Table in the living room," Lily told him.

He nodded, wormed his way through the women in the kitchen, and found the table where Lucas's presents had been deposited. A handful of kids were playing with a wooden train set on the floor, but for the most part, they ignored the presents. David was impressed. He had the vague idea that at six, no matter if it had been his own party or someone else's, he would have been tearing at the paper to get a peek inside.

There was an enclosed porch on the back of the house with a door that led outside. Half a dozen guys, including a couple he vaguely recognized, sat in some older furniture watching ESPN. One of them, whose name David thought might be Anthony, acknowledged him with a nod and a manly grunt. David nodded back, but he had never mastered the art of manly grunting, and so remained silent.

He finally found Geoff in the backyard tossing a Nerf football around with Lucas, half a dozen other kids, and another one of the dads. Geoff spotted him immediately and tossed the Nerf. David caught it and threw it to the kids.

"Lucas!" he shouted, adding a bit of drama to his voice.

The ball bounced off the boy's head and rolled across the grass. Two other children got into a tug-of-war over it, and a couple of the other fathers on the back lawn had to break it up.

Geoff shook his head as he walked over. "Nice going," he said, with a backward glance at the shouting kids.

"Not my fault your kid can't catch," David teased. But he said it low so that Lucas would not hear. It was one thing to give Geoff a hard time, another entirely to scar his son for life.

With a chuckle, Geoff flipped him the middle finger, low to his chest, out of sight of the kids. "Want a beer?"

"One beer wouldn't kill me."

Together they walked over to the two wide coolers that were propped against the back porch. Geoff reintroduced David to several people he had met at Lucas's last birthday. For the most part, when he saw the Kentons, it was just him, though for a while it had been him and Janine.

Just the thought of her made David smile.

"What's the grin for?" Geoff asked as he pulled a pair of Bass Ales from the ice.

Caught, David shook his head. "Nothing, really. Just . . . I saw Janine last week."

"No shit?" Geoff fished a bottle opener from his pocket—indispensible at such gatherings—and popped the caps off both beers. "What's she up to?"

A bit reluctant, David nevertheless caught Geoff up on Janine's recent tragedy, and the visit they'd had on the previous Saturday. Geoff was a guy's guy, for the most part, but the sorrow on his face when he heard about Janine's baby was not feigned. He had a good heart. That was why David had worked at maintaining the friendship, despite how differently their lives were turning out.

"Lily's going to be crushed if you start seeing Janine again," Geoff told him.

In the midst of a swig of beer, David almost choked. He lowered the bottle and wiped his mouth with the back of his hand. "Why? She liked Janine, I thought."

"She did. But she's got this friend from her book club that she wants you to meet. Samantha. I was against it, I want you to know."

David raised an eyebrow. "What's wrong with her?"

Geoff snickered nastily. "Nothing. She's completely smoking. I just didn't want you to end up having sex with her because then I'd be jealous."

They both laughed.

"Well, now I want to meet her," David said.

He made a show of glancing around, enjoying the chance to remind Geoff of the benefits of free agency. Though personally he thought people who were happily married were about the luckiest people in the world, it assuaged a certain amount of gloom that went with being single whenever he was able to take advantage of married guys' natural inclination to feel like they were missing out on something.

"What was her name again?" he taunted. "Samantha? Like on *Bewitched*? I like that."

"Fuck off," Geoff muttered.

David continued to glance around the backyard. A few of the mothers had come out onto the lawn now, but it was still mostly dads and the children. The Nerf was missing and in its place was a game of tag accompanied by giddy shrieks from the kindergartners.

Lucas streaked across the grass, attempting to avoid being tagged. As David watched the boy, a figure in his peripheral vision drew his attention. He looked up. There, across the lawn, just at the edge where the earth was shored up by a concrete wall and steps led down to the lake below, stood Ralph Weiss.

With the bright sun above, he seemed almost gray, silhouetted there at the far end of the property with the lake spreading out behind him. A cold wind rippled the surface of the water.

Paralyzed, David stared, unable to speak or even breathe. His eyes felt dry, burning.

Geoff stepped in front of him, cutting off his view. "Check it out. Here she comes with Lily. I told you she was going to play matchmaker."

David tilted his head to one side and looked past Geoff. Lucas had been tagged and was now "it." Another boy had fallen and his father rushed to pick him up.

There was no one at the edge of the lake.

"What the hell?" David whispered.

He set off across the lawn without hesitation. As he walked he glanced left and right; he studied the faces of the adults in the yard. Ralph Weiss was dead. He knew that, and doubted it not at all. David Bairstow did not believe in ghosts and he did not want to believe he could have been hallucinating, so he studied those faces closely, hoping that one of them would look even a little like Weiss. Enough to have suggested it to his subconscious.

None of them resembled the dead man at all.

Where the Kentons' property ended there was a six-foot drop, reinforced by concrete, down to the lake. The water lapped against the retaining wall, flowing over two of the steps. There were no boats in the water, nothing at all save a kayaker all the way on the other side of the lake. It was still early in the year for sailing.

David stared out at the lake for a long moment. Then he was startled by sixty pounds of human child colliding into him from the side. Panic surged through him as he nearly lost his footing. Both of them would have tumbled over the edge and into the shallow water if he had not thrown himself sideways just then.

"You're it!" Lucas Kenton cried out joyfully.

David laughed and ruffled the boy's hair, then set him aside and climbed to his feet. Then he reached out, tapped Lucas on the shoulder, and fled.

"You're it!" he called back.

Lucas shouted that it was no fair, but he was laughing so David thought that was all right. By the house, Geoff and Lily stood with a knockout redhead who looked much younger than any of them. Silently he cursed himself as he realized how rude it must have seemed, his just wandering off like that. As he approached, Lily whispered something to Geoff, and he felt guilty.

"Sorry about that," he told Geoff. "Just thought I saw some hawks across the lake. They're . . . really interesting."

Geoff frowned. "Never took you for a bird-watcher."

But Lily brushed it off, obviously glad for any excuse to give her friend that was better than he-saw-you-coming-and-ran-like-hell. "I've never noticed hawks back here before," she said. "I'll have to keep an eye out. They are beautiful birds."

The redhead was even more stunning up close. She had green-blue eyes and a sweet smile. Her hair was braided in the back and her oval glasses gave her an intellectual air that David found very attractive.

"Hi. David Bairstow. I'm not usually such a flake."

"Yes, he is," Geoff put in.

"Samantha Kresky." She held out a hand and he shook it. "I've heard a lot about you."

"All of it bad, I'm sure," David replied.

It was mild flirtation, but he was on autopilot. This was what Geoff and Lily expected of him, and he wanted to be polite. But his mind was elsewhere. Even if he were not still half in love—maybe more than half—with Janine, he was still rattled by what he thought he'd seen a moment ago, illusion or not.

It was not as though he could tell his friends that, for just a moment, he had thought he had seen a dead man standing on their lawn. It had been someone else, he was sure, and his mind had superimposed the suggestion that the figure looked like Ralph Weiss. After all, the man was on his mind. His funeral had been the week before, and both Geoff and Lily had also been taught by him.

But in that moment when the illusion had held, it had more than unnerved him; it had sent a chill through him that he still felt.

The conversation went on, and David made every attempt to be pleasant, but his eyes were drawn, again and again, to the place where the ground fell away and the lake began. He could almost still see the figure standing there, like the spots a quick glance at the sun left upon his vision.

Clouds began to gather in the early afternoon. By the time Annette picked Janine up, the day had turned gray and chilly, almost as though the beautiful morning had been an accident God now hurried to make up for.

To Janine's mind, God had allowed far too many accidents of late. She tried not to think much about the Almighty, however. When she did, it pissed her off. As far as she was concerned God was a sadist, and that was the end of that. He had provided her with friends like Annette and David, but that was about the best she could say about Him.

The car was mostly quiet on the way to the cemetery. Janine had felt a vague sort of unease since she had woken up that morning, but even more so after the conversation with her mother. It was the last thing she wanted to talk about. Life went on, or so people said. That was what she wanted. For life to go on.

Yet she was not willing to pretend that she had never carried the baby inside her, that it had not existed. Her loss was part of her now, the baby still with her, in a sense.

It seemed only right to visit him. Already she felt guilty about the days that had gone by without her doing so. Those days seemed like one long night to her, a restless night where twisted, disturbing dreams came too often to visit. Some sweet dreams, too, but those were the exception. She had stayed in the house, mostly, going out only to the store, speaking on the phone only to Annette and her mother and to Tom Carlson at the high school.

The entrance to Oak Grove Cemetery came into sight.

Her father had been born and raised in Medford. His parents were buried at Oak Grove, and when he died, he had been laid with them. Janine's aunts had been kind enough to offer to let her bury the baby in the family crypt, and to give her the place that had once been intended for her mother.

"It's sweet of you to take me," Janine said.

Annette nodded. "It's no problem."

Her smile was only halfhearted, though, and Janine frowned. "You all right?"

As though surprised by the question, Annette pushed a lock of her short hair behind her ear, and shrugged. "I'm good. Just . . ." She rolled her eyes. "Never mind. It's stupid."

"Not if it's bothering you."

Annette turned through the cemetery's gates, then glanced over at her. "Considering where we are and why we're here? It's stupid."

Janine glowered at her.

Finally Annette sighed. "It's just . . . I saw Melinda last night."

"You guys are getting back? That's great!" Janine said, trying to be encouraging, though she had not been overly fond of Annette's last girlfriend.

Annette kept her eyes straight ahead, slowly guiding the car up into the wooded hill at the back of the cemetery.

"I saw her at a bar. With someone else. Very much a couple."

Janine's heart sank. "Oh, Elf, I'm sorry."

But Annette shook her head. "It's nothing." She put the car into park. "I think about why we're here, and I feel like a moron, not to mention heartless, for even letting it get to me."

Janine reached out and squeezed her friend's hand. "I appreciate it. But just because I . . . just because this happened, that doesn't mean you're not allowed to hurt."

When Annette looked up, her eyes were moist. "Just gets lonely sometimes."

"Trust me, I know."

Janine squeezed her hand again, then opened the door and began to climb out.

She was half-in, half-out of the car when she saw a man in a long coat standing over the Hartschorn crypt. His coat flapped in the wind; his hands were jammed in the pockets.

The world fell silent around her. The rumbling of Annette's engine, the wind rustling mostly bare branches above, the sound of her own heartbeat; it all went away.

Janine stood up and stared at the man. A memory, or just the ghost of a dream, skittered across her mind like a squirrel darting into a tree for safety. Her lips felt cold.

Then the man turned.

It was Spencer.

Fury replaced dread within her. Her fists bunched as she glanced around and spotted his car a little farther up the hill. With her teeth gritted together, she strode across the lawn toward him. Spencer noticed her immediately, and he stiffened, eyes wide.

The sight of her made him nervous. Janine was glad of that.

"Son of a bitch," she whispered as she marched across the ground, still hard from the winter.

"Hello, Janine," Spencer said. He kept his expression neutral, and just waited.

Without pause, she slapped him. Her palm stung, and the noise of the blow echoed down the hill. Spencer rolled with it, eyes crimped with pain, and he swore under his breath as he stood up straight again, his hand over the red splotch on his cheek.

"You feel better?" His voice was like his expression, dead, hollow.

The corner of her mouth twitched up. "Not by half, but I liked it. Enough to do it again."

He retreated half a step.

"What the fuck are you doing here?"

Spencer lowered his hand. An angry red welt had risen on his cheek. He shook his head just slightly. "What do you think I'm doing here? You wouldn't return my messages, so I called the hospital. They told me where he was buried."

Janine pursed her lips, bitter. "Assholes."

"They had to tell me. I'm the father."

Bile rose in her throat and her breath came faster. She narrowed her gaze and, despite the burning in her eyes, commanded herself not to cry.

"You're nothing. You don't belong here."

Spencer's eyes grew hard. He straightened up even further. He put on the face he always used for clients, his fuck-you-I'm-in-charge face, and slid his hands back into the pockets of his greatcoat. Like the suit beneath it, there was neither spot nor wrinkle on the expensive fabric.

"It doesn't have to be this way, Janine. All right, I'm a shit. I didn't want to be a father. But I never stopped loving you."

Of all the things he might have said, that was the last one she expected. Janine laughed at that. It started in her gut and just came rolling out, hard enough to make her bend over slightly. Tears came to her eyes now and she wiped them quickly away. She was dimly aware that she might be hysterical, but did not care.

Spencer stared at her for a few seconds, then shook his head, turned on his heel, and headed for his car in long, stiff strides.

Janine saw Annette watching from the car, and her laughter began to subside.

Near the road, Spencer stopped and looked back at her. "On the headstone? It just says 'Baby Hartschorn.' You didn't give him a name?"

The muscles in her face ached from laughing, but now they went slack. "He has a name. You'll never know it."

Spencer turned away again. "I love you, Janine," he said, and then climbed into his car.

It unhinged her. "Fuck you!" she screamed at him as the car started and began to pull away. "You bastard, fuck you!"

Annette ran to her, and held her tight, but Janine went on like that until the car was out of sight.

CHAPTER 5

❧

With the exception of a convenience store and a coffee shop, the neighborhood around St. Matthew's was residential. Once upon a time the homes nearby had been inhabited by aging couples who had grown up in Medford, but over time, rents in Boston skyrocketed and it became both practical and trendy for young professionals to live in surrounding cities.

David remembered what it had been like twenty years before, and he thought the changes had stolen some of the character from the neighborhood.

Or perhaps it was just the rain. . . .

Wednesday was the third day in a row when morning never truly seemed to arrive. The sky was not simply gray, but charcoal black, and headlights were necessary at all times. In places, the rain flowed along the street like a stream, and puddles hid secret potholes that only grew larger as cars bounced through them, drivers unsuspecting.

The front right tire of David's Volkswagen splashed through a puddle and thunked into a pothole deep enough that the car bottomed out for a moment. He cursed loudly and bent forward to peer past his barely effective windshield wipers in search of a spot in the faculty parking lot.

When he found one, he had to roll the window down, rain spattering his face, in order to make certain he didn't hit another car while he pulled in. With a sigh, he killed the engine. The radio cut off abruptly, and only then did he realize how loud he'd turned it up in an effort to drown out the rain.

He ran for the back door with his briefcase on top of his head, and held the collar of his raincoat tight around his throat against the bitter cold. April showers. He knew how the song went. They brought the flowers that bloomed in May.

At the moment, David Bairstow could do without the damn flowers. In May, or ever.

At the foot of the granite steps was a wide puddle. He slowed only a little, then jumped for the first step: an easy distance if he had not been playing rain-dance contortionist with his briefcase and coat. His left foot landed in the puddle; the water came just over the top of his shoe, soaking instantly through the leather and his sock.

"Goddamn it!" Fuming, he lifted his foot as though he had stepped in dog shit and glared down at it. Then he shook his head and reached for the door.

Inside, several students glanced quickly away, their amusement poorly masked. With a self-deprecating grin and a sigh of relief, David entered the school and let his briefcase hang once again at his side.

"Good morning, Mr. Bairstow," cooed a sophomore girl he barely recognized. Not one of his students, but maybe the younger sibling of one of them.

"If you say so," he replied. "But then, you look dry."

The girl smiled at his sarcasm. "I brought an umbrella."

David smacked his forehead. "Umbrella! That was the secret all along." He started up the stairs, but glanced back at the student one last time. "Actually, I'm starting to think we may need an ark pretty soon."

On the second floor, he began to unbutton his raincoat one-handedly as he weaved amongst the students on their way to their homerooms. He did not have a first-period class, but had wanted to get out of the rain and dry off, then do some preparation for class. The students were due to begin presenting their final papers today, and he wanted to go over who was up at bat and what their topics were, so he could at least be ready to comment intelligently.

Down the hall, he saw Lydia exit the teachers' lounge with a load of books in her arms.

"Mr. Bairstow?"

David had the distinct impression that it was not the first time his name had been called. He had been distracted. Now he turned to find Brad Flecca watching him expectantly.

"Brad. Sorry." He shook his head. "What's up?"

"You got a minute?"

The kid was fair-haired and had gentle features but he was built like a tank. Brad was a star on the football team, the kind that came along maybe once every ten years. For the most part, he was also a decent student. Unlike the stereotypical jock, Brad was not stupid; he just never seemed willing to exert himself academically.

David slipped a hand into his pocket and pretended he had no idea what Brad wanted to talk about. "What can I do you for?"

The football star glanced away, fidgeted a little, then finally sighed and met his gaze again. "Listen, maybe you heard I got a scholarship to B.C. for football?"

"It was in all the papers," David observed.

Brad puffed up a little. "Yeah. Yeah, cool, huh? Anyway, look, I know I haven't been, y'know, applying myself all that much this term. But, the thing is, my scholarship is conditional, right? I've gotta keep an eighty average or better. If I get below a C in your class, I'm scr . . . uhh, I mean, I'm in trouble."

He smiled wanly.

David nodded, tried to put on an understanding face. "That would be bad, huh?"

"Yeah. Real bad."

They stared at each other for a few moments. Kids pushed by them in the hall, not paying any attention to them, all absorbed in their own dramas. David tightened his grip on his briefcase.

"You need a solid B on your final paper to clear

a C in my class, Brad. Maybe even an A minus," he said.

Brad winced.

"I guess it's safe to assume you're not going to be ready to present for the class on . . . what is it, Friday you're supposed to go?"

"Friday, yeah."

The boy's voice was shaken. David's heart went out to him. Brad had been slacking off since Christmas, no question about that. But he was a bright kid, and though it was football that had gotten him into B.C., David thought a school of that quality could really make a difference for Brad.

"Tell you what," he said.

Brad glanced up hopefully.

"You can go last. That's two weeks from today. I'm not going to do you any favors on the grading, though. You'd better work your butt off, knock us out, if you want that scholarship."

"Absolutely, Mr. Bairstow. I swear." Brad nodded enthusiastically. "I'm totally into it. It's gonna be great."

David found himself nodding in return. "Which topic did you pick, again?"

"Atavism in the works of Jack London."

He cast a dubious glance at the boy. "Brad, do you even know what atavism is?"

The student, who had an inch and forty pounds on his teacher, slapped David good-naturedly on the arm. "Not yet, Mr. B., but I will. I will."

They both laughed.

Down the hall, a girl cried out in panic. "Tim, no!" she wailed. "Leave him alone!"

"Son of a bitch!" a male voice snapped.

There came the sound of something slamming against metal, a body against a locker, David thought. He spotted a couple of guys shoving each other near the stairwell, back the way he'd come. Students started to circle around them like wild dogs, the pack observing a battle for primacy.

"Atavism," David said. "Come have a look." Then he started off toward the stairs without another word to Brad.

As he sprinted down the hall, David got a better look at the students involved with the brawl. Tim Ferris was a junior, an average student but a good kid. Vinnie Abate was a senior, and trouble on two legs. Thing was, the way things looked, this was all Tim's doing. Vinnie was bigger, but Tim had clearly gotten the jump on the senior boy. He choked Vinnie with his left hand and hit him once, twice, a third time.

Tim's girlfriend, Liz Rossiter, grabbed his wrist. "Tim, stop it! He didn't do anything!"

With a snarl of rage, Tim shook her loose. "Let go of me, you slut!" he shouted. He turned, raised his hand to her.

David grabbed his wrist before the blow could fall. "Don't you dare!" he shouted.

The crowd began to disperse immediately. None of them wanted to be asked to talk about what they had seen, who had started it. Liz started to walk away and David nailed her with a hard look.

"Not another step, Liz."

He pushed Tim up against a locker and held him there. For a second he glared at the kid; then he turned to Vinnie, who touched his swollen lip and held the fingers away from his face, checking for blood.

The bell for homeroom rang.

"Mr. Bairstow," Liz began.

He studied her closely, then let go of Tim and stepped back from the locker. "Why don't you tell me what's going on, Liz?"

Her gaze hardened and her expression soured. Petulant and childish, she looked away. David stared first at Vinnie, then at Tim, and finally shook his head sadly.

"Tell you what. I'll make it easy for you. I'll give you a hypothetical, and you tell me what I get wrong." None of them would look at him now; all three had retreated behind shields of sullenness.

"All right. Hypothetically, I'm guessing you, Liz, did

some things with Vinnie that maybe you weren't supposed to do, considering Tim here is your boyfriend."

"He's not my boyfriend," Liz muttered.

Tim glared at her. "Slut."

David nodded. "I guess that means I'm warm, huh?" He pinched the bridge of his nose, took a deep breath, and then reached out to tap Vinnie on the shoulder.

"Stunned as I am to admit it, Vinnie, you didn't start this. You can go."

"What?" Tim snapped. "Look, Mr. Bairstow, he—"

"Spare me the details, Tim. I don't need to know. Whatever he and Liz did or didn't do? That's their business. Much as you may want to resort to violence, you have no right to. That's what the law says, that's what school policy says, and that's what common sense says. I used to think you had some. Common sense, that is."

The boy glared at him with malign intention.

"Liz, you can go, too." He brushed at the air dismissively. "Maybe in the future you want to break up with one boyfriend before finding another. Just a piece of friendly advice."

The girl went, quickly and without comment. Vinnie caught up with her and they walked away together. David felt bad for Tim, understood what he must be feeling. But his feelings did not excuse him.

"What about me?" Tim demanded, still surly.

"It isn't up to me, but it's possible you'll be suspended," David told him. "Meet me in Sister Mary's office at the end of the day."

"The hell I will," Tim said with a sneer.

David blinked, astounded by the kid's audacity. All the sympathy he had felt evaporated.

"Tim, maybe you don't realize how much trouble you're already in, but if I were you—"

"You're not me, Mr. Bairstow. You don't have a clue. Just leave me the fuck alone!" Tim threw up a hand, turned, and started to walk away as if nothing at all had happened.

Before David could react, a voice boomed from the stairwell beside them.

"Mr. Ferris!"

Tim froze, then turned slowly. The expression on his face had changed completely. The kid nodded his head nervously, but he would not lift his gaze. He shifted uncomfortably as Father Charles stepped between them. The priest barely glanced at David before he went to the student and stared down at him.

Perhaps four inches separated them.

"I only caught the tail end of that conversation, Mr. Ferris, so perhaps I misunderstood your response to Mr. Bairstow. Did I misunderstand?"

The kid's lips pursed as though he'd just poured dry lemonade mix into his mouth.

Father Charles leaned in a bit further. "Did I misunderstand you, Mr. Ferris?"

"Yes, Father," the boy replied, barely above a whisper.

"I hoped so," Father Charles said curtly. Then he dropped his own voice to a whisper. "I don't care who your father is, or how much money he gives to the archdiocese, Mr. Ferris. Nobody speaks to a teacher that way in this school. You will meet Mr. Bairstow at Sister Mary's office at the last bell, at which time you will hand him a formal, written letter of apology for your behavior. At that time you may throw yourself on Sister Mary's mercy, but know this . . ."

The priest stood up to his full height again, and Tim looked up at him.

"I'm going to be there as well," Father Charles said. "And no one's ever accused me of being merciful."

Tim visibly stiffened. He looked scared, and David was glad.

"Go," the priest said.

Tim went, as fast as he could move without actually running. They watched him hurry away, and when he was gone, David stared in amazement at Father Charles.

The priest grinned. "It's the uniform," he said.

David laughed, and they fell into step together. Briefcase dangling from his left hand, David accompanied him as far as his office. They chatted briefly about the weather, but after three solid days of rain, there was little that remained to be said about it.

At the door, they paused.

"Quite a start to the day, isn't it?" Father Charles said.

"It can only improve."

"Wouldn't it be wonderful if that were true?"

David gave him an odd look, and the priest offered his trademark enigmatic smile in return. One of the unsettling things about Father Charles was his barebones approach to life, his unwillingness to allow platitudes to survive.

"You know what you should do?" the priest said abruptly.

"What's that?"

"Call Janine Hartschorn and ask her to join you for dinner this weekend. What are you waiting for?"

For a moment, David's mouth hung open in surprise. Then a little voice told him how stupid he must look, and his mind began to work, cogs turning.

"You've been talking to Annette."

Father Charles smiled mischievously. "Miss Muscari may not be the president of my fan club, but we are forced to collide in the halls and cafeteria from time to time. When we do, the only thing we can safely talk about without an argument is you."

David rolled his eyes. "You're just a big yenta in a white collar."

"You'll call her?"

"Today," David agreed.

"You're welcome to use the phone in my office," the priest suggested. "I happen to know that she doesn't start back to work at Medford High until next Monday, so she's probably home."

He gestured toward his office door. David chuckled softly and went in to use the phone.

*   *   *

They tried their best to pretend it wasn't a date.

Janine sat across from David at a small, unsteady table in the Border Café and ate popcorn shrimp with a swiftness that was almost greedy. The restaurant had been a favorite of theirs in the old days because it was in the middle of flashy, edgy Harvard Square in Cambridge, where it was always fun to people-watch, and because it combined the best of Cajun and Mexican cuisine.

The popcorn shrimp was Janine's favorite. The Border was decorated to look as if it sat right on the edge of the bayou, as though the things tacked to the walls had been dredged up from the water or found on the side of the road. Cajun trash chic. From tables to menus, everything had a kind of sticky glaze on it, the air redolent with enough spices to make her eyes water almost perpetually. They had always thought of it as a kind of paradise, and it hadn't changed.

It was Saturday afternoon—she thought it likely David had chosen lunch to make it seem less like a date—and more than two weeks had passed since she had come home from the hospital. Though her grief was still powerful, it often receded enough that an entire hour might pass without her thinking once of the baby. That was probably her prescription at work, she thought, but if so, she knew she would happily declare herself an addict.

Janine was not ready for this. Not able to even conceive of opening her heart up to anything or anyone. It was already shattered, and if she took away the shield around it, her heart might simply wither and fall to the ground like leaves in autumn. She was not ready, but she was terrified also that she might never be. Once upon a time she had made a horrible mistake with David Bairstow, and here was the possibility of rectifying that mistake.

Ready or not, she was not going to let that go.

The waiter brought her a cup of gumbo so tasty Janine practically moaned with each spoonful. After a minute she grew self-conscious and glanced up to see David watching her.

Embarrassed, she covered her mouth with a hand and laughed softly at herself. "God, I'm such a pig, I know. The food here is just so amazing."

"It is," David replied, deadly serious. "And you are. A pig, I mean."

Janine's mouth dropped open. Her nose wrinkled with the nasty look she gave him, and she leaned over to whap him on the shoulder.

"Jerk," she said, though she knew it was unconvincing given the smile on her face.

David's eyes had a mischievous twinkle that she had forgotten all about, but that she now realized she had missed terribly. It occurred to her then that, much to her surprise, she was not pretending. No longer was she an imposter, going through the motions. It frightened her, made her feel raw and exposed. David must have seen some of that in her face, for he frowned deeply and leaned toward her.

"Relax, Janine," he said softly. "Take a breath. It isn't like you have to worry about making a good first impression."

He blinked awkwardly, then shook his head. "Wait, not what I meant. Of course you make a great first impression. I just mean that, y'know, this is me. You know me. And I think I know you almost better than anyone. You don't have to worry about being on your best behavior."

Yes, I do! a little voice cried out in the back of her head. The last thing she wanted was for him to come back into her life and then wonder what he'd seen in her in the first place. Janine was not going to make any assumptions about lunch with David, but even if he was just a friend, she needed that desperately.

It didn't hurt that he looked great. Though he was dressed so softly, in a V-necked cotton jersey and blue jeans, she found her mind flashing back to the feel of his muscles under her caress.

Zoloft, she thought. *Blame the drug for everything.*

David watched her with a curious smile.

"What?" she asked, as she finished the last spoonful of her gumbo.

"You look happy. Just glad to see that, I guess."

"It's an illusion. Trust me. But I am glad you called," she confessed, avoiding his gaze. "I wanted to see you again, talk some more, but I felt weird about calling."

"Why?"

With a frown, she studied him, reluctant to say more. "I just . . . things didn't end well with us before, and I . . . I mean, it was my fault, but I just wouldn't want us to have any misunderstandings right now. I don't think I could take that."

The waiter interrupted with their meals, blackened catfish for Janine and crawfish étouffée for David. After he had refilled their water glasses, he disappeared once more into the crush of lunch patrons. For a moment Janine and David just looked at each other. He licked his lips and smiled weakly.

"You don't have to worry, Janine. No misunderstandings, okay? No assumptions. If we're going to be friends, we have to be able to be honest and open with each other, right?"

Friends, she thought. *So that's the object of the game, then?* Yet she did not put voice to those words, did not ask for clarification. She realized how ironic her thoughts, considering David's words, but could not control them. It was too early for her to be even thinking that way, and she was in no state to begin a new relationship, or even rekindle an old one. But still, she was disappointed.

"Exactly right," she lied. Her smile was halfhearted, but he did not seem to notice.

"So what's your plan now?" he asked. "A little birdy told me you're starting back to teaching on Monday."

Janine rolled her eyes. "Annette."

"Actually, no. It was Father Charles. Who, no doubt, heard about it from Annette."

Janine raised her eyebrows. "They're talking?"

"Only when they can't avoid it," David confirmed.

She laughed then. "You'd think a man of God would have other things to do than meddle in matchmaking."

David's smile faltered a second, and Janine froze inside. *Matchmaking* implied so much.

"Look at us," David said. "Fumbling around each other like high school kids."

"*Junior* high," she corrected, shaking her head. Then she grew serious again. "I'm so sorry I hurt you, David."

His expression was grave. "You had to find out what could be," David said, his voice low. "If you'd chosen to stay, you would've resented me eventually, wondering what it would have been like with Spencer."

"Even so, it would have been better if I'd stayed."

Their eyes met and Janine felt both her heart and stomach flutter.

"So," she said, too brightly, "how 'bout those Red Sox?"

"Umm, they're gonna choke by the All-Star break?"

The tension of the moment evaporated. They both dug into their lunch, and talk turned to work and their respective colleagues at Medford High and St. Matt's. Only in talking to David did Janine realize how much she was looking forward to Monday morning.

"Teenagers can be brutal," she told him, "but I really think they'll be sympathetic."

David nodded, though a mouthful of fish made him pause before he could answer. "I'm sure they'll be good to you. But only for a week or so. After that, the gloves'll be off again."

It was after two when they left the Border, and they linked arms as they walked up the side street that led back into the center of Harvard Square. The sky was blue and clear, and the sun glinted off windshields and storefronts. A chilly breeze blew through the square, and Janine sneaked under David's arm. He seemed more than pleased by that.

At the newsstand on the corner, they ducked in for a quick glance through the magazines. David bought her a semiwilted red rose and was as nonchalant as possible when presenting it to her. Janine wanted to call him on it—*If we're not on a date why are you buying me flowers?*—but she didn't dare.

Across the square, perhaps fifty yards apart, a man with a Hammond organ and a microphone sang Beatles songs in musical combat with a robed Hare Krishna who chanted and shook cymbals.

"God, how do you stand it?" Janine asked the man behind the counter.

"At least you get to go home," he told her, wincing as if in pain. "Thing is, the Beatles guy is so fucking out of key, but the Krishna's got a decent voice. If you just teamed 'em up, probably wouldn't sound half bad."

Out in the square, the throng meshed and flowed: students from Harvard and MIT and Tufts, aging Bohemians, Cambridge locals, and tourists galore. Punks with green-dyed hair, software salesmen in wool, homeless men wearing huge filthy parkas because they had nowhere to leave them. A beautiful Asian girl as petite as a twelve-year-old strode hand in hand with a blond woman who was model gorgeous and as fit as an Olympian.

Music blared from cars and floated sweetly from sidewalk-strummed acoustic guitars. The smell of incense was overpowering as they entered a small shopping mall called the Garage, where they bought big Ben & Jerry's waffle cones. Janine was already very full, but she could not say no to Ben & Jerry's.

We should go home now, she thought. *If it really isn't a date, we should go.*

They stayed. More than stayed, however; they strolled away from the square toward the Charles River. With all its wonderful, eccentric visitors, Harvard Square could become almost claustrophobic. Janine loved it, but she was happy when they began to leave the crush of people behind.

As the river came in sight, the wind picked up and she shivered. Her black leather jacket was stylish, but not very warm. David was in the midst of catching her up on what she'd missed in the time since they had last spoken, not just in his life, but in the lives of his sister and other people she had known only through him. When they stopped on the corner of Memorial Drive, across from the river, to wait for the light to change, he must have noticed how cold she was, for he offered his jacket.

Janine declined, but David insisted. A few minutes later, as they walked slowly along the river, side by side but not touching, his hands were jammed in his pockets and it was obvious he could barely keep his teeth from chattering, but he refused to take his jacket back. Refused, even, to admit to being cold.

My chivalrous man, she thought.

Yet even the warmth of his jacket over hers was not enough to keep away the strange chill that came over her whenever she glanced at the water. David called her on it only a few minutes after they had reached the river.

"Hey," he said softly, neck muscles taut as he tried to hide his shivering, "you wanted to come down here, right?"

"Yeah," she said, too quickly. She would not meet his eyes.

He stopped walking. With one hand on her arm, he turned her to face him. "Am I pushing too much, Janine? You're looking around like you can't wait to go home. I know we're dancing around some things here, but I am really happy you agreed to come out today. The last thing I want to do is make you uncomfortable."

A jogger ran by with a CD player clipped to his pants. A couple on bicycles approached from the other direction. Memorial Drive was thick with cars. There were plenty of people around, and yet Janine felt unnerved by her surroundings.

She reached up to touch David's face, just a momentary caress of her fingers on his cheek. "It isn't you, David. It's . . ." She glanced around, gestured at the river, then looked up at him again. "I thought it would be nice to walk down here together. Maybe it's just too cold still, or too early in the season, but it's sort of creepy. It's been weeks, but ever since I came home from the hospital, I haven't been sleeping well. Bad dreams, y'know. And for some reason, this . . ."

"Oh, hey, no. Come on, no problem. Let's go back," David said quickly.

With a single motion, Janine slipped his jacket off and swung it behind him in a flourish. She leaned in to pull it snug over his shoulders, and felt a hot spark shoot through her. Her breasts pressed for just a moment against his chest, and the intimacy of that closeness, the feel of his warm breath on her face, was enough to make her blush.

With a swift motion, she darted forward and kissed his cheek before she was even aware of what she was doing. A little laugh escaped her lips and she covered her mouth and raised her eyes heavenward as she turned away.

"We should *definitely* go," she said, surprised at herself.

David did not follow as she started to walk away. Janine froze, there on the bank of the Charles. All the noises of the world seemed to go away save for the sound of the river lapping against the shore as it lazily followed its course.

"Janine," David said.

There was something about his voice that seemed exposed, like copper wire stripped of its plastic sheath, ready to connect, to channel music or images . . . or to electrocute.

She blew out a long breath but did not turn.

"It isn't fair to you, after what you've been through," he said. "I promised myself I wouldn't do anything stupid. But I've got to say this. I don't know how much longer I can pretend I'm not still in love with you."

Startled, completely off balance, Janine spun to face him. David gazed at her. He took a shuddery breath and stood up a little straighter. Janine tried to speak, but found she could not. Instead, she ran to him and crumbled into his embrace. She held him so tight that her arms hurt.

The tears came, as though all along Janine had been holding them in, waiting to cry them in David's arms.

"You don't ever have to pretend with me," she whispered minutes later, as she wiped her eyes.

With her pressed against him, his arm around her, they walked away from the river.

From behind them, the sound of metal clanking against wood rolled up from the river. In the distance, almost as though it were the whistling of the wind, there came the sound of a baby crying.

Janine shut her eyes and pressed herself more tightly against David, and did not look back.

The wind. Just the wind.

CHAPTER 6

∾

There were bookstores that were closer, but Annette always preferred Bookiccino on Massachusetts Avenue in Arlington. As long as she did not try to drive over during rush hour, it took her only fifteen minutes or so. The mall bookstores were usually so cold and sterile, not to mention staffed by people who knew little to nothing about books. Bookiccino, on the other hand, was a wonder to behold.

It sat on a corner only a few blocks up from the legendary Capitol Theatre, an old-time movie palace that showed a combination of current and art films. Bookiccino billed itself as a "book boutique," and it appealed to the same crowd. Two-thirds of the sizable corner storefront was taken up by the books, most of which were novels. No self-help guides at Bookiccino. The nonfiction they did carry was mostly travel books, biographies, and true crime.

With novels, they weren't quite so discriminating. The only rule the management had was *no category romances*. Annette had never figured out if this was practicality due to the tastes of their clientele, a way for them to get attention, or an actual prejudice. But according to the owner, they'd never had any complaints about that particular bit of bigotry.

The third of the store not given over to books accounted for the *-iccino* part of the place's name. It was a warmly decorated café and bakery that specialized in exotic coffees and pastries Annette had come to admit she would kill for if necessary.

So when the urge to browse for books overcame her, or if she simply had a couple of hours to kill and wanted a cup of great coffee, she would find herself in her little SAAB on the way over to Arlington. Not so often that they would remember her name in the store, but frequently enough that they always recognized her face.

That Sunday afternoon, with the air turned chilly and the sky stingy on sunshine, she cranked the heat and the radio and drove out Route 16 to Massachusetts Avenue. In a few days it would be May, and she cursed the weather. It was too cold by her estimate, far too cold for this time of year. All the more reason to head to her favorite spot for a mochaccino.

Behind the wheel, Annette grinned. *Maybe with whipped cream.*

It truly was *her* spot. Though she had been going to Bookaccino for four years, she had never once asked anyone to go along with her. Until she found someone she wanted to share it with, she never would. In her sourest moments, she suspected it might be forever.

Such thoughts were unwelcome. Annette found a parking space on the street half a block away and felt a tiny burst of contentment at the knowledge that the meters were dormant on Sundays. Sometimes the smallest things could give her a lift.

It was almost two-thirty when she killed the engine, cutting Sarah McLachlan off midsong. Almost unaware she was doing it, she took a moment to check her appearance in the rearview mirror. Then she slipped her thin purse over her shoulder and got out. All day long the clouds had been rolling in and then thinning out again; at the moment, they were high and wispy, and the sun was dimmed only a little by their gray presence.

The Sarah McLachlan song was still in her head and she hummed along as she pushed open the door into Bookaccino. *Your love is better than ice cream. . . .*

I don't think so!

Annette smiled to herself, then plunged into the books. The latest legal thrillers were on prominent display, but she ignored them and instead made a beeline for the science fiction section. Though she enjoyed a good mystery now and again, science fiction appealed to her mathematician's mind.

Just a few minutes after she began to scan the shelves, an older woman with her hair dyed screaming red appeared nearby. She hovered a moment before smiling sweetly.

"Can I help with anything?"

Annette batted her eyelashes. "I'm looking for something romantic."

For a moment the woman seemed at a loss. Then she caught on, and they shared a brief chuckle.

"If you have any questions, let me know," the woman said. She moved on to help a younger couple, a thin, stylish black girl and her huggy blond boyfriend.

Though she wandered for more than twenty minutes, only one book caught her attention, an odd combination of fantasy and science fiction about a female space pilot who discovered a parallel world filled with dragons. Not usually her sort of thing, but for some reason it appealed to her.

Soon she was settled at a table in the café with her mochaccino and a sinfully rich apple cinnamon muffin, the book open before her. With the smells of the coffee and pastries filling the place, it was sheer paradise. It occurred to her, as she paused between the first and second chapters, that part of the reason she never brought anyone with her was that she was able to indulge without having to make excuses.

"Is it good?"

Annette glanced up, her mouth half-full with muffin, then tried to chew more quickly in order to reply. The woman who had spoken—or girl, for she looked barely old enough to be out of high school—smiled awkwardly at having caught her like that. She had long blond hair halfway down her back, sparkling blue eyes, and a dimple on her left cheek that lent her an air of mischief.

"The muffin or the book?" Annette finally asked.

The girl uttered a soft, pretty laugh and leaned on the back of the other chair at the table. "The book. I know the muffins are good."

Annette closed the book and glanced at the cover. Then she shrugged. "I'm not sure, actually. I just started it. Moves pretty fast, though, and the main character's a kick. I like novels with sexy, smart-ass women protagonists."

"Me too," the girl said. Her smile grew wider, her dimple more defined, and the mischievous air around her was even more pronounced. "Too bad life isn't more like that."

A slow, sly grin crossed Annette's features. With her right hand she tucked a lock of her short hair behind an ear and regarded this fascinating new arrival with a frank stare.

"I'm Annette," she said.

"Jill," the girl replied. "I'm Jill."

"Want to sit down, Jill?"

What are you thinking, Annette? She's a kid. Nineteen, tops.

With a toss of her swaying hair, Jill swept around and planted herself in the chair opposite Annette in one swift motion.

"I'd love to," she said. "So is this your first time here?"

"Not at all. I'm in here all the time."

Jill glanced around, gestured with a flap of her arms. "This place is like my second home. Books and coffee go together like movies and popcorn. Weird that I've never seen you here before."

Annette became uncomfortable. She grew oddly shy and sipped at her coffee. For a moment Jill frowned and watched her closely. Then she leaned in, snatched up Annette's book, and began to silently read the back cover. Fascinated by the girl, Annette studied her.

As if she sensed the attention, Jill's gaze flicked toward Annette.

"Twenty-two," she said quietly.

Annette blinked. "I'm sorry?"

The sultry, presumptuous smile that split Jill's features in that moment took Annette's breath away.

"My age," the girl said. "You didn't ask, but I figured you were wondering. Someday I'll be glad I look younger, or so I'm told. Usually it's damned inconvenient. Like now, for instance."

For a moment Annette only gazed at her. Then her eyebrows went up and she shook her head. "Twenty-nine," she said softly, as she raised her cup to her lips again.

"What do you say I grab a café latte and we go for a walk?" Jill asked.

Annette knew she ought to have been put off by the girl's—the woman's—forwardness, but she was too busy being enchanted by everything about her, including that brazen quality.

"I think I'd like that."

The students at Medford High gave Janine all of three days to adjust to being back at the front of a classroom. By Thursday morning, whatever break they had given her in sympathy had eroded completely. She knew that part of that was her own fault; she had worked hard to convince faculty and students alike that she was doing just fine. They took her at her word that day. Seven students showed up without the brief essay assignment, two earned detention for talking incessantly in class despite her many admonishments, and one girl became hysterical for no apparent reason when Janine called on her.

At lunch she broke up a fight between two junior girls that had something to do with cigarettes and slander. In her final class of the day, Andy Watkiss asked her straight out why she bothered to come back when half the kids didn't give a fuck about school and only showed up because their parents made them.

"You don't really believe that," she told him. "This is Medford, not some inner-city school. Most of you guys care even though you pretend you don't. I came back for the ones who do. The ones who don't can stay home as far as I'm concerned."

They all went quiet then, that last Thursday class. For the rest of the period they listened, and even participated.

Janine was back, and each time one of her students asked a pertinent question, or expressed an opinion, she realized that she had missed it very much. Certainly not all of them were intrigued by their class discussions. Some showed absolutely no interest in most of what she said. But there were moments, sometimes entire minutes, when she had the attention of every single one of them. In those moments she discovered that teaching meant more to her than she had ever known.

At three o'clock that afternoon, she met with Tom Carlson in his office. The principal of Medford High was a bearded, somewhat rotund man whom students thought of as a stiff, a stern and humorless commandant whose attention to even the tiniest of rules seemed both intolerant and intolerable to the young people in his charge.

Fortunately, Tom Carlson was the principal and not standing at the front of a class. Janine imagined he had once been a perfectly horrible teacher. Carlson communicated very well with adults, but was completely incapable of doing so with teenagers. He was aware of it, too, which was perhaps his saving grace.

When she rapped on his door a few minutes after three, he called out immediately for her to enter. Carlson stood by the windowsill behind his desk, a watering can in his right hand. With a smile, he glanced over his shoulder at her.

"Hi, Janine. Have a seat, why don't you? I'll be through here in just a moment."

As though the plants were all delicate and exotic hothouse orphans, he sprinkled water in a gentle shower of droplets above each plant. Janine watched him as she slid into a leather chair facing his desk. She was fascinated by his obvious affection for those plants. She thought he probably talked to them. Probably communicated with the plants a lot better than he did with the students.

Carlson set the watering can on the end of the windowsill, then stood back to gaze at his babies. He pruned a wilted leaf off one, a flowering thing Janine could not identify. Then, with a self-satisfied grin, he turned to regard her again.

"Sorry. Once I start my routine, I'm always afraid if I stop I'll forget I didn't finish, and—"

"It's fine, Tom. No worries." Content with the way her day had gone, and yet also tired from work and insufficient sleep, she settled more deeply into the chair, relaxing back into it with a catlike stretch.

Carlson fixed her with a steady, sympathetic gaze. "You're haunted."

Janine flinched. "What?"

"Haunted," he repeated, and nodded as if to underline the point. "It's something in your eyes, in the way you walk around the halls. Not that I blame you, but you seem so far away. I haven't audited your classes, but—"

"Maybe you should," she interrupted angrily.

The principal blinked, taken aback.

"It took some adjusting. Probably will take some more. But I had a good day today, Tom. All right, it took a couple of days, but I'm fine. I don't think it's fair to—"

"Janine."

His voice was firm, but kind. It drew her gaze to his expression, and she saw the confusion and sadness there. Since her loss, Carlson had been nothing but sweet and helpful to her. Janine had needed his sympathy then, but at the moment it was too much. It made her feel vulnerable.

Eyes pinched closed to hold back tears, she put a

hand over her mouth and let her chin fall. After a moment, embarrassed, she opened her eyes again.

Carlson got up from his chair and stepped around the desk. Despite his girth, he crouched beside her, his hand on the arm of the chair.

"I probably chose my words poorly," he began. "I didn't mean to upset you."

She shook her head. "No, you're right. This is ridiculous. The last thing you need is a teacher who can't control her emotions."

Janine felt his warm, surprisingly strong fingers grip her hand. Reluctantly she gazed up into those sad eyes again.

"Seems to me you're doing an admirable job so far," he said. "And in front of your class, that's good. In here, though, you don't have to hide your feelings. I can't even begin to imagine what you're feeling, Janine. I'm glad you're back, the students are glad you're back, the other teachers are glad you're back."

Hopeful, she offered a tentative smile. "I thought you were going to tell me to take more time."

With difficulty, he stood up and leaned against his desk, releasing her hand. "If you need it, you can take it. That's what I was about to say. You do seem haunted by what happened to you. How could you not be? But it seems to me that you're getting a handle on things. Unless you tell me different, I'm going to assume you can handle all your regular duties."

"I can," she said quickly. Then, after a moment's contemplation, she nodded slowly. "I can."

A broad smile spread across Carlson's face. "Excellent."

Janine was troubled, however, and the man saw it on her face.

"What is it?"

She shrugged almost imperceptibly. "What you said. I feel like I am haunted, in a sense. By this image I had of the way things should have been."

"My dear Janine," Carlson said sweetly, "that specter haunts us all. It's the Ghost of Christmas Past, or something like it, I think. But I don't think you have to worry about the other two spirits. I have a feeling you're going to be just fine."

Janine nodded. "Me too. I have some good friends watching out for me, coaxing me along. Without Annette Muscari, I would've been lost."

"And I hear you're seeing David Bairstow again," Carlson observed.

"Gossip hounds, all of you, I swear!" Janine cried. But she shook her head, amazed at how quickly word had gotten around. "We've been out twice."

"In five days, that's pretty good." Carlson waggled an eyebrow suggestively. "That's nice, though. I always thought you two made a great couple. I'm glad that you had Annette and David to help you through this."

"And you, Tom," Janine said softly. "You helped, too. A lot. Thank you."

He seemed stymied by her gratitude, and only nodded a bit shyly. "This school needs you, Janine."

"Not half as much as I need this school." She stood up, went to the door, and then turned to face him again.

"Glad to hear it," Carlson replied. "Tell David I said hello."

"Will do."

Janine opened the door and stepped into the outer office. While Carlson's inner sanctum was overrun by plants yet otherwise neat, the outer office—lair of the receptionist—was a vast array of in and out boxes, file cabinets, folders, and an enormous jar filled with rolls of SweetTARTS candy. Janine had often wondered why SweetTARTS but had never remembered to ask.

No one sat at the reception desk, but as she stepped out, past the Poland Spring water dispenser, a tall, thin man with wispy hair and a red tie and a rumpled suit stood up from a chair near the door to Carlson's office.

"Janine Hartschorn?" the man asked.

A student's father, she thought. But she did not recognize the man.

"I'm Miss Hartschorn," she replied, relying upon the school's traditional formality within those walls.

The man reached inside his jacket pocket and for some reason she stiffened. A breeze whistled through the slightly open window nearby and it sounded almost like crying. A child crying.

He handed her a folded sheet of paper and, by reflex, Janine took it.

His smile was like a shark's.

"A summons, Miss Hartschorn. Have a good day." The man turned on his heel and marched stiffly out of the reception area.

"What?" she whispered, mystified. The breeze from the open window slipped tendrils of cool air around her, and she shivered as she unfolded and read the summons.

She forgot to breathe. The tears she had held back in Carlson's office began to flow and she put a hand to her mouth again. A tiny grunt escaped her, the smallest of breaths, as though she had been punched in the gut. As if it burned her, she dropped the paper and took several steps back as it fluttered to the carpet. Her legs went numb and collapsed beneath her, and Janine found herself sitting in the middle of the floor. She cradled herself, rocking just a bit.

"Bastard," she whispered. "You evil bastard."

"Hey," a gentle voice said.

Janine glanced up, and Carlson was there, stroking his beard, his brow furrowed in profound concern.

"What was that about? What's happened?"

"Spencer," she said, and fought for breath, struggled to keep from hyperventilating.

The clock on the wall ticked loudly, proof that she was still alive, that the world was moving on. Somewhere out the window, out in the parking lot somewhere, a car engine roared to life and the radio was up too loud. From the hallway, a girlish giggle.

The words that came out of her mouth seemed so

foreign to her, as though someone else were speaking them. Distant and hollow and metallic, the way it sounded if she tried to talk while underwater.

"He's suing me for custody of . . . of the baby. It says I buried my son without his consent. He . . ." She gazed up at him, the horror of it all dawning fully on her now. Nausea roiled in her belly and then vomit rose in her throat. Only with effort did she manage not to puke, but she could taste bile in the back of her mouth.

"Jesus, Janine, how can he do that? The baby's already buried." Carlson gazed at her awkwardly, perhaps unsure how to help, or unwilling to admit that he couldn't.

Long, shuddering breaths escaped her and her whole body shook. The tears on her cheeks seemed to burn. She felt a lump inside her, but not in her stomach this time. Lower, deeper. Janine could feel the weight in her uterus, feel the distended flesh stretched across her belly, where baby David had once breathed and thrived, her blood his blood, her breath his breath.

Hollow, now. Hollow inside.

Now he rested in the cold ground beside the bones of her father, who had held her in his arms when she was a little girl and told her it would be all right. He could never have known how wrong he was. She had thought, in some crazy way, that he would watch over his grandson now.

But he was dead. Her father was dead, and her son was dead, and it was all she could do to keep her spirit from withering and decaying along with them, to keep her soul from becoming as hollow as her belly.

"Janine?" Carlson prodded.

Cold, empty, she turned her eyes up to him again. Her hand was across her mouth and nose as a mask, and she gazed at him over her quivering fingers.

"Spencer wants to . . . to dig him up. To . . . exhume him so they can put the baby in his family crypt."

She threw up then, there on the floor in the reception area outside the principal's office.

CHAPTER 7

❧

*T*he smell of popcorn.

Janine sat in the passenger seat of an old Monte Carlo, just like the one her mother had driven when she was a girl. Through the car's windows she could see the parking lot of the drive-in all around her. There were dozens of cars, each with dark figures inside, illuminated only by the softest glow of dashboard lights.

Her window was down and the breeze swept in. Somehow she could not feel it. The sensation of her hair moving with the wind, yes, but not the caress of it on her face. It carried with it the smell of popcorn, however, and she found herself craving its salty flavor.

With a grin of anticipation, she glanced toward the driver's seat.

It was empty, and she frowned, wondering why she could not remember who had driven her here. On the driver's door, however, hung a speaker that was meant to pipe in the audio from the movie showing on the enormous screen.

The screen. Had she even been paying attention to the movie?

Only static issued from the speaker, and Janine grumbled with frustration as she realized she had no idea what movie she was at. Must have drifted off to sleep, she thought.

The breeze blew the popcorn smell into the car again and, reminded, she climbed out. With a sense of determination, she slammed the car door behind her. In synch with the clank of metal as the door banged shut, the wind died.

Janine glanced around and saw that the cars were now all empty. That soft glow from the dash still lit each vehicle, but there was no one within them. Just empty cars, all around, lined up and down the cracked, weedy parking lot.

Static hissed from the speakers that stood atop metal posts. It occurred to Janine that people didn't go to drive-ins anymore, that there were only a handful left in America. But there was this one, and it had plenty of business. Where were the people, though?

Popcorn. They smelled the popcorn. The thought seemed to satisfy her, and she glanced across the lot at the concrete projection building where the concession stand windows were wide open, yellow light pouring out. Yellow like butter.

A gust of wind blew up suddenly, and those yellow lights winked out as though they were the glow of flickering candles. The back of the parking lot was cast in darkness. An instant later, the row of cars farthest to the back went dark, all of them at once. Without the dash lights inside, they seemed almost to disappear, gobbled up by the dark.

Then the next row.

The darkness seemed to flow toward her.

Janine shivered. The smell of popcorn came to her on the renewed breeze again, but this time her craving was gone, replaced by a revulsion that made the gorge rise in her throat.

Anxiously, she stumbled back toward the car she had left. Though she had slammed the door, it hung open, awaiting her, beckoning her to the safety and warmth it represented, a haven from the encroaching dark.

Static hissed from speakers all around.

As though the eyes of the actors on the screen stared at her, she felt self-conscious and turned to gaze at the broad expanse of flickering black-and-white images that loomed above her. Jack Klugman and Tony Randall were on the screen. It made no sense, because that show was on television, or it had been once upon a time. Yet she loved them, and so that was all right.

The only problem was she could not hear them, only the hissing. On the screen, the two men talked, lips moving without words in a kind of manic pantomime.

Out of the corner of her eye, she saw the blackness enfold the row of cars just behind her. A single pop, and all of them went dark.

Janine ran, pursued by the hiss of static and the sickly sweet smell of popcorn. She slid into the car seat and yanked the door closed, and stared out at the big screen with the two men miming comedy, and she refused to turn around. Refused to look back at the darkness.

Something shifted beside her and she turned quickly to look. The driver's seat was no longer empty. A fat tub of gooey, buttered popcorn sat there, gleaming almost obscenely in the light from the car's instruments. With a little chuckle at how silly she had been, Janine reached out and grabbed the popcorn. She rested the tub on her lap and ate a few kernels. It was heavenly, just as she had imagined.

She stared at the silent screen and tried to read lips.

The static on the speaker was interrupted by the sound of a baby crying.

Janine flinched and turned to stare at it, but the speaker only hissed, and then began to jitter, to clank against the glass. Something shifted in her arms and she glanced down . . .

. . . and a sweet sense of peace descended upon her, calming her nerves and soothing her heart. Her baby lay there, in her arms, eyes bright and gleaming. He suckled on her bared breast contentedly, squirming to get in closer to her body heat. As he fed, her nipple began to ache, but it was a good, pure feeling unlike anything else she had ever known.

It was bliss. His eyes fluttered closed and the sucking slowed as he began to drift to sleep in her arms. Janine smiled and cooed softly, filled with a love she had never imagined.

She closed her eyes.

Her nipple burned. With a gasp, she opened her eyes quickly and stared down at the baby. His eyes were still closed, but he was not so peaceful now. He sucked hard on her nipple with lips that were blue and cold, his face pale white and frosted with ice.

Janine tried to pull his mouth away from her, but his icy lips stuck to her frozen nipple. Her flesh tore as she tugged harder and she screamed.

In a panic, she glanced around, desperate for help.

She was nude inside a long, wooden boat, surrounded by nothing but churning black water. Alone and filled with dread. She wished that she did not know where she was headed, but was afraid that she might.

The river rushed around her. The boat was swept on blindly into the darkness, only the lantern on its prow to light the way. Janine clutched the icy infant in her arms and began to weep.

Long, slender fingers lay upon her shoulder.

A cold voice spoke to her. "I will care for you."

Her eyes snapped open and she stared briefly at the ceiling of her bedroom. Then the tears began to flow and she lay on her side and cried herself back to sleep. It took more than twenty minutes of weeping before she at last drifted off again.

After that, she dreamed no more.

"Twenty-two?"

David stared at Annette in disbelief. It was Friday afternoon and they were alone in his classroom. She sipped a cup of coffee and leaned on the radiator by the window as he collected his papers to go home.

Or that was what he had been doing when she had mentioned the age of the new woman in her life.

"Twenty-two?" he repeated, though this time without quite so much judgment in his voice. He had not been able to edit out the astonishment, however.

Annette frowned at him over the rim of her coffee cup as she took a long swig. David was fascinated by her in that moment. All week she had seemed different to him, happier. When they had lunch together or even just stumbled across one another in the corridors of St. Matt's, her eyes had a faraway quality that had been a mystery to him.

Not anymore.

Though her clothes were not very much different from what she usually wore—today she had on a burgundy cotton V-neck and beige capri pants—somehow she looked better. Sexier.

Only now did he realize that there was a reason she looked sexier.

"Wow," he whispered.

Annette's expression changed, and now she looked almost hurt. "Y'know, try to be a little open-minded, David. If one of your penis-equipped friends had met a cute twenty-two-year-old girl, you'd be high-fiving him in the hallway. She's not *that* much younger than me."

The desk was not much neater, but he had gathered the things he needed. David clicked his briefcase shut and offered a sheepish look by way of apology.

"Just doesn't seem like you, Elf. Took me by surprise."

That faraway look that had been with her all week returned then, accompanied by a grin both coy and mischievous.

"Only 'cause you haven't met her."

"She must be really something," he said.

"Oh, yes. But you can find out for yourself at my birthday party tomorrow night."

"I'll look forward to it," David told her. "Then I can be all jealous and sulky that you're with the hot barely-out-of-college babe and I'm not even allowed to watch, never mind touch."

Annette laughed and pointed at him. "See, there you go! That's the reaction I was expecting. Jealousy! Well, you've got a woman, mister, and a great one at that."

"Point taken." He shrugged with faux innocence. "Still, if you ever need someone to videotape . . ."

She batted at his arm as they walked out of the classroom.

"So I guess I'm supposed to high-five you now," he teased.

"You will when you meet her. Looks like we've both been lucky in love lately. It's about time."

David thought of Janine and smiled, but with a bit of melancholy. He wished he could believe that things were really going to work out with Janine, but he dared not be so optimistic. She had retreated within herself after this latest blow, and he had been delicately attempting to get her to open up again since then. What Spencer Hahn had done to her, suing for custody of their dead child, was the cruelest thing he had ever heard of anybody doing to another short of violence.

Janine had broken his heart once already. David wanted to be cautious this time around. Or as cautious as he could be, considering how deeply he loved her.

"What's her name, anyway? This college girl?"

On the stairs, headed down to the double doors that led out to the faculty parking lot, Annette jabbed him in the ribs with a finger.

"She's not in college anymore, David. Don't make me have to hurt you."

"It's envy," he confessed.

Which was partly true. He loved Janine, true, and she was beautiful; there was no doubt about that. But he was a man, after all, and the idea of making love to a gorgeous twenty-two-year-old woman had its appeal. Of course, the idea of Annette making love to her had almost as much, perhaps even more. Not that David would dare say such a thing to Annette. He had guy wiring, simple as that. Those prurient thoughts were merely that, thoughts, and they did not undermine how deeply he felt his friendship with her.

Or, at least, not much. He tried to push the images in his head away, told himself to grow up.

"So what's her name?"

They pushed out through the double doors into the lot. It was warmer than it had been that morning, above sixty, and David slipped his jacket off, juggling his briefcase in order to do so.

Annette grinned happily. "Jill. Her name's Jill."

"You can't even say her name without that cat-swallowed-the-canary smile," he marveled. Then he lowered his voice. "Guess that answers my next question."

"Guess it does," Annette teased. "And just FYI? She was great."

David let his head loll forward. "You're killing me, Elf."

"I live for your torment."

A sense of camaraderie filled David. It was a feeling he often had with Annette, yet he never allowed himself to forget how rare that was. As a child, he had wandered this city in a small tribe of boys and girls among whom he had almost always felt that almost indefinable sense of kinship. But as he grew older it had become a precious commodity. As an adult, he had that sense of comfort with his sister, Amy, and with Annette.

No one else.

Not even Janine.

Particularly not Janine, if he were honest about it. His love for her craved intimacy, but it also created a distance between them, a gap to be bridged only in time. He suspected it was that way in most relationships in the early going, tiptoeing around each other, not daring to reveal any flaw or blemish or even concern. True intimacy came only in time, if ever. Which made the risk he felt now with Janine all the greater. They had shared that sort of closeness once, and she had hurt him profoundly.

Yet here he was, risking that pain again.

Guy wiring.

Only about half the spaces in the lot were full. Several cars jockeyed for position for departure through the only exit like planes without an air-traffic controller. David and Annette walked across the faded gray pavement to her SAAB, which was parked under an oak tree whose leaves had begun to fill in early.

Something fluttered in the branches of the oak, and David looked up to find a pair of bluebirds busy at something in among the new greenery. From the other side of the building, out on the main road, he could hear the heavy, lumbering groan of a bus engine, and then the hydraulic whine of its brakes. A bus from the public high school, he presumed, delivering its teenage payload. All the buses from St. Matt's had left half an hour or more earlier.

Annette unlocked the SAAB and threw her bag over the seat into the back.

"So, seven o'clock tomorrow night?" David asked.

"If you want to eat anything, be on time," she replied. "Jill's baking things for dessert, and I have no idea if she can cook."

"Seven it is."

He slung his jacket over his briefcase and used his free hand to dig in his pocket for his keys.

"You David Bairstow?"

A frown creasing across his forehead, David turned at the sound of the voice. Next to Annette's SAAB was a red Chevy Corsica with a dented rear fender that he thought belonged to one of the janitors. Behind the Chevy stood a man with shoulder-length blond hair and stubble on his chin. The stubble didn't make him look tough, though, not as well dressed as he was. The man wore a cotton shirt with an open collar and dark wool pants with sharp creases pressed in the legs and all about him was an air of hauteur and wealth.

Clearly, the Chevy didn't belong to *him*.

Annette climbed out of the car and glared over the open door at the newcomer. "What the hell do you want, Spencer?"

David stiffened. His hand slipped out of his pocket without retrieving his keys, and by instinct he switched both his briefcase and jacket to his left hand. This was the son of a bitch who had twisted Janine's life around, broken her heart more than once. Hell, this was the bastard who had stolen her away from him last time.

This was the guy who wanted to pay to have his baby's corpse dug up just out of spite.

Spencer gave them a wolfish grin. "Nice to see you, Annette. You look great."

"Fuck you," Annette snapped.

The words seemed to echo in the parking lot, but at the moment there was no one there to hear them. The first wave of departing teachers was gone, and no one else had come out yet.

Spencer's cell phone was clipped to his belt. It began to ring, an annoying, almost alien sound. One eyebrow shot up and he glanced down at the phone, obviously tempted to answer it. He didn't, and a tiny crack opened in the polished veneer that seemed to envelop the man. His appearance suggested the agonized preparation and purpose of a magazine advertising layout, but a ripple broke the surface of that strange, stylish bubble.

"Guess you spend enough time licking cunts, you start to act like one," Spencer said. His voice had dropped an octave. It was insidious now. Dangerous.

Annette laughed. "Explains why *you're* such an asshole."

But David wasn't laughing.

He dropped jacket and briefcase on the pavement, unmindful of where they might land, and strode around behind the Chevy. Spencer gave a shark's smile as he approached.

"You're the guy I came to see, anyway. Listen, we need to—"

David swung, hard. Spencer was fast. Fast enough to dodge the blow. But one punch was not what David had in mind, and he was already following it up with a left uppercut to the gut. Spencer grunted and began to double over. David caught him on the way down with a hard right jab that stung his knuckles but knocked the asshole back a step or two with a clack of teeth.

"You fuckin'—" Spencer sputtered.

David grabbed his arm, spun him around, and ratcheted the arm up high, and Spencer snarled in pain. The asshole swore again and tried to break the hold. Furious, David drove him facedown onto the trunk of the Corsica and held him there, pinned to the car.

"Apologize to Annette."

"You are going to pay for this, Bairstow," Spencer spat.

"What the fuck are you going to do?" David demanded. "Sue me?" He yanked up hard on Spencer's arm—any harder and he'd dislocate it—and the man actually cried out in agony.

"Apologize."

"Sorry!" Spencer growled in pain and rage and disgust. "I'm sorry, okay?"

"A little courtesy," David whispered. "That's all I'm asking."

Then he let go, backing off quickly just in case Spencer decided it wasn't over yet. Slowly Spencer stood and brushed at his shirt where it had been dirtied against the car.

"That was a mistake, Bairstow."

Even as Spencer said it, David knew it was true. The guy was a scumbag and what he had done to Janine was unforgivable. What he'd said to Annette . . . you didn't just walk away from that kind of thing. So maybe violence was not the answer. Maybe hitting the guy had been a mistake. But David knew he would do it again.

"You want to file charges against me? Fine," he snapped. "Sue me? Pretty much what I expect. See you then. For now, though, why don't you get the fuck out of here? Return that call you got."

Spencer nodded slowly, no trace of amusement on his face. A small red welt had begun to form high on his cheek.

"I came here to say something to you," he told

David, without sparing even a glance at Annette. "I took her away from you once. I'll do it again. All you're doing now is wasting everybody's time. She doesn't love you, Bairstow. If she did, she'd never have come back to me the last time."

"You arrogant, ignorant prick!" Annette shook her head in amazement. "You think after all this she wants you anything but gone? You used her, then left her pregnant. She almost died because of you. Losing that baby almost killed her, body and soul. Now you want to dig him up? You're not even human!"

With another slight nod, Spencer tossed back his too-long hair and puffed his chest up, as though the things Annette had said made him proud.

"Neither one of you really knows her. I do. It's never really been over between us, not since the first day we met on campus." He glared at David again. "Just stay away from her. Make it easy on all of us."

"You're insane," David muttered.

Spencer shrugged. "I tried, that's all. Now we do it the hard way."

Without another word he turned and strode confidently across the lot to a BMW convertible that was parked next to Sister Mary's Honda.

Side by side, David and Annette stood and watched him climb into the car and drive away. The cold rage within him turned brittle, and gave way to more heated emotions: grief and doubt, even hate. But there was a sense of satisfaction there as well.

He turned to Annette, all those feelings roiling within him.

She gazed at him fondly, slipped her arm through his, and laid her head on his shoulder.

"I wish I had that on videotape."

Janine stared across the table at David, certain she had to have heard him wrong.

"You did what?"

He dropped his gaze. "I hit him."

Gingerly she set her wineglass down on the creased

tablecloth. Around them, the little Italian restaurant bustled with activity. Asagio, as it was called, had been recommended to her by a colleague at Medford High, and Janine had seized upon it as something new. She did not want her dates with David to keep taking them back to places that had meant something to them before. If things were to work between them, they would have to create a new relationship.

No more than a dozen small tables fit inside the cramped confines of Asagio. It reminded her of some of the tiny restaurants she had eaten in during a trip to New Orleans some years earlier. Pressed white tablecloths were draped over the tables, and each was topped with a burning candle and a fresh red rose in a small vase. The waiters were very Italian. In the North End of Boston, that was almost required.

In the late afternoon, the sky had turned gray. Now, as she gazed at David's strong, kind features and marveled that he had any capacity for violence at all, rain began to fall lightly outside, to patter the window not far from their table.

A waiter brought a basket of bread and set it between rose and candle.

"Are you ready to order?" he asked in accented English.

Janine blinked and glanced at him, but could not seem to summon a response.

"We need a few more minutes," David replied.

The waiter nodded and went to clear a nearby table.

With a soft smile, Janine regarded this man whom she had known for so long, and yet perhaps not really known at all.

"You hit him?"

He nodded.

"Just once?"

Shamefaced, he shrugged. "A bunch of times, actually. Annette wanted to call you right away, but I told her to wait so I could tell you myself."

It had been a hard couple of days. All of that bottled up inside her, she did the only thing she could do: Janine began to laugh. First it was a tiny thing, a chuckle in the back of her throat that she hid with a hand over her mouth. Then it erupted out of her in a howl of laughter and tears sprang to her eyes.

At first, David obviously had no idea how to handle that response. He glanced around at the other patrons and at the waiters, likely worried that they would think her a madwoman. Janine thought they might be right to think that, and cared not at all if they did.

But then David began to laugh as well, the laughter expanding like a balloon around them. After a minute or so, it started to deflate and Janine sighed happily.

"You kicked his ass?" she asked.

David nodded.

"How did it feel?"

"Pretty damn good, I confess. Annette said she wished she had it on tape."

The last of the laughter between them died away, but both still wore wide grins. David sipped his wine.

"He threatened to sue, of course. Wants me to stay away from you because he expects that things will work out between you two eventually."

Her jaw dropped. Janine could feel the blood draining from her face as she stared at him. "He didn't really say that?"

"He did."

"Jesus, what a deluded son of a bitch," she whispered.

In the aftermath of that exchange, they retreated into silent contemplation during which they studied the menu. The waiter arrived a few minutes later and took their order: insalata caprese and ziti with chicken and broccoli for her, Caesar salad and veal parmesan for him. When the waiter had retrieved the menus and they were alone again, David reached across the table for her hand.

He slid his fingers over hers, twined them together, and Janine let him. It felt good and right. She ran her thumb over the back of his hand and he flinched. With a frown, she glanced down and saw that the knuckles were red and swollen.

"I'm glad you did it," she said, her voice low. "I'm afraid of what it might cost you, but I'm glad you did it. I would have done it myself if I could have."

David nodded. "Have you talked to a lawyer? About his lawsuit?"

"Today," she replied. "I'll tell you, David, after I got that summons on Wednesday, I really had to wonder if God had it in for me. I didn't tell you this, but I didn't go in to school yesterday. Tom Carlson subbed for me himself."

"He's a good man," David said.

Janine smiled softly. "He truly is. Anyway, I woke up this morning and I just felt . . . different. I've been having a hard time sleeping; I told you that. Bad dreams, even creepy dreams. Dreams about the baby. There's not much I can do about that. I can't bring my baby back. I can't go back in time and tell myself not to be a fool, to stay with you, to keep away from Spencer.

"But I can fight him. I've been hurt. Pretty badly wounded. It'd be easy to wander around like some emotional cripple, to just spend all my time crying about what a bastard he is. Even now. Even with this."

His fingers closed more tightly around hers and Janine leaned in closer over the table. Candlelight flickered off his eyes and cast his handsome features in waves of shadow. She could smell the rose.

"That's not me, David. This morning I woke up and I realized that it isn't me. I've had some pretty awful shit come into my life in the last year, especially in the last month. Every step of the way, he's had me in a situation where there was nothing I could do to fight him. But I can fight this. And I'm going to.

"I talked to my mother this morning. She and my stepfather have plenty of money, and they know a lot of lawyers, even up here. I talked to one of them, this woman Elaine Krakoff, today. She said the case was unusual, but she did find precedent. There was something like it in Virginia in the early nineties, but in that case the mother had moved to another city, where she became a crack addict, had the baby there, and it was buried in a pauper's grave."

"So she thinks you'll win?"

Janine sat back a little, let her fingers slide out of his. She reached out and traced one nail down the stem of her wineglass.

"No way to be sure. But, yeah, she doesn't think he's got a case. Even if I win, though, that won't make what he's done any less painful. If there were any way I could make him suffer for it, I would. Then again, maybe you gave him a little taste of his own medicine today."

David raised his wineglass in a toast. "Here's to fighting back."

Her fingers curled around the stem, and then Janine raised her glass as well, slowly, deliberately. "Here's to starting over."

"I like that one better," David whispered.

Their glasses clinked together, and they both sipped at the dry Italian wine. A moment later the waiter brought their salads and conversation turned to other things, particularly Annette's new girlfriend and the birthday party the next night. Both of them were looking forward to celebrating with their friend. Also, though, they were both insanely curious about the new woman in Annette's life.

The spatter of rain came and went quickly. After dinner they walked around the North End for a little while, enjoying the feeling of history in that old neighborhood. They had coffee and dessert at Mike's Pastry, which was legendary in the area. By the time they found their way back to the car, it was ten-thirty.

When David unlocked her door before walking around to the driver's side, she stopped him with a soft touch on his arm. He glanced down at her, and in his eyes she saw love and warmth and hope and fear.

Their lips met, and Janine laid her head on his chest a moment and listened to his heartbeat. It made her feel safe.

All the way home, David drove with one hand, his other clasped in hers.

When they pulled into the driveway at Janine's apartment house, the headlights washed over the old barn in back and the trees beyond it. Behind the barn, not far from the trees, the lights momentarily illuminated a lone figure, a man who stood frozen there.

Janine clutched David's fingers tightly. "Did you see that?"

He slipped his hand away and placed it on the wheel. "I saw something." Quickly he turned the car so that the lights again shone upon the backyard.

Nothing. The figure was gone.

"You don't think it was . . ." Her words trailed off.

"Spencer?" he finished for her. "It could have been."

"Bastard." She sighed. Janine could not even muster the anger she knew she should feel.

"You should call the police, at least have a report on it. Otherwise if you need to bring it up later, in court or whatever, they're going to ask why you didn't call."

He parked the car and they both got out. David walked her to the door, where he paused to push her dark hair out of her eyes and to kiss her, first on the forehead, and then on the lips. The kiss went on awhile.

The backyard was not visible from the front steps, but David cast a concerned glance in that direction regardless. Then he studied her closely.

"I'm not assuming anything, Janine, but . . . do you want me to come up? Just until the police come?"

Janine slipped an arm behind his back and pressed herself against him, molded her body to his. To think she had given up this man for Spencer . . . it was enough to make her cry. Or it would have been, if not for the fact that whatever shitty things God had done to her lately, He had seen fit to give her a second chance with David Bairstow.

She didn't know if she was ready for what came

next, but it scared her to wonder if she would ever be. *Ready or not*, she thought.

"I want you to come up," she whispered, her gaze locked on his, making certain her intent was clear. "But not because I need you to protect me. In fact, I'm not going to call the police just yet."

A troubled frown creased David's brow. "But what about—"

With a kiss, she shut him up. He relaxed into her, and she pulled back to gaze at him again. They went upstairs together to her apartment. Once inside, they undressed one another slowly, without turning on the lights, only the glow of streetlamps to see by. With the languid, smoldering passion of former lovers reunited, they caressed and tasted each other, discovering new things, and rediscovering what they had nearly forgotten.

David touched her with a hunger that Spencer never had. Janine felt that same yearning for him in return. She wanted to stroke and kiss him, but he was coy and playful, and kept out of her reach, insistent upon pleasing her. He kissed and licked all of her, and she shuddered with pleasure and stroked his hair as he gazed up at her while he teased the insides of her thighs with his tongue.

Then he was through teasing.

Janine closed her eyes and shivered, weak with her ecstasy. But even that was not enough. She pushed him away and turned him over on his back, then crawled on top of him.

When she slid herself down onto him, Janine gasped at the feel of him inside her, filling her up. David sighed with pleasure and reached up to trace his fingers down over her breasts and belly, propped himself up enough to take her nipples in his mouth, each in turn.

They moved together and took their time, and Janine knew that this was what was meant to be. Making love could not erase her pain, but it could provide bliss as a counterbalance. All the hesitation and awkwardness that the past couple of years had built up between them was burned away in the heat they created.

Everything would be all right now, she was convinced.

They had a second chance.

David would drive the bad dreams away.

CHAPTER 8

∾

The brief rain shower on Friday evening was only a flirtation with the storm that rumbled in on Saturday morning. The sky was heavy with thunderheads, black and ominous as they roiled above, yet seemed to move so slowly across the sky, to linger with malicious intent.

David hardly noticed the rain at all. Though they had fallen asleep before two a.m., they were up again by eight. A crack of thunder greeted him when his eyes slowly opened, and then he focused on Janine, her raven hair splayed across the pillow, her luxurious curves peeking out from beneath the rumpled sheets. When he reached out to caress her face, her eyes fluttered open and she offered a sleepy smile.

Then she reached out to drag her fingernails suggestively down his chest.

It was well after lunchtime when they finally, reluctantly, got dressed. Somewhere in the middle of the morning there had been a shower, but as they were together at the time, cleanliness had not been the first priority. A little past one, David made them both chicken salad sandwiches at the kitchen counter while Janine blew-dry her hair in the bathroom. Though David had tried to follow her in, she had insisted that each of them take their second shower of the day alone.

They ate their sandwiches at the small table in the kitchen. An open jar of pickles and a bag of potato chips were arrayed on the table with an informality that David loved. It reminded him of the intimacy they had once shared, the comfort level that had once existed between them. Over lunch, they talked about Annette's party that night, speculated about her new girlfriend, and avoided any conversation about their hours of lovemaking, as though some third party had joined them in the room. Yet from time to time they shared a secret smile. A kind of giddy humor suffused David and yet he dared not speak to Janine about what he felt for fear that the heat that remained within him might rob him of the caution he knew was necessary. At least for the moment.

The last thing he wanted was to reveal too much of himself, to presume an emotional intimacy that could scare her off.

She had missed him.

For now, that was enough.

Aside from having one of the longest, steepest subway escalators in the Northeast, Porter Square had very little going for it. True enough, there were plenty of restaurants, both franchises and unique hangouts, and a wide variety of retail stores, but it was simply not the sort of place tourists went to wander. Close as it was to Harvard Square, there had always been the sense that Porter Square was the poor relation of Cambridge locales. Exacerbating the situation was the fact that Davis Square—just over the line in nearby Somerville—had inherited the trendy, Bohemian charm Harvard Square had increasingly abdicated over the years. Davis also inherited the trendy Bohemians that went with it, which left Porter Square smack-dab in the middle of two places most people would rather be.

A stop along the way, a place to do errands, and not to linger.

There were exceptions, of course. Porter Square was on Massachusetts Avenue, which was punctuated all along its length by fascinating little boutiques and pubs, bookstores and cafés. Among those exceptions, just a block or so up from the T station with the terrifyingly long escalators, was the Cayenne Grill.

The Cayenne was one of the quirkiest restaurants David had ever been in. Though its name was derived from the peppers most frequently found in Cajun and Creole cooking, only a portion of the menu focused on such fare. There were dishes from all over the country available at the Cayenne, whose interior reflected the diversity of its cuisine, decorated in an eclectic collection of styles from around the country. Somehow, it worked.

The owner of the Cayenne was Carl Montenegro—though David had always doubted that was his real name. Montenegro had been part of a program aimed at giving gay teens role models in the real world, people who were stable and successful and content in addition to being gay. It was through that program that he had first met Annette, argued with her quite loudly and publicly about her position as a teacher at a Catholic school, and how he felt that undermined everything gays were attempting to do. She was, in essence, working for the enemy.

David recalled the argument well, for he had had a ringside seat. It had begun while they waited for a table at the bar. Annette had promptly told the owner of the restaurant to fuck off, and then proceeded to explain that in her estimation, the only way to change the system was to infiltrate it and rebuild from within. Anything else, she told Montenegro, was cowardice.

First he threatened to throw them out. Then he gave them dinner on the house. Though David got along with the man passably well, he knew him only incidentally. Annette, however, had forged a strong friendship that night.

This was the third year running that Montenegro had hosted her birthday party in the second-floor function room at the Cayenne Grill. He kept the bar on a cash basis—he was not about to fund anyone's drunk-driving accident or arrest—but dinner for all the guests was on him. Every year David found himself speculating about the revenue the place must generate for the man to be able to be so cavalier about such an expensive proposition. And every year he found himself realizing that it may well have simply been that Montenegro loved Annette.

She commanded love from nearly everyone who knew her—love and loyalty—and she gave it in return. Father Charles at St. Matt's was the only exception he could think of, and that was more Annette's doing than the priest's.

David parked on Massachusetts Avenue and reached into the backseat for an enormous black umbrella. He got out and ran around to Janine's door to keep her from getting rained upon. Though he had run home to dress appropriately for the party, he cared not at all about getting a little wet. On the other hand, Janine had taken time to get her hair and makeup perfect, and the crimson dress she wore seemed too immaculate to allow a single raindrop to mar its perfection.

As he walked her the block and a half to the restaurant, he wielded the umbrella with almost absurd intensity, making certain she remained unsullied.

Inside the front door, they received a nod of recognition from the hostess, checked their coats, and headed up the stairs.

"You didn't come last year," David observed. It was something he had wondered a lot about.

Janine reached down to take his hand, tapped their clasped fingers against her thigh as they ascended. Her eyes appeared almost violet in the dim light of the stairwell, and the dress rippled over her as though she were an alluring phantom rather than flesh and blood.

"I didn't want to see you," she confessed. Then, quickly, she shot him an alarmed glance. "Out of guilt, I mean. I thought I'd hurt you enough. The last thing I wanted to do was show up here with . . ."

Her words trailed off. She didn't want to say Spencer's name. David reached out to slide his fingers beneath her hair, and he rubbed his thumb gently across the nape of her neck.

"Got it. And on that note, no more of the past tonight. Just the future."

"Agreed."

At the top of the steps, they pushed through a pair of French doors into a small room with windows along the front that looked down on Massachusetts Avenue. There were nine or ten round tables, each set for six, but most of the activity was around the bar. The people mingling in that room were a collection of Annette's friends who were almost as eclectic a grouping as the décor in the main restaurant downstairs. David saw Clark Weaver with some of the other teachers from St. Matthew's in a kind of tribal circle in one far corner. Clark laughed loudly and nearly spilled the martini in his hand. The sight made David smile. Clark had been struck particularly hard by Ralph Weiss's death, and it was good to see him loosen up.

Around the bar was a clutch of women, some of whom David recognized, most of whom he supposed to be gay. Along with them were a handful of men, including Montenegro's longtime companion, Alex Cotton.

"Looks like the party's well under way," David observed.

"We're fashionably late," Janine told him, squeezing his hand.

"Maybe late isn't fashionable anymore?"

"Yeah, then where's the birthday girl?"

David could not stop the devilish grin that spread across his face. "Getting her spankings?"

"If she's lucky," Janine replied, with a smile that matched his own.

They laughed and merged with the partygoers, began to mingle. Though he did not recognize her at first, David found himself talking to Annette's cousin Gwen, a recovering alcoholic and rabid Republican, and Gwen's boringly wealthy stockbroker husband. There were also a handful of friends Annette had picked up at college or at one of the various nonprofits she had worked for over the years. All in all, their coworkers and the gay couples were much better company.

He was relieved when Lydia Beal bustled up to him, knocking aside a textbook editor from Little, Brown and her accountant husband.

"David, I've been looking all over for you," Lydia told him in a hushed voice. "You've got to point out which of these guys are straight and unattached."

"I'm on the job," he vowed, and began to gaze around the room in earnest.

"Lydia!"

Janine had peeled herself away from Montenegro, who had proclaimed her a horrible person for not having visited him in nearly two years, then begun to regale her with his tales of trench warfare in the restaurant business. David had listened with one ear for the first few minutes and then tuned them out. If Janine had needed an escape from the conversation, Lydia provided it.

The two women embraced and cooed at one another. Janine thanked Lydia for the sympathy card and flowers she had sent, which caused a brief wave of gravity to sweep over them. It was gone quickly enough, however, as the two old friends began to gossip.

"Have you met Jill yet?" Lydia asked. "My God, she barely looks old enough to have graduated from college."

A frown furrowed David's brow. "You mean she's here?"

Lydia gave him a confused look. "Of course she's here. It's Annette's birthday."

"We haven't even seen Annette yet," Janine said with regret. "We thought she was late."

"She was," Lydia confirmed, her gaze beginning to rove over the people gathered around the room. "But she's here now. Somewhere." After a moment, Lydia's eyes brightened. "Over there. With that nice lawyer and his boyfriend."

Sure enough, they spotted Annette right away. The lawyer and his boyfriend weren't familiar faces, but Annette seemed animated enough talking to them. David had to assume the woman next to Annette was Jill, though she had her back to them. Still, even across the room, he could see that the woman with the taut body and long blond hair seemed young. Even in the way she carried herself.

Intrigued, he smiled.

"Lydia, do you mind?" he asked.

"Not at all. It's her birthday. Go say hello before she starts hunting for you."

Lydia began to mingle again, on the prowl for available men without appearing to be that interested. He silently encouraged her, hoping she would find what she was looking for.

Janine took his hand again and they nudged through the partygoers in a cloud of apologies and nearly spilled drinks. All the while, David peered in between bodies for a good look at Jill. The lawyer's boyfriend told a joke, and both Annette and her new lover laughed. Jill turned to gaze sweetly at Annette, gave her a soft kiss on the cheek.

David froze.

Janine's fingers slipped out of his. Eyebrows raised, she turned to stare at him with concern.

"What's wrong?" she asked. "David?"

Slowly he brought a hand up to rub at his eyes, and then he looked again. As if she had sensed his attention, Jill glanced over her shoulder at him.

"David?" Janine prodded, sounding even more worried now. "Are you all right?"

The lawyer added something else to the conversation, and Annette and Jill laughed again. The women's amusement was a lovely sound, a light, lilting melody. He saw that Jill had her arm around Annette. David could no longer see the girl's face, but he did not have to. Her image was etched on his mind's eye.

"Whoa," he said, letting out a long breath.

"Hey," Janine said, her voice gentle, but worried.

He met her concerned gaze and offered a wan, but nevertheless reassuring smile and a shake of his head. "Sorry. I just . . . it's impossible."

"What is?"

Awkwardly, he glanced around to make sure no one was listening, then lowered his voice anyway.

"This Jill? She looks exactly like someone I knew in high school."

"How exactly?" Janine asked.

"A lot."

"She's twenty-two, David."

He smiled weakly. "Yeah. Freaky, huh?" With a wave of his hand, he tried to push away the chill that had surrounded him when he had first seen the girl.

It was Annette's birthday. Time to celebrate.

And even if Jill had not been so young, she could not have been Maggie Russell. Maggie was dead.

David had killed her himself.

Fucking dyke.

Spencer sat in his Mercedes and glared out through the windshield at the face of the Cayenne Grill. He had left the BMW at home. They had both seen that car before. The dark blue Mercedes was beautiful, but inconspicuous enough. He had been parked half a block from Janine's apartment all night. That asshole teacher Bairstow had never gone home, not until the middle of the afternoon.

There were images in his mind, pictures of them fucking, but Spencer could not banish them. Janine and Bairstow, together. It killed him.

He hated them both. She had gotten herself pregnant, trying to lock him down, put him in a box; then she had let his baby die and buried it somewhere and he'd never even gotten to see it. Not that he'd wanted the thing, not after the way she'd gone about it. But he was the father, goddamn it. He had rights.

Without the baby, it could have been good with

Janine again. He would have laid down some new ground rules, but they might have made it work. All through college, they'd had a heat he never found again after. That had been why he'd tracked her down in the first place. Years later, and he had not been able to get her out of his head. Then she pulled the shit with the baby . . . but now, no baby.

It could have been good.

If not for Bairstow.

Still, he didn't blame the teacher. He was an asshole, but he had a dick, and Janine was an extraordinary piece of ass.

Bairstow would get his. Spencer would drag the fucker into court for assault, nail him to the goddamn wall. And Janine? He'd already hurt the bitch a million times over, but this thing with the baby? It'd tear her heart out if he got to exhume the kid. Not that that was his only motivation. His flesh and blood should be buried with his family. Period.

The only one he couldn't hurt was the one he blamed the most. That dyke, Annette. Spencer knew that she had been the one behind getting Bairstow and Janine back together. Little matchmaking twat had been working against him all along.

Fucking dyke, he thought again.

The rain blew in sheets across his windshield and turned his view of the restaurant into a bleary neon mess. Not that it mattered. Though he was parked in the strip mall parking lot across the street, a stone's throw from the T station, he had a good view of Bairstow's car. He would see them when they left.

But he would not follow. Not this time. Spencer had spent a lot of time ruminating about ways he could hurt Janine and Bairstow. There was plenty of time for that.

The dyke, though, that was something else.

Hurting her was going to require a more direct approach.

On the seat beside him lay a pair of leather gloves and a crowbar. In the glove compartment was a Frankenstein mask he had bought the previous Halloween but never worn.

Spencer sat back and listened to the patter of the rain on the roof as he waited for Annette's birthday party to end. Her biggest surprise was yet to come.

After a while, he grew bored and turned the key backward in the ignition. The dashboard lit up and the radio came on. An old Queen song. Nostrils flared, he punched the preset buttons until he came upon something a little more suitable to his mood.

Someone rapped on the window.

Startled, Spencer glanced over to see an old man peering in at him through the rain-slicked window, all weathered features and white Hemingway beard. It amused him how accurate the comparison was. The old man did look a lot like Hemingway. Contrary to Spencer's expectations, however, he was too well dressed to be some panhandler aggravating people until they gave him money. The old man looked sharp, and his eyes were warm and intelligent.

Worried that the crowbar might raise suspicion, or that the old man might remember it later, Spencer shifted forward on the seat before lowering the window.

"You're getting wet, pal. What can I do for you? You need a jump start or something?"

The old man was fast.

He thrust his left hand through the open window and grabbed a thatch of the long hair Spencer was so proud of. Then he raised the bowie knife in his right and punched it through Spencer's throat, rupturing his windpipe. The sound of it reminded Spencer of ripe watermelons and backyard barbecues.

The old man held on tight to his hair and drew the knife sideways. Arteries spurted blood in Rorschach patterns across the upholstery and windshield.

Spencer slumped down in the seat, on top of the crowbar and gloves. As the old man walked across the parking lot, he dropped the knife, and the rain sluiced the blood from the blade and from his hands.

*   *   *

The windshield wipers squeaked across the glass on high speed, but even then, David could barely see the road in front of him. His headlight beams refracted off the heavy rain and he sat rigid, back straight, fists gripping the steering wheel. The wiper on his side went too far when he had them set at high speed, and its tip kept pushing over the edge of the windshield, each time making a small popping noise.

"God, this weather is awful."

He said nothing. Though he could feel Janine's eyes upon him where she sat in the passenger seat, he had no idea how to express what he was feeling in that moment. The storm had him on edge, yes, but it was far more than the storm.

"David, hey." She put a hand on his shoulder and kneaded the muscles a bit. "Do you want me to drive?"

The suggestion was so ironic, he laughed a little. It allowed him to relax ever so slightly. "No. I'm all right."

"This is all about Jill? 'Cause she looks like some old girlfriend of yours? Don't tell me you're still in love with a girl you haven't seen in fifteen years."

An image of Jill swept through his mind, then seemed to freeze there, a face behind a curtain of ice. The line of her jaw, the flare of her nostrils when she laughed, the way the skin at the edges of her mouth crinkled just so when she smiled.

"She seems really nice," Janine added.

"No argument from me," he replied.

The front left tire plowed through a deep puddle and he could hear the water pummeling the underside of the car. A spray of it shot out and showered the sidewalk. For only a second, the car began to hydroplane.

David hung on to the wheel but didn't touch either of the pedals. It passed immediately, the tires gripping the road again, but now, as he drove through Medford Square, he tapped the brakes and went even slower.

Though other cars honked at him, he stayed well away from the curb and watched carefully for puddles.

"If you liked her, what's got you so spooked?" Janine asked.

He sighed. "It isn't just the resemblance. I mean, all right, it is pretty spooky how much she resembles Maggie. But it's more just that seeing her brought back a lot of old pain. A lot of guilt."

"Guilt about what?"

The light ahead turned red. That crimson illumination seemed not truly obscured, but spread by the rain on the windshield, as though the light had begun to bleed out from its encasement. David slowed to a stop. After a moment he glanced at Janine, then quickly looked away.

"I was in a car accident my junior year. Broke my leg and fractured two ribs. Maggie didn't have her seat belt on. Her head hit the windshield."

His knuckles hurt with the fierce grip he had on the wheel.

"Her skull was cracked. Her neck was broken."

"God, David," Janine whispered. She slid her hand down his arm.

Again he glanced at her. The red glow from the stoplight gleamed on her pale flesh.

"I'm sorry. It must hurt to be reminded of that loss. But . . . I know how hollow it sounds, but accidents happen."

David stared at the rainswept street in front of him. "We were drunk. I was drunk, Janine. I should never have been behind the wheel of a car. It was an accident, sure. I know that. But I killed her."

The silence between them then was electric. It lasted a trio of heartbeats, no more. Then the light turned green and David accelerated, still careful of the road. Again he could feel Janine's eyes on him, studying him. He turned up Winthrop Street, just a short way from her apartment building.

"You know you didn't really kill her," Janine said, her voice shaky.

"But I'm responsible," he said. A great sadness rippled through him, and yet it took some of his tension with it. He blew out a long breath. "I'm okay. I've lived with it a long time. Just . . . seeing Jill . . . it's just so bizarre. I swear if I showed you pictures . . ."

Again, there was silence between them. A few minutes later he turned in to the driveway beside Janine's building and parked.

"Want to come in?" she asked.

He smiled weakly. "Not tonight. I don't think I'd be very good company. We'll talk in the morning, all right?"

Janine wanted to reach out to him. David sensed that from her. But after a moment's hesitation, she nodded. He was glad. What he needed at the moment was just time to recover from the shock, time to get Jill's face . . . Maggie's face . . . out of his mind. Though he loved Annette, he secretly hoped this relationship did not work out for her. The last thing he needed was that constant reminder of his guilt.

Umbrella in hand, he left the car running and walked Janine to her door. He saw that she was deeply troubled as well, her eyes haunted and sad.

"Hey," he said softly, and lifted her chin so she would meet his gaze. "I'll be all right. Just need a little sleep, I think, and sunshine tomorrow. Hopefully we'll get it."

Her smile was clearly an effort.

"Janine?" he prodded.

"I just . . . I was thinking, wondering why in all the time we were together before, all the things we shared, you never told me that."

A tiny ball of ice formed in his stomach, and yet his face felt warm and flushed. Guilt. It was a familiar feeling.

"It isn't really something I talk about to anyone."

Hurt, confused, she looked up at him expectantly. "But we shared everything. Good and bad. You told me about some really painful things; I'm just surprised you never told me about Maggie. I don't even remember your mentioning her name. It's like, she was this girl you loved in high school and you erased her from your memory."

Pained, he glanced away. "I wish I could."

"Guess I didn't know everything about you after all."

"I thought I knew everything about you, too," David said quickly. "But I had no idea you'd just walk away from what we had if Spencer came back into your life."

Eyes wide, Janine reached for his face, stricken by his words. She touched his cheek. "I've paid for that, I think. What can I do to make *you* forgive me?"

His heart broke a little bit. That happened a lot, particularly where Janine was concerned.

"I didn't mean that. I do forgive you. I did even then. All I'm trying to say is that I don't know if anybody ever really shows all of themselves, even to the person they love the most. Maybe if you're married for fifty years, but even then, maybe not. That doesn't mean I don't love you. It just means there are parts of me that are just for me. Little painful things that are hurtful to me, or could be to you, things I hide away even from myself. It sounds selfish to say it out loud, but you can't deny that you're the same way. We all are.

"And let's not forget that I *did* tell you. I just told you when it seemed to become something you should know."

Water sluiced off the umbrella on all sides, raining down around them in a curtain. Janine smiled ever so slightly, which confused David even more.

"What?" he asked.

"You're right, of course. It just isn't something people talk about, you know? That internal landscape. But I'm actually stuck on something else you said, just a second ago."

He frowned. "What did I say?"

"That you love me."

"Which comes as a surprise to you?" he asked. The

tension and the guilt and the cold knot in his stomach all began to dissipate in the warmth of his feelings for her. "I never stopped, you know?"

Janine slipped her arms around him and laid her head on his chest. With the rain coming down at an angle, David's shoes and pants were getting soaked, but he said nothing.

"A long time ago, you told me you'd always be there to catch me if I was falling," she said, her voice tight with emotion. "Now I know you meant it. I just want you to know that the same is true for me. I want to be there to catch you if you're falling."

He stroked her hair and kissed the top of her head. "Sounds like a good deal to me."

After a moment Janine hugged him even tighter, then let go. She got her keys out and opened the door, then stepped inside.

"I'll talk to you in the morning?"

"Absolutely," he promised.

He waited until she closed the door before he turned to go back to the car. The image of Annette's new girlfriend still lingered in his mind, but it, and the guilt it had raised like a phantom in him, was ushered aside by his feelings for Janine and the memory of their lovemaking the night before, and all that morning.

The drive home took him past the Mystic River, whose waters had climbed higher on its banks in the storm. There were fewer cars on the road than before. It was late now, almost midnight, and the storm would have kept less motivated people home. He'd had only a couple of drinks over the course of the evening, but he wore his seat belt cinched tight across his chest and kept both hands on the wheel. The lessons he had learned fifteen years earlier had been reinforced tonight.

David was still careful as he followed the road that wound along beside the river. Streetlights cast a diffused glow at intervals along the street, but their light accomplished very little. The radio was on low, a soft-rock station to soothe him. Ahead was a curve in the river, and the road followed it. A yellow sign warned of the sharp turn, and he touched the brakes to slow down, careful not to brake too much in case the road was slick.

The headlights washed across the soft shoulder, the grass of the riverbank, and the water itself.

At the edge of the river stood the ghost of Ralph Weiss. As the lights passed over him, passed through him, the dead teacher lifted his right hand and pointed an accusatory finger at David, mouth open in an angry shout that was either silent or drowned by the storm.

"Jesus," David whispered.

A chill ran through him; his heart sped, his grip loosening on the wheel as he stared at the apparition. He steered the car to follow the road, but glanced to the right as he passed the spot where the ghost had been.

But the apparition was gone.

"Holy shit," he said aloud. *That was not my imagination.*

With a sudden flash of brilliance, headlights popped on behind him. They had not been there a moment earlier. A car roared up on his left on the curving road, the storm flashing lightning in the sky. The driver did not pass, however. It was almost as though he wanted to race.

"What the fuck?" David snapped, still reeling from what he'd seen.

He glanced over at the car beside him on the rain-slick road. Just as he peered through the dark, they passed beneath a streetlight and he was afforded a very clear view of the driver's features.

It was Steve Themeli.

Steve Themeli, who had been one of his students, a drug user he had tried but failed to reach. Steve Themeli, who had been murdered in a fight over drugs. Steve Themeli, who was dead.

Then they were in darkness again, rain pelting the car's roof, suddenly loud enough to drown the music.

David, eyes wide with terror and confusion, heard the rev of the engine of the car beside him just before it careened sideways. Metal screamed as the cars collided, and he grabbed the steering wheel, slammed on the brakes.

His tires began to hydroplane, the car to spin out of control.

The steering wheel felt useless in his hands as he worked the gas and the brake and the wheel to try to get the car back under his control. It slid onto the shoulder, tires tearing up the muddy grass.

Then it flipped.

The windshield splintered into spiderweb fractures when the car landed on its roof. David shouted his fear loud enough that his throat felt instantly raw. He watched through the shattered glass as the car slid on its roof toward the river's edge.

And stopped.

His chest rose and fell quickly, his eyes were wide, and he waited as though certain it was not over.

Yet it was. The car rocked slightly, but stopped there, half a dozen feet from the riverbank. Upside down, held in place by the seat belt he had cinched so tightly, David quickly checked to make sure he was all right. He had banged his head on the driver's-side window, and there was a lump rising there. Otherwise, to his astonishment, he was unscathed.

He began to weep.

CHAPTER 9

၈၅

The house on Briarwood Lane had been in David's family since the early 1900s. It had been built in 1887 by a local doctor by the name of Early, and above the door was a sign placed there by the historical society that announced it as THE DR. JOS. EARLY HOUSE. David had never liked the sign, but his parents had told him there was a tax break involved or some such. He never paid it much attention after that.

The old Victorian was a quarter of a mile from the Mystic River. Less than half a mile from the location of the accident. Its façade was both classic and quirky, with a restored turret to the left of a pair of high-gabled windows that looked down from the third floor. Though it was surrounded by less than half an acre—which for a city like Medford was substantial—the house was enormous and sprawling, much like those on either side of it and across the street. It was a creature of its times.

There were parlors on either side of the first floor, both with fireplaces, built-in cabinets, and ornate woodwork. The central staircase was grand. In the rear were a small formal living room, a vast dining room with tall windows that let in a great deal of sunlight, a small kitchen with outdated appliances and a back staircase for the doctor's help, and a small pantry and mudroom that opened onto the backyard.

The second floor featured three large bedrooms, two bathrooms, and a library that had been part of the house's original design. On the third floor were two more bedrooms and what had always been called "the turret room," a small space with steps leading up to a spot eight feet in diameter, just enough room for a desk and chair, and a couple of lamps to read by.

Though he did not visit the turret room often, it was David's favorite room in the house. He would go there to read, or just to look out the windows on the street below. If a melancholy mood took him, the turret room was almost certainly his destination. When it snowed, he liked to sit up there in silence and watch the flakes fall. Even as a small boy, it had been a place he and his sister, Amy, had felt happy and safe. Their private sanctuary.

After Janine had left him, there had been many nights David had fallen asleep up in that room, lost in whatever book he had escaped into at the time.

When he woke up Sunday morning, just after nine o'clock, he pulled on a pair of sweatpants, draped the bedspread over his shoulders, and went up to the turret room. He had not heated the third floor in years, but the heat rose from below, warming it enough that though the morning was chilly, the spread was sufficient to keep his teeth from chattering.

The chair at the desk was a high-backed leather thing with rivets. His father had used it in the late seventies and then abandoned it to the house, and David had been in love with it ever since. The smell and feel of the leather, even the way it seemed to absorb and retain the temperature in the house, it all reminded him of the most innocent of times.

He slid into the chair and placed his hand on the biography of Teddy Roosevelt he had been dipping into from time to time. Though he had no intention of reading from it now, he pretended to himself that it was why he had come up to that room.

Instead, he stared out the windows of the turret at the houses across the street, their faces dark, still sleeping; at the trees behind them, far older than the homes, reaching for the sky and falling short; at the clouds that were pasted in shattered pieces across the heavens. The rain had stopped about four that morning. He had been awake then, as he had been off and on through the night. Now the blue sky shone through breaks in the clouds, a struggle to reclaim what the storm had stolen the day before, to make the storm only a memory.

A door slammed. David leaned forward and glanced down to see Mrs. Dodolan across the street picking up the heavy Sunday *Globe* from her front steps. As she turned to go back inside, a fiftyish man with white hair but in great shape jogged by at a brisk pace, careful to avoid the large puddles that remained.

For more than an hour, David sat holding the book on his lap and stared out at his world. It looked much the same as it had when he was eight years old.

But he did not feel quite so safe anymore.

The paramedics had taken him to the hospital by ambulance. David might have argued, but his car was wreckage and so he could not drive himself. A nurse cleaned up the many scratches he had, but none of them was so serious as to require stitches. He had some serious aches and pains, but according to the staff at Lawrence Memorial, no concussion. The seat belt had saved his life. When a doctor finally looked him over, it took five minutes for him to be discharged.

The last thing he wanted to do was worry anyone, so he took a taxi home. By two o'clock he was asleep, as if the accident had never happened.

Yet it was not an accident. That was the part of it that had haunted his dreams. There were no ghosts in his dreamscape, no familiar faces at all, in fact. Just the rending of metal and the world turning upside down and the river coming closer. He dreamed he was drowning, and beneath the water was a face.

Smiling.

It was an image that woke him up several times, one he escaped only after the rain had stopped. Then, at last, he slept without dreams for a handful of hours.

When he woke, the faces returned. Ralph Weiss. Maggie Russell. Steve Themeli, driving him off the road.

A dead boy had tried to kill him.

Impossible, but there it was.

Shortly after ten-thirty, David watched a police car cruise slowly up Briarwood Lane and pull into his driveway. The front door was a long way down—too many stairs—but he dragged himself reluctantly from the chair and started down, leaving the bedspread behind. At the second-floor landing he realized that he still held the Teddy Roosevelt book in his hands, and he clutched it to him like a child's stuffed bear.

The doorbell rang as he went down to the first floor. Just as he was about to reach for the knob, the policeman on the other side knocked and David jumped a bit, startled. His heart sped and he took a long, shuddering breath, and wondered how long it would be before he stopped being afraid.

With a sigh, he hauled open the door. On the front porch stood a young police officer in uniform, trim and fit in an almost military fashion. Beside him, and obviously in charge, was a man in dark pants and an expensive-looking leather jacket. He wore a tie, but David had the idea that was only because someone in charge had told him he ought to. The man had the build of an old-time boxer, burly but not fat. His hair was a little too long, and there were bags under his eyes.

"Mr. Bairstow?"

David nodded.

The older man stuck out his hand. "I'm Detective Kindzierski. I hoped I could take a few minutes to talk about your accident last night."

"I told the officers at the hospital. It wasn't an accident."

When he spoke, David thought his voice sounded dull, as though he were drugged, or were trying to talk underwater.

Detective Kindzierski's eyes sparkled. "That's what I wanted to talk to you about. It's been a long night."

David stepped aside and the two cops entered. He knew, vaguely, that he ought to offer them something, coffee or tea. But he simply did not have the energy. Instead, he led them into the parlor on the right and gestured for them both to sit. The detective did. The uniformed officer stood at the door as though at attention.

"You can call me Gary, by the way. Or just 'Detective.' The name's a pain in the ass, I can tell you. Half the time I think the reason I'm not married is because no woman would want that name, even as a hyphenate."

Kindzierski sat on an antique sofa and grinned up at him. "Then I remember that I'm kind of an asshole and impossible to live with, and I figure that's a more logical explanation."

The uniform chuckled softly, the first sign of animation he'd given other than walking. The detective shot him an admonishing glance.

"That's Officer Simmons, by the way. He's my ride."

Simmons's smile disappeared.

David nodded at the uniformed man, then sat in a wooden rocking chair that had once belonged to Grandpa Edgar, book still in his hands. It gave him a perverse kind of pleasure, at times, sitting in that chair and knowing the old man would have cringed at the thought.

"What more can I tell you, Detective?"

With a nod, Kindzierski reached inside his jacket and pulled out a pad and pen.

"First, you should know that your story is as verified as we can get it. Nobody saw you take a drink as far as we can tell, no alcohol in your system, your car clearly shows signs of the impact of having been hit by another car. In your statement this morning, you said that you were sure the other driver ran you off the road on purpose, and that you got a good look at the guy."

A flash of memory went through him, a vague jumble of images from the crash, the ambulance ride, talking to the cops in the hospital.

"You said," Kindzierski continued, "that the driver was a kid named Stephen Themeli, a former student of yours. But you and me both know Themeli's dead. Want to elaborate on that?"

The detective frowned and leaned forward as though David were going to give confession. David grimaced, then worried that the half smile might come off as a little crazy. Kindzierski did not seem to be passing judgment, just doing his job.

"I . . . that isn't what I said, exactly," he said.

Kindzierski raised an eyebrow. "No?"

"No. I said he looked a great deal like Themeli, enough so that if you want to find him, you could actually use an old picture of Steve and try to find a close match."

"Weird that the officer who took the statement wrote it down without that distinction," Kindzierski noted.

David shrugged. "I was pretty shaken up. Not to mention tired. I might not have been completely clear."

"All right. We'll look into that. Meanwhile, there's something else."

The detective's voice had dropped an octave, and the change in his tone was revelatory. He had not come to talk about the accident. Not really.

"Yes?" David asked.

Kindzierski leaned back in the chair and studied him thoughtfully. "Last night, the officer who took your statement asked if you knew of anyone who might have a grudge against you, a reason to hurt you."

"I saw the driver," David interrupted.

The detective waved the statement away. "If he did this on purpose, it isn't likely it was just for fun. If you don't know him, chances are he was hired, or at least did it as a favor to someone. The only name you could come up with was Spencer Hahn."

With a nod, he offered a small shrug. Officer Simmons cracked his knuckles loudly and David flinched. He let out a long breath.

"Spencer and I had it out a couple of days ago. He's a low-life asshole who used to go out with the woman I'm seeing. And if you need testimony on just how much of an asshole, I'm sure you'll have no trouble finding it."

"I don't doubt it," Kindzierski said. "Thing is, I spoke to Miss Hartschorn this morning. I asked her not to call you, but she wanted me to tell you she'd be over as soon as she's showered and dressed."

David glared at him. "You told her about the accident?"

"Sorry." But it was obvious he was not. "I know you'd rather have told her yourself, but I have an investigation to conduct. Let me cut to the chase, here, Mr. Bairstow."

Mr. Bairstow. The way he said it reminded David of Ralph Weiss, and he shivered again, and forced himself not to think about what he had seen the night before.

"Please do, Detective Kindzierski."

Immediately, David regretted his tone, but it was too late to undo it.

Kindzierski drew a short breath. His expression was grave. "Last night, around the same time you and Miss Hartschorn left the Cayenne Grill, Spencer Hahn was stabbed to death in his car in a parking lot directly across the street."

David actually pulled away from the detective slightly, flinching back in the rocking chair and setting it in motion. His voice failed him and he turned to glance at Officer Simmons, who fixed him with an accusatory stare, his mouth set in a grim line. Slowly, David began to shake his head.

"Oh, wait," he said, voice a rasp. "Now just wait a minute."

"Relax," Kindzierksi said, and held up a hand. "You've got to understand, you and Miss Hartschorn would have been my primary suspects. With what happened with her baby, and Hahn's lawsuit—something that automatically makes him a lowlife in my book, by the way, no testimony necessary—both of you have motive. You and the victim had a fistfight in the parking lot of a Catholic school."

"Holy shit," David whispered.

"Whoa, there, Mr. Bairstow. No need for the divine manure just yet. See, I've got two witnesses who saw Hahn's murderer. Maybe not well enough to pick him out of a lineup, but enough for me to know it wasn't you. Guy was old, shorter than you, had a beard."

Confused, David shook his head. "If I'm not a suspect, what does his death have to do with me?"

Kindzierski raised his eyebrows. He slid back on the couch and steepled his fingers under his chin in consideration. After a moment's hesitation, he smiled without humor.

"Hahn used to be involved with Janine Hartschorn. You're currently—and were formerly—involved with her as well. An hour after his murder, possibly even less, someone tried to kill you. I'm just wondering if you know of anybody else in Miss Hartschorn's life who might want you *both* out of the way."

David stared at him.

Kindzierski grinned. "You can say 'holy shit' now if you want."

"Holy shit."

"There you go. So, any thoughts?"

"Jesus," David whispered. "Not a one."

Kindzierski stood, straightened his pants, and slipped the pad and pen back into his jacket. He had not written anything at all on that pad while talking to David. Officer Simmons stepped out into the corridor as Kindzierski offered David his hand.

"That's exactly what Miss Hartschorn said. Thanks for your cooperation. We may contact you again, particularly if we find the guy who tried to do you in. Meanwhile, do you have a cellular phone?"

David set the book he'd been holding on the

mantelpiece and shook his hand. The detective's grip was firm.

"Never had a need for one."

"Not a bad idea, if someone really is trying to make trouble for you," Kindzierski explained. He produced a business card as if from nowhere, then walked out into the corridor.

David gave the card a cursory glance, then followed. Simmons was already on the front porch. At the door, Kindzierski turned to glance at him again. For a moment David wondered if they had met before. The expression on his face, the hand gesture as he noted that he had one last question. Then he knew.

Det. Gary Kindzierski had seen one too many episodes of *Columbo*.

"One last thing, Mr. Bairstow. You know we could subpoena phone records. You're certain Miss Hartschorn didn't call you this morning after I'd been to see her?"

"Very certain," David said, a bit irked now, but pleased to find himself able to feel annoyance. Happy not to be numb anymore. "You can ask her yourself, though. She's here."

Kindzierski glanced out the door, saw Janine's car pulling up to the curb, and nodded. "So she is. Thanks for your time, sir."

David went out on the porch and watched the two policemen walk to their car. Kindzierski waved to Janine, whose expression was stricken as she hurried up the driveway toward the house clad in blue jeans and a dark green sweater. The clouds had cleared off quite a bit, and the sun shone down on her face and hair. Though she had showered, her hair was pulled back in a ponytail and she wore no makeup.

Her wave back to the detective was little more than an acknowledgment of his presence. Then she was rushing across the lawn and up the front steps to the porch.

"I was going to call," he said as she came to him.

Janine threw her arms around him, hugged him

tightly, then pushed him away so that she might examine his injuries. Satisfied that he was all right, she glared at him.

"Next time I tell you to stay over, you stay over," she snapped angrily.

Then she kissed him, deep and long, and her lips tasted of tears and joy, of fear and dread.

David did not bother to watch as the police car drove off.

"About Spencer—" David began.

She shook her head. "No. I don't want to talk about him."

Together they walked back into the house. In the foyer, at the foot of the grand staircase, Janine gazed at him again, reaching up to push her fingers through his hair.

"Do you think . . . I mean, do you really think there's any connection?"

He ran the backs of his fingers along her cheek in a gentle caress. "No. I really don't."

"Then why?"

He stiffened. Once more, images from the night before flashed through him. Jill's resemblance to Maggie Russell had to be coincidence. He had talked and laughed with her. But what of Ralph Weiss? Twice he had seen that apparition. And what of the driver of that car, the guy who tried to kill him? That was no apparition, but a flesh-and-blood person behind the wheel. It could not have been Steve Themeli.

Yet, somehow, he believed that it was.

A shudder passed through him as he reached down to take Janine's hand in his. He kissed her fingers.

"I don't know why," he rasped. "But I'm okay, Janine. I'm all right."

As though she were deflating, Janine let a long breath out and seemed somehow to diminish slightly, to become her own self again. She went and sat at the bottom of the steps. Her relief was palpable, and there was even a tiny, tired smile on her face as she looked around the foyer.

"I missed this place," she said. "I didn't realize how much until just now when I walked in."

A thought skittered across David's mind, and before he could stop himself, the words came out.

"You don't ever have to leave."

Janine blinked several times and stared at him in astonishment. Then she nodded slowly. "Whoa." Her smile changed, became one of surprise and wonder.

To his own surprise, David laughed. "Too fast. I know. But it's hard not to think in terms of picking up where things left off. I know it's not that simple."

"A conversation for another time, though," she replied earnestly. "I hope."

"Definitely."

"I do love this place. So many old homes seem musty and, y'know . . . haunted." She hesitated on that last word, and seemed almost unsettled by it.

David understood what she meant, though. The house felt alive, still, not drab and withered like a lot of homes from times past.

In this case, he thought, *it isn't the house that's haunted.*

It's me.

Even as the idea came into his head, he understood that it was meant to be a joke, something to make light of what he had experienced, to amuse him.

Instead, he shivered.

The neighborhood where Ruth Vale lived with her husband Larry was a haven for the wealthy. Ruth enjoyed the money and privilege; she enjoyed the freedom it brought, and the ability to surround herself with things of beauty, to liberate her from the more mundane things that most people took regretfully for granted: cleaning the house, washing the car, doing the laundry. Yet there were drawbacks as well. Nearly every day she walked up and down the streets of her neighborhood amidst enormous homes with no visible life within. Curtained windows, perfectly groomed yards, and no sign of humanity, most of the people hiding behind the gates of their castles.

The result was that Ruth did not very much enjoy being home. With all that she and Larry had, all the luxuries there, and the beauty of their surroundings, she would rather be in her Manhattan office. On the weekends, she and her husband kept busy. She walked, and gardened, and they entertained whenever possible.

More often than not, she thought about Janine, and wondered just when the distance between herself and her daughter had grown so wide and deep. They were always so tentative with one another now, and Ruth had no idea how to fix that.

Her mind was filled with bittersweet musings about her daughter when she finished her walk late that Sunday morning. Her red sweat suit seemed almost garish in the staid environs of Scarsdale, but she relished its outrageousness. Energized, despite the bit of melancholy she felt, Ruth jogged up the front steps and opened the door.

At the back of the house, Larry poked his graying head out of the kitchen. He held the phone against his ear, a troubled expression on his face.

"Look, Hugh, thanks for the call, but Ruth just walked in. Why don't we talk tomorrow about the Judson thing? Thanks."

As Ruth unzipped her sweatshirt, her elevated heart rate slowing to normal, her husband clicked off the phone and let it dangle in his hand. He had showered while she was gone, but not bothered to shave, and he ran a hand across the gray and black stubble there. Larry was aging, but with his wavy hair and Tom Selleck mustache, he was still a handsome man. At the moment, however, he only looked sad.

"What happened? That was Hugh Beaumont?"

Larry hesitated only a moment. He hefted the phone in his hand as if weighing it. "He was watching the news this morning up in Boston. Spencer Hahn was murdered last night."

Ruth brought a hand to her mouth and closed her eyes. "Oh, Lord," she whispered. "Oh, Jesus, not now. Why now?"

Eyes still closed, she felt her husband's hand on her shoulder and fell into him. His strong arms encircled her and Ruth laid her head on his chest. A long sigh escaped her.

"Hey. Not that I wish that on anyone," Larry said softly, "but if anyone had it coming to him—"

"I don't care about that son of a bitch," she snapped. "I hope he rots in hell. I'm just thinking about Janine."

Ruth opened her eyes and looked up at him. Larry nodded in understanding, but she wasn't sure he did understand. He was a good man—a bit stiff, but kind and genuine. Yet he and Janine had never really bonded, so Ruth did not believe Larry could feel what she was feeling.

"She still hasn't really come to terms with losing her baby," Ruth insisted. "I think she never had a memorial service because she's trying to avoid reality. Maybe she hated Spencer for what he did, but she loved him once; he was the father of that baby. Even if she hated him, she's got to feel like her whole world is falling apart."

Larry seemed thoughtful a moment. He put one hand on her shoulder and massaged gently.

"You should go back up there."

Ruth shook her head. "She doesn't want me there. I just get on her nerves. And we can't . . . it seems like we aren't able to really communicate anymore. Everything has to have other things weighing on it."

"Maybe," Larry agreed. "But maybe that's okay. Maybe it's all right for you to get on her nerves and for her to get aggravated at you. If that's what your relationship is, that could be what she needs right now. So you drive her crazy. You're her mother. That's your job. And even if you exasperate her, she loves you."

Taken aback, Ruth blinked and stared up at him. Then a small smile fluttered across her face.

"That's about the sweetest, smartest thing you've ever said, Mr. Vale."

"Why, thank you, Mrs. Vale."

Ruth kissed him quickly, then headed for the stairs. "I'm going to Boston."

Behind her, she heard Larry as he retreated into the kitchen. "Why didn't I think of that?"

On the bank of the Mystic River, Janine stood just a few feet behind David and stared at the water. They had driven over in her car, of course, because his was totaled. Now, having seen the skid marks and broken glass and the ravaged riverbank where his car had flipped and nearly tumbled into the river, Janine was even more unnerved, more horrified than she had been that morning when she had learned of the accident.

Though there were still some clouds in the sky, it had mostly cleared, and the sun shone in patches down upon the river. The wind blew, making the surface of the water choppy. Janine walked up behind David and slid her arms around him; she laid her face against his back.

"I feel lucky," she whispered.

Slowly he turned, took and held her hands, and gazed down at her. "Lucky? How's that?" he asked, his eyes doubtful.

"Somebody ran you off the road last night. Could have killed you." She smiled. "Killed your car. But you're right here with me still, no worse for the wear."

"Takes a licking and keeps on ticking," he replied, smile uncertain.

"Hey, I'm being serious; no talking about licking."

"No innuendo intended, I promise. Not today."

Janine nodded. "Not today. Anyway, I'm just glad you're all right. Now, can I ask you something?"

"Of course." He squeezed her hands reassuringly,

but his eyes flickered past her to the roadside, just a short way up from where he'd been driven off the pavement.

"What are you looking for down here?"

David flinched as though she'd pinched him. "What do you mean?"

"The police have been here," she explained, a deep frown creasing her forehead. "The car's been towed away. The drunken loony who did it is long gone. So why are we down here?"

He shrugged, glanced away, then met her gaze with a grim cast to his features. "I don't know. I almost died right here. When they took me to the hospital, I was so shaken up that I almost felt like I left something behind. I needed to *walk* away from it. Does that make any sense?"

"A little," Janine replied, though it really did not. What was important was that it made sense to him.

"I feel like I touched something here, like I came close to seeing whatever's waiting for me when the end really does come."

She swallowed hard, but found her throat was dry. His words made sense to her now, but a little too much sense. Ever since she had lost the baby, and almost died herself, she had felt somehow disconnected from reality. She shuddered, despite the sun.

"Can we go?" she asked, offering him a tired smile. "Why don't I buy you lunch?"

"I like that plan."

David turned to take one last look at the rushing river, and Janine stood beside him, an arm around his waist. He shook his head and muttered sounds of amazement at his narrow escape.

Janine glanced up at the opposite bank of the river, and she stiffened. A lone man stood at the water's edge, amidst the trees that lined the Mystic. The man stood perfectly still, as though a scarecrow had been erected by the water. It was quite a distance across the river, but she could see that he had a long beard. His face was very pale and he seemed to be staring at them.

She froze.

It's him! she thought in a panic. *From my dream.*

But after her initial reaction, she narrowed her gaze and studied the figure more closely. Though she could make out very little about him, he was clearly flesh and blood, and not some dreamlike specter. Those had been dreams. Janine considered herself an intelligent woman, and she realized that her half-formed impressions of the eerie man from her dreams would automatically be altered by seeing someone in real life who reminded her of those dreams.

Still, the way he just stood there and seemed to stare . . .

"God, he's creepy."

"Who?" David asked.

She glanced at him. "That guy on the other side. Gives me the creeps."

David stared across the water, his gaze scanning the opposite bank. Then he shrugged. "Guess I missed him."

When Janine looked again, he was gone.

Though he might have slipped behind a tree or something, she was forced to wonder if he had ever been there at all. It worried her to think that the answer might be no. She knew that she had been more than a little unstable lately, that the baby's death had been affecting her in a lot of ways she didn't want to deal with, but hallucinations would be very bad. In her exhaustion and her grief, she knew she had heard things that probably weren't there. But this was something else entirely.

A niggling thought wormed its way up inside her head, but she pushed it away, refused to listen to the frightened dream-voice in the back of her mind. The one that said it had to be a hallucination because David didn't see him.

But what if it wasn't?

CHAPTER 10

On Monday morning, an hour before the first bell would ring, Hugh Charles sat in his office and read over the notes he had prepared for the week's theology lessons. His window was open and the curtains were pulled back. Though the breeze that blew in was cool, the sun was bright and warm, the sky a vibrant blue, and the scents of spring almost intoxicating.

A small radio played on the bookcase in the corner, upon which also rested a leafy green monstrosity that would soon need a bigger pot. The tinny melody that came from the radio's speakers was old Motown, and it made him think of spring days just like this one from thirty-five or forty years before. He loved Motown.

His right foot tapped against the leg of his chair in time with the music, and he hummed softly to himself as he turned his attention to his plans for the final exam in theology.

Someone rapped on the frosted glass of his door.

Father Charles looked up to see David Bairstow and Annette Muscari standing in the corridor. The priest was alarmed by how pale David seemed, and Annette's worried expression only furthered his concern for the teacher.

"Have you got a minute, Father?" David asked.

"Of course. Come in, please."

David glanced at Annette and she squeezed his hand, then looked into the office, her eyes guarded as they always were around him. "I'll see you later, Father."

"All right, Annette. Don't forget, you promised to speak to that student for me."

Annette nodded and turned to walk off. Father Charles watched as David came tentatively into the office. He seemed unable to decide where to put his hands, and they fluttered into his pockets, then up to scratch his head, then down to his sides. His eyes were equally restless, taking in all of the office, and yet none of it. The teacher's demeanor concerned the priest greatly. He was very fond of David Bairstow. If he had a friend on the faculty, other than Sister Mary, of course, it was David.

"I heard this morning about your accident," Father Charles ventured.

David stiffened.

The priest gazed at him. "Sister Mary had heard about it from Lieutenant Garney. Though she said the word was you were none the worse for wear. Why do I have the feeling that might not be completely true?"

"Father, I . . ." David shuffled his feet a bit.

"Sit down, please. You wanted to talk, David. I'm sorry if I've put you off track."

A kind of sadness seemed to sweep through the teacher, but Father Charles thought there was more to it than that. Not just sadness, but anxiety, even fear, a kind of emotional static that resonated in the man like the sound of the ocean in a seashell.

"I got scratched up a lot, a few bruises, but I'm all right. The car isn't going to make it, though." David smiled for just a moment, unconvincingly, then turned away.

Father Charles waited. In a way it was much like confession. Sometimes a gentle prodding was required, as though the other person needed permission somehow, but he never pressed.

After a moment, David sighed and sat up a little straighter in his chair. As though he had regained some lost determination, he gazed directly at Father Charles.

"Do you believe in ghosts, Father?"

The room was silent then, save for the crooning voice of Smokey Robinson on the radio and a few chirping birds outside his window. Father Charles stared at David and attempted not to allow his expression to change. It was the last question he would have expected.

He picked up a pen and tapped it on the desk as he studied David's expression, wondering what had prompted such an inquiry.

"Well, the Church believes—"

"I'm not asking what the Church believes," David interrupted. "I'm asking what *you* believe."

Father Charles leaned back in his chair and put his hands up under his chin, fingers steepled in an unconscious expression of prayer or concentration, or perhaps both.

"During my time in seminary, I saw several things that I would be hard-pressed to find a nonsupernatural explanation for. Do I believe in ghosts? Let's say I'm inclined to believe, but I'm still formulating an opinion."

With a long sigh, as though something that had been dammed up within him had broken free, David shuddered and put a hand to his face. He nodded slowly. Then, though he spoke haltingly, pausing to find the right words every few moments, he told a most extraordinary story that began with the death of Ralph Weiss and concluded, at least for the moment, with his car accident two nights before.

Throughout David's story, Father Charles listened without comment, save for a nod now and again that he added only to encourage the man, in a sense to give permission for him to continue. Again he was reminded of confession. When David finished, he seemed tired, and yet somehow refreshed.

"You haven't talked to anyone about this?" the priest asked.

David shrugged. "Janine, a little, but not the ghost part. She thinks this Jill looking like she does is a coincidence. But last night I looked at the yearbook I dug out of the library, Father. It isn't a coincidence. Maggie Russell's been dead a long time, but this Jill? She's a dead ringer."

The teacher uttered a little morbid laugh. "Bad choice of words, huh?"

Again the priest allowed his thoughts to drift, turning the story over in his head. It was far from the craziest thing he had ever heard. Though he had never witnessed an exorcism, he knew older priests at the seminary who had. Their tales were chilling. Ghosts, however—that was something else. He had been vague with David, but this was not the first time he had run across a ghost story. Some of them had even turned out to be true.

"You think I'm crazy?" David asked.

The words were not bitter, but sad and anxious. Father Charles looked into his eyes and saw the earnest faith and hope in them, and a sudden dread filled him.

Sometimes the stories were true.

"I don't think you're crazy," the priest said. "But I do think we need to talk more about this. To investigate a little more, find out what's really happening. I'm a priest, David. No one needs to convince me of the existence of supernatural power. As a Catholic, I believe in one God, and yet historically that is a relatively young theory. I believe in angels and demons and in heaven and hell. That's what they teach you in the seminary. I had a proctor there, though, who had some other theories that he expressed outside the classroom from time to time. He suggested, more than once, that perhaps all of those things are just part of this being we call God."

"Where do ghosts fit into that? Lost souls? Spirits revisiting Earth from heaven or before going on to their final rest?"

The priest laughed lightly. "You have a lot of faith

in my ability to provide answers, David. The problem is, no one can. You know that. Those sound like reasonable possibilities given the other things we believe, but who can say for certain? What I will say is this: Ghosts, if they do exist, have never been known to drive cars. They're also not generally known to be corporeal enough to attend birthday parties where they eat and drink and bump shoulders with flesh-and-blood people. I'm troubled that this one . . . manifestation . . . appears to be Steve Themeli. If these things are real, we'll have to find out what they are, and why they're preying upon you."

The grateful expression on David's face evaporated after a moment, and he frowned. "What about Mr. Weiss? I saw him at least twice, maybe three times. And he wasn't flesh and blood."

Father Charles glanced out the window. On such a perfect day, with reality so tangible, it was odd to be having this conversation. And yet he knew well enough that humanity defined reality by its experience, by its five senses, and there was far more to the world than that.

"I've been wondering about that myself, ever since you mentioned it," the priest said thoughtfully. "The ghost, if ghost he is and not some manifestation of your subconscious—always a possibility—has not tried to harm or even harass you in any way."

"Then what's he doing?" David asked.

"Have you considered the idea that he may be attempting to warn you of danger? If there is a ghost in this, David, it sounds to me as if he's on your side."

For several minutes, both men were lost in their thoughts, and the room was silent save for the Supremes on the radio.

Janine shifted uncomfortably on the sofa in her living room. Her gaze flickered downward a moment. The expression on Annette's face might have been comical if it had not been at her expense. It was Monday night. There were dirty dishes on the table from the dinner she had made for them, but neither woman moved.

•"You've got to forgive me, okay? Just trying to wrap my head around all this," Annette said. "I mean . . . you're still taking the Zoloft, right?"

Exasperated, Janine nodded.

"Don't get upset," Annette chided her. "What do you expect me to say? You had this . . . near-death experience, or whatever, then nightmares, and now, what? Hallucinations? Too strong a word, maybe, but maybe not. Janine, don't you think you should talk to someone?"

"You mean a psychiatrist." She pursed her lips and sighed a bit.

"Well, someone. I mean, there are things that can cause hallucinations, you know? Medical conditions. Chronic insomnia, for one."

"Brain tumors for another."

Annette blanched. "Hey. That's not what I'm saying. I just think that for your own sake you should make sure that this is just your imagination and not something actually *wrong* with you. If you don't want to see a psychiatrist, though, you should at least talk to David about it. I can't believe you haven't mentioned any of this to him."

Horrified, Janine stared at her. "How can I? God, Annette, we're just getting things going again. What am I supposed to say? 'Hey, I know I broke your heart, and you've kind of forgiven me, we're working on rebuilding love and trust and, okay, having completely rocking sex, but by the way, I'm either a delusional, paranoid freak or I'm being stalked by some bogeyman from the afterlife'?"

Annette shrugged, doing her best not to laugh. "That'd be a start. All I'm saying is, it can't be helping things if you have all this shit in your head and you can't even talk to him. He loves you, Janine. He always has. And for a guy, he's pretty perceptive. Maybe he can help."

"Maybe," she grudgingly allowed.

It felt absurd to Janine to even talk about it, as though she were watching a film of someone else's life. Yet this thing that had been haunting her dreams—and then appeared at the river's edge—inspired a dread in her she could not escape. Thoughts of it, images of the Ferryman in her head, had begun to eclipse things that ought to have been far more important.

The dreams she had been able to rationalize away, and she could ignore the chill feeling of being watched that came over her from time to time. But on Sunday morning, she had *seen* him. Spectral, in some way, but still substantial. Whatever it was, she refused to believe it was some sort of mirage.

With a shuddering sigh, Janine smiled. "You know what? It would be a relief, to be honest, to find out it was all in my head. I just . . . I haven't been able to shake this feeling that someone's watching me."

Annette leaned toward her, putting a comforting hand on her leg. "Janine. Listen to me. Someone *was* watching you. When he was killed, Spencer was across the street from my party, sitting in a parked car facing the door. You think that was some sort of coincidence?"

"Maybe not," Janine allowed. A chill ran through her again and she hugged herself. "But Spencer's dead, Annette. He was a fucking bastard, but I thought I loved him, once upon a time. It's just awful and creepy that someone murdered him with me so close by. So he was following me, all right. I thought I saw someone out in the yard the other night, and I've been kind of assuming it was him.

"But what if it wasn't?"

Janine reached down and took Annette's hand in hers as though she could somehow share in her friend's warmth and strength. The world continued to roll on without any notice of her anxiety. Reality was inflexible. That ought to have comforted her, knowing that despite her eerie dreams, bizarre thoughts, and the fright she'd had on Sunday, everything around her remained mundane and painfully normal. David loved her, and though she still felt terrible guilt for having hurt him in the first place, she had begun to allow herself to love him again as well.

There was comfort in his arms, and in his bed. There was shelter in her work and the faces of her students.

But at home, at night, she was frightened.

"Janine."

She did not respond at first, her gaze drifting, lost, to the darkness outside her window.

"Hey," Annette said, and gave her hand a squeeze. Janine finally looked at her, and in her friend's loving eyes she found the refuge she sought.

"Spencer probably was stalking you. But he isn't anymore. You've had a lot of bad things happen to you in the last year, but good things are happening now. You can put it all behind you. It may take a while, but you can. And I'll be here to help you every step of the way."

Janine smiled softly, sadly. "I don't think I could do it without you," she said, her voice hitching with emotion.

With a sigh of relief, she leaned in and Annette opened her arms. Janine laid her head upon her friend's chest, her mind awhirl with images from her dreams and the lone figure on the riverbank the day before. Annette held her gently and kissed the top of her head, and they fell silent for several minutes.

Janine had hoped that having Annette there would somehow help her clear her mind, drive away the ghosts in her head. But the fear did not leave her.

"It's going to be okay. You'll see," Annette told her.

"See, the thing is, that feeling, like someone's watching?" Janine said softly. "Spencer's gone, but that feeling's still there. I can feel his eyes on me. He's waiting for me, Elf. And he's not going away."

Annette lived in a two-bedroom apartment above a hair and nail place in Medford Square. They had changed the name four times in the two years she had lived in that particular apartment, and she had a hard time remembering what it was called. Part of that was probably also because she had never actually gone inside.

That night, her concern for Janine still lingering with her, she parked as usual in the municipal lot two blocks away and walked to her building. A sliver moon hung in the sky and stars shone brightly above. The night was clear and warm enough that it was possible for her to believe that spring was really here. No more freezing rain, no more reminders of winter.

Her jacket was slung over her arm as she walked to the door that led upstairs to her apartment. The salon was long since closed, but someone waited in the shadows under the store's awning.

She hesitated, more deeply affected than she had realized by Janine's fear, and what had happened to David.

Then a smile blossomed on her face.

It was Jill. She looked extraordinary, her long hair falling in a blond cascade across her shoulders and back. With her full lips and wide eyes, she looked like a porcelain doll. She was breathtaking. Part of that, Annette knew, was that though she was twenty-two, she barely looked that, and there was a part of her that felt wanton and indecent when she thought about the things she had done with this girl.

Wanted to do, even now.

"Hey," Annette said, her voice barely above a whisper. "Fancy meeting you here."

Jill smiled, her sensual lips parted slightly. "You said you thought you'd be back around ten. I thought instead of calling I'd just come by."

A flash of guilt went through Annette. It was almost ten-thirty. "Have you been waiting long?"

"Fifteen minutes. It's a nice night, though. And you're worth waiting for." Jill seemed a bit uncomfortable then. "I hope it's okay, me coming by. I wanted to surprise you."

Annette stepped in close, slid her arms around her lover, then let her lips brush against Jill's, gently suggestive. "It's more than okay," she said.

The smile on Jill's face was conspiratorial, and urgent.

Together they went up to the apartment. Annette turned the lights on at first, but the place was a mess. There were three pairs of sneakers in the foyer, jackets and skirts draped over chairs, videos piled on the coffee table. She turned the lights off again and with just the stars and moon and the lights from the street, they stood close in the living room and touched and kissed and caressed one another.

Breathless, Annette pulled away. She went to the kitchen to retrieve several candles and a book of matches. Without a word she went to her bedroom. The bed was unmade, but otherwise it was clean and tidy. She placed the candles about the room and lit them. Dave Grusin was already in the CD player and she turned the music on. Sweet, soft jazz piano came from the small speakers.

When she turned, her breath caught in her throat. Jill stood in the open doorway of her bedroom, completely nude. The gentle glow of candlelight flickered off her milky skin, made shadows around her small, perfect breasts. Jill's eyes smoldered and she gazed at Annette intensely, no trace of a smile on her face now. Her hair was swept back, and she walked into the room without a sound.

Annette uttered a tiny gasp as Jill came to her and kissed her, then began to undress her, her lips brushing tiny kisses on each newly exposed area.

"Is Janine all right?" she asked breathlessly.

The incongruity of the question was jarring. Annette blinked. "What?"

"You said she was upset about something."

Jill kissed her throat as she removed Annette's bra. Then she traced circles on Annette's back, raising goose bumps. Her mouth moved lower, but she gazed up, waiting for an answer.

"She's spooked about . . . her ex getting killed. She's all right."

With a shy grin, Jill slid her tracing fingers around to caress Annette's petite breasts. Then her mouth descended and Jill began to lick her nipples, slowly, teasing.

Then she stopped. Again she gazed up at Annette, but now her face was a bit sad. "You love her, don't you?"

Annette stiffened. Her head was swirling with passion, her chest rising and falling quickly with her arousal, but Jill's question seemed almost to cut her.

"No, I . . . She's straight, Jill. She'll never be anything but."

"So you can't have her, but you do love her?"

"She's my friend."

As if Annette had not spoken, Jill let her tongue trail down Annette's gently sloping belly and worked her fingers to unzip her lover's jeans.

"You don't want her?"

Jill slid the jeans down and she stepped out of them. Annette shivered as her young lover slipped her fingers into the waistband of her panties and began to slide them down as well.

"No," Annette said, feeling her legs grow weak. She reached out and ran her fingers through Jill's long, silken hair. "I . . ."

Jill stood, then, and pressed her body against Annette's, her breasts warm and her hands moving tenderly over Annette's curves.

"Prove it," Jill whispered. "Show me."

Then Annette was lost in her arms, and for a long time, all thoughts of Janine were banished from her mind. Later, though, as they lay tangled together in bed, with Jill just beginning to fall asleep, her mind went back to her best friend. She felt a strange kind of guilt, there in the exhilarating aftermath of making love with Jill. Janine was profoundly troubled, frightened.

Now, though she was not alone, Annette remem-

bered her friend's apprehension all too clearly, and a
frisson of fear went through her with a shudder.

The glow of flickering candles cast haunting shadows on the walls. Annette was suddenly, uncomfortably aware that the fear she felt was not merely for
Janine, but now also, inexplicably, for herself. The
feeling Janine had described, like malevolent eyes
upon her; Annette thought she now fully understood
what that meant.

Not since she had been a little girl, afraid of the
open closet door or the scrape of a tree branch against
the window, had she felt the sort of unfocused dread
that suffused her now.

Jill's breathing changed; she slept peacefully in the
crook of Annette's arm. It ought to have given Annette a kind of serenity. Instead it unnerved her even
more. Though Jill aroused in her a lust and a sense
of playfulness that she had never felt before, in that
quiet moment she was ill at ease, as though a stranger
slept in her bed.

This was her place. Annette had never felt afraid in
her own apartment.

Until now.

A myriad of regrets accompanied Ruth Vale on the
long, lonely drive to Boston. Though she had tried her
best to get away earlier in the day, her commitments
at work could not be so easily circumvented. Meetings
had to be rescheduled, fires had to be put out, and
she had reluctantly agreed to go into the office for a
few hours in the morning to take a look at the mock-
up art for a new magazine campaign for a cosmetic
company that was one of her biggest clients.

It was after three o'clock before she got out of New
York City. Ruth cursed herself all the way home. She
had packed her bags the night before, and so they
were waiting for her when she arrived. Larry was still
at the office, and she called him before getting into
the car, just to remind him that she loved him and to

call her at the Parker House in downtown Boston if anything came up that required her attention. He promised that he would not allow the agency to disturb her, that the time up in Boston was for her and Janine. But Ruth knew that vow would last only until something truly important came up. She did not blame Larry, though. Ruth was sure he meant it when he said it. It was only that, for both of them, business had always been a little too important. The truth saddened her, but she had long ago resigned herself to it.

By the time she hit the Merritt Parkway north into Connecticut, it was after five o'clock. She hated to drive at night, but there had been no way to avoid it unless she wanted to wait until the next morning. Shortly after seven, she stopped to eat dinner at a strip-mall steakhouse. Ruth could not bring herself to eat fast food, not at her age.

The entire ride, she chided herself for not calling Janine first. It was unlike her to simply show up unannounced, and she doubted her daughter would appreciate the surprise. At the same time, she knew that if she called, Janine would tell her not to come. That was the thing she regretted above all else: that her little girl was hurting, and would not turn to her mother for comfort.

The here and now was immutable. There was no going back to fix the mistakes she had made as a mother. But that did not mean she could ignore her child's pain.

It was a Monday night, so there was very little traffic on the road. She made good time despite her dinner stop. Shortly after nine-thirty, she checked into the Parker House. The rooms were beautiful, as was to be expected given the cost and history of the grand old Beacon Hill hotel. There was a phone beside the bed, and after she had used the bathroom and washed her face, she lay on the thick, floral spread and stared at it.

I should call. It's too late to just go over there.

After only a moment's hesitation, she got up and left the room. Ruth had the overwhelming sense that her daughter needed her, and she was not going to be held back by the fear that Janine might tell her to go home.

The drive to Medford took twenty minutes. Though Winthrop Street, where Janine's building was situated, was a main road, it was quiet enough at that time of night. When she pulled into the driveway and saw her daughter's car there in the gleam of starlight, a sigh of relief escaped her lips.

She's all right, Ruth thought.

Part of her was tempted to just turn around, drive back to the Parker House, and phone in the morning. But Janine would be at the school early, teaching, and they would not have time to speak until after the end of the school day.

She parked next to Janine's car, slung her purse over her shoulder, and stepped out. With a flick of her thumb, she armed the car's alarm system and then dropped the keys in her purse.

A light, warm breeze rustled the leaves of the trees at the edges of the property. The barn at the back of the house was dark, its open doors revealing only blackness within, unmitigated by the moon and stars.

Ruth strode across the pavement, headed for the front of the house.

From the darkness of the barn came a baby's cry.

Startled, Ruth frowned and turned to peer into the night at the ominous face of the barn. She was inclined to treat the cry as something born of her imagination, but then it came again. The whimpering of an infant curled out of the barn and reached out to her heart. Horrified, fearful for the child, Ruth started across the small parking area toward the barn.

No doubt someone had abandoned the child, a drug-addled teenager, more than likely. Ruth was filled with righteous anger at the imagined mother, and also bitter when she considered the purpose of a

God who regularly gave children to such women and yet had denied her lovely, intelligent daughter the joy of motherhood.

Her wrath dissipated as she neared the barn. She peered into the dark recesses of that structure, and her footsteps faltered. It was as though the light of the heavens simply stopped at the entrance to the barn, as if it were somehow eaten by the darkness within. She knew what was inside—lawn mower, snowblower, yard tools, storage, and an old car of the landlord's, among other things—but that abyss yawned open before her, and for an instant, the crying child seemed less important. Not her responsibility. Not when it meant going into that darkness.

Then the cry rose higher, the infant's voice ululating with fear and longing, perhaps hunger.

"Is anyone in there?" Ruth asked, her voice a bit raspy from unuse.

Only the baby's cries in response.

She stepped into the barn.

The crying stopped.

CHAPTER 11

❧

By late Tuesday morning, the anxiety caused by the accident—a word that David doubted would ever quite fit in his mind—had receded somewhat. His scratches had begun to heal, the insurance company had agreed that the car was totaled, and he had even allowed himself to begin thinking about what he was going to buy to replace it.

Thoughts of shopping for a new car and the conversation he had had with Father Charles the previous morning gave way, as almost everything did of late, to thoughts of Janine. David was not blind. He had been aware on Sunday that she seemed almost as remote and contemplative as he did, even more so in some ways. But they both had plenty of reason; the car accident and the mystery of Spencer's murder, and his activities before the killing, were enough to ruin anybody's week, month, maybe even year.

David was not going to let it get that far. When he had spoken to her on Monday morning and found Janine still in that melancholy state, he had talked to Annette about it. With the wild, disturbing things going on in his own head, he thought it would be better if Annette tried to cheer her up. Annette had instantly agreed, as he had known she would.

Now he stood in the cafeteria just before the first lunch period bell rang and waited for sight of her. Since Ralph Weiss's death, the lunch monitor schedule had been jumbled around quite a bit. David and Annette did the first lunch period together.

The bell rang. A low rumble of voices and laughter and a stampede of feet began to rattle the corridors out in the main school. Moments later, the first of the students began to spill into the room. Behind the counter, a trio of women who reminded him of Shakespeare's witches—the maiden, the matron, and the crone—prepared to serve up heaping helpings of mystery stew or processed stuffed manicotti.

Annette walked in five minutes after lunch had started. Dozens of students were already seated, digging into their meals as though they were unaware that it was awful, tasteless fare.

He greeted her with a hesitant smile. "Good morning, Miss Muscari," he said in his teacher voice.

"Good morning, Mr. Bairstow," she replied in hers.

It was a familiar bit of sarcasm for both of them, but it seemed weak that day.

"So, how did it go with Janine last night? I talked to her this morning and she seemed . . . I don't know, brighter. Like she was all there. I think you really cheered her up."

Annette nodded. She glanced around at the tables, at the line of students still waiting for meals. There was a gravity to her expression that made him uncomfortable, but also somehow reassured him.

"You should talk to her, David," she said, her voice low. "I'll be blunt, because I care about both of you. She wants us all to think that she's dealing with having lost this baby, but I think she's really just pretending. Now this thing with Spencer . . . I told her I thought she should see somebody, a professional, someone she could talk to without feeling inhibited. All this grief and death, it's haunting her, giving her nightmares."

A trio of freshman girls walked by, and one of them glanced at Annette and whispered something to the others. They giggled behind their hands and Annette pretended not to notice. She had always amazed David that way. There was certainly plenty of gossip about her amongst the students, but she took their childishness in stride.

Then he noticed one of them staring at him, as well. A sly, knowing smile reached the girl's lips and David blinked and looked away. High school kids flirted with their teachers. It happened every day. But he would never get used to it.

Annette glanced around again, taking pains to make sure their conversation was private. With the girls settled at a table, they could speak again.

"Until she resolves all this, you two don't have a chance. She's got to get through the things that are haunting her before she can really dedicate herself mentally to the idea of a real relationship."

Haunting her, David thought. The irony of Annette's choice of words chilled him.

His mind began to wander, and his gaze to rove across the gathered students. Annette tapped him on the arm. When he turned to look at her again, her expression was intense.

"You need to talk to her, David. This crash thing is making you just as remote as her grief is making her. All of a sudden you guys are not communicating. Time to start."

He nodded slowly.

"You get it?" she prodded.

"I get it," he agreed.

"Good," she said, nodding with satisfaction. "So what time tonight?"

He blinked. "I'm sorry?"

The cafeteria was filled with the almost ear-shattering chatter of over a hundred students. At one table, a group of boys threw rolls and bits of stew meat at each other. In a moment he'd have to go over and break it up. David noticed that his tie was skewed, and as he gazed at Annette, trying to make sense of what she was saying, he straightened it.

"Tonight?" she said. "You talked to Janine this morning, yes?"

"Yes."

"But she didn't mention tonight?"

He offered his most baffled look.

Annette sighed. "I made plans with her last night for Jill and me to take you two out to dinner at the Harlequin tonight."

A chill went through David; his face went a bit slack. "Oh."

"Oh? What's that all about?"

Annette was clearly hurt, and David tried his best to smile. A picture of Jill—really an image of long-dead Maggie Russell—appeared in his mind, and he knew that his smile must look forced. He was a rational man. No matter how creepy it was, no matter how sure he sounded when he talked to Father Charles about it, in the back of his mind he knew that Jill's resemblance to Maggie *had* to be nothing more than coincidence. But it was an uncanny resemblance, more like twins than even mother and daughter, and it spooked him.

"Nothing," he said quickly. "No, I'm just . . . we had talked about a quiet night at home tonight. But, y'know, with what you were just saying it would probably be really good for us to get out."

"How can you not like her, David?" Annette said. "She's sweet, and cute, and smart, and all she wants is for my friends to like her. It's all I want, too."

Her voice was as close to pleading as he had ever heard it. He felt guilty for having hurt her.

"Hey, Elf, it isn't like that," he began. A temptation rose in him to just tell her, to explain why being near Jill unnerved him so. But then he realized that no matter how he phrased it, "Your girlfriend gives me the creeps" was the last thing Annette needed to hear.

"I'm a little freaked out by how young she is," he lied. "She seems really sweet. It'll take some getting used to, but once we get to know her, I'm sure we'll love her, okay? What time tonight?"

With a flicker of a smile, the familiar sparkle returned to Annette's eyes. She tucked an errant lock of hair, the same one that always seemed to get loose, behind her ear.

"You swear?"

"I swear."

"Good, 'cause, y'know, if you guys didn't like her, I could never be happy with her," Annette said.

David's stomach dropped. He hated to lie, hated to pretend in any way. Annette was not always so open, so vulnerable, but he knew that she spoke the truth. If he and Janine said, "Stay away from this girl," Annette would. They were her best friends, and she trusted their opinions and instincts.

"It'll be great. What time?" he asked.

Though, inside, even the thought of seeing her again filled him with trepidation and a creeping sort of dread that would linger for the rest of the day.

The Harlequin was a European restaurant that offered a nicely varied menu of dishes culled from across Europe, with a dash of individuality from the chef who had created the menu in the first place. Apparently the owner had chosen the name and décor as testament to her love of clowns and jesters, so that the walls were festooned with photographs, paintings, carnival masks, and circus posters from various nations.

Janine was terrified of clowns, but by some perverse logic, she loved the place. It was almost impossible not to be cheered by their surroundings. She wondered if that had been Annette's intention in suggesting it.

If so, she doubted it would work.

From the moment David had picked her up in the rental Ford the insurance company had provided to him, the atmosphere between them had been heavy and ominous, as though some invisible force were driving them apart. He smiled at her, said all the right things, kissed her on the sidewalk before they went into the restaurant, but there was a sort of forced quality about it that tainted everything.

Yet David was not the only guilty party. Janine also felt a certain reserve. She was troubled, and it seemed that Annette had been correct. In attempting to keep her anxieties to herself, she might have been cluttering up her relationship with David rather than keeping it clear of debris, as had been her intention.

I'll talk to him, she vowed as they walked into the Harlequin. *And I'll find a shrink, too, if that's what it takes.*

Life had battered her, of late, but somehow she managed to keep getting back up again after being knocked down. Even that, though, had been mere survival. Now it was time to fight back, to seize control.

Which was all well and good for her, but even if she succeeded, it would solve only half the problem. That faraway look that had been in David's eyes the past few days would have to be dealt with as well.

The hostess informed them that the rest of their party had already been seated. The warm atmosphere of the restaurant, its bright colors and calliope music, the wonderful old posters, all combined to lift Janine's spirits just a little.

"There they are!" she said happily.

The hostess, menus in hand, led them toward the table. Jill wore a light cotton dress with a lavender floral pattern. With her hair curled and her makeup just so, she looked far more mature than Janine remembered her from the party. Jill had a hip, edgy style that she seemed, at least for tonight, to have abandoned completely. Annette, on the other hand, wore a black suit whose jacket hung halfway to her knees, a modern cut that might have seemed severe on another woman, but which was cute and sexy on her. They looked good together, not only in the sense that they seemed to fit in some way, but in that they appeared happy and content.

Annette saw them first, and waved.

Janine reached out to take David's hand, to lead him to the table, but he hesitated a moment, hung back.

With a frown she turned to look at him. His face was so pale she worried that he might be sick.

"What's wrong? Don't you feel well?"

"I'll be all right," he promised. "Just a little oogy all of a sudden. I'm going to hit the men's room, okay? I'll be right back."

For a moment, she watched him as he weaved through tables toward the back of the restaurant. David glanced at Annette and Jill, then quickly looked away.

"Is he all right?" Annette asked when Janine sat down at the table.

"He's not feeling well suddenly," she replied with a small shrug.

Jill smiled warmly. "I hope he feels well enough to eat. Annette tells me the food here is great."

Their waitress appeared then, as if on cue, to see if Janine wanted a drink. Janine glanced at the table and saw that neither of the other women was drinking alcohol. She hesitated, then laughed softly.

"Y'know what, I could really use a drink. Rum and Coke, please."

The other two laughed easily with her, but Janine noticed that Jill reached for Annette's hand on the table and held it almost protectively. Though she had never been overly concerned about public reaction to displays of affection between herself and a girlfriend, Annette's gaze flicked self-consciously toward Jill, then back to Janine.

"So," Annette ventured, "are you feeling better today?"

"Much. In fact, I think I'm going to take your advice."

Satisfied, Annette relaxed back into her chair a bit. She still held Jill's hand, but now their grasp was hidden from direct view by the table.

"See? I don't know why my friends can't make things simpler, and just follow my wise counsel."

"You mean obey your commands, Queenie?" Janine teased.

Jill slid a bit closer to her lover. "I think I like the sound of that."

Annette blushed a bit. Her ears turned red. Janine was amazed, for she did not remember ever having seen her friend blush before.

"So you slept all right, then?" Annette asked, in an obvious gambit to change the subject.

"No dreams, good or bad, that I can remember," Janine confirmed. It was true. She had slept soundly the previous night and woke feeling more refreshed than she had in a very long time, perhaps since before she had become pregnant in the first place.

David arrived at the table a moment later. Though he greeted Annette warmly enough, and was polite to Jill, he was still a bit pale. After they had ordered their meals, he was uncharacteristically quiet and spoke only when spoken to. Janine did her best to keep the conversation going, but Annette and Jill clearly noticed his reticence, and she imagined they were as uncomfortable as she was.

When the food arrived, David barely picked at his shrimp Creole. He ate a little bit, then prodded at what remained as if testing to see if it were still alive.

In the midst of a story Annette was telling about a gay freshman girl she was counseling, David cleared his throat and interrupted.

"So, Jill, I don't remember if Annette told me where you went to school," he said, his voice a bit jittery.

His face had grown even paler.

A sweet smile fluttered across Jill's face. She seemed pleased that he had become a bit more animated, that he had addressed her at all.

"I went to Suffolk," she said. "I'm thinking about going on to law school, but I haven't quite decided yet."

"What are you doing for work in the meantime?" David asked.

Janine flinched. It was less a question than it was a demand for information. She glanced at Annette and saw a flicker of anger in her friend's eyes. David was interrogating her girlfriend. Janine did not blame Annette for being mad. Then again, Annette had no idea that her girlfriend bore a disturbing resemblance to another girl, long dead.

Though she had been aware that the resemblance spooked David, Janine had thought he was over it. It was odd, sure, but certainly did not warrant the way he had been behaving tonight. If his preoccupation this evening was that and nothing more, Janine was going to be pretty pissed at him later.

Jill, for her part, did not seem bothered by David's manner at all.

"I'm working as a receptionist for a software company in Harvard Square," she said. "Not something I'll put on the résumé, but it's an income while I'm trying to figure out what's next."

Janine forced a smile. "Take your time, Jill. Figure out what you really want to do. You've got your whole life ahead of you."

The legs of his chair squeaked on the floor as David slid back from the table and stood up. He looked worse than ever.

"Excuse me. I . . . I'm really not feeling well."

He rushed off toward the rest rooms again. Janine glanced at Annette, afraid that she might still be angry. Instead of anger, however, she saw only confusion and concern.

A few minutes later David returned. He did not even glance at Jill.

"You know what, I'm really feeling nauseous," he said. "I'm sorry, but I think I should really get home and lie down. I've been poor company, I know. Another night I'll make it up to all of you, I promise."

Janine was not convinced it was only his stomach bothering him, but she was not about to question him there in the restaurant. "All right. Let's just settle the bill and we'll go."

"No way," Annette said. "I said this was our treat and it is. Next time, you two can pay. And hopefully David won't be so overwhelmed by the presence of three gorgeous women."

"Thanks," Janine said. "Both of you."

"You know what? Why don't you stay, Janine? You shouldn't have your night ruined because I've got some kind of stomach bug. I'm sure Annette wouldn't mind dropping you at home after."

He looked expectantly at Annette, who nodded her agreement.

"No problem."

Janine was about to argue, but found to her surprise that she did not want to. She loved David, and cared about him, but it was clear he intended to keep to himself about whatever was freaking him out. In truth, she thought he was acting like a jerk.

Whatever his problem was, there was nothing she could do for him until he decided to talk to her. She had planned to speak to him later that night about her own concerns, but it would keep until another day. Then she would find out what was really on his mind. More and more, since speaking to Annette the night before, Janine realized that her relationship with David might actually depend upon their opening up to each other. This was only more proof of that.

"I hope you feel better," she said.

His expression of relief that he could depart alone stung her. She hoped he would regret it.

That dress.

From the moment he walked out of the Harlequin, David had tried desperately to think of something other than the dress Jill had been wearing at dinner.

Jill? he thought now as he got into his car. *Stop kidding yourself, Dave.*

During the meal, he had the bright idea that in the morning he might check out her story about attending Suffolk University in Boston. An old college friend worked in admissions there. David also had friends at the Registry of Motor Vehicles and the state police. It would be a relatively simple thing to find out more about her, to find out if she was what she claimed to be.

Then, as he went through his mini-interrogation, she had glanced up at him with an almost petulant expression on her face. Though he had known the moment he walked through the door and saw her in that dress—the dress so similar to the one she had been wearing the first time they made love, his junior year at St. Matt's—it was that look that shook him of his illusions. Up to that point, he had tried to deny the truth to himself. The dress had shocked him, chilled him, but it could have been coincidence, could even have been him remembering wrong.

But that look, that knowing smile.

Her name was not Jill.

David slipped the key into the ignition and the rental car gave a tame little growl as the engine purred to life. There was very little traffic as he pulled away from the curb, but he drove slowly, just in case. Every couple of blocks he glanced in the rearview mirror and looked over his shoulders to check his blind spots.

His breathing seemed too loud to him. A chill came over him that raised goose bumps on his flesh, but he could not shake it. His grip was tight on the steering wheel and he sat forward a bit, as though he were navigating through a blizzard.

But the night was clear.

The only storm was the one in his heart and soul.

Though he had been drunk that night, all those years ago, certain things lingered with harsh clarity in his mind. The flash of streetlights across the windshield. Maggie telling him he was too drunk to drive, that he should give her the keys. The way her sweater stretched across the top of her breasts. How much he wanted to get her away from that party, somewhere he might get that sweater off. The copper taste in his mouth that he always associated with both beer and blood.

Past and present seemed to converge upon him now, the road ahead now two roads, the car two cars, and he himself two Davids: a young, drunken boy and a man, haunted and afraid.

"Jesus," he whispered, low and harsh. While it was indeed a curse, it was also, in some way, a prayer.

The headlights of cars going the opposite direction passed like a lighthouse beam across his windshield, and the illusion was complete. It was not enough that he should be confronted with this specter, whatever she was, but the night around him now seemed almost transformed into the ghost of that fateful moment back in high school. Though he knew that this phantom, at least, was the product only of his mind, it chilled him nevertheless.

David never liked to think about that night. It was something he had lived most of his life trying to forget.

Laughing, bleary-eyed, drunk, and horny, he had been driving too fast. Maggie had asked him to slow down, but not angrily. They were in love. She was nervous, but along for the ride. Lynyrd Skynyrd had come on the radio, his favorite band back then. The song was "Sweet Home Alabama." Right after the first guitar riff in the song, Skynyrd's front man said, "Turn it up."

"Fuckin'-A right," David had muttered.

He had leaned over to fiddle with the volume control, trying to comply.

There was a curve in the road.

When Maggie screamed, he looked up to see a telephone pole looming up in front of him. David had jerked the wheel, afraid but numb from alcohol. The front bumper missed the pole. For a split second he had thought they would be all right. But he had cut the wheel too far, and the car slewed sideways, slammed into the pole.

His forearm had slipped into the opening of the steering wheel. Upon impact, he was thrown to one side and his arm had broken with a grinding snap. He tore something in his shoulder. The combined pain was enough to burn off some of his inebriation. The car was not moving. The engine had died, and it ticked several times.

"Sweet Home Alabama" still played on the radio.

His teeth gritted against the pain in his broken arm, it had finally occurred to him to glance at Maggie, to see if she was all right.

At first he had thought she was unconscious. The telephone pole had buckled her door and splintered her window. Her head lay against the glass. Then, in the light from the streetlamp above, he had noticed the blood that had seeped into the million tiny cracks in the webbed glass. It crept and seeped along ridges of glass shards that barely hung intact.

The music had kept playing on the radio.

"Jesus," David whispered again.

With a jerk, he clicked on his turn signal and pulled over to the side of the road. A car that had been following too close behind him beeped as it went around him. He reached out and punched the button to turn the radio off with a kind of horror. A sickening feeling roiled in his stomach as he rolled down the window and laid his head on the steering wheel.

The sweet spring air blew in, and the weird sense of displacement that had enveloped him began to dissipate. His breathing returned to normal.

He understood nothing.

There was freedom in that.

Jill did not exist. Somehow it was Maggie, a bit older, but nowhere near the fifteen years that had passed. Questions churned in his head like the nausea in his gut. *What is she? Why is she here now? What does she want with Annette?*

They were questions he could not answer. In the morning, first thing, he would call Father Charles and ask if his research had turned anything up. If that led nowhere, he realized that he would have to confront this creature, this ghost, this thing that now haunted him.

David doubted he would be able to sleep that night.

CHAPTER 12

❦

He was wrong about sleeping.

Upon arriving at home, David had slumped fully clothed onto the couch, channel-surfed for twenty minutes, and then fallen fast asleep in front of a documentary about old Hollywood. A short time later, he woke just long enough to reach for the remote and shut off the TV, but made no effort to relocate.

When his eyes flickered open again, the clock on the DVD player read 12:17. Though he was cramped on the sofa, and had the urge to pee, neither issue was urgent enough to move him just yet. His gaze flicked from side to side. His thoughts were muddled by sleep, a kind of curtain of warm, stupefying static that lay over his mind, and yet it occurred to him, just for a moment, to wonder what had woken him.

Then, as he had ignored the demands of his body, he shrugged the thought away and resettled himself on the sofa. His eyes closed once more, and he drifted into sleep.

A stair creaked.

David's eyes opened again. The clock read 12:18.

Quiet, heart thumping in his chest, he sat up and listened to the darkness. Every nerve ending seemed to be attuned to changes in the air around him, an alteration of the atmosphere in this house, where he had lived off and on for his entire life. It was a noisy old house, true enough. Pipes rattled and walls creaked in a heavy wind. Changes in season made the wood pop loudly as it expanded or contracted with the temperature.

But David knew all of the noises in his house.

The stairs did not creak unless someone trod upon them.

He breathed through his mouth and his tongue and lips became dry. He dared not even blink as he glanced around the darkened room again, still listening. His chest ached, so hard was his heart pounding.

Nothing.

Adrenaline began to subside and he relaxed a bit, the pressure in his bladder suddenly more insistent.

Then he heard it again.

For just a second, David pressed his eyes shut with his fingers, attempting to calm his mind and heart. With a long breath, as quietly as he was able, he stood and looked around the room for a weapon of some kind.

When he was eleven, a burglar had come to the window and startled his mother into a scream. He had been sleeping at the time and her cry of alarm had woken both him and his sister, Amy. But this was something else. This was no face at the window.

Another creak, this one farther away, and a rustle of clothing.

Two of them,, he thought. *Fuck.*

One man, without a gun, he thought he might do all right. But two? With greater desperation he searched for something, anything, to fight with, and his eyes settled on a small bookshelf near the windows. On top of the antique piece of furniture sat a half dozen dusty leather-bound volumes bookended by a pair of heavy granite gargoyles.

Careful not to make a sound, David hurried across the room and hefted one of the gargoyles in his right hand. It was no Louisville Slugger, but it was better than nothing.

"Don't fight," a voice whispered.

He stiffened.

It had not come from the hall, but from there in the room with him, almost right beside him. David glanced over his right shoulder and a tiny gasp escaped his lips as he saw the ghost of Ralph Weiss up close for the first time. The old man's eyes were wide with alarm, his face etched with sadness. Through his ephemeral form, David could see the window and the street outside. The spirit shimmered and drifted, and for some odd reason he was reminded of a jellyfish, buffeted by the water around it.

"Don't fight, Mr. Bairstow," the ghost repeated, and now its voice sounded as though it were inside David's head. *"Just run. You are not prepared to face Charon's creations."*

David swallowed hard, took one last look at the ghost, then headed for the hallway. This was no ordinary burglar, then.

He had known that from the moment he had opened his eyes.

Don't fight, run.

Just inside the TV room, he leaned against the door frame and peeked out. A low, almost inaudible creak came from the corridor. The intruders had stopped just outside his bedroom.

If I hadn't fallen asleep on the couch . . . he thought. Then he pushed it away. No time for "if."

A single light fixture burned out in the hall. David pulled back a second, took a breath, and then peeked again. They stood in the corridor just across from the TV room, stood just outside his bedroom door. In the half dark, and from behind, he could make out only silhouettes. A teenager with dark hair, short but with clenched fists. He bounced on his toes like a boxer about to enter the ring.

For a second, the kid glanced at his companion and that half-moon glimpse of his face was enough to confirm David's instinct.

Steve Themeli.

For real. He was not sleeping now; there was no rainstorm, no car accident, nothing to confuse him.

The most frightening thing was that he was not surprised. If he could have dinner sitting across from the girlfriend whose death he had caused in high school, why not a late-night visit from a teenage drug dealer who, as a teacher, he had reached out to and failed to save?

The gargoyle felt heavy in his hand. How could he fight this boy, this thing? Whatever it was, it wore the face of this kid he had wanted so badly to rescue. Then he remembered the accident, his fear as the car had slid and then rolled, the river so close he held his breath.

His fingers tightened on the stone bookend.

But what of the other? The much older man with white hair and a thick beard. He was taller than Themeli, more broad-shouldered, a powerful figure despite the age revealed by the color of his hair.

Move, he whispered to himself. In another second they would enter his bedroom and see that he was not there. Then they would begin to search the house. He would have the element of surprise for a few more seconds; that was all.

Run, the ghost had said. *Don't fight.* But in order to run away, he first had to get past them. Whatever they were, they were solid enough to hurt him, kill him.

David patted his pocket gently to make sure his keys were still there. Had he gone to bed, he would be lying defenseless and naked in the other room just then. He did not even want to think about it.

Jaw tight, heart racing, he shot out of the door and into the corridor. The older man was nearest to him. David shot out his left hand, grabbed a fistful of white hair, and slammed the intruder's face against the wall, hard.

Themeli began to turn.

Even in the dim light, there was a spark of malevolence in his eyes that drove an icy spike of fear into David's brain. He almost faltered, but then instinct took over. They would kill him; he was sure of that.

"Get the fuck out of my house!" he screamed, and his voice sounded cracked and hysterical to his own ears.

He brought the gargoyle down hard. Themeli attempted to parry the blow, but he was too late, too slow. The stone bookend crashed across the bridge of his nose and bone gave way. With a scream of pain, the dead kid fell back into the bedroom.

David clutched the gargoyle in his hand as though it were a crucifix and ran for the stairs.

A deep, bass voice rumbled behind him. "This is not *your* house, boy."

Four steps down, David stopped, nearly toppling over as he whipped his head around. The voice was familiar. It had always filled him with fear and dread, made him feel small and useless.

The silhouette came back to him, the beard and white hair, that strong back and powerful build.

"Grandpa Edgar," he whispered, the words like ghosts themselves as they slipped from his lips.

David felt weak, small again. Confusion rippled through him and tears sprang to his eyes. His grandfather strode to the top of the stairs with fury blazing in his eyes, his thick, meaty hands closed in massive fists.

"You little shit," Grandpa Edgar said in a sneer. "Drop that goddamn thing right now and come on up here. You been nothing but a thorn in my fucking side since the day you were born. You soured it all. Now you've put your stink on my house, boy. *My* house."

The undead thing pointed angrily at the landing. "Get your ass up here and take what's coming to you."

It was not that absurd request that made David act, nor was it the fear of his grandfather, or whatever this revenant was that even now tried to intimidate him. It was the tone of his voice.

The same tone he had always taken with David.

Fury welled up within him from deep inside. His fingers tightened on the gargoyle.

"Asshole!" he roared.

Hand on the rail to steady him, he used all his strength to hurl the gargoyle at his grandfather's chest. It struck the dead man with enough force to make him stagger backward and nearly fall. The surprised look in his eyes gave David an almost perverse pleasure.

But he saw it for only a second. Then he was leaping down the stairs two and three at a time, and damn the risk of snapping an ankle. He leaped the last five steps to the foyer, lost control of his momentum, and his arms pinwheeled until he slammed hard against the heavy wooden door.

His grandfather shouted obscenities after him and David could hear two sets of feet pounding the stairs. They were both coming for him now. Themeli's face was crushed, but somehow he was up and in pursuit. David did not want to turn and see them, did not want to see what sort of damage his blow had done to the kid's face.

He worked the two locks, hauled the door open, and ran out, slamming it behind him. The moon and stars were bright above, and yet there was nothing beautiful about it. Tree limbs above and the house itself, outlined in that sickly yellow glow, threw creeping, insidious shadows.

Maggie. Themeli. Grandpa Edgar. David knew he was not safe, even if he escaped them now. There could be many more where they had come from. And that was the question, wasn't it? Where had they come from?

Charon's creations, the ghost had said. *What the fuck was* that *all about?*

Keys jangling, he pulled open the door to the rental car and dropped into the driver's seat. Then he reached to pull the door closed, and finally glanced back up at the house.

The ghost of Ralph Weiss stood on the front porch. The specter seemed almost to be grinning at him. Unable to stop himself, David smiled in response.

The front door opened. Wan light spilled out from within. David started up the engine and slammed his door shut, put the car into reverse. One last time he glanced up at the front porch.

The thing that was silhouetted in the open door was not his grandfather.

It was inhumanly tall, its face pale and lined like marble. Its eyes burned, even from that distance, and its long, thick beard was gathered by a metal ring perhaps six inches along its length. In its upraised left hand, the apparition held a heavy iron lantern whose light shone as green as its eyes.

David's mouth hung wide. The need to urinate had left him before, driven away by his terror. But that was nothing compared to this. This creature, this manifestation, whatever it was, seemed like a wound on the face of the world. Its presence seemed to suck at the available light with the power of the void, a black hole replacing the light it stole with the greenish taint from its lantern.

Upon the porch, the ghost of Ralph Weiss turned toward this phantasm, cowered, and screamed silently.

It raised its lantern and the ghost shuddered. The diaphanous mist that made up Ralph Weiss's spectral form took on the same verdant hue as that otherworldly light. Then, abruptly, the ghost was torn from the porch, sucked into the lantern, its mouth open in a silent scream.

David cried out in terror and grief, even as he reversed out of the driveway with a squeal of rubber on pavement.

As he raced off down Briarwood, he tried to blot the picture of the thing with the lantern from his mind, tried not to think about what price Ralph Weiss's soul might even now be paying for trying to help him.

As houses flashed by on either side of the car and other vehicles passed him on the road, the surreality of the entire episode began to unravel him emotionally. This was not merely fear, but a kind of terror he had never imagined. Everything he knew about the world was wrong. Whatever this thing was—demon, monster, walking nightmare—it was after him. Yet David had no idea why.

He had to run.

But he had nowhere to go.

Janine is submerged beneath the rushing waters of the river. Though it is dark above, she can see. The river carries her along and she drifts with it, arms outstretched as though she is flying. A smile spreads across her features. The current caresses her entire body, swaying her from side to side, teasing and touching her, arousing her.

Though she is reluctant to surface, she knows that at some point she will need air. Precious air. Without it she will die. Somehow there is something amusing about that. Still, with languorous strokes, she pulls and kicks her way upward. A moment later she thrusts her head up from the water. Suddenly she can stand, and she rises, nude and glistening in the green starlight. With a laugh she tosses back her hair and it sprays water in a gentle arc onto the nearby shore.

The wind touches her and she shivers with a delicious chill. Her nipples are taut, erect, and she is extremely aware of them. Gently she strokes them in soft circles, glances down to see that her breasts are full and heavy with milk.

A warm light falls over her from behind, casting an erotic shadow image onto the riverbank, her own picture, a shadow of her caressing herself. Though a small twinge of fear runs through her, there is a yearning in her that overwhelms any hesitation. She hears the lap of the river against the side of the boat, then the swish of water as he slips out of the boat.

A moment later he is behind her. She can feel the rough cloth of his robe as he presses himself against her naked flesh. Tenderly, he caresses her shoulders, then her arms. His arms encircle her and with long, almost skeletal fingers, he strokes her breasts, makes soft circles on her sensitive nipples. Janine arches her back and stretches out her arms as she leans back into him, giving herself over to him just as she did in the river, for this is much the same.

Precisely the same.

He is the river.

When she leans her head back, he half turns her so that he can gaze down into her eyes. His long beard is soft as it trails across her naked chest, the steel ring tied into it cold against her skin. In his eyes there is a longing unlike anything she has ever known, save that in its way it is much like grief.

He is gentle, otherworldly, not ugly but delicate. And in the way of dreams, she discovers that she knows his name.

Charon.

"You were meant to be with me," he whispers, his voice the cascade of the river over stone. "But you still breathe, and so I will stay here with you. Nothing will stand between us."

Charon's hands stroke her, but they are cold now. She shudders.

The phone rang. Her eyes snapped open and she inhaled harshly, as though for a time she had forgotten to breathe. The ringing echoed in the room. Heart fluttering anxiously, Janine began to sit up, mind still in the midst of the transition from sleep to wakefulness. The spread was bunched down at the footboard and the sheet was wrapped around her legs. She had twisted around so much while sleeping that her blue cotton nightshirt was rucked up nearly to her breasts. Otherwise she was naked, and it made her feel vulnerable. The warm tingle between her legs, arousal left over from her dream, only added to that feeling.

As the phone rang a third time, she pawed at her nightshirt to pull it down. The ring was cut off as the answering machine down in the kitchen picked up the call.

Janine blinked as she reached for the phone, peering at her alarm clock. It was after twelve-thirty. Panic and anger warred in her briefly. That late, the call could only be something bad, or someone unpleasant.

"Hello," she rasped into the phone.

"Janine. Gosh, I'm sorry to wake you. I'd never call so late, but I'm just . . . I'm pretty worried."

Still a bit disoriented from sleep, she did not recognize the voice at first.

"When did you speak to your mother last?"

She frowned. "Larry?" she asked. Then his tone, and the question, got through to her, and alarm bells began to go off. "Larry, what's wrong? What's going on?"

"Have you seen her today?" Larry pressed on, oblivious to her question.

"I haven't talked to her since last week. Maybe Thursday?" Janine said. "What's *wrong*?"

But there was a sudden silence on the other end of the line.

"Larry?"

He sighed heavily. "Oh, God," Larry whispered. "Janine, listen to me. Your mother was worried about you, after what happened with Spencer. She was going to surprise you. Last night she drove up to Boston. She checked into the Parker House late, but according to the concierge, she left shortly after that, I assume to go by to see you. As far as I can tell, no one has seen her since. The hotel manager says the bed was not slept in. You're sure you haven't heard from her?"

There was a desperation in his voice that made Janine want to lie, but the urge was ridiculous. Her mother. Something had happened to her mother.

"Not since last week," she repeated, a kind of numbness creeping over her. "Are you . . . I mean, you're sure there's no mistake at the hotel?"

"I'm sure. I've already called the police but they won't do anything for another twenty-four hours. I could . . . God, Janine," he said, his voice tortured, "I could tell they were patronizing me, like they thought maybe Ruth was off having some torrid affair."

Are you sure she isn't?

It was the first thing that went through Janine's mind, but she would never have said it. She was not fond of her stepfather, but she certainly did not want to hurt him. Even if she believed her mother capable of such a thing, she would not bring it up.

"I'm sorry I woke you," he said. "I . . . I should have waited until morning. I'm just . . . this is too much. Ruth would never just disappear without calling me first. I'm not stupid enough to think the idea of an affair is impossible, but I know this much: if Ruth were to do something like that, no way would she let it be discovered this way. Something's happened to her, Janine. I'm sure of it."

"Mom," Janine said softly. "Oh, God."

No, she thought. *Not now. Not one more horrible thing.*

"I'm driving up there tomorrow, Janine. I'll go to the hotel first, talk to the police, and then I'll call you with an update. If anything happens, of course, I'll call right away."

"Thank you," she said, a bit hoarse. "I'll . . . I'll talk to you tomorrow."

Janine felt as though she were still asleep. Her hands seemed a bit swollen and her body felt awkward, as if she had detached from it somehow. Her mind had become a tiny thing, lost in the immense, dull, immobile cage of flesh that was her pale, quivering form. Her throat was dry, yet so were her eyes. She felt as though she were observing herself at a distance, and it surprised her that there were no tears in her eyes.

A twinge of pain cramped her stomach and she brought her hands to her belly and bent over slightly on the bed. She stayed like that a moment, then sat up again. Now she felt cold. Alone and helpless, just as she had so often in her dreams. Terrible things were happening in the world around her and yet she could do nothing to stop them, to influence the outcome, nothing even to slow the dark current that seemed to be carrying her along.

"Oh, Mom," she whispered, squeezing her eyes shut tight, covering them with her hands.

When she dropped her hands and opened her eyes, she froze, her mouth open in shock, her breath coming in hitching gasps. The room was bathed in a dim green light.

Charon the Ferryman stood at the foot of the bed.

Dream and reality shifted and seemed to merge. Charon was a figure of hallucinations and nightmares, a mirage, Janine thought. Or she had never woken up at all. Though she had always thought she knew the difference between the tangible world and the subjectivity of dreams, all the skeins that tied her to what she knew were coming unraveled.

The Ferryman was so tall he nearly reached the ceiling. In his left hand he held the lantern that she had seen—when had she seen it?—clanking against the prow of his boat. A green flame flickered within, casting warped shadows through ancient, hand-blown glass. He stared at her with those eyes—enormous black pupils, rimmed with fire—each one a solar eclipse.

The air shimmered with the dream light, the death light from that lantern.

It isn't real, Janine thought. And yet it was hyper-real. She felt the cold that seemed to emanate from him and she blinked away the light from the lantern. Her eyes could pick out every detail of the room around her, every chip in the paint, every uneven slant of a picture frame; just as she could also see each fold of his robe, and the bit of tarnish on the iron ring he wore in his beard.

Charon gazed at her. The suggestion of a smile appeared at the edges of his mouth and he tilted his head to one side.

"Janine," he said. *"Do not fear simply because you*

do not understand. You have welcomed me in your dreams. I know the essence of your being. I have dared much for you."

Though she heard the words, she could not make sense of them. Bathed in that ethereal light, she found herself unable to move. Perhaps that was Charon's doing, or perhaps it was simply her fear, her terror that what she was seeing and hearing might be real.

Charon opened his robes and slipped the lantern inside. It disappeared there, though the Ferryman himself was suffused with its green glow. He crossed the room toward her with a swish of robes that sounded like the surf, a confident stride that bespoke his power, the arrogance of a king.

Janine tried to inch backward on her mattress. She tried to close her eyes to blot him out. She tried to open her mouth to scream. Tried, but failed. Instead, she sat paralyzed as the creature leaned toward her, long robes brushing her face. Skeletally thin fingers, long and sharp, reached out to caress her face.

They were cold and damp.

Her eyes were wide. They burned, as though tears would fall, but even that she seemed incapable of. Her heart thundered wildly in her chest. She could hear its manic rhythm inside her head.

The Ferryman's skin was like stone polished clean by the river, lined with blue veins and shadowed by his long mane and beard. He brushed her own dark locks away from her face, ran his fingers through her hair.

His breath was the breeze off the river. Those burning black eyes seemed to widen as though they might drink her in.

"So strong. So defiant. Though you had no reason to stay, though your body was ready to give in, you fought. You threw the coins back at me. Others have seen me and not crossed the river, but none have ever done that before, thrown away the fare for their passage. You would not come to me, but having seen that

fire in you, that life, I knew that I could not forget. I had to taste it. So I have come.

"You fear. But you have left this world once already. You know there is more than this. Life exists beyond what you know. Remember what you have already seen, and you will learn. Oh, the things I can offer you, Janine. No more fear.

"You do not belong among these, the living. They can never feel for you as I do. What I offer . . . is eternal. You will see that their love is not worthy of you. An ephemeral, gossamer thing. Then you will realize that I speak true.

"One way or another, you belong to me."

He leaned over her further, hair brushing her face, and cold lips touched her forehead. Charon kissed her above each eye. His talons slid down her face, her throat, her nightshirt, and skeletal fingers traced lines along the roundness of her breasts.

It was like the dream.

But not the dream. She did not yearn for him. The twisting in her stomach was fear, not desire.

Above her, so close, those blazing eclipse-eyes stared down into hers. A tear slipped from her right eye and ran, hot and salty, down the side of her face.

"No," she whispered, softly.

She could speak. She could cry. She could move.

Janine screamed as she thrust her hands out and shoved him away. Under her touch, his robes felt like damp, slick moss, and she shuddered with revulsion even as she tumbled out of bed and staggered backward, away from him.

"My God, what are you?" she rasped, her chest heaving with panic.

But she knew what he was. Impossible, but she knew.

Charon raised himself to his full height. For the first time, his huge black pupils diminished and the fiery corona around each one expanded. His body still glowed with the infernal light from his lantern, and the Ferryman extended one long finger to point at her in accusation.

"You belong more to me than to this place. You will be with me. Your precious few shall only suffer should they stand between us."

The voice was like the cry of a drowning man.

Janine stood with her back to the bedroom wall, trapped.

The crackle of supernatural energy in the room, the surreal tension that connected them, was interrupted by a sudden buzzing in the room. Janine blinked several times before she could turn her gaze away from Charon. Her mind backtracked to that sound, tried to put it in a real-life context.

The door.

It was going on one o'clock in the morning, but someone was down at the first-floor landing, buzzing for her to let them up.

The buzz came again.

Charon snarled softly, then reached into his robes to retrieve the lantern. Its iron and glass cage barely contained the green flame within, which roared up as he retrieved it, as though it had been waiting to be free again.

The light flashed so brightly that Janine had to cover her eyes. When the light subsided and she looked around the room, the Ferryman was gone. Janine gasped for breath, certain that at any second he would appear again, his image still outlined against the backs of her eyelids.

It can't be, she thought. *I'm losing it.* But she knew that was not the truth, that the truth was something she was incapable of confronting alone.

The buzzer sounded a third time.

Her fear remained upon her like a morning frost, and Janine tried to shake it off as she ran for the door. Anything to be out of that room, away from the moist echo of him that seemed to linger on the air. Her gaze flicked from side to side, searching for some sign that Charon was still in the apartment. In a frenzy, she brushed her hand through her hair . . . and found it wet.

Charon had touched her there, and now her hair was damp as though from a shower. Disgusted, and frightened by this lingering evidence of his presence, she glanced down in the dim hall light and saw that the front of her shirt was also wet, where he had fondled her.

"Jesus," she whispered.

At the door, she pressed the speaker button.

"Who . . . who is it?" she asked, her voice cracking.

"Hey. Sorry to wake you. Can I come up?"

David!

A hand flew to her mouth and she felt something crumble inside her.

"Oh, thank God," she whispered, then flinched, startled by her own voice in the darkened apartment.

Janine had never been so happy to hear the voice of another human being in her life. Though the warnings and vague threats of the Ferryman echoed in the back of her head, she needed nothing so much at that moment as her lover's arms around her. Her true lover, not some nightmare suitor.

She did not even bother to reply. Instead she buzzed him in, then feverishly worked the locks. Without thought as to how little she was wearing, Janine threw the door open and rushed down the stairs.

David stopped short halfway up and stared at her. His hair and clothes were disheveled and his eyes were bloodshot. There was a frightened, lost expression on his features that she knew must be at least the match of her own.

"David," she said again, voice barely above a whisper.

"Janine, I . . . What happened?" he asked.

With abandon, she threw herself into his arms, nearly knocking him back down the stairs. He used the railing to steady himself, and then he held her as she wept in great, heaving sobs, her face buried in the wonderful warmth of his shirt. It had the smell of him, and that was an enormous comfort to her.

That was *real*. David, and what she felt for him. That was real.

"Janine?" His voice was gentle, but there was a quaver to it as well.

She pulled back and gazed into his red-rimmed eyes. Though she wanted to ask what had happened, why he was there in the dead of night, why he seemed so distraught, she could not even begin. Her own fears were too fresh, nearly spilling over with the urgency she felt.

Dreams. She had fooled herself into thinking they were just dreams. And that day by the river, she had *seen* him. It was not in her mind. She knew that now.

"I had . . . an intruder," she ventured.

Immediately he tensed, muscles flexing. David was not an inordinately large man, but he was powerful and quick. Absurdly, it made her feel immediately safer, though what he could do against the nightmare that had visited her she had no idea.

"Is he still—"

"He's gone," she said, unsure how to begin. "I . . . I think he's gone."

Together they went back up the stairs. David led the way, alert for any sign of an intruder. One by one, they turned on all the lights. Soon they were both satisfied that the apartment was empty save for the two of them.

At last, David seemed to deflate. They sat down together on the couch in the living room. He ran a hand through his hair and she saw a bit of gray there she had not really noticed before.

"Did you get a good look at him?" David asked.

She bit her lip and nodded.

"You need to call the police."

"There's nothing they can do," she said.

Perhaps it was something in her tone, but he looked up sharply and a kind of shock spread across his features, as though he had just realized a horrible truth.

"Tell me," David demanded.

So she did.

When she was through, she was shaking all over. He slid closer to her and held her, but she shook her head.

"I know you probably think it's all in my head—"

"No. No, I don't," he assured her.

Stunned, she gazed up at him. "I don't understand."

"I've seen him, too," David explained. He glanced away, the memory causing him to flinch. "But there's more. A lot more to this than you realize."

The things he told her, about ghosts and walking dead men, cultivated a new terror that blossomed even colder in her heart. But when he told her that one of the intruders in his own house had been his grandfather, that his Grandpa Edgar had tried to kill him, a deep, abiding sadness settled into her bones with an ache she doubted would ever go away.

"And Jill?"

"It's Maggie," David said firmly. "I was sure last night, but how could I have said anything? You would just have thought—"

"You should have," she told him.

"We both should have," David replied softly.

"So what do we do now? These . . . the people he's sent after you. They may be trying to kill you, but he hasn't tried. You're still in danger."

"You spurned him," David reminded her. "I'd say we're both in danger." He leaned back a bit, almost collapsing into the sofa. Then his eyes roved around the room. "We should get out of here. Go to a hotel. He could come back at any time. Hell, we don't even know if he's really gone. In the morning, we'll go see Father Charles."

"Do you think he'll believe us?" she asked.

Something flickered across his eyes then, a sort of curiosity, maybe. "Yes. I really think he will. I get the idea from talking to the padre that he's heard his share of weird stories."

"All right. Let me pack some things," she said.

Janine got up and went toward the bedroom. Outside the door she paused and stared into the room. A moment later David came up behind her and she breathed a sigh of relief as he followed her in. She did not want to be in there alone.

When she had thrown some overnight things into a bag, Janine went to the phone.

"Let me just call Larry and let him know where I'll be," she said.

"Why call Larry? It's only for a few hours."

"Just in case he hears anything about my mother."

Silence. Slowly Janine turned to find David staring at her. It hit her, then, that in all their conversation, their shared fears and the nightmarish spectacle they had each been through that night, she had not mentioned the call she had received earlier, not told him about her mother.

"What about her?" David asked.

Janine swallowed hard, pieces of a puzzle beginning to click together in her head.

"She's missing," Janine said, her voice catching in her throat.

They stared at one another, both chilled by those words.

CHAPTER 13

The morning ought to have brought solace, but the world still seemed off-kilter, as if the sunlight were filtered through a dusty curtain.

David stood just inside the front door of his home, stared around with eyes wide, and wondered why he was not crying. The house remained intact, true, but *his* things, the parts of this house that were him, had been destroyed. Paintings and plants, knickknacks and books; some of the furniture had been shattered, scattered across the floor, broken and torn and even pissed on. The smell of urine was strong in the foyer.

Underneath it, though, was another smell, not unlike the ocean at low tide.

"David. I'm so sorry."

With a deep breath, he collected himself and then glanced back at Janine, who had come in behind him. Though the night had passed, they had agreed that neither of them was going to stay at home until they found some answers, but David had wanted to at least get some clothes. They recognized that there was risk involved in returning here, but the coming of the dawn had mitigated their fright. Now, though, it seemed foolish to have assumed that the arrival of morning would have chased away the darker shadows of the night.

They had been cautious as they entered, and ready to flee.

Now this.

"Stay with me," he said, his voice numb.

Then he started up the stairs. The second floor was not in quite as much of a shambles, but it still pained him. Soon, when he was able to return here again, he would put things in order.

At the moment he could not bear it.

In his bedroom—which was littered with broken things and torn clothing—he managed to find three days' worth of clean clothes. He stuffed them into a bag as Janine stood with him in silence, and they returned to the first floor. For several long minutes they stood in the foyer again and he stared up the stairs.

The morning had brought bright sunshine and blue sky, the bustle of human activity, and a new perspective. He was still afraid, of course, but now he was angry. More than angry. Whatever these manifestations were that were fucking with his life, David wanted it to stop.

A sigh escaped his lips and he grimaced as he ushered Janine out the door onto the front stoop. Just before he would have turned the key in the lock, the phone rang within. For just a moment he paused, head down. Then he glanced at Janine and she shrugged.

David nodded, walked back through the house to the kitchen, stepped over pots and pans, and picked up the phone.

"Hello?"

"Mr. Bairstow, hello. This is Gary Kindzierski from the Medford P.D. At St. Matt's they told me you weren't coming in today. I'm glad I've caught you at home."

With a frown, David switched the phone from one hand to another and glared at it as though it had done him some personal slight. "You must be a mind reader, Detective. I was just going to call you."

A pause, as the policeman considered that statement. "Oh?"

"I wasn't home last night. Someone's vandalized my house."

"I'm sorry to hear that, Mr. Bairstow," Kindzierski said. "I find it pretty interesting, though. Is Miss Hartschorn there with you right now?"

David stiffened. "As a matter of fact, she is."

"I'll send a couple of guys over to have a look around your place and take a statement. Meanwhile, I'm meeting Miss Hartschorn's stepfather at the Parker House in Boston at one o'clock to talk about her mother's disappearance. I think it would be helpful for both of you to be there as well."

Janine had come back in while David spoke to the detective, and now she stood in the kitchen, attempting to avoid stepping in whatever foods from the refrigerator had been strewn around, and tried to catch David's eye, to get a sense of the conversation he was having.

David stared back at her blankly.

"I'm glad you're on it, Detective," David said. "But Larry said you couldn't do anything for forty-eight hours."

Kindzierski paused again. When he spoke this time, it was in measured tones, as though each word had been carefully considered.

"That time period is set up to weed out the cranks, Mr. Bairstow. One-night runaways, cheating spouses, miscommunications. Given the other things that have been happening around you and Miss Hartschorn in the past week or so, well, I think you see what I mean."

"I do," David told him. "And thank you."

"I'll see you at one," Kindzierski said.

After they hung up, he related the conversation to Janine. She turned and walked back through the house in silence. Just inside the open front door, she stared out at the street. David glanced around the kitchen and felt the urge to begin to repair the damage done to his home, but he pushed it away. There would be time later. Not to mention that the police would likely want to see it the way it had been left.

"Janine?" he asked as he walked up behind her.

The sun shone brightly through the door and he lifted a hand to block the glare. She faced him.

"It's a waste of time. There's nothing the police can do to help us," Janine said, her voice hollow. "She's dead, isn't she, David?"

"You don't know that," he said quickly. "We don't even know it's connected. Maybe Kindzierski can't help us, but that doesn't mean he can't find your mother. We'll go into Boston, and stop to see Father Charles on the way back."

Janine nodded, then turned to gaze back out at the street again. It was quiet, serene. Springtime. The world had been invaded, tainted by something that did not belong there. Yet it seemed unchanged, unaware, just the same as it had been the day, the week, the month before.

Except through our eyes, David thought. *Through our eyes, everything looks different now.*

Beacon Hill was one of the oldest sections of Boston, and among the trendiest and most expensive to live. Its winding one-way streets were considered by out-of-towners to be a labyrinth worthy of the Minotaur. Yet it was also among the most picturesque spots in the city. Boston Common's green parklands gradually ascended toward the pinnacle of the hill, the Massachusetts State House, itself topped by a golden dome. Government buildings were merged there on Beacon Hill with old neighborhoods and enduring establishments such as the Parker House hotel.

David and Janine hurried up from Park Street station toward the State House, and then down the narrow side street. While they had waited for the police to show up to investigate the vandalism at his house, Janine had called Larry Vale on his cell phone and got him in the car, somewhere south of Hartford, Connecticut. It turned out that sleep had been hard to come by for all of them the previous night. Larry had risen at six-thirty and been on the road north by seven.

He had made a reservation for himself at the Parker House, and planned to stay as long as it took to find Ruth.

When Janine related the conversation to David, he tried his best to hide his reaction to Larry's vow. Not that he needed to, for Janine spoke the very words that had gone through his mind.

"He may be here forever," she'd said.

So often, when he was a child, the terrors of the nighttime would be dispersed by the coming of the dawn. It ought to have been the same now, in a place like this, with the woman he loved. Yet the surreal frights of the previous evening seemed almost compounded by the perfection of the day, perhaps, he thought, because these things were supposed to go away in the morning, but he knew that was not going to happen.

Hand in hand, they strode purposefully up to the door of the Parker House. He held it for her and then followed her inside. They found Kindzierski already speaking to Larry at the bar. When he saw his stepdaughter, Larry Vale heaved a sigh of relief, rose, and went to her. Though he and Janine had never been close, she allowed the embrace. More than that, she seemed to hold on to him as though each could not survive without the other.

Neither of them wept, though. David suspected that they both would feel that was too much like surrender.

"Janine. How are you faring?" Larry asked. He held her at arm's length and studied her.

Her smile was fleeting. "I'll get by. Let's not worry about me right now, though, okay?"

"Right."

Larry nodded once in affirmation. He offered his hand to David and they shook firmly.

"You both know the detective already?" Larry asked.

Greetings were exchanged all around and David and Janine pulled bar stools out so the four of them were arranged in a rough circle. Kindzierski was quieter than

David had expected, and he looked as tired as he had the last time they'd met, with dark circles under his eyes. Yet the detective was very clearly observing them, and there was a dark intelligence in his eyes. David wondered what it did to a man's soul to always have to consider everyone a suspect.

"Everything squared away at your place?" Kindzierski asked.

David nodded. "Much as it can be at the moment. Some of the furniture and a few paintings were destroyed, a lot of knickknacks, that sort of thing. After your people were done, we picked up as well as we could for the moment. Obviously there's a lot more to do."

There was a pause as the detective studied the three of them. Then he let out a breath and raised an eyebrow.

"I'll be blunt. I don't want to waste your time. I'd rather be out there trying to figure out what happened to your mother, Miss Hartschorn. To get there, I'm going to ask you some questions that might sound a bit abrupt or unfeeling given your situation. I'm sorry for that, but it can't be helped."

Janine reached out and took David's hand, rested their clasped hands on her leg. "It's all right. Whatever you need."

Kindzierski nodded. His hand went to a small notepad on the bar that David hadn't noticed when they had first sat down, but he did not pick it up. The detective's eyes were still distant, observant, but his expression was kind and his hesitation seemed genuine.

"Mr. Vale and I were just discussing whether or not there was anyone who might, for any reason, want to hurt Mrs. Vale," he said, moving on quickly so as not to be interrupted. "We also talked about the possibility of kidnap for ransom, though since no one has been contacted, I think it's safe to say that isn't likely."

The bartender arrived then. David ordered a Samuel Adams, Janine had wine, and Larry asked for another Seven and Seven. The detective drank soda water with a twist of lime, and seemed a bit cranky that he could not also have a drink. When the bartender had gone, Janine frowned and gazed at Kindzierski.

"I can't imagine anyone having any reason to hurt my mother," she said, her voice hitching a bit, but still strong. "Also, I'm sure it's another thing you have to cross off your list, but you can forget about affairs. My mother's in love with Larry. They're partners. And . . ." She paused, glanced a bit sheepishly at her stepfather, then looked back at the detective. "I've been thinking about this, and I don't think she's ever been that interested in sex, so you can probably rule that out."

"Not completely. I don't want to rule anything out completely," Kindzierski said. "But I appreciate the insight. It helps."

"You're leading up to something," Janine observed.

The bartender delivered the drinks. They all paused a moment to take a first sip, and then Kindzierski regarded them each in turn, finally settling on Janine again.

"Your ex was murdered in a parking lot across the street from a party you were attending. Your current boyfriend, Mr. Bairstow here, was run off the road and nearly killed. Days later, his house is vandalized. I notice neither one of you went to work today. That means someone had to sub for your classes, which just from what I know of you I'm gonna guess both of you take pretty seriously. I'm sure that vandalism was traumatic, but why *both* of you?

"I think you both can see where I'm going with this. I'm sorry for saying, Miss Hartschorn, but bad things are happening around you lately, and now your mother is missing. Has been missing, apparently, since she left this hotel on her way to your apartment. But you didn't know she was coming and she never arrived."

Kindzierski took a breath, chuckled softly at himself, and leaned forward on his stool. "You know what? I said I had questions. I guess what I've got instead is some curiosity, a bunch of facts, and one big question.

"What aren't you telling me?"

A million replies bounced through David's mind in an instant. He saw in Janine's eyes that she was taken equally off balance by Kindzierski's approach. She glanced at him, but David thought that the detective might think it odd if he responded first, so he said nothing.

With her fingers steepled under her chin, hands together as though in prayer, Janine regarded the man a moment. Then she shook her head and dropped her hands to her lap.

"There's nothing, Detective. Honestly, I wish there were," she added, her voice cracking. Her lips pressed together as she forcibly composed herself. "I'm afraid for my mother, more afraid than I've ever been in my entire life." Her voice hitched. "But I don't have anything that would help you."

"Your point is taken, though," David added.

Larry and Kindzierski both seemed a bit startled when he spoke. The detective narrowed his gaze as he glanced over.

"It seems almost impossible for these things to be unrelated," David continued. "Sure, they might be, but we'd be idiots not to look for a connection. Whoever ran me off the road that night, I'm sure it was no accident. I've got to figure that's the same person who trashed my house. I don't know why. But I'd like to get my hands on him."

David shivered a bit. The lie had been easy because it was so intertwined with the truth. His frustration and anger were very, very real indeed.

"You have no idea who that might be?" Kindzierski asked.

"Other than the description I gave you, no," David said.

Obviously troubled, the detective only nodded. "I

don't suppose either one of you can come up with anyone who might want to hurt you?"

Janine gave a sad, morbid little laugh. "Only Spencer, and he's dead."

"All right," Kindzierski said. "Please keep in touch with me. Meanwhile, I know that Mr. Vale has plans to aid in the search for Mrs. Vale. The Medford P.D. would appreciate being part of any independent process so that we're not working at cross-purposes."

"Of course," Janine replied.

It was clear from the cop's expression, however, that they weren't done quite yet. The bartender cruised by, glanced down to see if anyone needed a fresh drink, then continued on. A trio of professional women at a table in the restaurant laughed uproariously at something. They drew the detective's attention, but when Kindzierski cast a quick look back toward them, a pair of fiftyish men a few stools down turned away as though caught at something.

They were listening, David thought.

Kindzierski slipped a hand inside his leather jacket and came back out with a small wallet. He flipped it open, revealing the gold shield that identified him as a detective.

"Hey," he said, voice low.

The two men, probably lawyers or politicians, considering the neighborhood, feigned surprise as they looked up. One was bony-thin, the other a ruddy, jowled, thick-bodied man.

Kindzierski hung his badge out. "Clear out."

The big man, clearly the more senior of the two considering his bluster, sat up a bit straighter. "Excuse me, Detective, but we're about to have lunch. I'm not sure what right you think you have to—"

"Don't fuck with me. I'm not in the mood," Kindzierski snapped, loud enough to draw attention. Loud enough to make the politician blush. "You want lunch, go somewhere else or find yourself a goddamn table."

The men both gawked at Kindzierski as if the cop

had dropped his pants. Then the bony one began to stand up. The other clapped a hand on his shoulder and kept him seated.

"We're fine just where we are, Detective. I'd be careful how I proceeded from here if I were you."

Kindzierski turned his back on the two men, his jaw tight with anger. Without looking at them again, he spoke just loudly enough for them to hear.

"In five seconds, if those two eavesdropping assholes are still there, I'm going to make an arrest for interfering with an officer in the course of an investigation," he said. "If I have to go, we can pick this conversation up again later. Now, I'm gonna count. You let me know if they're still there when I'm done."

The big man's jowls shook and his ruddy complexion darkened further. "Listen here, you little prick. This isn't even your jurisdiction. I saw your ID. There's nothing you can—"

"One," Kindzierski interrupted, his back still toward them. "Two. Three. Four . . ."

Enraged, the one with the jowls caved. He stood up, muttering obscenities under his breath, and Bony followed him as they made their way to an available table, drinks in hand.

"They're gone," David said quietly.

"Good," Kindzierski said.

Janine and Larry exchanged an anxious glance, but David smiled. He liked the cop a hell of a lot more, all of a sudden. There were secrets to be kept, and that had created within him a kind of adversarial attitude toward Kindzierski. Now that disappeared. He was almost tempted to let the man in on the truth. But Kindzierski wasn't his friend and he wasn't a theologian like Father Charles. There was nothing David could tell him that the detective would find even remotely believable.

Or is there?

Before David could speak, Kindzierski cleared his throat and sat up a little straighter.

"One last thing," the detective said. "Mr. Vale tells

me that the two of you spent the night at a hotel. That's why you, Mr. Bairstow, weren't home when your place was trashed. Not to pry into your personal lives, but you both live alone. If you wanted some time to yourselves, why would that require a hotel room?"

David blinked, speechless a moment. The question threw him off. At the bar, Larry Vale blushed deeply and studiously avoided looking at his stepdaughter. Janine was flustered, completely caught off guard. Her reaction was sure to raise Kindzierski's suspicions, take up more time, and David felt it was far more important that they get to their meeting with Father Charles.

"Tell him, Janine," he said.

Kindzierski raised a curious eyebrow. Larry stared at Janine. Her mouth was open in an almost comical expression as she gazed at David in confusion.

"Tell him about the stalker."

"You have a stalker?" Kindzierski asked. "And you didn't think to mention this to me before? Why am I not buying that?"

Janine shrugged slowly, at a loss.

David fumbled to cover for them. "He's not a stalker, necessarily. Just this creepy guy who's been hanging around near her place lately. Probably nothing. Certainly not the guy who ran me off the road, and he doesn't match your description of the man who . . . who killed Spencer. Could just be some homeless guy, but she saw him in the yard last night and just wanted to stay somewhere other than home."

Kindzierski frowned, suspicious. "Why not your place, then?"

Janine jumped in, then, and David was glad. It seemed awkward for him to speak for her.

"If he really is stalking me, I was afraid he might already know where David was. I just wanted one night in a place where no one could find me," she said.

"That's why you called me so late about going to the hotel," Larry Vale put in. "Why didn't you say something?"

The slick ad executive's voice was usually commanding, arrogant. Today he just seemed lost in his fear for his wife.

"You had enough on your mind, Larry," Janine said gently. She laid a hand on his arm to comfort him.

"But this 'stalker,' he hasn't done anything to threaten you in any way?"

Janine hesitated. Then she shook her head. "No. He's just . . . creepy."

Kindzierski seemed even more frustrated now. "I'm still getting the feeling there's something you two aren't saying. I mean . . . I just can't believe with all these 'coincidences,' it didn't occur to you that you should mention this guy to me right off. Whatever you may think, he could be the source of all your problems. You're upset enough to spend the night in a hotel, but you say nothing to me about it. What am I missing?"

"I'm sorry, Detective Kindzierski," Janine said, her voice shaking. "I guess we're just not thinking very clearly."

Kindzierski sighed and shook his head. He studied them both for a few moments as if waiting for one of them to say more. Then he shrugged.

"All right, look, there isn't a lot I can do about him right now. If he doesn't match the description of either suspect and he hasn't actually done anything, the best I can say is that I can have a patrol car swing by Miss Hartschorn's apartment hourly. If you see the guy again, call me immediately. Even if he hasn't directly threatened you, I can bring him in for questioning about all of this. If I could catch him on your property, that would be even better. At least that would give me enough to hold him on.

"I just need a description."

As they rode the T back to Medford, Janine sat silently beside David, her hand gripping his, and they both stared straight ahead at some curious bit of nothing in the distance. There were not very many people on the train at that time, mostly college students, but Janine did not want even to whisper to David with others so close. She was reminded of the two men who had been listening to Detective Kindzierski in the restaurant and she held David's hand more tightly and waited as though she were holding her breath.

They got off the train at Davis Square Station and went up the escalator, still in silence. A guy with a boyish face and innocent blue eyes played acoustic guitar and sang high-pitched folk blues like he really meant it. Janine watched him recede as the escalator drew her up and away, and she wished she had stopped to throw a dollar in his guitar case, just to let him know that someone heard him.

There was a bank of phones upstairs in the station. A couple of kids who probably shouldn't have been out of school just yet skateboarded past the glass-and-steel doors. Janine and David went to the phones. He picked one up and began to dial, then hung up and glanced at her.

"We blew that, didn't we?" he asked.

Janine stared at him a moment, then nodded. "Big-time. There's no way that he doesn't think we're hiding something. But what else were we supposed to say?"

"I should've just kept lying, but he already knew there were holes in what we were telling him," David said.

"There's nothing we can do about it now," Janine told him. "And it isn't like the cops can help us."

David took a long breath, then picked up the phone again. He fished in his pocket for some coins, slid them in, and dialed Father Charles at his office at St. Matt's. Janine listened as he spoke to the priest. Since David had not gone in to teach that day—though the vandalism to his house was a solid excuse—he did not want to be seen in the halls of St. Matthew's.

Just a few moments later, David hung up.

"He wants us to meet him at the rectory."

"Now?" Janine asked.

"I think now would be good, don't you?"

It took them only a few minutes to drive from Davis Square to St. Matthew's. When they rang the bell at the rectory, the door opened quickly, as though the priest had been waiting just inside for them. Father Charles greeted them with a tumbler of Crown Royal in one hand and a cigar in the other. Black pants and a black sweater were Hugh Charles's idea of dressing down, but he still looked like a priest.

The woman who worked in the rectory office was on the phone as they walked by, and did not even glance up. Father Charles led them to a study on the second floor with a quartet of old leather chairs around a small round table. An enormous masonry fireplace took up one side of the room, but it was dark and dormant that day.

The priest offered them both a drink, but they declined. Thereafter, he did not touch his own drink, and even put out his cigar.

At first, Janine was hesitant to relate the events of the previous night. David, however, had already broken the ice with Father Charles about the bizarre nature of their recent experiences, and he was quick to describe what had happened at his house. She had been caught up in her own fear, in the numbing chill that went through her when she thought about Charon, or about her mother's disappearance. Now, though, Janine truly saw David's fear for the first time.

When he spoke, she reached out to hold his hand.

Listening to him broke down her own reluctance, and she finally opened up to the priest. She left out much of the sexual context of her dreams, but aside from that, she was even more open with him than she had been with David.

Like a confessional, she thought.

Yet she did not feel the sense of judgment with Father Charles that she would have felt in confession. It amazed her how open he was. The words *insane* and *lunatic* had been swirling around in her mind for a while, but with Father Charles, a man she respected as both intelligent and logical, she was able to push doubts about her mental condition aside for the first time.

She told him about her dreams, about the things she had seen and heard that she had at first thought she had imagined. She told him about seeing Charon that day on the riverbank, at the spot where David had been forced off the road. Together, Janine and David told him about her mother's disappearance and their meeting with Detective Kindzierski. Father Charles listened with very little comment save a gentle prodding for further detail, until they both had sort of run out of steam.

"And you *gave* him a description?" Father Charles asked, aghast, when she revealed the end of their conversation with the detective.

Janine shrugged. "Not an exact description. Not the way I just described him to you."

At length, when Janine was all talked out and she sat back in the leather chair, the priest reached for his whiskey and took a slow, contemplative sip, watching her over the rim of the glass.

Then he sat forward, his eyes upon her as though David were not even in the room. Janine shifted a bit, suddenly uncomfortable under that intense gaze. His eyes were kind, set in a wide, friendly face. Yet they sparkled with a kind of exhilaration. He took another small sip of his drink, then set it aside.

"I think we should take a ride," Father Charles said lightly, as though nothing they had told him was at all out of the ordinary. "There's someone I want you both to meet. I'm sorry to say that you may have to tell those stories all over again."

"Who are we going to see?" Janine asked, mystified.

"An old teacher of mine, actually," Father Charles replied.

"The one you told me about," David said quickly. "From the seminary."

"Indeed," the priest said. "Father Cornelius Jessup. Since David first talked to me about the things that were happening to him, I've had several conversations with Father Jessup. He'll be very interested to meet you."

Once again, a kind of impatient silence descended upon them. Father Charles attempted to distract them both with talk of the day-to-day goings-on at both St. Matt's and Medford High, but to Janine that entire part of her life, the real world, seemed to exist in some far-off land now.

The tires thrummed on the road, bumped through potholes as they drove out to Route 16 and followed it all the way into Everett. David was behind the wheel and he kept the window open to give them fresh air, but it could not wash away that feeling of unreality.

It was Father Charles's fault, actually. She had expected him to require more convincing, if he were able to be convinced at all. At the very least, she had thought he would interrogate them a little more, try to find holes in their stories. But he had not done that.

He had not done that, and the only thing Janine could think was that perhaps that was because he *believed* them. Somehow, that made the fugue she was in so much worse. For if he believed them, it might all be true, and if it were, what did that say about everything she had believed about the world her entire life?

"Here," Father Charles told David. "Turn in here. You can park in back."

Janine glanced up as they pulled into a long drive that led into the rear lot of a large, faded brick building. It was a retirement home for priests in the archdiocese of Boston, and the first thing she saw when she caught sight of it was that it wasn't worthy. With all that priests did to serve their communities, it seemed unfair to her that they should be tucked away in a crumbling neighborhood with graffiti on the walls, in a building that might have been a jail once upon a time.

Inside, the receptionist told them that Father Jessup was expecting them. Janine hated the sterility of the place, the antiseptic smell that reminded her of a hospital. Of the hospital, the one that had been both retreat and prison to her after her baby had died. As though he sensed her discomfort, Father Charles laid a comforting hand on her shoulder and they followed a disheveled orderly whom the receptionist had instructed to take them to see Father Jessup. David walked quietly behind them.

"You must be important visitors," the orderly said. "Father Jessup was holding court with some of the other residents before he got your call. He's been in the library ever since."

"I've asked him for his opinion on a matter of theology," Father Charles explained.

Janine snickered, a bit madly. It sounded so innocent, and also so hollow.

"Yeah, well, prepare for a lecture," the orderly said with a laugh. "Cornelius has no problem offering his opinion when he hasn't been asked. I don't want to think about what he's like when people *want* to know what he thinks."

Father Charles stiffened.

"Young man," he snapped at the orderly, though the heavyset man with his untucked shirt and unruly hair hardly seemed of an age to warrant the description.

The orderly turned quickly, but did not raise his eyes. Father Charles's tone had been enough to tell him he had crossed a line. Enough for him, at least, but not for Father Charles.

"Cornelius Jessup, whom you so casually dismiss, is a brilliant man. He was my teacher. To this day, he is still my teacher. There are untold volumes of knowledge that you might attain simply by standing by to catch the pearls of wisdom that fall from his most august lips, and yet I daresay you would hardly recognize them. You know what they say about pearls and swine."

The orderly knew he had been chastised, but seemed to have only the vaguest notion that he had also been insulted. "Sorry," he said halfheartedly, "just kinda the impression you get, the way some of the other priests act around Father Jessup. They treat him like he's a crank, you know?"

Father Charles sighed. "I'm sure they do. Perhaps, however, one day you'll realize that it is possible to make up your own mind about your charges here, rather than relying upon the prejudices of others."

"Sorry, Father," the orderly said again.

"Let's move along," Father Charles replied, giving the man not an inch.

After a moment, the orderly shuffled along the corridor again and they all followed.

The library turned out to be much larger than Janine would have expected, and much more richly furnished given the rest of the facility, particularly its exterior. There were high-backed leather chairs, and some softer ones as well, and at least two sofas that she could see. One entire wall was made up of high windows so the daylight shone in, but the other walls were lined with books, mostly hardback volumes.

The place was empty save for an attendant who sat behind a desk near the door.

"Father Jessup here?" the orderly asked.

"In back," the attendant replied.

"We're all right from here," Father Charles said, in a tone that would brook no argument.

Not that the orderly had any interest in giving him one. He glanced once at Father Charles and then fled the room, likely more than happy to return to changing bedpans or mopping floors if it meant not having to bear up under Hugh Charles's admonishing gaze.

A number of tall shelves on the far side of the enormous room created the illusion that the place was far closer to an actual library. Beyond those shelves, they found a long oak study table surrounded by plain wooden chairs quite different from the plush, comfortable furniture near the door. This was an area for study, Janine thought immediately. Not enjoyment.

The books also seemed different. The spines of a

great many were leather, and some appeared to be quite old. Even newer-looking books shared one element, however. As Janine scanned the titles she realized that all of them were volumes on mythology and comparative theology.

At the far end of the long table sat a lone figure, a tall, thin man in dark pants and a green cardigan sweater. He had wispy white hair, pale skin, and a thin mustache, and he reminded Janine quite a bit of the late British actor David Niven, though he wore glasses with square, wire rims. This had to be Cornelius Jessup, and though he seemed quite spry, she gauged his age to be in the mid-seventies.

"Father Jessup?" Father Charles ventured.

The old man glanced up quickly, his eyes bright and alive behind his glasses. When he stood, however, it was with great difficulty. Pain flickered across his features before he pushed it away.

"Hugh, my boy," Father Jessup said, his voice the rasp of a lifelong smoker. "You're looking well."

"And you're still as dashingly handsome as ever. Still breaking the ladies' hearts, I'll wager," Father Charles said.

Janine blushed, a bit taken aback by this exchange between the priests. As if he sensed her discomfort, Father Jessup glanced at her, then held out an age-mottled hand in her direction.

"Don't listen to him, my dear. I'm quite dedicated to my vows."

"That's what breaks their hearts," Father Charles retorted.

But the moment for humor had passed. Once Father Jessup had looked at Janine, he had not looked away. He studied her now with an intensity that made her squirm uncomfortably. All trace of amusement had gone from his face, to be replaced by a gravity that seemed dreadful to her.

"Seen something you can't explain, haven't you?" the old priest asked. Then he glanced at David. "Both of you."

Father Charles gestured toward them. "This is David Bairstow, Father. A colleague of mine at St. Matthew's. And the young lady is Janine Hartschorn, formerly at St. Matt's and now at Medford High."

Father Jessup nodded grimly. "Teachers. Well, I guess we'll find out what sort of teachers you are."

"How do you mean?" Janine asked, surprised to find herself speaking at all.

But the old priest grinned. "Too many think once you can teach, you don't have anything more to learn. I guess you've already learned how wrong that approach is, just by what Hugh here's already told me."

With a tiny grimace at the pain in his lower back and legs, Father Jessup reached out to shake both their hands. "Well, sit, then, and tell me what it is you've come to tell me. Trust me when I say it can't be any crazier than a lot of the things I've heard over the years.

"Fortunately for you two, I'm about the craziest old coot in the place." He winked at Father Charles as he said it, but there was a bitterness in his voice as well. "Ask anyone; they'll tell you."

So the four of them sat at the long oak table in the back of the library, and Hugh Charles slipped his old teacher a few cigars that Father Jessup quickly hid inside his sweater with a conspiratorial glance. The two men bemoaned the lack of good whiskey in the place.

And then Janine and David told their stories.

Father Jessup listened intently throughout, and Janine noticed that Father Charles was also paying close attention, though he had heard it all before.

When they were through, Cornelius Jessup leaned back in his uncomfortable wooden chair and rubbed his stiff back. His gaze drifted from Janine to David to Father Charles and then off to some distant point where only his eyes could see anything of importance. He reached inside his sweater and drew out one of the contraband cigars, peeled the crinkling plastic wrapper off it, and sniffed it exotically.

Then he clenched the cigar between his teeth and rose with difficulty from his seat.

"Give me a moment, would you?" he asked.

Then he began to drift amongst the books. For more than twenty minutes, while the rest of them made lame efforts at small talk, the old man puttered amongst the books, reading titles and, from time to time, pulling a volume off the shelf to peruse a few pages.

Then, abruptly, he abandoned the shelves and returned to the table. He slid in painful increments into the seat, cigar still jutting from his lips. Then he removed the cigar and placed it carefully on the table in front of him, lining it up as though he were a carpenter taking invaluable measurements.

Finally, he regarded them again. His eyes were narrowed slightly, deepening the lines on his face as he adjusted the square glasses that sat on the bridge of his nose, his hands shaking slightly.

"Let me first say that I believe you," Father Jessup told them. "Everything that you've told me would be dismissed as ridiculous by the Church, of course, but that's good for business, isn't it? For us, I mean. The Church. In the fifty-seven years since I was first called to the service of God, I have seen a great many odd things. Sought them out, I should confess. It has earned me a reputation that is not entirely flattering."

Father Charles began to speak, but the old priest shot a finger out toward him.

"Not a word from you," Jessup commanded, and Father Charles obeyed.

"I have given my life over to the study of faith, my young friends," Father Jessup continued, his eyes flashing and alive now with a renewed spark. "To belief. To spirituality and what is often perceived as the supernatural. So, yes, I believe everything you have told me.

"But there is one part of this story you've left out. It's a vital part, I think, and before I can formulate a hypothesis, it's a tale I should like to hear."

Janine raised her eyebrows. Out of the corner of her eye, she noticed David watching her. She shrugged.

"I don't know what you mean."

"The first time you saw him, Janine," the priest said gently. "During labor, when you lost your baby. You haven't talked about that at all. Tell me about that. Talk to me about what it was like to die."

CHAPTER 14

❧

On the way home from the school, Annette stopped to pick up a few things at the grocery store. She had subbed for one of David's classes and had not been able to eat lunch as a result. It was never a good idea to go to the supermarket when she was hungry, so rather than just the milk, bread, and juice she had intended to buy, she also had a block of cheddar cheese, a bag of cookies, brownie mix, and a frozen pizza she knew she would regret buying.

Tired and hungry, she lugged her groceries from the parking lot to her building and managed the acrobatic feat of fishing out her keys and opening the doors without bothering to put anything down. Upstairs, however, her arms began to weaken and she was finally forced to put the bags on the landing to unlock her apartment.

Even as she swung the door open, the phone began to ring.

She grabbed two of the bags and used her foot to slide the other over the threshold. With a flick of her wrist, Annette tossed her keys onto the table and then slammed the door shut behind her. The phone on the wall in the kitchen was on its third ring when she snatched it up.

"Hello?"

"Hey, sexy."

Annette could not have said why she blushed. Under normal circumstances, she was a hard woman to fluster. But ever since she had met Jill, that had changed just a little. There was something about this amazing, passionate woman that had her constantly off-kilter, butterflies in her stomach, as though she were back in eighth grade about to go onstage in the school play.

"Hi," she replied, her voice almost unconsciously dropping to a low, feline rasp.

"What are you up to?" Jill asked, her tone playful as always.

"Right now?"

"Right now."

"About to put some groceries away. Then . . . it was kind of a long day, so I thought I'd jump in the shower."

"Want some company?"

Annette leaned against the wall in the kitchen and crossed her legs. As though Jill were right there in the room with her, she smiled shyly and glanced at the floor. Her voice sounded so close, Annette could almost feel Jill's hands on her.

"I'll wait for you," she said.

Talk to me about what it was like to die.

Janine flinched and looked away. Though she certainly understood what had happened to her—what had *almost* happened—no one had ever stated it to her so plainly, so boldly, before. It brought her back to that time, to the lost, drifting sensation that had overwhelmed her when she had . . . almost died.

It was as though the memory enhanced her senses. All around her, the library seemed to come alive. Her hands touched the arms of the chair and found the wood hard and dry. A shiver ran through her. With amazing clarity, she glanced around at the wood and glass and leather-bound books in the room, so warm and masculine, and every line was visible to her, each a work of art. David gazed at her with love and concern, and she saw her own stricken reflection gleaming in his eyes. Father Charles had small crinkles at the edges of his eyes and mouth, and a spatter of white hair amongst the auburn at his temples. It was as though she could see each wrinkle, each strand of hair. He nodded for her to go on, as if to tell her it was all right to share this now, this pain of hers.

Father Jessup reached out and laid a cold hand, soft and dry as tissue paper, over hers. "I've upset you," he said with that smoker's rasp. "I'm so sorry."

"No." She held up a hand almost as though she were blind, and shook her head. "No, it's okay. It's just . . . I felt strange, suddenly. When I think about what it felt like . . . then. To be so lost, everything so unreal, not like a dream, but like, I don't know, finding yourself part of a play, when you know it's not real but you can't seem to stop acting in it."

Janine shook her head. She looked to David for support. "I'm not making any sense."

"No, you are," David insisted. "Okay, none of us has ever gone through what you did, but we all know what it's like to have a dream. I've had dreams where I consciously knew I was dreaming, and still didn't wake up right away."

Somewhere far off a phone began to ring.

"Yes," Janine said, as she turned her attention back to Father Jessup. "It was a little like that. But I didn't wake up at all. It seemed to last forever."

The old priest settled back in his chair and gazed at her expectantly. Father Charles watched her with almost paternal concern.

Janine closed her eyes and remembered. A muscle in her shoulder twitched and started her shivering. Eyes closed, only the scents of the room and the silent knowledge of the presence of the three men to comfort her, she brought herself back to that horrible day.

Lights above her. Doctors and nurses snapping at each other. Machines beeping angrily.

But no crying. She was supposed to have a baby, but there was no crying. Her body had suffered so much trauma that by the time the baby was removed from her womb, it was dead.

Though she sensed much of that, even while unconscious, she did not really know it until she finally came around. It was what happened during the procedure, while her baby was dying . . . while she was dying . . . that Father Charles wanted to hear about.

"They lost me," Janine whispered, her eyes still closed. Vaguely, she felt David's hand cover her own, there on the arm of the chair. But she was lost in the past now, in the memory of something she had been trying so very hard to forget.

"One minute I could sort of hear voices, and the machines, and I could smell that awful ammonia smell in hospitals, where it's meant to be clean but it's really just them trying to cover up the smell of sickness and dying.

"Then I was awake. I . . . I was in this place. A very dark place with trees all around. The ground was soft and damp and there was a river, and the sound of it was so loud in my ears. There were stars in the sky, but they were red, like blood, and the sky seemed too close to me, too low. That's what I meant, I guess. It was like the sky was a prop and I was on some stage somewhere.

"But the river . . . the river was real. I knew I was lost. I wasn't supposed to be there, but more than that, no one was supposed to stay on the riverbank. Like the water was magnetic, dragging me in. But I didn't want to go. All I wanted was to find my way home, and I kept trying to get away from the river and I'd just come back to it."

Eyes still tightly closed, Janine paused a moment. She realized that her breathing had changed. Now her chest rose and fell with the dread that filled her. The picture was so clear in her mind it was almost as though she were there again in her mind.

"I can almost smell the river, even now," she whispered. "The water."

Clink-clank!

At that sound, a jolt of fear shot through her and her eyes snapped open. Then she saw that it had been nothing but Father Jessup setting his glasses on the table, and she felt foolish.

"Janine?" Father Charles ventured.

"I'm all right. Just . . . nothing. Never mind." She closed her eyes again. It was as though she slid back into that death-dream, as though with her eyes closed, darkness inside her mind, she could paint on the canvas of her conscious mind the things she dredged up from her subconscious.

Janine was cold all over. Her hands were damp. She could almost feel the weight of the silver coins in her pocket, the ones with which she was meant to pay the Ferryman.

"Through the mist on the river, I could see the light from his lantern across the water. I heard it kind of banging against the wood as the current rocked the boat. The sound echoed. I fell in the water, or stepped out too deep from the riverbank—even though I was moving away from it. The water pulled at me, like it was trying to drag me in. I felt so heavy . . . so cold . . . and when I looked up, the boat was there. And so was he. He had a dark red robe on, with a hood, but then he took it down and he was just as I described him. Those eyes . . ."

Her voice failed her a moment. She felt small and afraid, a little girl again. It was a feeling she hated, a helplessness she had made up her mind she would escape.

Janine cleared her throat. "He wanted the coins. I knew who he was. Somehow I just knew. He asked for the coins, the fare for me to cross. But I refused. I . . . I took the coins out of my pocket and I threw them into the water."

David clutched her hand a bit more tightly, but she went on without responding.

"I ran. It felt as though, having thrown those coins, I was free. I turned away from the river and took off. Then I tripped and fell facedown in mud and I couldn't breathe. I thought for sure I was dead. And then, all of a sudden, I tasted air. It rushed into my

lungs and it burned and my eyes hurt 'cause of the
bright lights. . . .

"And I was in the hospital again. And they told me
my baby was dead."

While she waited for Jill to arrive, Annette picked
up in the living room and made her bed. Even as she
did so, she knew it was a bit silly, given that the bed
was likely to be a mess again shortly. But there was
something about mussing a made bed that was alluring
to her.

With that little bit of neatening done she resisted
the urge to continue onto a full-scale assault against
her imperfect living space and drifted into the kitchen.
Her anticipation of Jill's arrival had taken the edge
off her hunger, but she was still aware that she had
eaten nothing since that morning, and her stomach
rumbled the minute she opened the refrigerator. Since
she was not sure how long it would take Jill to get
there, she decided against making a sandwich and instead opted for a yogurt with granola sprinkled on top.

Jill had not arrived by the time she tossed the empty
yogurt cup into the garbage, so she grazed about the
kitchen. A handful of Cheerios. A banana. Lipton
chicken noodle Cup-a-Soup.

As she sipped from the mug full of soup, the doorbell rang.

From the moment she had hung up the phone, Annette's skin had prickled with excitement. A cynical
thought about Pavlov's dog went through her head as
the buzz from the door echoed and died, for that
crackle of sexual energy that seemed to course
through her immediately increased in intensity. A delicious thrill made her quiver a bit, and as a wanton
smile creased her lips, she uttered a tiny chirp of
pleasure.

Then she laughed at herself. "Jesus, Elf," she whispered aloud. "Rein it in."

But, though the words registered in her mind, her
body did not heed them. No one had ever had this

effect on her before. Quickly, almost shivering, she went to the door and pressed the buzzer next to the intercom. Then she opened the door and waited.

Annette heard Jill's footsteps on the stairs. She knew that she was getting carried away, both physically and emotionally. The long-term prospects of a relationship with a twenty-two-year-old were dim. With that in mind, Annette was at last able to rein herself in.

This isn't love, she told herself.

Then Jill crested the landing, and Annette's throat went dry. Jill wore soft, black, calves'-leather pants and a matching jacket that hung to her thighs, her blond hair fanning out over her shoulders in a cascade of silk. Beneath it she wore a blue T-shirt with Superman's trademark *S* stretched across her breasts. The shirt was cut off above her newly pierced belly button. A mischievous smile played at the edges of her lips.

Annette stepped out onto the landing and grabbed for her. She pulled Jill into her arms and kissed her long and deep. Jill responded hungrily, and their hands roamed over one another. When the kiss ended, Jill giggled softly.

"You ready to get wet?" she asked, a bit breathless.

A small chuckle escaped Annette's lips and she smiled shyly. "I've been wet since I hung up the phone."

Jill gently pushed her back into the apartment and closed the door.

Janine kept her eyes closed. Her lips were dry and she darted her tongue out to dampen them, and only when she tasted salt did she realize that she was crying. Her eyes fluttered open and she wiped warm tears from her cold cheeks.

Beside her, David crouched and held on to her hand. He had moved closer while her eyes were closed. Father Charles leaned over in his chair and regarded her closely. Father Jessup studied her, an expression of fascination on his face, as though she

were some sort of laboratory experiment. Then the
old priest blew out a long breath and reached out to
pat her other hand.

"I'm so sorry for your loss, Janine. I know the
wound is still very fresh for you."

She nodded.

"Please, Father," David said, almost curtly. "I know
it all sounds insane, but if there's anything you can
tell us, we'd be grateful."

There was something strange in David's voice, Janine thought. Something other than just his sympathy
for her and the stress and fear that had been building
in both of them. Janine turned to him, but David's
eyes were on the two priests who sat across the table.

"Father Jessup has already said he believes you,"
Father Charles said. "So do I."

David's hands flew into the air. "I don't get it,
Hugh. I really don't. I've seen this stuff, and so has
Janine. But you're both just taking our word for it.
How can you do that?"

Father Charles raised an eyebrow at the outburst.

"Sorry," David muttered. "I just don't get it. I
mean, you said you saw a ghost one time, and Father
Jessup saw some other things, but—"

"I saw an angel," the priest said abruptly.

Janine blinked. "I'm sorry, what?"

Father Charles laughed. "With what you're telling
me, you find *that* hard to believe? It's true, though.
When I was twelve years old, I saw an angel, standing
right in front of me, no farther away than you are
now. I've always hoped to see another one, but never
have. It's why I became a priest, to be perfectly
honest."

Fascinated, and filled with hope, Janine stared at
him. "Would you tell us about it?"

"Sometime, I will," Father Charles replied. "When
this is over." He smiled as though recalling some distant memory. "Back to the business at hand, though.
Father Jessup?"

The old priest was watching his former student with

a benevolent warmth that Janine envied. But then he glanced at her, and she felt as though a portion of it had been transferred to her. It felt like a gift.

"I believe that during your near-death experience, you confronted Charon, a creature from ancient Greek mythology," Father Jessup said. "And I believe that he is somehow here, in our world, haunting both of you."

Janine could only stare at him. It was true. She had no doubt of that. She had been living the truth of it for weeks. But like her brush with death, it seemed more frightening and also somehow more incredible to have it said aloud.

"How can that be?" David asked.

Father Jessup glanced at the younger priest a moment. He seemed to hesitate, as if what he had to say was even more difficult to believe than what they had told him. After a moment he smiled sheepishly and turned his attention to them again.

His smile was unnerving.

"I've been tarred and feathered a dozen times over for discussing my theories, and according to the archdiocese, I'm not to speak to anyone about them. So much for that," the old priest said with a smoky chuckle. He toyed with the cigar on the table in front of him a moment before sliding it back inside his sweater.

"I believe that all religions spring from the same source, that God, or what you and I would call God, is the collective spiritual energy that not only began but that now powers this universe. That same school of thought suggests that human beliefs actually mold God to fit our faith and perceptions. God remains a constant, but how we see Him defines . . . well, how we see Him. The trappings and manifestations of His power are malleable, possibly even *sculpted* by faith.

"Once upon a time humans believed in many gods. According to this theory, that would have meant that though they were all in some way part of a greater whole, there *were* many gods at that time. Some mythological creatures may also have actually existed as a manifestation of that omnipotent god-power here on Earth.

"It's a paradox of the highest order, you see. God is eternal and constant in purpose, yet fluid and ever-changing in presentation. In that sense, it may be that all religions are in some way true."

At his first pause, Janine and David both glanced over at Father Charles to see his reaction to all this. It was clear from his expression that he had heard it all before, and that if he did not believe it, he was at least not prepared to disbelieve it.

"Angels. Demons. The deities of ancient Rome, Egypt, China, and Greece. Everything," Father Jessup added.

"So . . . this Charon is . . . part of God?" Janine asked.

The old priest shook his head. He looked almost angry. "It's just a theory. If it's true, then this creature is a manifestation of God's power. Part of what I'll call god-energy, but not in a way that implies that the Almighty is responsible for or even aware of this being's actions. For all intents and purposes, whatever the fabric of his being, whatever he's made of, Charon exists, and obviously has both a function and a will of his own."

Janine shuddered.

"I'm confused," she admitted. "If all this is true . . . Jesus, I can't even believe I'm saying that. But I guess if *you* can, then so can I. So let's say it is. Wouldn't Charon have been . . . outmoded a long time ago? Wouldn't he have gone the way of Bast and Odin?"

Father Jessup nodded slowly, studying her thoughtfully with his old man eyes. "It follows, yes. That would be logical."

David snorted. "As if any of this is logical."

There was silence then for a few moments. Father Charles shot an annoyed glance at him, but Father Jessup barely seemed to notice.

Janine slid to the edge of her seat and clasped her hands together on the table. For a moment, David seemed surprised that she had pulled away from him, but when she looked at him, he must have seen the intensity on her face, for he said nothing.

"Maybe he was forgotten," she suggested.

"Forgotten?" Father Charles said doubtfully.

She nodded. "Maybe Charon was insignificant, really. What if it takes a long time for this . . . deity . . . to evolve. Or maybe nothing ever actually goes away. Maybe all these old gods are lying around, mostly dormant, created but forgotten, cast away like a child's toys and left to collect dust in the basement or under the bed."

"God's basement?" David asked, a slight smile on his face.

Janine chuckled, realizing how silly it sounded. But she was on a roll. It felt right to her, all of it.

"I see your point," Father Charles said. "Once something is manifested by God's power, it always exists, but loses prominence as faith in it withers."

"Precisely!" Father Jessup snapped excitedly. Then, like a wayward child, he glanced across the library to make sure he had not roused the attendant. When he spoke again, his voice was far more subdued.

"Some of these entities go away, perhaps even fade to nothing, to be reabsorbed into the greater whole, though it's possible there's some sort of spiritual realm where they still exist, I suppose. But given Charon's emergence here, it's clear that at least some of them . . . linger."

The image of the Ferryman was suddenly clear in her head. Janine closed her eyes a moment and she could see his burning black eyes, his carved marble flesh.

"He still has a purpose," she said. Her eyes snapped open and she found them both staring at her. "He does. Like the Angel of Death or the Valkyries in Norse mythology."

"Yes," Father Jessup said excitedly. "Maybe there'
a heaven. Maybe there's a hell. But we can all agree
there's an afterlife of some kind."

"Across the river," Janine said.

"In ancient Greece, that was known as the nether
world. But as Catholics began to believe in heaver
and hell, it would have splintered. Maybe purgatory is
the ancient netherworld, the way the Greeks knew it.'

"And Charon takes people across the river . . . to
purgatory?" Janine asked slowly. "Which would mean
that's where I was headed."

Again, they were quiet.

Janine stood and went to the window. For several
long moments, she stared out at the lengthening afternoon shadows on the yellowed lawn in front of the
building.

"I have two questions," she said quietly, as she
turned to them again. "First, why me? I mean, this
ancient creature found some way to get into our world
just so he could . . . be with me? Touch . . . touch
me. Just to give me these erotic dreams. I don't get it."

David held up a hand. "That one's easy," he said.
"He fell in love with you."

"Maybe," Father Charles mused. "But why Janine?
There have been a great many near-death experiences reported."

"None of them talk about *him,* though," Janine said
softly. And then she remembered the words of the
specter from the night before, and she knew. "Nobody
ever threw the coins away before. He said that. He's
been denied, but not like that. Not so completely."

"So, what are we saying, the Ferryman liked your
spunk?" David asked, incredulous. Then he softened.
"Not that I blame him. And it makes a certain amount
of sense. While you were talking about . . . what happened to you, and the baby and all, I was thinking.
Something disturbing occurred to me.

"Something *else* disturbing, I should say."

Janine frowned and studied his face, saw pain in
his eyes.

"These people I've been seeing . . . the dead people from my past . . . I've got to figure he brought them back. Went and found them wherever they were and somehow brought them back from the dead, back to the world. He's tormenting me. Even trying to kill me. And there's something else. The witnesses who saw the guy that killed Spencer? The description matches my grandfather."

Janine shook her head with a frown. "But . . . why?"

"This . . . creature. This monster. If it loves you, maybe it thought it was doing you a favor, or maybe it thought Spencer was in the way. Why else would Themeli have run me off the road? Why did they try to kill me last night? It's the only thing that makes sense. Anyone who cares about you, anyone you might turn to, competition for your affection . . . Charon wants you all to himself."

A horrible, icy chill spread through Janine's gut, and her eyes slowly widened. Though there was no way Detective Kindzierski could have known what was really going on, David had just unconsciously echoed the policeman's words. She looked at Father Charles, hoping he would argue the point, but he nodded.

Father Jessup cleared his throat. "It does make a certain sense, if my theories about Charon are correct."

"My mother," Janine whispered.

"I know," David said, and he reached out to clasp her hand firmly in his own. "But there's more to it than that. Themeli and my grandfather came after me. But if this 'Jill' really is Maggie Russell . . ."

"Annette," Janine said slowly. "David? What do we do?"

Father Charles stood up quickly. He reached across the table and clutched his old teacher's hand. "I'm sorry, Father, but we've got to go. A friend may be in danger."

"Go, Hugh," Father Jessup replied fondly. Then he

glanced around at them as they all rose from their chairs. "Please let me know how this all turns out. It represents everything I've believed for so very long. In the meantime, go with the knowledge that whatever you want to call Him, however you want to picture Him, God is there.

"I will pray to Him for you."

Annette lifted her chin and let the shower spray her face. Steam swirled around her and water ran in hot streams down her body. As she stood there, Jill reached around from behind her and languourously soaped her breasts and belly with a bar of soap. Annette relished her lover's touch and arched her back. She half turned and Jill quickly kissed her, blond hair darkening with the water.

Her hands slid down Annette's belly, fingers sliding between her legs, and she gasped a tiny moan into Jill's open mouth.

The water beat a rhythmic massage down upon them and the steam swirled into a cloud above. Annette turned fully, retrieved the soap from Jill's hands, and began to return the favor, washing her lover slowly and gently, yet with a quiet, burning urgency that she had never felt before.

Not love, she reminded herself. *Maybe. And if not . . . God, who cares what it is?*

Grinning, she glanced up to find Jill's eyes filled with sadness. She could not be sure in the spray from the shower, but Annette thought she might be crying. Jill held her gaze a moment, then glanced away, her beautiful mouth twisted with despair.

"Jill?" Annette asked, taken aback by the sudden shift. "Honey, what is it?" She slipped her hands behind Jill's back and gave her a little shake. "Hey."

Jill glanced up at her briefly with an expression of such profound regret that it broke Annette's heart.

"What did I do?" Annette asked softly, unable to keep her pain out of her voice.

"You?" Jill asked, her voice cracking with bitterness. Then she shook her head, her long hair pasted in thick, wet strands on her shoulders and chest and back. "Nothing. You're . . . you're the greatest thing that's ever happened to me."

Annette flinched. "I don't understand."

At last Jill straightened up and met her gaze. She reached out and pushed her fingers through Annette's short, spiky, sodden hair. "I love you, Annette. I want to make sure you know that."

Though her heart beat wildly at those words, and she realized that she had indeed hoped to hear them, Annette did not let them distract her. "That's a reason to be upset? Is it such a tragedy, to be in love with me?"

Again, Jill could not face her. "You have no idea."

Annette stared at her as the spray pounded them both. All the eroticism of their shower together had dissipated, carried away on the steam or down the drain with the soapy water.

"I don't want to," Jill whispered.

"Don't want to love me?" Annette asked, stricken by the words.

Then Jill looked up, but this time she was not looking at Annette. Rather, she stared past Annette, through the smoky glass into the bathroom beyond. Annette was confused, and more than a little distraught herself. Then she noticed the soft green glow on her lover's face.

"I don't want to," Jill said again, her voice barely a whisper.

Slowly, Annette turned. Through the faceted glass door she could see a dark figure standing just outside the shower, some kind of green light in its hand.

"Damn you!" Jill cried out, with a shriek that sounded as if had torn up her throat.

As Annette turned back toward her, Jill grabbed her around the throat with both hands, slammed her against the tiled wall of the shower, and began to squeeze. Her hands were impossibly strong. Annette's eyes widened and the curtain of water separated her face and her lover's, even as Jill cut off her air.

Annette tried to gasp for breath, tried to call out, to scream in fury, to plead for some explanation. Her eyes darted to one side to peer out through the glass again, desperate and confused. The dark figure was gone, as was the green light.

Her vision began to dim. Multicolored spots on her eyes gave way to a momentary darkening. Oddly, her skin felt supersensitive, as though she could feel every line of grout in the tile against her back, every pin-prick of water upon her chest.

She still held the soap in her hand, but it slipped from her grasp and thumped to the floor.

Jill leaned in, her face pushing through the curtain of shower spray, and Annette saw grief in her eyes. Even as Annette began to weaken, Jill pushed in further and her lips brushed Annette's.

"I'm so sorry. I loved you," Jill whispered.

Something inside Annette snapped. A rage swept through her unlike anything she had ever known. With whatever life remained in her, she struck out at her lover's face and arms, but she was already too weak.

Her legs gave out and she collapsed toward the glass. Jill tried to hold her up, but the water and the soap on her body made her skin slick. With one last effort, all that remained to her, Annette reached out and grabbed a fistful of Jill's long, wet hair. Jill tried to pull back, but lost her balance.

Together, in a twine of limbs, the lovers crashed through the door of the shower stall in a barrage of shattered glass. Annette's back hit the toilet but she barely felt the pain of the impact. It served to turn them around, however, and so it was Jill who landed on the glass instead of her.

Jill cried out, but she did not bleed.

Annette gasped, hot air burning her throat as she gulped it down. But weakened as she was, she felt as though she were moving underwater. She began to get to her feet, barely feeling the small pieces of glass that cut her, but Jill was upon her in an instant.

"Why do you have to make it so hard?" Jill pleaded. "I never . . . I never wanted this."

With a grunt, she struck Annette across the face. Annette's head rocked back and struck the toilet tank. Her ears began to buzz, and she thought she heard a kind of hammering somewhere.

She waited for the next blow, but it did not come.

Ears still ringing, she glanced up. Jill stood over her. Tears streamed down her cheeks and she shook her head, then gazed down at her own hands.

"No," she said.

Her face was etched with agony, a sadness that welled up from deep inside her, that went to the bone. Trembling, Jill reached out for her face and Annette flinched.

"Oh, God, send me back already!" Jill wailed. "Nothing's worth this."

The hammering sound came again and they both truly heard it for the first time. Then there was a thunderous, splintering bang, followed by shouts and the pounding of footfalls from the living room. Voices crying out her name.

Annette could not respond.

She did not need to.

The bathroom door was not locked. As Jill backed toward the ravaged shower stall, hot water still pouring down, steam swirling around them, obscuring the mirror with moisture, the door slammed open.

Janine stood just outside the door with David beside her. Someone else was there as well, but Annette could not really see through the steam that rushed out into the hall. Sobs began to rack her nude body, and for the first time, she truly felt the cuts on her feet and back and arms, and the pain in her throat.

"David," Jill said. A dark look crossed her features.

"Maggie," David replied. "Keep the fuck away from her. She's done nothing to you."

"You fucker!" Jill . . . Maggie . . . shouted. "I never

wanted this. It's all on you. You didn't even cry after you killed me, David!" she screamed in anguish. "You didn't even cry."

It was a standoff, then. Nobody wanted to move. Jill did not try to attack her again, but David and Janine seemed so stunned, so horrified, that they froze there, just inside the door.

Then the figure Annette had not been able to see, out in the hall, pushed his way through into the bathroom. Father Charles was dressed in priestly garb, all in black, his white collar a spot of purity beneath a grim, stern visage. He wore a silver crucifix on a chain and held a leather-bound Bible in one hand.

Jill laughed. "I'm not a vampire, priest. What the hell do you think you can do to me? I'm already in hell, don't you get it?"

"You do not belong here, Maggie Russell. Your presence is a blasphemy in the eyes of God. If you truly are Maggie Russell, you'll know that. Do not let this creature mold your soul, Maggie. It will make you a monster. You know this isn't hell. You can still be forgiven."

"Bullshit!" Maggie screamed.

She raised her arms over her head, her body perversely beautiful, despite what she had done, despite the shards of clouded glass that jutted from bloodless wounds all over her body.

"All I wanted was my life! Another chance!"

Annette stared at her in horror. This woman . . . Maggie . . . glanced down at her, lost and alone and in pain. Damned.

"This isn't life," Maggie whispered.

She stepped through the shattered glass door and into the shower. Tendrils of steam seemed to wrap around her and droplets of water bounced off her skin as the spray cascaded over her again.

Janine rushed to Annette's side and crouched by her, cradling her gently. But Annette's attention was on the girl in the shower.

Maggie melted.

As the shower rained down upon her, Maggie's body turned to water, mixed with that spray, and swirled down into the drain. The shards of glass that had jutted from her wounds broke into even smaller bits as they fell to the tile floor.

Annette stared at the empty shower, at the water flowing in circles toward the drain.

Father Charles began to pray.

CHAPTER 15

It should be dark out, David thought. He sat on the couch in Annette's apartment and stared out the windows at the long afternoon shadows falling over Medford Square.

Shit like this isn't supposed to happen during the day.

But he knew that sort of thinking came from movies and television, and what was happening around them wasn't a movie. Movies could not kill you. They didn't run you off the fucking road or choke your best friend half to death in the shower.

"Jesus," he whispered to himself.

Annette was off in her bedroom getting dressed. She had taken Janine with her because she did not want to be alone, not even for a second. The only other person in the room was Father Charles, who stood with his arms crossed like an angry parent and stared at nothing as though he'd gone catatonic.

He twitched when David spoke, a sign of life, and then actually glanced over at him.

"I hope that was a prayer, my friend. I'd say we're going to need some."

David nodded slowly, out of respect for the man. It did make sense to him, though. For if Father Jessup's insane theories were true, if faith, simple belief, was what created the world's deities and their minions, prayer might actually be the only weapon they had. Yet what would they pray for? That Charon had never been created?

The Ferryman's very existence proved that faith endured. What once was worshipped could not be erased except by time and circumstance.

"How do we fight something like this?" David asked, surprised to find his voice steady and strong.

Father Charles began to reply, but then his gaze flicked toward Annette's bedroom. David rose from the couch and turned to see the two most important people in his life, his lover and his best friend, coming into the living room. Janine was pale, shaken, but she was being strong for Annette, who was a wreck. Her eyes, always so bright, seemed dull and lifeless to David now. Annette seemed tiny, dressed in jeans and a sweater, with Janine's arm around her.

David went to her. Annette gazed up at him, searching his eyes for something, perhaps strength. Whatever it was, she seemed to find it, for she nodded once as if to silently reassure him that she would be all right. There were bruises on her throat, and several small cuts on her skin, but beyond that, she seemed all right.

"I'm sorry, Elf. Sorry you got caught up in this."

There was so much more he should have said, but Annette was well aware of what this truth had cost her: love, and trust, and a taste of happiness. The last thing he wanted to do was rub it in, even unintentionally.

Annette reached out to lay a hand upon his chest. "This . . . Maggie?"

David nodded.

With a sad shake of her head, Annette turned to include the others. "Janine's told me a lot about what you've all got figured out."

"What we think we've got figured out," David corrected.

Annette nodded. "All right. And an hour ago I'd have said you were out of your fucking minds." Her eyes flicked toward Father Charles. The barrier that she always put up between them was still there, but perhaps not quite so solid now. "Except you, padre. I would have found a more polite way to call you crazy. Now, though . . . it all sounds a little too logical to me, now that I've got all the pieces of it in front of me. But here's what I don't get. Jill . . ."

Her expression tightened painfully and she took a breath. "Maggie. This Maggie . . . what the hell is she? She turned to water, you guys. And excuse me again, Father, but what the fuck is up with that?"

For a moment it was so quiet David could hear the clock ticking on the wall and the sound of music coming down from the apartment above them. His heart broke for her just then, for though somehow Annette had found the strength to face this thing with them and not simply shatter, he knew that it had to be a near thing.

They all looked to Father Charles for an answer. The priest raised his eyebrows, and then sighed.

"I don't know," he said. "I'd say there's plenty of room for speculation, however. Maybe these things are just manifestations from David's subconscious mind—"

"No," David said quickly. "That was Maggie. Didn't you hear the pain in her voice? And I saw my grandfather. It's him."

"The . . . the girl I was with wasn't just some mirage," Annette added, a bit of defiance in her voice, as if daring the priest to bring her sexual preference into the equation.

"All right. All right," Father Charles said slowly. "Perhaps, then, if Charon is really bringing these . . . spirits . . . back from the underworld, he's somehow created bodies for them out of water. This sort of wild speculation is not my bailiwick, my friends. I've always indulged Father Jessup's expeditions into logic and theology, but this . . . I'm as baffled as you all are. Still, water is Charon's element, isn't it? So that's a bit of logic in itself."

"But why would they do it?"

Janine had asked the question, and they all turned to look at her. She sat on the arm of the couch hug-ging herself as if cold. Her eyes were distant, and David knew that her mind was working, turning it all over, trying to make sense of it.

"Good question," Annette said. Then she glanced at David. "Why would they?"

A chill ran through David. He felt their eyes upon him and turned away, strode toward the window. Pain and guilt began to boil over inside him, but they had been simmering there for some time . . . since the truth of all this had begun to present itself. He planted his hands against the window and the glass was cool, soothing.

Outside, the sky had begun to darken as the day slid toward dusk.

That would be better. It would be right, he thought.

A prickle of heat ran across the back of his neck, as though he could feel their attention on him, and he closed his eyes.

"You're wondering how my grandfather could kill someone. He killed Spencer, right? And Steve Themeli tried to kill me. Twice. And Maggie . . . God, poor Maggie. I can't tell you if my grandfather ever killed anyone else, except in the war. I guess what's important is that he has always hated me. Even when I was little, he hated me. He was a sadistic old fucker even then.

"You all know what happened with Maggie. She died because of me.

"And Themeli? I wanted to help him get off drugs and I tried to reach out to him, and when I couldn't help . . . I turned him in. I thought even if he went to jail, at least he'd stay alive. Maybe it'd just be rehab, maybe not, but one way or another, he'd have a chance to get clean. He was stabbed in jail, died there.

"So they all have reason to hate me. Somehow Charon found them, gave them a chance to hurt me. Maybe to drive me away from Janine or maybe to kill me to get me out of the way."

His eyes opened. It had grown even darker outside,

the night coming on inexorably, sucking the life from the day. David could see the reflections of his companions in the glass. All three of them were staring at him.

"I never knew that about Themeli," Janine said, her voice low. "You never told me."

"It wasn't something I was proud of," David confessed.

"But it was the right thing. You tried to help. It wasn't your fault," Janine went on.

David knew that. It didn't help.

Annette went to him, leaned against the wall between the windows. He could see her staring at him in his peripheral vision and his gaze was at last drawn away from the window. David turned toward her.

"Hey," Annette said. "For . . . for what it's worth, Maggie doesn't want to be here now. She said some things that have me thinking maybe this Charon offered her something to do this. Maybe offered it to all of them. All right, they weren't hard to convince, but . . ."

She shrugged.

Father Charles cleared his throat noisily. Though he had seemed as disturbed as they all were by what had happened, what they had seen, he had gained some of his dignity back. There was power in the symbolism of his priestly garb, and he stood straight and noble as he regarded them now.

"It's possible he offered to let them stay when he was through with them."

"God," Janine whispered. "Can he do that?"

She moved to David and slipped into his arms. It felt so good to him to have her there, as if the two of them together were somehow safer, stronger. It wasn't true; not really. He knew that. But it felt true, and he thought maybe that was enough. It was about faith, after all.

"I guess he can do just about anything," Annette said, her voice haunted.

"Not anything," Father Charles said confidently. "He can't kill."

"What about Spencer?" David replied, frowning. "What about—" But he stopped midsentence. He was going to mention Janine's mother, but did not want to hurt her. From the look in her eyes, however, she had gotten his meaning. She flinched and glanced away.

Father Charles walked across the room, deep in thought. He spoke as if to an empty room, as though they were not there at all.

"The Ferryman hasn't killed anyone yet. Your grandfather killed Spencer. The attempts on your life, David, and on yours, Annette, were made by these . . . revenants of his. If all that we've theorized is true, what would happen if a creature responsible for shuttling human souls from this plane to another were to start killing people?"

David frowned, not sure where the priest was going with that.

But Janine got it. A tiny "hunh" escaped her lips. David glanced down at her.

"Well," she said, "if he exists, it stands to reason that there are other things like him, some kind of hierarchy. Call 'em angels if you want to. Whatever this enormous God-being is, it might not notice if Charon starts to kill people. But these other things, the things that are supposed to watch out for humanity's well-being, to guide our souls . . . they might have a problem with that."

"Excellent," Annette said.

They all looked at her. She shrugged.

"Hey, it has a weakness. That's good, right? I mean, okay, he's in love with Janine. In love enough to torment her and do all this shit. But he can't kill anybody."

"Unless he stops caring about the consequences," David said, his voice low, almost hating himself for saying it.

"Thanks for that thought," Annette snapped.

Several moments of silence ticked past before Janine spoke. "So what now?"

"I want to call Father Jessup again," Father Charles said. "And possibly some old friends from my days in seminary who also gave his theories a bit more credence than the Church would like. I'll have to pose the questions hypothetically with them, of course. But we may be able to learn something."

"Good," David said. "You can do that from my place. Take some clothes, enough for a few days away from home. We'll stop at Janine's, then the rectory."

"Why your house? He's already been there," Annette reminded him, a frightened look in her eyes again.

"He's been here. He's been to Janine's. I doubt there's anyplace he can't be. But we've got to figure out what we're going to do about this . . . figure out if there's anything we *can* do about it. Anyway, my house is the only place big enough for us all to stay together."

"And we've *got* to stay together, protect each other," Janine added. Her eyes locked on Annette's.

"We're all targets now."

The thing that amazed Kindzierski most about David Bairstow's neighborhood was how quiet it was. Medford wasn't exactly Boston or Cambridge, and there were plenty of well-groomed side streets, but the city was usually pretty active. On Briarwood Road, though, with the tall trees all around and the river not too far off, they might have been in New Hampshire, it was so peaceful.

Peaceful was bad. It lulled him, made his eyelids droopy, and he yawned in spite of the surplus of Dunkin' Donuts coffee he held between his legs in the biggest travel mug on God's green Earth.

He was parked three houses down and on the opposite side from Bairstow's in an aging Toyota he'd borrowed from the pool. The view of the front door and driveway was decent, and he had not dared park any closer during the day. Now that it was dark, he'd thought a dozen times about moving up, but did not want to draw the attention of the neighbors. Better to just stay put, see what turned up.

So far, nothing at all.

While it was still light out, he had been able to read the sports page and a film magazine he'd brought with him. Now that it was dark, though, Kindzierski simply sat and stared at the house up the street. The window was down and the night had grown cool. His light jacket was just enough so that he was not cold, and the air felt good on his face, helped keep him awake.

The coffee, though, wasn't helping. He had more than two hours to go before Simmons would arrive to take a shift on surveillance, and he did not want to have to leave his post to piss, so he was nursing the huge mug.

Boredom was the biggest enemy on a surveillance gig. Kindzierski knew that from long experience. A couple of times, on past details, he had actually fallen asleep briefly. Fortunately, both times he had woken up pretty quickly and hadn't missed anything vital, as far as he could tell.

As he sat and watched Bairstow's house, he fought to avoid falling asleep a third time. With the quiet neighborhood and the pleasant weather, though, it was a tough fight. The only thing that saved him was that as soon as it began to get dark, the frequency of cars down Briarwood increased, people coming home from work. Each time a fresh set of headlights lit up his windshield, Kindzierski went on alert, and a bit of adrenaline shot through his system.

But, so far, none of those cars had been Bairstow.

It was his case, and Kindzierski couldn't get the kind of manpower he would have needed to stake out both of the people he wanted to keep an eye on—Bairstow and his girlfriend, Janine Hartschorn—so he had been forced to choose. Instinct made him go with Bairstow. Hartschorn had a stalker, maybe that was true, but twice, someone had supposedly tried to off her boyfriend.

Kindzierski didn't have the first clue as to what was

actually going on, but he had a very strong suspicion that at least one if not both of them knew a hell of a lot more than they were letting on. Maybe the Hartschorn woman had a stalker; maybe she didn't. Bairstow could be the guy, might even have trashed his own place, but he sure as hell had not run himself off the road. He hadn't killed Spencer Hahn, either.

At the moment, though, Kindzierski was mainly concerned with only one part of this bizarre tangle of interrelated events, and that was the disappearance of Ruth Vale. He had a pretty good idea Ruth Vale was dead, but if he was wrong about that, he would need to find her soon.

So he sat and sipped at his coffee and tried to keep his eyes open as the cool breeze carried the rich scents of spring into the car.

As it neared seven thirty, the flow of after-work traffic onto Briarwood dropped off to nothing. Despite the cool night, Kindzierski began to feel warm all over, and several times his eyes fluttered to stay open. His head began to bob as he tried to stay awake.

"Shit," he muttered as he sat up straight.

Though he was trying to quit—and knew it was more likely he would be noticed if he smoked in the car—he pulled a partially crumpled pack of cigarettes from his jacket pocket and lit up. The nicotine gave him an instant rush and he stretched a bit. After a moment, he turned the key backward in the ignition, not wanting to start the engine but needing at least the temporary company of the radio. He did not want to drain the battery, so he would not leave it on for long. But a few minutes of classic rock would help him clear his head.

As he fiddled with the search buttons, trying to find a station to his liking, headlights washed across the windshield and he could hear the sound of an engine approaching. More than one, actually.

Kindzierski ground the cigarette out in the ashtray and slid down slightly in the seat so he could just see over the dash. Beneath the streetlights, he saw that the first car was the rental Bairstow had been driving. Both vehicles pulled into the teacher's driveway, and then Kindzierski got a good look at the second, a mid-nineties-model SAAB.

Doors opened. Bairstow and Hartschorn got out of the rental, then went around to the trunk where the woman retrieved a small suitcase. The driver of the other car was a petite woman with her blond hair cut short. Though he could not make out her features very well in the dim light from the streetlamps and from that distance, Kindzierski figured from what he could see that it had to be Annette Muscari. Bairstow and Hartschorn had been at her birthday party the night Spencer Hahn had been murdered.

The Muscari woman opened the back door of her SAAB and took out an overnight bag.

Whaddaya know? It's a sleepover.

Muscari was not alone, either. A tall man in a long black coat emerged from the passenger side of her car. This was new, and Kindzierski narrowed his eyes and cursed under his breath because he could not really make out the man's features. Muscari's boyfriend, maybe.

The man in black opened the rear passenger door and pulled out a small case as well. It was getting stranger by the moment. The women both lived nearby, in the same city even. Unless they were all having some kind of fucked-up sex party, Kindzierski could not imagine why they would all stay overnight at Bairstow's house.

The four walked up to the front steps together. Bairstow pulled out his keys and unlocked the door. As he did, the man in black turned to say something to Hartschorn, and Kindzierski got a better look at him. At his throat, the man wore the white collar of a Roman Catholic priest.

Kindzierski grunted softly in surprise. "Now what the hell is *that* about?"

To Janine, stepping into the foyer of David's house was always a little like stepping back in time. Despite the damage that had recently been done to it, the house was truly beautiful, and her memories of it were comforting. Though it had been violated, even worse than her apartment and Annette's had, the house felt safe to her somehow.

"It's a lovely place, David," Father Charles said as Annette closed and locked the door behind them.

"Thank you, Father. Though I have to confess, most of the furnishings were picked by my parents years ago. I just sort of keep it up as best I can."

Father Charles peeked into both of the front parlors, then went to stand by the grand staircase. "You grew up here, I know. But doesn't it ever seem too big for one person? I think I would get lonely in a place as big as this, by myself."

A twinge of sadness touched Janine and she glanced at David. He gazed back at her and a silent communication passed between them; he had never wanted to be alone in this house. More than anything, he had wanted to marry her. If she had not left him for Spencer, they might have been living here as a family even now, perhaps with children. None of this would have happened. She might never have lost her child.

But there was no blame in their tacit acknowledgment of that hard truth. David was not accusing her of anything. It was simply that they both now wished things had been different.

A small, ironic grin touched his features as he glanced back at the priest. "There have always been ghosts in the house, I guess. But up until now, they've been good company."

Father Charles did not seem to notice the awkwardness of that response, entranced as he was by his exploration of the house. He wandered off into the kitchen.

"Dibs on the turret room," Annette announced.

"God, you'll be freezing up there," Janine said. "It's not *that* warm yet."

David grabbed both their bags and moved toward

the stairs. "Actually, Elf, I'm thinking maybe we should all stay on one floor. The closer the better."

Janine expected Annette to fire off a volley of innuendo in response, but she said nothing. Her silence was disturbing. They were all afraid. Janine knew that. But she wanted to pretend as best she could that they could face this thing without crumbling. It was important for her to fake it, at least to herself.

After David had settled his guests in—Father Charles and Annette in the other bedrooms on the second floor and Janine in with him—they gathered in the dining room. The priest carried a stack of books he had retrieved from the rectory, as well as his small personal phone book. Among the books were Greek histories and mythologies, as well as several comparative theologies and a three-volume set on the belief in an afterlife.

"What are we looking for, exactly?" Annette asked.

Father Charles paused thoughtfully, his brow furrowed. After a moment he shook his head. "I wish I could narrow it down for you, but, really, anything on Charon. If there's a story or reference to him that indicates a weakness or how someone might avoid traveling across the Styx, that's the kind of thing we want. Even if it sounds ridiculous, it might have a deeper meaning from which we can draw something."

He stood and watched as they began to pick through the books, and tried not to reveal his own fear and anxiety. More than that, though, he tried to hide from them the awe that he felt at what they were dealing with . . . and what it meant.

In some way he was still trying to fully grasp this horror, the vicious creature who had visited erotic dreams upon Janine and had raised revenants from dead souls to torment David . . . in some way, it proved to him that there was indeed a God.

As a priest, he had always had faith.

But this was more than faith. This was truth. At

first he had thought that it made a mockery of his priesthood, made all the Roman Catholic dogma he was supposed to preach into nothing more than a flight of fancy. But while they had driven around, gathering clothing and books, and then driven over to David's house, something else had occurred to him. This meant not that what he had always been taught was bullshit, but that it was completely and totally true. And so was everything else.

What it meant for him, for his vocation as a priest, his calling . . . Father Charles could not say.

Let's live through this, and then I'll figure it out, he thought as he watched them begin to page through the books he had brought.

"I'm going to make those calls I mentioned," he said. "If I can manage not to come off like a complete lunatic, I hope to learn something."

All three of them laughed politely, but they were already intent upon their research, driven by their fear. There had to be an answer, a way to escape or destroy this creature. And they knew they had no choice but to find it. The other option was unthinkable.

Annette could hardly concentrate on the book in front of her. She kept having to reread paragraphs or even entire pages. The sting of the cuts on her skin was a distraction, but not because of the small pain they gave her. Rather, they were a reminder that created a constant undercurrent, a buzzing in her head like static on the radio, that brought her back to the shower. To Jill.

Not Maggie, but Jill.

She understood what was going on. Theoretically. But in her heart she knew that the woman . . . the girl . . . whatever this being was that had made love to her and tried to kill her and then transformed itself into water . . . she *knew* that Jill felt something for her. That *Maggie* felt something. Charon had ordered her to kill Annette, and Maggie had refused.

In her heart, Annette knew that was true, and it only made the pain worse. She ached more deeply than she had ever imagined possible, not because her love for this woman had been so profound—it hadn't had time to become that—but because of the tragedy of it all. The dead girl's pain, David's pain, and Annette's own. And Janine's as well, she could not forget Janine. No matter what she herself had been through, Annette knew that Janine had suffered most of all.

There in David's dining room, with what remained unbroken of the crystal and china on display in beautiful cabinetry, a dark wooden table that gleamed with polish before them, lights sparkling in the chandelier above, they seemed an entire world away from the terrible events at her apartment. And yet somehow *this,* the normalcy of this room, seemed like the dream to her, and the terror and grief that echoed in her mind seemed like the waking world, the reality that they would be forced to return to all too soon.

The thought made her shudder.

"Hey," Janine whispered.

Annette looked up to find both of them, her best friends, watching her.

"You doing all right?" David asked gently. "I mean, considering?"

"Considering?" Annette replied with a grim chuckle. "All things considered, I think I'm doing fucking smashing, don't you?"

They all smiled tiredly at the dark humor in her voice. David shook his head, looked at her another moment, and went back to his book. Janine gazed at her a moment longer, and Annette could see the love in her eyes. The warmth of it was almost more than she could bear. There was no use wondering what the world would have been like if things were different, but still, nothing meant more to her than what she saw in Janine's eyes just then.

They had all lost far too much recently, and yet they had survived. She had an idea that the one thing none of them could survive the loss of was each other.

A thought whispered across her mind and she glanced again at David. After a moment, he seemed to feel her gaze on him and looked up.

"Annette?"

"Sorry," she said. "I was just thinking about Ralph, you know?"

"What about him?"

"Well, he came back for you, didn't he?" Annette said. "I mean, think about it. I know you're hurting, David, with all this shit. But Ralph was dead. Who knows how it happened, but somehow, over there, maybe when he was passing over or whatever . . . somehow he knew what was going on."

"Maybe Charon approached him," Janine suggested.

Annette nodded. "I'll bet he did. Everyone thought you two hated each other, David. Everyone except Father Charles, that is. So maybe Charon asked him, 'Hey, Ralph, come help me fuck with David Bairstow and you can hang out on Earth a while longer.' But the thing is, Ralph told him to screw, then found a way to come back as a ghost or phantom or whatever and *warn* you. I've just been thinking that ought to count for something, y'know? All these people are haunting you, but we all have relationships that turn bitter in our lives, we all fuck up, make enemies we never even understand how we made.

"But Ralph Weiss came back for you."

David nodded slowly, a melancholy smile on his face. "Thanks, Annette. Thank you."

As Annette watched, Janine reached out and squeezed David's hand. They locked eyes for a moment; then David sighed and they all drifted back to the books in front of them.

After a time, Father Charles came in and cleared his throat.

"Hey, padre, what've we got?" Annette asked.

The priest swallowed, then shook his head slowly.

"Nothing, I'm afraid. Father Jessup's theories are

merely that, theories, and he knows nothing more specific about Charon. The others I spoke to thought I needed time off. And I don't suspect you're going to find anything in those books, either. Needless to say, I waltzed around this subject as best I could, but nobody has ever heard of anything like it. I asked an old friend, a Greek Orthodox theologian who also knows his mythology, how you would stop a creature out of legend, like the Medusa or what have you, if it wanted to hurt you. I asked hypothetically, of course. He reminded me that Medusa was defeated by having her own power turned against her. Her own reflection turned her to stone. Somehow, though, I doubt we're going to be able to drown Charon the Ferryman."

"Shit," David said, his voice low.

"That's what I said," Father Charles replied.

"Wonderful. The priest is swearing. That's a great fucking sign," Annette muttered.

They were all silent for several moments after that. At length, Janine rose from the table.

"I'm going to check in with Larry, see if he's heard anything from the police about my mother."

A now familiar dread had seeped into Janine as she had listened to Father Charles speak. Now she went upstairs to David's bedroom and picked up the phone, barely aware of what she was doing.

Escaping, she thought. It was not only that she wanted privacy to speak with her stepfather. It was that she was running away from the ominous truth the priest had revealed without actually speaking the words.

They were fucked.

Nothing, not even a clue how to deal with Charon. No way to defeat him. He could come for them at any time. In truth, she wondered why he had not done so already.

Distraught, she wandered the second-floor corridor as she dialed the number of the Parker House. The front desk rang Larry's room for her, and as she listened to it buzzing in her ear, her eyes chanced upon the stairs that led up to the third floor.

Escaping, she thought again. And what better place than the one to which David had always retreated to think, or to be sad, or simply to relax or wax nostalgic.

The first time they had made love, years earlier, had been in the turret room. David was not the only one who felt safe there. The urge to retreat there now was too much for her to resist.

Janine went up the steps to the third floor.

"Hello?"

"Larry, hi."

"Janine. Have you—"

"No, no. I just . . . I wanted to check in with you. So you haven't heard anything either?"

A pause. In his silence she had her answer, and she could hear all the pain that he would never put words to.

"Nothing. I talked to the police again, and they're looking into it. I've got people putting flyers up. And I was on the news tonight. Channel five."

"I didn't see it," Janine told him as she reached the third floor. "But that's great, Larry. If anyone saw her, they'll call."

It sounded hollow even to her, and Larry didn't respond.

"Anyway, look, I just wanted to tell you I'm at David's. Do you have a pen?"

As he searched for something to write with, she wandered around the third floor. It was chilly up there, and the rooms were little more than storage space, which she thought was a shame. In the back of her mind, Janine could not look into those rooms without seeing children's bedrooms, even a study room, or a sort of rec room for the kids she hoped to one day have with her lover.

She squeezed her eyes closed as she thought of the child she had carried in her belly, the one who had died. The one she had wanted to name David. Janine bit her lip and pretended that the numb, dead space inside her was only temporary, that it would go away.

"Okay," Larry said.

She gripped the phone a little tighter as she gave him David's phone number. There was an awkward moment before they hung up, as though each of them knew there was something missing, some endearment they ought to trade before signing off, but their relationship had never included that, and so eventually they said only good-bye.

With a sigh, Janine turned and walked up the few steps to the turret room, with its windows all around, its view of the night and the moon and the stars.

Her mother's corpse lay sprawled in a chair, positioned in a grotesquely lifelike fashion. Ruth Vale's eyes were wide and staring, almost completely white, and her mouth was slightly open as though in shock. Her flesh was blue and bloated, her skin the texture of raw dough, as though she had drowned and then been dredged up days later.

"Mom," Janine whispered, her throat burning with the word. "Oh, God, Mom."

As if to make certain it was not a ghost before her, or some abhorrent hallucination, she reached out to touch her mother's arm. At that gentle prodding, the corpse's head sagged to one side and stagnant water poured out of her mouth.

Someone screamed.

It took a moment for Janine to realize that the voice was her own.

CHAPTER 16

๛

Kindzierski jerked awake, banged his knee on the underside of the Toyota's dashboard, and swore loudly. Then he frowned deeply, blinked a few times, and listened to an echo that lingered only inside his head. He had turned off the radio so as not to drain the battery, and the street outside was quiet, almost eerily so.

Silence.

But a moment before, there had been a scream. It had cut through the veil of half sleep behind which he had retreated. Even while dozing, his mind was attuned, listening for something out of the ordinary.

A scream fit the bill.

"What the fuck was that?" Kindzierski muttered, rubbing his sore knee.

He bent forward to peer through the windshield at David Bairstow's house just up the street. Some of the lights were on, but nothing seemed out of the ordinary. In the windows of the turret room at the peak of the house, shadows moved in partial darkness, a zoetrope of flickering motion, but he could not make out any more than that.

Still, the sleep-memory of the scream was fresh in his mind, and it had not been a dream. Of that he was certain.

Even as he mentally cataloged the various excuses he might use for dropping in on Bairstow unannounced, Kindzierski grabbed the keys from the ignition and stepped out of the Toyota. He craned his neck, trying to get a better view of the turret room, but could not. It was simply too high.

Reluctant to reveal to the subjects of his surveillance that he had been observing them, he knew that he had no choice but to investigate that scream. It was possible that it might have come from another house, but every instinct he had honed during his years on the job told him that was just whistling in the dark. His scalp tingled as though an illicit lover had been running her fingers through his hair, and his stomach felt as though he'd swallowed half a dozen live goldfish.

Something was going on.

Kindzierski bounced on his feet several times before finally making up his mind. Then he strode across the street and began to walk along the sidewalk toward Bairstow's place.

Two houses away, he halted and shook his head, disgusted by his own foolishness. Whatever lame excuse he might make up to explain his sudden appearance at the door, it wasn't likely to be convincing if he left his car parked down the street. Somehow his error seemed to increase his anxiety, for he hurried now as he jogged across the road toward his car, a big man in a dark leather jacket who was obviously a stranger to the neighborhood. Too conspicuous, yet somehow he was no longer worried about attracting unwanted attention.

The door was locked.

Kindzierski cursed himself in a low voice and fished his keys out again. He had programmed himself to always lock the car. Usually it wasn't a big deal, but more and more, a dark urgency filled him.

He slipped the key into the driver's door and unlocked it.

Then he froze. A shudder scurried up and down his spine. Kindzierksi frowned, wondering where the sensation came from. It did not go away, either. Instead it lingered like skunk scent, carried to him on some malevolent wind. But it wasn't an odor. It was a feeling. And there was no wind. In that moment there was no breeze, no rustling of leaves in the trees, not even the distant barking of dogs.

Headlights washed over him where he stood by the driver's door of the Toyota, but Kindzierski had heard no engine. Though he knew he ought to pretend he was leaving, get in the car and watch the other car pass from inside, something stopped him. Drew him with as much magnetic pull as a strikingly beautiful woman or the wreckage on the side of the highway after a car accident.

He turned, blinking away the brightness of the lights as the car slowed soundlessly to a stop in front of David Bairstow's house. It was only when the headlights snapped off that something else occurred to him: The engine had made no noise at all.

With the headlights off, Kindzierski could make out the vehicle. It was a brand-new powder blue Lexus, just like the one Ruth Vale had been driving when she disappeared.

Get in the car, he chided himself. *Watch from the fucking car.*

But he couldn't look away. The doors on Ruth Vale's car opened, and three men stepped out. Even from that distance, Kindzierksi suspected he knew who they all were. The driver was a black-haired kid, maybe eighteen, who perfectly matched Bairstow's description of the driver who had forced him off the road. The guy in the passenger seat was much older, late sixties at least. The old guy had white hair and a beard, but he didn't look a damn thing like Santa unless Santa had slimmed down and was seriously pissed off. He matched the eyewitness description of the man who murdered Spencer Hahn behind the wheel of his car in a Cambridge parking lot.

Riveted to the pavement, Kindzierski stared openly at them, almost guaranteeing that they would see him. In his mind, he scrambled frantically to put the pieces together, to try to figure out what the hell these people were doing at Bairstow's house, if it meant Bairstow was involved, or in trouble. But neither his astonishment nor his confusion accounted for the way he abandoned all common sense, not to mention his training as a police officer, and just stood there out in the open.

No, his seeming paralysis, the shutdown of the part of his brain that dictated logic and self-preservation, could be attributed to the third guy, the one who climbed out of the backseat and followed the other two across the driveway and the front lawn toward Bairstow's front door, none of them sparing even a glance for the linebacker-sized middle-aged cop in the leather jacket who stood staring at them sixty yards away.

The third guy was Spencer Hahn.

But Spencer-fucking-Hahn was dead, his throat slit by the white-bearded guy with whom he now seemed pretty damned chummy.

"Holy shit," Kindzierski whispered.

The sound of his own voice was the catalyst he needed. The astonishment that had frozen him shattered and he could move. A minivan came down the street from the other direction and with it the world came back to life. A door slammed somewhere nearby, and in the Federal Colonial his car was parked across from, the radio began to blare, much too loud.

Kindzierski hurried across the street again, picking up speed as the three men went up the front steps of David Bairstow's house. The other two hung back as if intimidated by the old man, who rapped angrily on the door. As he jogged faster, Kindzierski reached into his back pocket for the small leather wallet that held his badge. Almost unconsciously, he reached inside his jacket and unsnapped the tiny strap over his gun. He had always thought it strange how, with the strap on, he could forget all about the gun. Yet with it unsnapped, the sensation of danger emanated from the weapon all through him.

The old man knocked harder now, impatient. The

other two grinned at each other. Kindzierski's gaze was drawn again and again to Spencer Hahn. Someone in Cambridge P.D., never mind the M.E.'s office, had seriously screwed up.

No one in the house seemed to be responding to the knocking. The old man raised his fist a third time, but by then, Kindzierski had reached the edge of Bairstow's lawn, maybe forty feet away from them. He slowed to a walk, took two long breaths.

"Good evening, gentlemen. Can I help you with something?" the detective asked. He hung his badge out for them to see as he walked across the grass.

Hahn and the kid glanced up at the old man, who rolled his eyes as though he found Kindzierski's arrival tiresome.

"Get rid of him," the old man said.

Kindzierski frowned, but before he could even respond, Hahn and the kid started down the steps toward him.

"You picked a bad time to get curious, Officer. The wrong place. The wrong time," Spencer Hahn said.

There was something off about his voice, something bizarre. Like a ventriloquist drinking a glass of water while the dummy talked. But the observation had no time to take root in Kindzierski's brain. The two of them strode toward him with malice gleaming in their eyes.

The detective felt the ominous weight of his gun. He reached up and drew it with a speed he knew surprised anyone who saw him do it. These guys didn't even blink.

He leveled the gun at Hahn. "Not another step."

Hahn laughed as he swung a roundhouse punch. Kindzierski saw it coming, tried to dodge, but Hahn was faster than he looked. The blow rattled Kindzierski's cage, sent the cop sprawling back on his ass on the sidewalk. But even on the way down, Kindzierski controlled the fall, kept his gun firmly in his grip. His teeth clacked together as he landed and a scowl split his features. Both hands on his weapon now,

Kindzierski steadied the gun, its barrel ticking back and forth from Hahn to the gleefully grinning teenager who accompanied him.

Nearby, he could still hear the old man pounding on the front door of Bairstow's house. "Let me in, goddamn it! This is my house, you little shit!"

Kindzierski cocked the pistol, aimed at Hahn again. "I'm almost happy you did that," he said in a growl. "Take one more step and I will put a hole in your left shoulder."

"Boo!" Hahn whispered, both hands up as though it were a playground taunt. He took a small, almost dainty step toward the detective.

Kindzierski shot him in the left shoulder. The bullet slammed into Hahn, spun him halfway around. It should have dropped him. Even the kid stared at Hahn in disbelief as the man turned once again to Kindzierski, still grinning.

There was no wound on him, not even a hole in his jacket where the bullet had punched through.

"That was unique," Hahn said, fascination in his voice.

"Cool," the kid mumbled, staring at his associate. "Do it again."

Slowly, the two men turned their malevolent gazes upon Kindzierski again. The detective blinked several times in astonishment, but he was no fool. Hahn had no more than begun to step closer when Kindzierski fired again, this time into the man's leg. Something wet sprayed from the entry wound . . . and then the wound was gone. The bullet had been swallowed up instantly.

Kindzierski shot Hahn dead center in the chest, then through the forehead.

Hahn only laughed.

The detective's eyes were wide but he was numb all over. Part of him, the part that would have tried to make sense of the world despite the circumstances, seemed to have shut down entirely. Through the numbness, though, his fear remained. When Hahn reached out to grab him by the hair, Kindzierski closed his eyes like a small boy trying not to see the face at the window, to imagine away the thing under the bed.

Spencer Hahn was a dead man. Of course he could not be killed again. Gary Kindzierski had never backed down from a fight in his life. But this was not a fight. It was a visit from the bogeyman.

Kindzierski bit his lip, kept his eyes pinned shut, and silently prayed they would just go away. There were more bullets in his gun but he no longer had the strength to lift it. Then the decision was taken from him; the gun was torn from his hand. The detective's eyes snapped open just in time for him to see Hahn point the gun at him.

This isn't happening, Kindzierski vowed to himself.

His denial was not strong enough to stop the bullet. It went through his right eye and blew out the back of his skull.

Normal.

David meandered about his kitchen, searching cabinets for something to snack on. He had put a kettle of water on the stove, though he was still uncertain if its destiny was to become tea or hot chocolate. Father Charles had wandered off into the house, upstairs to his room perhaps. Annette sat hunched over the kitchen table, chin resting on her crossed arms, and watched David's quest.

There was something pitiful about it, he thought, this attempt of theirs to pretend this was all *normal*. The four of them, here in the house, with all the doors and windows locked up tight, behaving as though hiding out this way were perfectly reasonable.

But the alternative was panic, and that wouldn't do them any good. If there was a way to combat this thing, Father Charles would find it. David believed that, and he also believed that when morning came, it would help to give them all a new perspective. David had no idea why he believed that. After all, morning was a long way off, and even then, there was no reason to think the Ferryman was any less powerful.

But we won't be as afraid, he told himself. *The dark makes us like children.*

With a sigh, he leaned against the counter and stared at the contents of the open cabinet above the microwave. "What do you think?" he asked Annette. "Oreos or Pepperidge Farm goldfish?"

"Wow, talk about options," Annette replied, feigning boredom.

David smiled wanly as he drew the package of Oreo cookies down from the cabinet.

Far, far upstairs, Janine screamed.

For a moment, David and Annette both seemed to hold their breath. He glanced at her, paralyzed for what could only have been a single heartbeat but which seemed like so much longer. Then David raced from the room, the bag of Oreos dropping from his hand, splitting, spilling cookies and crumbs all over the tile. Annette was behind him by three or four paces, no more.

Hand on the railing, David took the steps two at a time. On the second-floor landing he saw Father Charles heading for the stairs to the third story. There was a grim expression on the priest's face that he envied, as though the clergyman had received a call to arms in a battle he had been waiting his entire life to fight.

David felt only fear. For Janine. For himself. Fear that all the madness that had been lurking in the shadows about them these past weeks had finally overcome them all.

They hurried up to the third floor, where Janine sat against one wall, hands in her lap, tears streaming down her expressionless face. David rushed past Father Charles and went to kneel by her.

"Janine. What happened? Was he here?"

Her lips pressed together as though she feared the words that might come out. One hand fluttered at the air, then came to rest over her mouth. Whatever had caused her scream, in that moment, it held such power over her that she could not speak of it.

"There's nothing here now," Annette said softly.

David sensed her behind him, was comforted by that presence. He knew that he had to be strong for Janine right now, but he did not know if he could have done that without Annette there to help him, to share his fear and his love for her.

He turned to face Annette, his hands resting gently on Janine's legs. "The other rooms?"

Father Charles started up the steps to the turret room. "No need. She was staring up here. Whatever was—"

The priest paused just inside the room and his words simply stopped coming. David felt too warm, suddenly, and damp.

"What is it?" he asked.

Father Charles came down from the turret and sat on the steps facing them. He gazed gently at Janine for a long moment before glancing at David again.

"There's a dead woman up there. She appears to have drowned."

"Drowned?" Annette replied, almost angrily. "How could . . ."

Her words trailed off as Father Charles and David both turned toward her. Annette cursed under her breath, looked as though she might say something more, and then hugged herself and moved to lean against the wall.

"Your mother?" the priest asked Janine.

She nodded, still mute. Then her eyes widened a bit and she shook her head. "Why?" she finally said. "I mean . . . why put her here?"

David reached out and touched her arm. "God, Janine, I'm sorry." She slid into his arms and he held her there. Her tears began again, but she did not sob. Rather, she stared past him at the entrance to the turret room and wept silently. David could think of nothing to do except hang on. He turned to glance at

Father Charles, but could not keep from staring past the priest, up into the darkened turret room.

"This isn't our world," he whispered, uncertain where the words had even come from.

Father Charles started. "What do you mean, David?"

He shrugged, released Janine, began to stroke her hair. Then he looked around at the others. "I don't know. I mean, listen to us. We're not questioning how Ruth died, or how a drowned woman ends up four stories off the ground. We've come so far from what we've always known to be true . . . it's like he's blurring the lines, pulling us into this gray place, like a no-man's-land between everything we've ever known and this netherworld where he exists, where he has power."

"It's *his* place," Father Charles agreed, his voice cold with certainty. "Between this world and the next, the physical plane and the spiritual, that's where the river flows. The river Styx."

"But this isn't the goddamn river!" Janine shouted abruptly, snapping off each word. "This is real, earth and stone and wood and . . . and flesh and blood. Our world. He doesn't even belong here!"

Out of the corner of his eye, David saw Annette stiffen. He glanced at her and saw alarm on her face. A deep frown on her forehead that almost erased the sweet, elflike cast of her features, she turned to gaze down the stairs toward the second floor.

"What was that?" she asked.

David only looked from Annette to Father Charles and back again, though his ears were now attuned, listening for any unusual noise. They all waited as though listening to the ticking of a clock.

"I didn't hear a thing," the priest said.

His words were followed by a distant, muffled thumping from below. Someone was banging on the front door. They all stared at each other, none of them wanting to move.

David stood abruptly, glanced at Annette, and a

wordless communication passed between them. She moved to stay by Janine's side as David ran up into the turret room. Father Charles stood aside to let him pass, then followed him up. To one side, Ruth Vale's waterlogged corpse slumped, eyes open and staring. Her mouth gaped, but within her distended lips there was a darkness deep enough that David had to force himself to look away from it. Water still dripped from her clothes and a stain had begun to spread across the floor.

He shook himself. Decisions about Ruth Vale's corpse were for later. Father Charles stood just behind him as David leaned over and peered out the window into the yard below. The first thing he saw was Detective Kindzierski. Then a couple of dark figures trotted toward him from the front of the house, where David could not see. One of them, he was sure, was Steve Themeli. They menaced Kindzierski, who drew his gun.

For just a second, the other man glanced up enough that the dim glow of streetlights lit his face.

"Jesus," David muttered. He glanced over at Father Charles. "That's Spencer Hahn."

"Apparently Charon is still recruiting," the priest said dryly.

Something in David's stomach rolled over, and he stepped back from the window. He had been unable to see the front step, to see whomever was pounding on the door, but he knew who it was. Grandpa Edgar and Steve Themeli and Spencer Hahn were dead . . . they were creatures of water now, lost souls crafted into undead things by Charon's power. Just like Maggie.

But Maggie wasn't there. He did not know what to make of that.

A gunshot split the night outside the house.

David swore again and stumbled back out of the turret room, ignoring Ruth's corpse now. Father Charles followed quickly.

"Wait," the priest said.

The two men faced one another, a kind of electric circuit locking them together. Another gunshot echoed outside, and then another.

"You can't help him," Father Charles said. "Not without letting them in."

"You're a priest, Hugh!" David snapped. "You can't just leave him out there!"

Father Charles did not waver even the slightest bit. "If I thought we could save him, I'd risk all our lives. You know that, David."

A fourth gunshot, this one dull, somehow distant.

Janine's tears were gone, and a kind of cold determination was etched upon her face when she stepped between them.

"He's right, David," she said. "Right now, the only thing we can do is try to keep them out. Keep Charon out until we can figure out how to destroy him."

"We haven't got the first fucking clue how to even fight him, never mind destroy him!" David snapped. He looked to Annette, trying to find someone who would listen to reason. "We're screwed if any of them get into the house. Unless someone feels like jumping out a second- or third-story window and trying to make a run for it."

"Not very likely," Father Charles said.

David bit his lip a second, then threw up his hands. "Shit!" he cried as he turned and started down toward the second floor. "Father, stay here with Janine. You're the only one with half a chance. Annette, help me!"

As though she could fly, she was suddenly behind him, crowding him as he hustled down. Ten steps from the first floor, they could hear the voice of David's grandfather roaring outside the door. It rattled on its hinges as he pounded furiously upon it, crying out vile, belittling slurs against his grandson between every blow.

At the bottom of the steps, David paused, the fear suddenly bounding out of the jungle of his mind with a ferocity he had never before experienced. It drove the breath out of him, made his knees weak, made him flinch with each thump against the door.

Wood splintered. The door frame.

Somewhere on the side of the house, a window shattered.

"They're coming in," Annette whispered at his side. "What do we do, David? They're coming in."

Her fingers twined with his, but David was frozen.

Janine stood in the third-floor hall staring at the gloomy stairwell where David and Annette had disappeared only a moment before. With a long, deep breath, she turned to face Father Charles. His auburn hair was graying, his face a bit too fleshy, and yet those seeming concessions to age did nothing to undermine the strength that she had always seen in this man. He was unsettled, yes. Afraid, but he'd be a fool not to be. But his eyes were strong and he held himself with a power given him by his faith.

She envied him that.

Janine pushed her dark hair away from her face, wiped drying tears from her cheeks, and stared at the priest.

"There's got to be something," she said, her voice a tired rasp. "Something you can do. Isn't there some . . . I don't know, some invocation or something you can do to keep him away?"

Her voice quavered and she knew how desperate she sounded. But desperate was exactly what she was.

Father Charles shook his head, the apology in his eyes before it ever reached his lips. "I'm sorry, Janine. I'm not a sorcerer; I'm a priest."

Janine sighed. She was about to reply when, out of the corner of her eye, she saw something move up in the turret room. Her lips parted and she felt her grief welling up in her again. There came a thump and something in that room slithered across the floor with a wet squelch.

"No," she said, shaking her head. "Not this."

Father Charles spun toward the steps that led up

into the turret room. Janine stared at the opening at the top of those steps, the half-open door. She had to turn away, knew that she could not bear to see the horrid thing, the wide-eyed, river-drenched corpse of her mother that she knew would emerge any moment at the top of those steps. But she could not move.

"Not this," she whispered.

The priest backpedaled, reached toward her without turning around, arm waving, gesturing for her to stay behind him.

With a wet laugh, the thing came down the steps. Hot bile rose in the back of Janine's throat but she choked it back down along with the scream that wanted to tear from her lips.

Mother?

But it wasn't her mother.

It was a thing shaped something like her mother, but made entirely of dirty river water. But her mother would never have accepted Charon's offer, any more than Ralph Weiss would have. It had no real cohesion, and could not even pretend to life like Maggie and the others. Just water, somehow coalesced into a monstrous form that came slowly toward them, dragging something heavy behind it.

Her mother's corpse. The vile thing, this creature of Styx, had been forged from the water in which her mother had drowned, now pulled from her clothes and from her lungs and from the stain around her body. Yet it was still connected to her by some hideous umbilical that strung from her dead mother's mouth to the head of the creature. It tugged her along and then Ruth Vale's dead body tumbled noisily, wetly, down those few steps.

At last, Janine could scream. But there was rage in her cry now, not merely grief and horror. Rage.

"By all that's holy . . ." Father Charles began.

"Do something!" Janine snapped at him. "Something! You're the one who's supposed to have the power here. You're the one with the faith."

The thing flowed across the floor toward the priest.

Janine knew he would be dead in an instant. Charon wanted to cut her off from anyone who cared for her, anyone who might help her. But the Ferryman would not risk her own death. While she was still alive, he might be able to sway her, but if she died . . . Charon's craft was not the only means of travel to the afterlife. Her death might put her out of his reach.

She threw herself at the undulating monster, and felt herself glide halfway through it, splashing. Then, suddenly, there was resistance. It pushed her away, but Janine blocked its path.

"You'll have to kill me!" she cried. "Do you hear that, Charon? I'll die first, and then where the fuck will you be?"

The filthy liquid thing drove against her, pushing her hard enough to drive her against the wall. An oceanscape painting fell off its nail.

Father Charles raised his right hand and quickly drew the sign of the cross in the air. He began to intone a prayer in Latin, rushing quickly through it but without tripping over a single word. The thing that drooled from her dead mother's mouth lurched back; then it flowed through the air, across the hall toward Father Charles, and struck the priest like a massive wave. It spun him around, tried to force its way down his throat. He gurgled out the last few words of the blessing.

Suddenly released from its form, the water splashed to the ground and flowed across the floor, harmless and inert.

Janine stared at the priest. "How did he do that?"

Father Charles spat dirty water from his mouth and pushed his wet hair back. "I don't know. The river he controls, Styx, isn't part of our reality. But this . . . I have no idea how far his influence extends."

A sudden squeal of strained wood and metal filled the hallway, accompanied by loud pops in the walls. Together, they turned toward the open bathroom door at the end of the hall, just in time to see the toilet and sink shattered as the pipes exploded. Porcelain tumbled down and cracked the floor tiles as water gushed from the exposed pipes.

Too much water. Too fast.

The lights flickered and went out, and Janine felt certain that the electricity had been shorted by water somewhere. The gleam from the streetlights came through the windows at the end of the hall, but then another light seemed to flicker to life, illuminating the third floor.

The water flowed, spread, became a river. Where the bathroom had been, the entire hall seemed to disappear, no longer a part of the house. It was a river that flowed beneath red stars like bloody wounds in the sky where the roof used to be. The house was still there, around Janine and Father Charles, but only ten feet away the floor became a river, water gushing up over the edge and soaking through her shoes.

Mist rolled across the surface of the river and within it, the sickly green glow of the Ferryman's lantern. Janine could hear the clanking of the lantern against the prow of the boat as he came near.

She squeezed her eyes closed. "It isn't real," she said. "He can't do this. No fucking way!"

She felt Father Charles's hand grip her arm. "What if he can? Maybe we're not even in our world anymore."

Janine opened her eyes. The river still flowed. The mist parted and Charon became visible, though still a distance away. Somehow, in spite of that distance, she could see the burning coronas around his enormous black pupils, and the blue lines marbling his flesh. She remembered the dreams of his hands on her, his cold lips suckling her breast, the way she had yearned in her dreams.

This wasn't a dream. But she would not allow it to be real, either.

Charon raised an arm and pointed at Father Charles. *"You try my patience, priest."*

His voice was cold, dead . . . but he came no closer. And that was when Janine knew.

"He's afraid," she said.

Father Charles started and glanced at her. "What?"

"You freaked him out!" she said, excited. "He's afraid."

"Soon, Janine Hartschorn," Charon said. *"Soon we will be together."*

"You're not even here!" she snapped.

Forget the water. Forget the mist. It's solid floor, a house, rooms I've been in a thousand times.

Janine ran toward Charon as though she could shoo him away like a flock of birds. Water soaked her feet, flowed past her ankles, but it was just the water from the pipes. She was certain.

She ran to the edge where the floor gave way to the river, and she fell, went under, arms lashing out around her, splashing and trying to find some purchase. Water filled her lungs quickly. Her fingers caught hold of the edge of the wooden floor and she pulled herself up, gasping.

The water surged up out of the river in ropy tendrils that snatched Father Charles and dashed him against the wall. The priest cried out in pain, but then he began to pray aloud in Latin.

"No!" Charon thundered.

Janine screamed for David.

The box windows in the front parlor on the first floor shattered and glass rained down on hardwood and carpet, along with a dull thump. In the foyer, only steps from the bottom of the grand staircase, David swore again.

"They're in," he said softly, mostly to himself.

Annette stared at him for just a second, alarm flaring in her eyes. Then she reached out to grab his hand and together they sprinted back up the stairs. On the second floor, they glanced back down. Grandpa Edgar stood in the foyer, staring up at them. The old man shook his head as though his grandson had performed some small, aggravating misdeed.

"Hello, Davey," he said, his voice deep and resonant, just as it had been when he was alive. "Might as well quit now, boy. Don't you think you've pissed me off enough as it is? You've never been much for the nasty stuff. Just all that goddamn whining."

In that moment, Spencer Hahn emerged from the front parlor. Steve Themeli appeared in the hallway coming out of the kitchen. It had been him smashing a window at the back of the house.

"Tell ya something, gents, when Davey was a kid, he whined so much he coulda driven Christ off the cross," Grandpa Edgar added.

All three of them grinned cruel, empty grins. David put an arm behind Annette and took off along the balustrade, hustling her along, headed for the door to the third-floor stairs. It hung open. Annette nearly fell as David rushed her up the stairs, then followed. He slammed the door closed, then slipped the dead bolt that locked it. He had installed the lock in high school, when he had wanted privacy up there on the third floor. With an errant mental whisper, he thanked the teenage boy he had once been.

David could feel Annette's hot, sweet breath on his neck. He glanced up at her. Her skin was pale, her eyes wide, and he thought she looked like a porcelain doll. But there was something there in her gaze, her pupils sharp as pins, that belied that apparent fragility. Annette was anything but fragile.

"What now?" she asked.

His eyes flicked upward, toward the third floor, where Father Charles and Janine waited with Ruth's corpse. Their situation was desperate. From where they were, there was no way out. Detective Kindzierski was likely dead, or at least so badly injured that he could not help them, and he had just locked them away from every phone in the house.

Desperate, he gripped the doorknob. "We hold them here. If we can't do that . . ."

"We're done," Annette said softly.

"Yeah."

The entire house seemed to groan and creak. A

loud knocking in the walls made them cringe, and David held on to the knob even more tightly. A loud clamor came from upstairs, a crash and a clatter, and the sound of rushing water.

Just as David turned to look up toward the third floor, water spilled over into the stairwell and began pouring down the steps in a small but powerful water-fall. A wave became a gush and soon it sprayed them as it fell, though they were all the way at the bottom.

With a loud pop, the house went dark, all the power going out at once.

"David," Annette said through gritted teeth. "I can't stand the dark."

A strange glow seemed to come down upon them from above, then, and when they looked up, they could see that water flowed past the top of the stairs. Janine shouted something angrily, and Father Charles began to recite in Latin.

Which was when the dead men, the hate-filled ghosts of David's past, began to pound on the locked door. The knob twisted, and he was not strong enough to hold it. It was banged upon, kicked, but the dead bolt held.

More water poured down the stairs.

From above, Janine screamed his name.

David glanced at Annette.

"Go!" she shouted.

For only a moment, he hesitated. Then Annette shoved him out of the way and gripped the doorknob herself, her jaw set with anger and determination. The echo of Janine's scream seemed fresh in his mind as David turned and ran up the steps to the third floor. At the top, his eyes were met with a sight that stopped him cold, forced him to grab the door frame to steady himself.

One half of the third floor had been sheared away and a river flowed in its place. Mist rolled across the floor and crimson stars burned in the sky. The Fer-ryman stood in the prow of his boat, one arm up as though to shield himself somehow.

Janine pulled herself out of the rushing river, drag-

ging her body onto the sodden floor of the hallway.
Father Charles stood over her, bruised, bleeding from
a large welt on the left side of his face. The priest
called out in a hoarse voice, Latin words that seemed
vaguely familiar to David. Then Father Charles made
the sign of the cross in the air before him.

"I'll see you on the water before long, priest!"
Charon rumbled.

But the river slowed, began to recede, revealing the
floor again, not so much beneath it as instead of it.

The Ferryman lifted the lantern from the prow of
the boat and raised it high. Its green flame blazed up,
and David, who had seen what it could do, cried out
to Janine and Father Charles to take cover. But this
assault was over. Charon blew out the green flame
and they were all thrown once more into darkness
broken only by the gleam of streetlights outside.

The river was gone. The mist. The Ferryman himself. Water still flowed uninterrupted from the burst
pipes in the bathroom, spreading across the floor and
spilling down the stairs, but it was merely water now.

David helped Janine up. She leaned on him as she
gazed around in amazement. Then she stared at Father Charles.

"You did it," she said. "You drove him away."

Father Charles nodded. "For now."

"How?" David demanded. "I mean, what did it?"

The priest shook his head. "I'm not sure. This isn't
his world. I don't understand how he can *intrude* upon
it so much. The only answer that makes any sense is
that he's anchored here somehow, and it isn't just his
obsession with Janine. Whatever this anchor is, it's
allowing him not only to be here, but to have a physical effect on our world. The way he can control the
water like that. There's no way to know how powerful
he is, but I get the feeling it's new to him, too, like
he's just finding out."

"That makes sense," Janine put in. "I mean, if he's
got some anchor here now, like you said, that's got to
be new to him. He's testing his boundaries."

"And ours," Father Charles replied with a grave nod of his head. "I'm beginning to think that every time he touches this reality, his ability to influence it grows a little stronger. He's trying to blur the lines between our world and his."

David was still reeling from what he had seen. He leaned against the wall and nodded slowly. "Oh, yeah, I'd call that a pretty major blur." Both hands came up and he covered his face, then slapped his cheeks as though trying to keep himself awake.

"Where's Annette?"

His head snapped up and he stared at Janine, then turned to look at the steps leading down to the second floor. David pushed off the wall and ran to the top of the waterfall stairs. The narrow stairwell itself was dark, but in the wan light from the windows on both floors he could see that the door was splintered in two, had been caved in, and lay in awkward ruins on the steps.

Annette was gone.

CHAPTER 17

༜

I'll see you on the water before long.

Janine knelt by her mother's body and stared into her dead eyes. A tear slipped down her cheek and she wiped it angrily away. She was through with crying. Her fingers encircled her mother's cold, still hand, and Janine simply sat like that, alone, for several minutes.

Through with crying. It felt as though she had made one simple mistake in judgment: she had trusted Spencer Hahn. And she had been paying for that error ever since. Her heart and mind had been ravaged by cruelty and tragedy, terror and loss. Until now, she had thought that her survival alone was an achievement. But that wasn't enough now. All this time she had struggled to withstand a maelstrom of emotion, but it had never occurred to her to strike back.

That time had come.

Charon. The fucker had murdered her mother, had tormented David in a way that still had him questioning his own worth, and now the Ferryman had taken Annette. If she closed her eyes, she could still recall the dreams she'd had of Charon, his hands upon her, his lips. . . . Janine shuddered now as she remembered the pleasure she had taken from those dreams. Her entire life had been out of focus, a sort of fugue of grief and despair, and Charon had used that, played with her, tried to coerce her into seeing him as an escape from her pain.

But all was in focus now. Janine saw with perfect clarity how she had been invaded, violated.

She squeezed her mother's rigid fingers; then she rose and went down to the second floor, where she stripped the spread from the bed in the guest room. Water had seeped through the ceiling from the burst pipes above. David had succeeded in shutting off the flow, but the damage was done. Tens of thousands of dollars in damage to his family home. Yet that was the last thing on any of their minds at the moment.

It infuriated her that they were still reacting. But there were things that had to be done.

With the bedspread in her arms, Janine walked back up to the third floor. She glanced once at the turret room, then draped the spread over her mother's corpse and left Ruth there. At the bottom of the steps, where the remnants of the shattered door still lay in the hall, she thought again of Annette, and wished that David and Father Charles would hurry.

Almost as though summoned by her thoughts, the front door opened downstairs.

"Janine!" David called.

"Up here!"

From the top of the grand staircase she could see them both. David had put on dry blue jeans and a knit sweater, his hair had been wet and dried wild, and he had a bit of stubble on his chin. He looked older, somehow, gaunt and haunted, and yet he walked with a determination that reflected what she felt in her heart. Father Charles was all in black, his priestly garb still damp. He seemed almost skittish, glancing into the parlor as he passed it, his eyes roving around, peering into every shadow.

"Did you find Kindzierski?" Janine asked, her voice echoing, hollow and cold in the large foyer.

David nodded. "He's dead. I . . . I don't know how many people heard those gunshots, or if they called the police, but we couldn't take any chances."

Janine kept her hand on the banister, her gaze locked on them. "What did you do?"

"There's a Toyota parked a couple houses down with magazines and empty Doritos bags in it. It was unlocked. I'm guessing he was watching the house. We—"

His words were interrupted by a bright light flashing past the house outside. David started and went to the door again, peered through the windows on either side of the door.

"Just in time," he said, his voice tired. "That's the police. Let's just hope no one actually saw anything, and they don't notice the broken window."

His fingers trailed along the splintered wood where the force of a dead man's hammering had caused the dead-bolt lock to tear through the wooden frame.

"What did you do with Kindzierski?" Janine asked again. Her eyes flicked toward Father Charles.

The priest crossed himself, but slowly, as though he had a new appreciation for the power in that gesture of faith.

"We put him back in the car," Father Charles said. "We were careful not to leave fingerprints on the door handle." The priest moved nearer to the bottom of the stairs and stared up at her, grim-faced, and yet somehow his eyes glistened with sympathy. "But that's only half of the problem, Janine. Once the police find Detective Kindzierski's body, they're sure to check in and realize he was watching this house. They'll notice the damage. They'll want to search the house."

David moved up beside him, as though they appealed to some goddess or queen.

"What are we going to do about Ruth's body, Janine?" her lover asked. "How do we explain that?"

She saw right away where they were going with that. "You want to dump her somewhere? In the river, right? Not going to happen, David. The police already know someone's been terrorizing us. With Father Charles to back us up, we could easily say we found her here. The front door's been broken in; there are smashed windows. We'll explain it. We've got witnesses. But I'm not going to take my mother's body and . . ."

Emotion choked her and she forced herself not to let it overwhelm her. "I couldn't stand waiting around until they found her. I can't pretend I don't know what happened to her. Not to the cops, and certainly not to Larry."

The two men stood in the foyer amidst antique furniture and arched doorways, all familiar and solid, and yet Janine could not help but think of the river that had flowed within that house, the way that Charon had been able to force his own nether realm into the real world. Janine shuddered, then pushed her wavy raven hair away from her eyes and started down the stairs.

"All right," David agreed. "All right."

He met her at the bottom of the steps and they embraced. It was brief, but there was a sweetness to that moment that gave her strength and succor. Janine broke away from him and reached out to take Father Charles's hand. She squeezed it, smiled weakly, and then let it go again.

Janine took a deep breath, then gazed purposefully at David. In every word and glance, there hung an ominous knowledge, unspoken.

"What about Annette?" she asked, a quaver in her voice.

David nodded slowly, then glanced at Father Charles as though he might have an answer. The priest said nothing, as baffled as they were. These dead things Charon had drawn from the afterlife had battered their way into the house and taken Annette away with them. The image of her mother's corpse was fresh in Janine's mind, and she tried unsuccessfully to avoid putting Annette's face there instead of her mother's.

"We have to find her," David said softly.

Dark circles under his eyes only punctuated the sadness in them. He blamed himself, Janine knew. Annette was his best friend, and hers as well. Finding her would have been their first priority, if they had had any idea where to look. Their helplessness was crippling.

Father Charles cleared his throat to draw their attention. "He's not going to kill her, I don't think."

"What makes you say that?" Janine asked.

The priest scratched his head. "His power in this world is still tenuous. It's growing, but it's unfamiliar to him. He may be anchored here but he's unsure of himself. He needs you vulnerable. Charon could have had them just kill Annette right then and be done with it. But they took her instead. He wants you to come to him."

A chill raced through her as she relived, in an instant, the moment during labor when she had almost died, the vision of Charon and the river Styx and the afterlife she had had then.

"I can't go to him without dying, Father. And, for that matter, how would he get Annette there without killing her?"

David began to pace the foyer, banging his fist unconsciously against his leg. "Not there. Not in his . . . place. Somewhere in our world, but where he feels like he's got power."

He stopped, glanced up at Janine.

"The river," she said. "I saw him that day, the morning after your crash, on the other side of the river."

" 'I'll see you on the water before long,' " Father Charles said. "That's what he said to me. Perhaps he meant it literally."

They drove to the river in silence. Though they did not discuss it, David's instinct led him to the spot where the revenant of Steve Themeli had driven him off the road. It was a reminder that though Charon was after Janine, these were David's ghosts that had been raised, phantoms of hatred dredged up from his past. He wanted to believe that they were not real, that they were merely echoes cast into the world to torment him. But Maggie—or Jill, as Annette had known her—she had had emotions. That knowledge tore at him as though he were Prometheus, hung from the mountain, fodder for birds of prey.

David held Janine's hand as he drove. Father Charles was curiously silent in the back, a Bible in his hands. They followed the twists and turns of the road alongside the river, and as they approached their destination, the place where he had nearly been killed, a fine mist appeared atop the rolling water.

None of them reacted to the phenomenon. David suspected it was what they had all expected to find there. It was not terribly late, but still, few cars passed them. Another vehicle was already parked on the side of the road, and he recognized it as Ruth Vale's car. Though Janine must have known it as well, it was yet another realization that went unspoken. He pulled over onto the shoulder, across from the riverbank, and they all got out. David jogged over to Ruth's car, but it was empty.

Headlights cut the slowly expanding, enveloping mist and they waited for the car to pass before crossing the street. Above, even through the fog, David could see the bright crescent moon and the stars. The air was cold and crisp, despite the damp of the mist, and David shivered. It felt good, though. Awake. Alive. His senses seemed somehow sharper as tendrils of mist swirled around them. He and Father Charles flanked Janine as they crossed the road. In the soft earth of the riverbank there remained a deep rut that had been carved out of the ground by his car. The smell of the upturned soil was strong, almost rejuvenating.

David thought of Janine's description of her brush with death, of the river Styx, and he felt the urge to hold her. It was absurd, given their circumstances, but he had never felt the need to have her in his arms more acutely. He reached out and touched her arm, felt the smooth softness of her leather jacket. She gazed out over the mist-shrouded river. Her dark hair framed her face, made her seem almost a ghost herself.

This, he thought. *This is what's real.*

"I don't see anything," she said, her voice tinged more with frustration than fear.

"There," Father Charles said, his voice so low it was below a whisper.

Out on the river, in the mist, an eerie green light began to glow, diffused and refracted into the fog. Even as they watched, it began to glide closer to them, cutting across the river unmindful of the current, as though it floated above rather than atop the water.

The smells of the earth and the river were strong, and David breathed them in, anchoring himself to the world he knew. Whatever lay out on that river, perhaps even the river itself, was something else entirely. Not a different place, not the netherworld, but perhaps a blurred place in this one, where Charon's river—in the borderlands between tangible and intangible, between reality and faith—flowed into this one.

David started as Father Charles gripped his arm from behind. He spun around to find the priest gazing at him intensely. There had always been something admirably haughty about the man. That arrogance was gone, but his dignity remained.

"Stay here. Protect each other," the priest said, his eyes blazing beneath his heavy brows. "Janine, use him as a bargaining chip if you need to. Your companionship for David's life."

Janine gaped at him, horrified. She began to shake her head. "Father, I—"

"Lie," the priest told her.

"Where are you going?" David asked, his mind racing. Without Father Charles, they had no way to defend themselves. Only his blessing had had any effect on Charon.

The priest hesitated, and David saw fear in those intense eyes. "Into the river," he said.

Then he turned and strode upriver along the bank,

disappearing into the mist within moments. Janine reached out and grabbed David's hand. Both of them looked out at the water, where the green light of the Ferryman's lantern glowed brighter, floated closer. They could hear the slap of water against the boat's wooden sides.

"Jesus, David," Janine whispered. "What are we doing here?"

He swallowed hard. "What we have to do. Even if he didn't have Annette, there's nowhere to run. We'll face him together. Somehow we'll get out of this, Janine. You have to believe it."

"I do. I have faith."

Ten feet from the riverbank, the rushing water began to ripple in two places, as though there were rocks just under the surface. The effect lasted only an instant before Themeli and Grandpa Edgar broke the surface. They rose slowly from the river, emerging as they strode calmly yet inexorably toward the bank, as though they had walked all the way across the river bottom at that same pace. Perhaps most disturbing was that neither of them seemed to be at all wet.

Fear and denial wrought within David a powerful temptation to simply flee, to run away like a child, like the very same little boy to whom his grandfather had always been so caustic and cruel. But he was not a boy anymore.

"Stay behind me, Janine," he said.

Her dark eyes flashed with alarm. "David, don't—"

"They're my ghosts," he told her. "It's time I fought them."

The two revenants, one a grinning, hollow-eyed old man and the other a sneering teenager, stopped at the river's edge, still ankle-deep in the water.

"Getting brave now, are you, boy?" Grandpa Edgar scoffed.

Themeli snorted at that, then shook his head. "What the fuck's the matter with you, Bairstow? Just walk away. Don't you get it? He doesn't care about you, just her."

A muscle twitched at the corner of David's eye, but there was no other outward sign of his terror. He stood firmly in the ragged grass and stared at them, not even sparing a glance at Janine.

"You're a little puke, Themeli," he said. "I reached out to you, tried to help you, but you were so in love with how tragic your life was, being a junkie was the only identity you could hang on to. You're not pissed because I didn't save you; you're pissed because I turned you in, I fucked up your ride. Boo-hoo."

Themeli frowned deeply and stepped out of the water, only to have Grandpa Edgar grab him by the arm and haul him back. Both of them glanced over their shoulders nervously, and David realized that they had not attacked yet because Charon had told them to wait.

"Touching," Grandpa Edgar said. His eyes glistened and the mist seemed to caress his face, the same white as his beard. "Is it my turn now, Davey? Have you got some bullshit psychology to explain why your old grandpa would come back to haunt you? Was I a product of a different era? Did my father's cruelty prevent me from showing the love in my heart? Maybe I secretly longed to tell bedtime stories and go on fishing trips?"

"No," David replied flatly. "You were just a prick."

Grandpa Edgar laughed uproariously at that, nodding in agreement. Even as he did, the mist on the river began to thin a little, the curtain not to rise so much as to become transparent. All of David's focus was on the creatures in front of him, the things that wore the faces of dead men, but Janine squeezed his hand and he glanced across the river. Green light spilled through the mist and glinted off the water.

The Ferryman was there, no more than twenty feet away. Though the current washed all around his long boat, it merely rocked in place. Whatever familiarity had lingered in the world around them seemed to be extinguished by Charon's arrival. David shivered. The ground beneath his feet seemed to dampen further, almost to squelch under his weight, though he could not have said whether that was only his imagination. He dared not look up for fear that the stars might have gone red at last. The fog enshrouded them, wrapped all around them, and though he had heard several cars pass by before, he did not dare turn around to look for the road now, for fear that it might be gone.

What world is this? he asked himself, afraid that the answer might not be what he hoped. But it had to be. They had not gone anywhere. Yet the feeling of otherness, of elsewhere, had come upon him so abruptly, as though he had suddenly become aware of being drunk.

No, he thought, and shook his head to clear it. *Maybe nobody can see us from the road, but that's only the fog. This is the Mystic River, not the Styx. It isn't his.*

Yet David could not deny that there, on the water, Charon had power.

That's why we're here, he reminded himself. *Why he took Annette here.* For there she was, seated behind him in the boat, a black hood pulled over her head and her hands tied behind her back. The resurrected Spencer Hahn sat at her side, poking and touching her so that Annette squirmed and shied away from him.

"Annette!" Janine cried out, and started to move toward the water.

"Yeah. Come for a swim, girl," Grandpa Edgar said with a grunt.

Janine flinched and drew back. On her face David could see how much it hurt her to be so helpless. Though he knew Father Charles must have some plan, in that moment he was furious with the priest. A tiny sliver of doubt cut through him as he considered the possibility that Father Charles had simply walked away.

No, he thought. Then, without looking around, David sent a small prayer out into the ether. *Whatever you're going to do, Hugh, make it good.*

The Ferryman swayed with the motion of the water

beneath the boat. His cowl was drawn back to reveal the twin eclipses in his eyes. More than ever, his blue-veined flesh seemed to have been carved from cold white stone. His beard swung ponderously, anchored by the metal ring tied near the end of its length. The lantern that sometimes hung from the prow of the boat was in his hand, its green flame flickering in the mist.

"Damn you!" Janine railed at him, biting off every word as though a sob hid just behind her teeth. "The only reason you still exist is because you have a job to do! Why don't you go and do it and leave us alone!"

Charon did not smile, but his eyes opened a bit wider. He raised the lantern a bit higher so that his face took on its greenish tint.

"This is not the first time I have abandoned my purpose for another," the Ferryman said, his voice insinuating and arrogant. *"I have always returned and so shall I do this time. But I will not return alone. How could I go if my heart is here?"*

Something unraveled in David. All the hesitation, all the contemplation, all the fear and doubt and sadness in him simply seemed to give way, washed downriver in a torrent of adrenaline and emotional debris.

"You don't have a heart, you dumb fuck!" he roared. "You're a myth!"

Janine hissed air in through her teeth. Grandpa Edgar laughed, but Themeli's eyes went wide with surprise. Out in the boat, Spencer Hahn turned his gaze downward so he would not have to look at Charon in that moment.

The Ferryman's black pupils shrank to pinpoint dots then, and the burning coronas that surrounded each of them flared like dueling suns. The stretch of river that separated him from the shore began to churn. David steeled himself for retaliation.

Yet before that retaliation could come, a jet of water surged up just beyond the boat. It took form in the air. First it was a silhouette, a sculpture made of water. Then it had color and weight and real shape.

"Maggie," David whispered.

Whatever dark power Charon had used to give Maggie Russell's soul new form, it remained. She had fled when confronted, but now she had returned. From the river water, she twisted herself into life yet again, landing on her feet in the boat with enough weight to rock it heavily to one side. Spencer had to grab the creaking wood to keep himself from going over.

The Ferryman rode the swaying vessel without effort, and laughed when he saw her.

"I wondered where you had gone," the creature said.

"I won't let you hurt her," Maggie told him.

She had shed the identity she had used when she had seduced Annette. In that moment, she looked to David precisely as she had on the night she died, the night his drunkenness had cost her her life. Of all of his ghosts, Maggie was the only one whose emnity he could not dismiss.

On the boat, Annette bucked against her bonds and shouted something beneath her hood that was muffled by the cloth and dulled by the distance and the rumble of the river.

"This is it," Janine said at his side.

David turned to gaze at her, saw the intensity in her countenance and her carriage, and knew that she was right. At the house they were only trying to defend themselves. But now Annette's life was at stake and there would be no hiding, no running away. Not anymore. This was the time. Perhaps the only chance they were going to get at surviving this thing. Themeli and Grandpa Edgar had turned to stare in astonishment at events unfolding on the boat twenty feet away. Themeli had even begun to wade into the river again as if to go to his master's aid.

This was the time.

With a nod, David ran the three steps to the river's edge and careened into his grandfather's back. The old man grunted and went down. Went under, with David on top of him. As they fell, David saw Janine leap on Themeli's back, one arm around his neck, choking.

The water was cold and soaked through his clothes as David grappled with his grandfather. He scrambled to get his feet beneath him, then hauled the old man up by his clothes. Edgar Bairstow's eyes glistened ice blue and he smiled with jagged, yellowed teeth. So real, so nightmarishly true, this grinning ghoul forced David to feel again all the humiliation and self-loathing the old man had drummed into him as a child.

He held on tight with his left hand and struck out with his right, the desire to shatter that smile so savage and primal in him that he had lost all control. But Grandpa Edgar's face collapsed around his fist, flowed around it. David cried out and withdrew his hand and the old man's face reformed, just as it had been.

"You really are as stupid as I remember," the old man croaked.

Themeli shrugged Janine off, her arm sliding through the liquid of his throat, and she fell to her knees in the river.

In the boat, Charon held up his lantern. The mist had always been thinner in the area around the boat, but now it dispersed almost completely, as though they were in the eye of a hurricane, the fog encircling them all around. A green light arced from the lantern and struck like lightning at Maggie's chest. She stiffened a moment, and then she was only water again, splashing all across the boat as the emerald energy sizzled, then returned to the lantern. Spencer laughed.

Suddenly David could hear Annette's muffled cries more clearly, could make out her voice.

"Jill?" she cried out. "Jill!"

Grandpa Edgar hit him then, drove him down into the water so he was on his knees only a few feet away from Janine.

Damn you, Hugh Charles, he thought desperately. *Where are you?*

David nearly lost faith then. It would have been so easy. He had been responsible for cutting Maggie's life short, and ever so briefly she had been given another chance at life. At love. Now she'd lost it all again.

They could not destroy Charon. Hell, they could not even touch his creations if they did not allow it. Not here on the water. In their element. *His* place. And where was the priest, his friend, who had the power at least to deprive Charon of his servants?

"David." Janine coughed, spitting river water.

He looked at her, saw in her eyes all that she felt for him. Though he loved her and knew she cared for him, David had always harbored doubts about the depth of her feelings. In an instant, that changed. He reached for her, and his grandfather kicked his arm away. David would not grant him the satisfaction of the merest grunt of pain.

"That will do," Charon said simply, his eerie voice now a rush of sound, as though the river itself were speaking.

The Ferryman stepped out of his vessel and walked across the surface of the swirling water. The river held him up, solid beneath his stride. Janine moved closer to David, and this time the revenants did nothing to prevent it. Grandpa Edgar and Themeli moved aside as Charon arrived before them. The creature's otherworldly gaze fell only upon Janine, and as David watched, she lifted her chin to stare back at him as though she could not resist his presence.

"I know that you think me a monster. I would show you other worlds, magic things. I would prove otherwise," the Ferryman promised, long robes whipping about him with the chill wind.

The mist enveloped them all, then, closing in, creating an unwelcome intimacy.

"No," Janine said simply, softly.

Yet the word rippled the mist around her.

Charon touched the metal ring on his beard, twisted it as he considered that response. Bargaining. Yet what, David wondered, could a creature like this bargain with? The thought was harrowing. The wind and the mist and the river went on, but everything else seemed to pause in that moment. Then, at length, Charon inclined his head toward her and nodded.

"Accompany me from this place," the creature said, *"and I will return your infant to you. You never held him in your arms. I can give him back to you."*

CHAPTER 18

❧

Hugh Charles was a man of God. A man of faith. But he could not keep the doubt from rising within him as the Mystic River swept him up in its current. Though spring had arrived, the water was cold, and as it saturated his clothes, weighing him down, Father Charles felt sluggish and heavy and very, very old. He had removed his shoes on the shore before slipping into the water and swimming out away from the bank, but now he wished he had removed most of his clothing as well. It was not modesty, however, that made him stay dressed in his black garments, his white collar. Rather, it was that, clad in the vestments of the clergy, he felt like more than he was, like a soldier of his faith. It was a uniform, in its way, and it lent him a confidence he feared he might not otherwise possess.

The clothes did not make the man. He knew that old adage well. But sometimes, he believed, the clothes might make the man something more.

"Fool," he muttered to himself, struggling to keep his face above the water. He was too old for this sort of thing, too out of shape. The water pulled at him, swirled around him. Father Charles could barely see the stars through the mist. The far shore of the river was blotted out entirely, but he could make out the dim outline of the bank from which he had pushed off. Somewhere, just up ahead, was the spot where he had left David and Janine alone.

Abandoned them, he told himself.

But he had not abandoned them. He had simply made a mental wager that the Ferryman's affections for Janine would keep her alive, and that David's wits would serve the same purpose for him. The moment Father Charles had seen the tainted green light of Charon's lantern approaching through the mist, he had known that he must act. If they were to have any chance at all, not only of saving Annette but of surviving themselves, he had to get closer. Close enough to *touch*.

So now he floated along with the current, expecting at any moment to come in sight of Charon's ancient vessel.

What are you doing, Hugh? What in God's name are you doing?

The question reverberated in his mind, and the first answer that came back was a bitter, frightened one. *Drowning*, it said. But he was not drowning. Not yet. He had not wanted, not dared, to strip his clothes off, but he had put his wallet and watch and keys inside his shoes back on the riverbank, and he sure as hell planned to go back and get them later. So drowning was completely out of the question. But all his thoughts about the weight of his sodden clothing and how deplorably unfit he was physically, all of that was merely his own way to distract him from the business at hand.

Then there was no more time for distraction.

The Ferryman's boat bobbed on the water just ahead, miraculously unaffected by the current. The mist thinned as Father Charles was swept closer, and he saw that Charon was not in the boat, but standing atop the water ten feet closer to the riverbank. David and Janine were at the monster's mercy, on their knees in the water. Two of his lackeys were there as well.

With a frown, Father Charles worked against the weight of his drenched clothes and began to swim nearer the shore. He glanced around for the third of Charon's servants. An idea struck him, and he looked back at the boat. Through the mist, he had thought it empty at first glance. Now, as the water rushed him closer, Father Charles saw Spencer Hahn seated in the boat, one arm slung around a diminutive, hooded figure, as though the two were great friends.

Annette, the priest thought.

For a moment he allowed himself to continue to merely float. Father Charles wore a crucifix on a chain around his neck, and its familiar weight was a comfort to him as he summoned his strength. Then he began to swim, positioning himself in the river so that the current would sweep him right up to the side of the boat.

He opened his mouth to intone the blessing and dipped under the surface a moment. When he emerged he was sputtering, choking a little on the river water, but he tried to be as quiet as possible. The boat, frozen there on the roiling surface, seemed to rush toward him, though of course it was the current that swept *him* toward *it*. He was running out of time. Chin up, out of the water, he spoke the Latin rite that would transform ordinary water into holy water. The blessing gave the water over to God, made it His tool. Once before it had shaken the Ferryman's power over his natural element. It had to work again, or they were lost.

The river seemed to drag him faster. Anxious, Father Charles hurried and stumbled over some of the words as he gazed at the riverbank and prayed Charon would not harm his friends before he could help them.

Then the boat loomed up in front of him. Silhouetted there against the mist, Spencer looked roguishly handsome, and for a moment it was impossible to believe the man was dead. Father Charles kicked his legs beneath the water and spread his arms out, swimming to the left to make sure he was precisely on target. If he missed the boat, he wasn't likely to ever get another chance.

Spencer frowned and cocked his head, as though he had heard something. The splashing the priest had made while swimming? Whatever caught his attention, it did not matter, for Spencer turned and looked down into the water, and he *saw*.

A grin split his features and he said something, though the priest could not make out the words as he swam. The hooded figure perked up and Father Charles felt hope surge within him. It was Annette, he was sure now, and she was not only alive, but aware.

Three times he repeated the last line of the Latin rite. He was a dozen feet away. Nine feet. Six.

Spencer stood up shakily in the boat and began to unzip his pants. "Come for a swim, Father."

Three feet, and now the priest was close enough to understand every word. Spencer intended to piss on him. The boat rocked as he pulled his pants down just a bit, laughing.

Father Charles lifted his hand from the water and made the sign of the cross in the air. Then he slammed into the side of the boat and grabbed hold. It rocked with the impact, and Spencer began to tumble over the side.

Even as he fell, whatever power had held his body together was thrown off. The water that comprised Spencer Hahn's form splashed down into the river with a slap, merged with the eddying current and had no more identity of its own. God had taken that water back from Charon, and taken back Spencer Hahn's soul as well.

Hugh Charles hung on the side of the boat for a long moment, panting, exhaustion creeping into his bones. Yet he no longer felt cold. A kind of warmth and light had filled him, for he had witnessed, first-hand, the power of faith. Though he had not always been certain of it, he believed now with all his heart that his faith would not fail him.

A thin smile on his features, Father Charles hauled himself up over the side of the boat.

"What the hell are you doing?" Annette snapped, her voice muffled beneath the hood.

"Annette," he said. "Just hold on."

He scrambled carefully across the ancient timber of the boat and drew the hood off of her. Father Charles flinched when he saw the deep purple bruise on her mouth and a long cut above one of her eyebrows, but Annette barely seemed to notice that she was hurt. Her green eyes were bright and alive.

And angry.

"Janine and David," she said, glancing quickly around.

"They need our help," Father Charles told her.

"Damn straight."

I can give him back to you.

The words echoed in Janine's mind. Her skin seemed to tingle with them. Her mouth was dry with the taste of them. The soft soil of the river was like quicksand beneath her knees, pulling at her just as the water did, just as her grief did. Janine had never felt so human, so physical, so of the flesh. Her bones felt heavy, her limbs and her breasts and the tight fist of confusion and pain in her gut all took on a ponderous weight that threatened to drag her under.

Her mind reeled for several moments as she tried to put a name to that feeling, tried to understand this horrible, carnal weight. Yet somehow, deep within her soul, she knew precisely what it was.

It was life. The burden of living. Once upon a time Janine had been young and happy and not too modest to admit that she was beautiful, at least to some. Now she saw that woman she had been through the haze of her grief. The world around her had been reduced to little more than a fading façade, a collection of pitiful stage props. Her baby had been a miracle, a spark of something true and good within her, but the baby had died. Now her mother was dead as well.

And Janine knew that death would come for her as well. If not today, well, it was only a matter of time. The days and years in between consisted of little more than treading water until the day. And if that were true, then what was the point of it all, really? Once upon a time she had believed that death was the end, that only oblivion awaited beyond the world she knew. Now that she knew—knew absolutely for certain in a way that most people never would—that there was an afterlife, another world where the souls of her son and both her parents now resided . . . why live?

Tears began to stream down Janine's face. She tasted the salt on her lips and savored it, for with the mist all around and the river soaking her pants and rushing past her legs, her tears were the only water not under the control of the Ferryman. Of death.

Her knees were weak and yet somehow she managed to stand. The water came halfway up her calves, but instead of backing toward the shore, Janine moved deeper, wading in until she was nearly waist-deep. In the starlight, she could see that the edges of Charon's robe hung right down to the surface of the river, floated and swirled with the current around his legs, and yet never seemed to become wet.

She gazed at Charon then. A tiny smile played at the edges of the creature's cold, white lips. His black eyes followed her as she drew within a few feet of him.

Janine closed her eyes.

"No," David cried, off to her left. "Janine, don't do it! Don't go with him! I love you. He can't take you if you don't want to go, don't you see? Just like when you almost died. You wouldn't go with him and he couldn't take you. Don't go!"

Her heart ached with love for David, but Janine did not open her eyes. She inhaled deeply, had the scent of the river in her nostrils, and she focused on the feeling of the water rushing around her waist, pulling on her, urging her to follow the path of the river. To give in to it.

In her mind's eye, she saw again myriad images from the erotic dreams visited upon her by Charon, felt his hands upon her again and the yearning within her as she arched her back, her body reaching toward his touch like flowers to the sun. His cold lips upon her breasts.

"The coins," Charon whispered now, his voice the river itself.

Sure enough, Janine could feel the sudden weight in her pocket of a handful of silver coins. Her eyes fluttered open. The breeze ruffled her hair as she stared up at the Ferryman. The metal ring in his beard gleamed. He held his lantern aloft with one hand and held the other down to her and there was a hunger in his eyes now. A hunger for her, passionate and dark. A hunger to taste and feel her, as if she were life itself.

To him, perhaps she was.

"Janine!" David cried again.

She glanced over at him, where he knelt in the water, flanked by his grandfather and Steve Themeli. David's brown eyes were desperate, filled with fear and love. There was beard stubble on his chin, and she could imagine it, could practically feel it, scratching her face when they kissed. His sodden sweater dragged off him. David looked drowned, beaten, but in that very same moment he forced himself to stand and rushed toward her, too fast for Grandpa Edgar or Themeli to grab him.

With a flick of Charon's wrist, a jet of water shot up from the river and drove David back toward the ghosts, the dead men who had tormented him. His grandfather struck him in the face and David cried out. Themeli punched him in the kidneys and David bent over, tried to stumble away from them.

He shouted her name again.

Janine could not bear to see them hurt him anymore. With the exception of the love of this man and of her best friend, Annette, all the world had given her in the past year had been pain and sorrow. Her hand slipped into the water and, with some difficulty, snaked into the pocket of her jeans. Despite the chill of the river, the coins felt warm as she withdrew them.

Charon gazed longingly at her.

"Yes, Janine," the Ferryman said, his voice a silken whisper. *"Come into the river with me."*

She rubbed her thumb over the coins in her palm and gazed at the twin eclipses of his eyes. "Eternity with you, not alive or dead, drifting on the river between this world and the next?"

Janine threw the coins into the river.

She could hear the Ferryman gasp. It was almost comical.

"You dare?" he roared furiously.

Her tears still flowed, but now she took strength from them. Janine brought a hand to her cheeks and wiped them, licked the salt from her fingers. This was her life. Her power.

The Ferryman's creations gripped David on either side and stared at her in astonishment. Even David seemed stunned.

"Sometimes living hurts too much," Janine said, her voice ringing clear over the water, echoing back from the encircling shroud of mist. "But my heart beats and my blood flows, and it's warm. And your river is never that. You've taken so much from me, but I still feel love. The sun will still rise. It's life. Something you could never understand."

The blue veins in Charon's face seemed almost to sink into his flesh, somehow pulled taut beneath that pale skin. He raised his lantern above his head and tendrils of emerald flame shot from it, dancing in the air around the Ferryman's head. He sneered and for the first time she saw that his teeth were the silver of the coins, yet stained with brackish green, like the bottom of the river.

He meant to kill her, she was sure. If she would not accompany him, he no longer needed to hide his presence in this world. And if punishment resulted, so be it.

Janine saw all of that in his polished black eyes.

Off to her left, the long-dead Edgar Bairstow was the only one who spoke. A single word.

"Fuck."

Something in his tone forced Janine to glance his way. The Ferryman turned toward him as well, rage simmering. But Grandpa Edgar was not looking at either of them. He was staring farther out on the river. Janine gazed past the Ferryman, trying to see what had so astonished this dead man.

Amidst the swirling mists, Father Charles stood in the prow of Charon's ferry with Annette seated behind him in the boat. Spencer Hahn was gone. Annette's short-cropped blond hair looked unruly, even wild, and in that moment Janine thought she looked like some elfin warrior, eyes blazing with rage. In Father Charles's outstretched hand, she saw a glint of metal. The boat was forty-five or fifty feet away and it was dark, but Janine thought perhaps it was a cross on a chain.

The Ferryman thundered his rage.

Father Charles lifted his chin defiantly. "You said you would meet me on the water. Here I am."

The river seemed to boil beneath Charon's feet and then it rose up, a spout of frothing water that hoisted him aloft and bore him toward the ferry.

"You are in my realm now, priest," Charon said in a snarl, his voice now the torrent of rushing rapids. *"I'll take your soul across the river without a single coin in payment."*

The water to either side of Charon rose up and he moved his hands as though conducting an orchestra. Tentacles of river water lunged in long arcs toward Father Charles and Annette.

The priest sketched the sign of the cross in the air.

The water splashed harmlessly down again to mix into the river.

"It isn't your realm," Father Charles called across the river. "You don't belong here. This water isn't part of your world, but man's. God's."

The Ferryman roared furiously and attacked again, waves growing on either side of the boat, rushing toward it as though they were enormous hands about to slap together, crushing the vessel and the humans between.

Father Charles blessed the waves and they fell.

A smile of wonder spread across Janine's features. "Faith," she whispered.

With a rumble that shook the entire river, Charon moved toward the boat, but slowly now, cautiously. Father Charles blessed the water around the small craft, and it began to float away, moving down river.

"Impossible!" the Ferryman said with a snarl.

"Apparently not, you ugly fucker!" Annette cried happily from the boat.

Then she jumped into the river with Father Charles close behind. They stayed near one another and began to swim, moving toward shore—toward the Ferryman—rather than away.

Father Charles began to shout so loud it sounded as though his voice was going. The words were Latin. Janine had heard them before. She laughed and turned to see that David was still held fast by the dead things, the ghosts of his past. But Edgar and Themeli were staring in horror and awe at the priest in the water, at their master's fruitless attempts to harm him.

She wondered.

As the priest intoned the words in Latin, Janine repeated them to herself, though she had no idea what they meant. Shuddering with the cold of the spring-evening breeze and the chilly river, she waded closer to shore, moved right up next to David and his captors. So intent were they upon their master that they did not even notice her.

Her lover stared at her, silently urging her to stay away.

Janine reached out and, with her thumb, made the sign of the cross on Steve Themeli's forehead.

He spilled into the water and was washed away.

Grandpa Edgar sensed her, then. He turned, alarmed, and he lashed out with a vicious backhand that caught her across the face. Janine felt her lip split, tasted blood, but she smiled as she fell backward into the cold river.

David had watched it all unfold in silent amazement, paralyzed with the magnitude of his emotions, each one like a separate string attached to his limbs, and he dangling there like a helpless marionette. When Janine blessed Themeli, destroying the creature, he wanted to laugh. Then Grandpa Edgar hit her and all the emotions that had strung him up fell away.

"Bastard!" David cried, and he struck out.

His fist connected solidly. Edgar Bairstow's head rocked back and he stumbled in the water, then turned to stare at his grandson.

"How . . ." the old man muttered.

A smile crept across David's features. In a single instant, a sequence of deductions skittered across his mind. Charon had created solid-water constructs to house these souls, to draw them from purgatory. Without his immediate influence, what control did they have over these bodies?

The answer was, apparently very little.

Grandpa Edgar rubbed his chin, but then he grinned as well, and David saw with horror that this white-bearded Ernest Hemingway face would likely be his own reflection in the mirror thirty or forty years hence.

"All right, Davey," Edgar said with a grunt. "Let's see what kind of a man you are, once and for all."

David steadied himself, ready for the old man to attack him. He could hear Hugh Charles's voice resonating over the noise of the river, Latin words, but more than words. Ritual. Belief. It was all about faith. Not God, but faith in his world and himself and the love that he felt.

"Come on, then," Edgar said, fists up, beckoning with them.

David dropped his hands and stood up straight. With pity in his heart, he looked down upon the ghost of his grandfather and shook his head.

"I've got nothing to prove to you, old man," he said. "I forgive you. And in the name of God— whatever God may be—I bless you."

Grandpa Edgar dropped his fists and stared at him,

wide-eyed with surprise. A kind of sadness crept into the old man's features. Then he fell away into the water like a cascade of tears.

David turned quickly and saw Janine standing just behind him. With a soft smile, she reached for him. He touched her outstretched hand. She was warm.

Hand in hand, they turned to see Charon sweeping down upon Father Charles and Annette. The Ferryman had ceased his attacks and now went at them himself. Green fire arced from the lantern in his hand. Father Charles continued his Latin chant, but the emerald flame did not dissipate. It did not turn away.

The priest tried to shield himself, there in the water, but the otherworldly flame seared his arms and set his auburn hair alight. Annette screamed and reached for him, drove him under to douse the fire. For a moment the green flame could be seen burning even under the water, but then it was out and they were drifting away on the current. They came up perhaps seven feet from where they had gone under, Annette holding on to the priest, who coughed water from his lungs.

Father Charles was alive, but they were no longer able to swim toward shore, and the Ferryman pursued them downriver, walking across the roiling surface of the water with an ominously purposeful gait.

"Swim," Janine said.

David did. He did a ridiculous, high-stepping run deeper into the river and dove, and she was beside him the whole way. He was submerged for a long moment and then he broke the surface, blinking water from his eyes. The current had him now, and Janine as well, and together they swam after Annette and Father Charles.

Hugh. Jesus, Hugh, be all right.

"Hey!" Janine screamed after the Ferryman. "What's the matter, you bastard? You don't love me anymore?"

With a flourish that sent a fan of water slicing up into the air, Charon turned toward them. His eyes were all black now, gleaming and dark, no more blazing coronas, no more eclipse. Or rather, a full eclipse now. All the light had gone from them.

David wanted to stop, to back away, but he could not. Janine swam on, right for the Ferryman, and David followed. The river carried them with all the inexorable strength of the natural world. Of time. Beyond the Ferryman, this monster who had so cruelly scarred their lives, David saw Annette swimming toward a bend in the shore. Father Charles paddled weakly beside her, one side of his face charred, his hair singed to ragged stubble.

But the priest began to chant again, his voice strong and clear.

And at last David began to realize what he was doing, over and over and over again.

Hugh Charles was blessing the entire river. He was turning the Mystic River itself into an unending flow of holy water.

Ahead, the Ferryman raised his lantern again, but now when David looked at the creature standing there above the water, his unwillingness to let it flow over him took on new meaning. Before it might have been to show his mastery of the river. But now? He wasn't part of this world. Didn't want it to touch him, except in the form of Janine's hands. Charon had been forced to create hard-water forms for the souls he dredged from purgatory, but what of his own form? What had it required for him to exist here? He thought of what Father Charles had said, about Charon needing an anchor here, and wondered just what that anchor was.

"What's he made of?" David muttered, even as he kicked and thrust himself through the water.

He ducked his head under, reached out with his arms. and pulled, swimming as fast and far as he could beneath the surface. He opened his eyes and looked up and above him he could see green light shimmering on the water.

Despite the water soaking his clothes, bogging him down, David kicked and pulled and thrust himself out of the water. The Ferryman was above him, emerald fire arcing all around his lantern, his power. David grabbed him, felt the tug of the river as he held on to this new anchor. Charon roared his outrage at this blasphemy, but David held on with one hand and reached out with the other.

He snatched the lantern from the Ferryman's hand, cocked it back, and shattered the blazing light across the creature's face. For a second, David thought he saw the ghost of Ralph Weiss silhouetted in that flash of brilliance, but then it was gone. Liquid fire showered bright green across the water and all over Charon himself. His robes began to burn, but only for a moment.

Water shot from the river and doused the flames.

David let go and began to swim toward shore, toward Annette and Hugh. Not all of the river was blessed, of course. It had to be constantly redone, replenished. But it was a matter of faith.

As Father Charles shouted out the blessing in Latin, David repeated it. He heard Annette doing it as well.

Without the lantern, there was only starlight now. The mist that had surrounded them like the eye of the storm began to thin, to spread toward them all now.

Charon turned on Janine, who swam toward him. *"I loved you, wretched thing!"* he cried.

"You *wanted* me," she snapped. "That's all. And you can't have me."

The Ferryman gestured toward the river and the water came up in crashing waves again. This time they did not fall away, but drove down upon Janine, forcing her under, pushing her with such power that she was forced upriver, back the way she'd come, against the current. David saw this and screamed her name. He stopped in the river, floated right by the spot where Father Charles and Annette watched, horrified, from the shore. David caught Annette's eye, and together they began to repeat the priest's Latin words again.

The water, David thought. *It's not his.*

When he looked again, the Ferryman was shouting

his rage. The river would not respond to his commands. Janine surged up from the current, splashing and flailing and choking. But that lasted only a second. She had been forced upriver, but now she swam with the current again, her hair slicked down her back, her eyes glistening with anger.

She grabbed hold of the Ferryman, and she pulled him down.

Charon cried out again, alarmed by this loss of power, but then Janine clutched at his long beard and she drove him under the water.

The river swept Janine along, but she held on to the Ferryman. His eyes stared up at her from beneath the water, wide and enraged. Then they began to whiten. He tried to pull her hands away from his throat, but she held on until the flesh gave way, soft and rotten, and she realized that somehow this was a corpse in her grasp. The remains of some poor dead creature that had provided an anchor for Charon on this plane. Now the Ferryman's anchor was crumbling. And still he fought her.

Drowning.

Charon, the Ferryman of the Styx, was drowning.

In that last moment, she thought to pull him up, but he stopped fighting. As though scoured by the river, the flesh seemed to flake and peel from the bones, and the bones themselves turned to powder and the robe was little more than a rag that began to sink.

The river had swallowed him, and now it bore away what little remained.

Janine let the current drag her for several moments, elated and yet somehow also horrified. Then she glanced back up the river, where Annette and Father Charles sat on the shore. She heard a shout and looked up to see David running along the riverbank near her. The mist had cleared enough that she could make him out fairly well, and beyond him, she thought she saw headlights speeding by on the road.

The water swirled around her, tugging at her still, hoping to carry her along forever.

With a kick of her feet and a stretch of her arms, Janine began to swim for shore.

EPILOGUE

❧

The third Saturday in May, Annette drove out to Bookiccino in Arlington. It was still early in the season, but the owners had put a few tables outside the door, creating a sort of faux café, trying to take advantage of the beautiful weather. It was in the mid-seventies and the air was crisp and clean, the breeze carrying the threat of sweltering summer days right around the corner. Days when only the ocean or the air conditioner could relieve the prickling heat of the sun on your skin.

Annette looked forward greedily to July and August, to lying on the sand and letting herself be cleansed by that heat.

Still, a day like today was a nice beginning. The sun glinted off her windshield and she had to hide her eyes behind silver-rimmed specs Janine had left in her glove compartment the previous summer. When she climbed out of her car on Massachusetts Avenue and went up into Bookiccino, it felt, in some ways, behind those flashy sunglasses, that she was a stranger to this place, coming to it for the first time.

The feeling took her by surprise, but she relished it.

Inside, the sound system filled the store with lilting old blues riffs. The song was one she recognized. "Trouble No More," it was called. Annette smiled at the refrain.

She took her time roving through the new releases and the mystery section, but in the end she felt the need for a change. The book she plucked off the shelf was *Lonesome Dove,* a Pulitzer Prize winner by Larry McMurtry. It was over a thousand pages long, and it was a Western, and if anyone had ever told her that she would someday read such a book, Annette would have laughed right out loud.

But the title drew her, and the images in her head of men off on the range somewhere, in a simpler time when people had the courage to shake off the trage- dies that befell them and soldier on.

What a strange choice of words, she chided herself. *Soldier on. This isn't a war. It's your life.* And yet sometimes it did feel a little like a war. An eternal struggle against the passage of time and the shadows that lingered in the corners of life, a fight to find some way to endure, someone to endure with.

Annette took the book to the counter and bought it, along with a cappuccino of enormous proportions. The woman who made the cappuccino was a fortyish redhead who offered Annette a tired smile when she handed the enormous mug and saucer over to her.

"There you go," the woman said. "Nice to see you in here again. Don't be a stranger."

"Huh?" Annette mumbled, surprised. It took her a moment to replay the words in her mind, so distracted had she been, and when she did, a smile spread across her face.

"Don't worry," she said. "I can't stay away from here for long."

They both smiled politely and then Annette took the cappuccino and her book to an inside table—none of that sidewalk café stuff for her until summer finally arrived. As she began to read the first few pages of the book, she was warmed again by the woman's kind- ness to her. There wasn't anything to it but courtesy, a pleasant demeanor, but still it touched Annette. She had been recognized here, and she was welcome.

A tiny thing, but it made her feel just the slightest bit less alone.

On the way back through Medford she took a detour, and drove down toward David's house to the spot on the Mystic River where it had all come to an end. Annette parked on the soft shoulder, but she did not get out of the car. Instead she merely sat and stared out at the river flowing by and she let the tears come again.

She hoped that if she cried now, she could be strong for Janine.

After perhaps twenty minutes she pulled away from the shoulder, turned around, and then drove out to Oak Grove Cemetery.

The gathering was small, and Janine was glad. Her mother's funeral had taken place two weeks before in Scarsdale, and she had been inundated with sympathy from what seemed to be hundreds of people she had never met but who somehow thought they knew her. Clients and coworkers of her mother's, relatives of her stepfather's who clung to her as though it had been their mother who had drowned.

Drowned.

If only it had been as simple as that.

Janine had been as patient with the mourners at her mother's wake and funeral as she could manage, if only because she had to be strong for Larry. Other than his work, Ruth had been everything in his life, and he admitted to Janine in the funeral home after everyone else had left the wake, with her mother's body only a few feet away, that work was going to be hollow now without her there.

For the first time since her mother had married him, Janine found that she loved Larry Vale. The irony was cruel, but she took the result for the precious gift it was. She would keep in touch with Larry now, would check in with him regularly, would take care of him one day if it came to that. He was really the only family she had.

Now, weeks later, they stood in another cemetery. Larry stood to her left, eyes rimmed with red but grimly fighting back tears, trying to be strong for her.

Annette was with him, her arm linked through his, and Janine silently thanked her.

Annette had always been the strongest among them.

David stood on her right, his arm tightly around her shoulder, stiff in his black suit. He held her firmly enough to let her know that she could turn to him if she needed to, if she wanted to rest her head or hide her eyes or simply be lost in his love for her. The day of her mother's funeral, she had done just that. But now, today, she was all right.

The grief was in her, a cold hollowness just at the pit of her stomach, a hesitation in the back of her throat. It was something she would carry with her always, the burden of her mourning, the loss of her child. But she would heft that burden and carry on, knowing that when she grew tired, there were people who would willingly volunteer to share it.

Tom Carlson was there, along with some of the other teachers from Medford High. The principal from St. Matt's, Sister Mary, stood with Lydia Beal and Clark Weaver from her own faculty. There were a handful of other people, but Janine had been very specific about who she wanted to know about the service.

Hugh Charles stood over the grave where two months before her son's remains had been laid beside her father's bones. The priest had always carried himself with great dignity and ceremony, but there was a grace about him now that gave Janine comfort.

Father Charles had endured a great many questions from police about the vandals who attacked David's house, and the stalker who the authorities believed had killed Ruth Vale, as well as Detective Kindzierski and Spencer Hahn. The cops looked into students from both schools who might have had a grudge against one or both of the teachers, but came up with nothing. Which made them very grumpy. Yet Father Charles had committed a great many sins of omission, even outright lied numerous times, in order to protect them.

It was, he said, simply the right thing to do.

Janine gazed with open admiration at Father Charles as he blessed the grave of her dead child. Silently she thanked him for the solace he had given her.

And yet she knew that, in the end, despite all the love and support she received from her friends, even from David, the modest peace she had achieved was something all her own.

"Amen," murmured the gathered mourners.

Father Charles gazed at Janine and she nodded a silent thank-you. The priest raised his hands to thank the people clustered around the grave on her behalf, and then they began to depart in twos and threes.

Janine looked up at David. All through the memorial service she had avoided doing that. He would give her every ounce of strength and courage and love he had if she needed it. David had said as much, but even had he not, Janine saw it every time she looked into his eyes.

But she did not want it. Janine knew, if they were to survive together, that she could not look to him for those things. Strength and courage and love, yes, but only if she returned it in equal doses. To do that, she had to find them within herself.

She would.

After what they had been through together, nothing would ever be the same. Not in the way they saw the world around them, or the things they believed in. But the key was that they did believe. In life. In living. In each other.

The day had grown even warmer, and a trickle of sweat ran down her back as she turned to walk across the grass toward the line of cars. All around them the earth was alive again and the wind carried the odor of freshly mowed grass and the scent of lilacs and jasmine in bloom.

A piece of her heart would always lie in the grave behind her, but with David beside her and her friends around her, Janine could not help but believe that this was not an end to things, but a beginning.

She had faith.

"Hey," she whispered to David.

He glanced down at her.

"No more cemeteries for a while, okay?"

David only smiled. He loved her too much to lie to her, but Janine knew that for her sake, he would pretend. Time and again, in their lives, they would return to these granite and marble fields, until at last they came and never left.

Meanwhile, though, Janine thought, and she smiled to herself. She liked that word, and all it entailed.

Meanwhile . . .

PENGUIN PUTNAM INC.
Online

Your Internet gateway to a virtual environment with
hundreds of entertaining and enlightening books
from Penguin Putnam Inc.

*While you're there, get the latest buzz on
the best authors and books around—*

Tom Clancy, Patricia Cornwell, W.E.B. Griffin,
Nora Roberts, William Gibson, Robin Cook,
Brian Jacques, Catherine Coulter, Stephen King,
Ken Follett, Terry McMillan, and many more!

**Penguin Putnam Online is located at
http://www.penguinputnam.com**

PENGUIN PUTNAM NEWS

Every month you'll get an inside look at our upcom-
ing books and new features on our site. This is an
ongoing effort to provide you with the most
up-to-date information about
our books and authors.

Subscribe to Penguin Putnam News at
http://www.penguinputnam.com/newsletters